Drizzle, Dreams, and Lovestruck Things

Drizzle, Dreams, and Lovestruck Things

MAYA PRASAD

HYPERION

Los Angeles   New York

First Edition, October 2022
10 9 8 7 6 5 4 3 2 1
FAC-004510-22238
Printed in the United States of America

This book is set in Adobe Caslon/Monotype.
Designed by Marci Senders

Library of Congress Cataloging-in-Publication Control Number: 2021060841
ISBN 978-1-368-07580-0
Reinforced binding

Visit www.HyperionTeens.com

For my siblings:
May we always dream big for
ourselves and one another

Prologue

ove is garbage.

It clearly didn't exist. Not if Rani couldn't find it on Orcas Island, where the waves and the sun and the pebble beaches stretched across the horizon, a cinematographer's dream. Summers here were nothing but endless idyllic moments: lazy kayaking through protected inlets and lush berries from help-yourself farm stands and the scent of the neighboring lavender field tickling your nose. Romance felt like a nutrient in the soil, a fragrance in the air.

Rani had been certain Raj was going to kiss her that last morning of his family vacation. A wedding had kept everyone dancing in the barn late into the previous night, and her family's inn sat still and silent. Raj and

Rani were the only ones up, sipping coffee from thermoses and sharing a plate of pain au chocolat on the porch hammock.

"I'm really going to miss . . ." He'd leaned toward her, the blush of sunrise painted across the sea.

"Yes?" Rani licked her lips, hungry for more than breakfast. All sixteen years of her life had led up to this moment, to be kissed by the sweetest guy she'd ever met.

"Your dad's gulab jamun," he finished.

Seriously? He was going to miss *the dessert*? Yes, the gulab jamun were puffy and soft and melted in your mouth in syrupy yumminess. But they were also just fried dough. So much for being the sweetest guy she'd ever met. More like the most clueless.

It was now the last weekend of August, junior year about to begin. Raj had returned to his home on the mainland, and Rani was stuck on this godforsaken rock with the aforementioned dessert as her only solace. She and her three sisters had squeezed together across the length of the non-romantic hammock Raj hadn't kissed her on, their elbows and knees bumping each other in the usual tangled mess. (Why the Singh sisters enjoyed sitting this way was a mystery.)

Rani sighed loudly into the hint of lavender and cumin in the gulab jamun, complemented with freshly churned vanilla ice cream. She'd better load up, because fall was coming and there wouldn't be any strong arms to keep her warm.

"Are you still wallowing? There will be other boys, you know," Nidhi said.

Of course, her eldest sister's practicality was exactly *not* what Rani needed right then. About to start her senior year, Nidhi was all lanky limbs and big, dreamy eyes and lashes for days. Even though she'd be turning eighteen in a few weeks, she still styled her hair as if she was a child, in two long braids.

Rani's fingers itched to free those curls, but she resisted. "Easy for you to say. You *have* a boyfriend."

Despite Nidhi's unfortunate taste in hairstyles, *she* was the one with a cute guy attached at the hip. The universe was so unfair.

"You're being dramatic." Nidhi poked her with a bony elbow.

"You always say I'm being dramatic!"

"Because you always are!"

Rani looked to her twin for help, but as usual Avani wasn't paying attention. Even in shorts and a T-shirt, hair in a careless ponytail, Avani effortlessly pulled off her charming outdoorsy look. It really wasn't fair because Rani was a good two inches shorter, and she didn't have the same easy, breezy girl-next-door face. Her own delicate features had to be coaxed out with the right hair and makeup and outfits—such as the unfortunately itchy lilac blouse Rani wore today.

Her twin was busy scribbling in her journal and simultaneously texting while her own bowl of gulab jamun perched precariously on the porch railing. Uh-oh. Rani reached out to stabilize it, but Sirisha beat her to it. They exchanged a quick smile. Avani was always doing twenty things at once, a whirling frenzy of unrelenting energy that Rani admired—even when she had to take cover from any unintended side effects.

Sirisha was the only one who would listen to Rani talk for hours on end without getting exasperated. The youngest of the Singh sisters was only fifteen, petite with long straight hair generally in a wild tangle from traipsing through the woods with her beloved camera. Rani had told Sirisha she'd look amazing in a bob so many times, but would any of her sisters listen to her sage advice? No.

But now Rani could tell that even Sirisha was getting impatient with all the moping, her sympathetic noises receding as she got up to focus her DSLR toward the sea. Telltale plumes of water shot into the air, a school of whales on the move.

Click. Click. Click.

The Songbird Inn faced south over the craggy edge of a cliff, with panoramic views that allowed the Singh sisters to enjoy both sunsets and sunrises over the Salish Sea. They would often retreat to the hammock on the peaceful southeast corner of the wraparound porch, tucked away from the large southern outdoor deck filled with tables for the inn's guests.

Though the inn now boasted a robin's-egg-blue exterior, tons of oversize windows, and restored Craftsman elegance, Rani hadn't forgotten the crumbling monstrosity that Dad purchased nearly ten years before. Still grieving for Mom after she'd passed, he'd needed a project and a change of scenery. And Rani had to admit that he'd transformed this place into a cozy haven.

It was beautiful, but the thing was: Nobody ever stayed. And the end-of-season emptiness of the inn had stolen into Rani's soul.

She wiped a tear from her cheek, feeling completely and utterly sorry for herself.

And that was when a thick yellow envelope came hurtling toward the porch, rocketing out from the island mail truck that had just arrived in the inn's parking lot to the east. The sisters shrieked and scrambled to get out of the way, but Rani fumbled at the edge of the hammock and the package ended up landing smack dab in the center of her dish. Syrup and ice cream splattered everywhere, while the mail truck sped away without a pause.

"Perfect," Rani grumbled, dabbing ineffectually at a stain on her blouse. (Despite being itchy, Rani had saved a lot for it, and she hoped it wasn't ruined.)

The package was soggy and torn, so Rani unwrapped it to reveal a shiny wooden plaque.

Nidhi peered over her shoulder. "Hey! The Songbird won an award for the Most Romantic Inn in America? That's amazing!"

Goose bumps raced across Rani's bare arms.

"Ooh, really?" Avani tucked her journal shut and nudged Rani with sudden interest. "What if the Obamas come stay here?"

"That would be pretty cool," Rani admitted. "They're basically royalty."

"What if actual royalty came?" Sirisha squealed. "Like a princess from some tiny nation nobody's heard of! Or a prince, if that's what you're into."

Nidhi laughed. "I'll settle for a boost in business. We need the extra cash flow."

"Don't be boring." Rani elbowed her. "We're dreaming here."

"In that case, I'm rooting for the Obamas."

Possibilities splashed among the sisters like baby seals, while late summer sunshine dripped deep into their brown skin. They had to make the most of it before the infamous rain and clouds of the Pacific Northwest returned. But suddenly, the changing of the seasons didn't seem quite so daunting to Rani.

The Most Romantic Inn in America. It really was, wasn't it? The award, the prospect of a little publicity, the sisters' fanciful predictions of fame and fortune shifted something inside her, driving away the vestiges of an unkissed summer. In its place, an unshakable feeling settled into her bones, the sweet conviction that interesting things really were headed their way.

And also interesting someones.

Part One:
Fall
Nidhi

Chapter One

The lights from the vintage chandelier in Nidhi's fourth-floor attic bedroom in the Songbird Inn flickered. The windows rattled like old bones, pine trees outside rustled, and rain pounded the roof as if the inn were being stampeded from above.

What a storm! Her sisters never failed to bemoan the coming of fall, the shortening of the days, the inevitable gloom of the Pacific Northwest. But Nidhi secretly reveled in it. There was nothing like curling up inside her small hexagonal turret of a bedroom, cozy and warm as the weather raged outside.

Working on her laptop in bed, she sat back against the pillows and wrapped her rose-dotted duvet around her shoulders. It had been her mother's, a lingering memento from a woman that Nidhi barely remembered. Her fingers flew fast as she revised an essay for English Lit, tapped out a few easy algorithms for her Comp Sci class, and then turned her attention to her beloved personal planner app. September was inching to an end, and senior year was full of so many responsibilities. Yet Nidhi wasn't worried. She could handle it all, as long as she stayed organized.

She glanced at this week's to-do items:

- Complete college essays? Check. They weren't due till December of course, but why wait if you knew what you were writing about? She'd laid out her dream to open a bakery, and her plan to major in business as preparation.

- Officially accept summer residency in Paris at the elite Siècles du Sucre? Check. Apprenticing under renowned French pastry chefs was the opportunity of a lifetime.

- Finalize the schedule for the weekend's big event? Check. The Songbird was set to handle a sizable Indian American family's reunion, complete with three birthdays, an anniversary, and a mundan ceremony.

Nidhi closed the laptop with a satisfied sigh. Was there anything better than checking off every item on a list? Of course, when the reunion family had called to book, she'd been too embarrassed to admit that she had no idea what a mundan ceremony actually was. Some kind of special baby haircut, apparently. A Hindu tradition. Dad had promised to handle the details of it, though, so she could focus on the fun part: the cake. Baking had always been Nidhi's escape, the perfect place to experiment and try new things—with the comforting road map of a tried-and-true recipe as a base.

As she sketched out a decadent four-tiered design, an ominous creak sounded from outside. Nidhi tensed under her mother's duvet, though it was probably nothing. The trees often made eerie noises, and she was way too old to be scared of a little storm.

But then the creak drew out into a groan, slow and loud, as if something very ancient and very large was creeping toward the inn. Nidhi set down her sketchbook. What was that? Perhaps she should look out—

A bellowing crunch erupted above. Water droplets and pine needles and splinters showered down. Time stretched and contracted, pausing and fast-forwarding and perhaps even rewinding as an enormous Douglas fir tore through the ceiling. And half the wall. As the tree hurtled right toward Nidhi's bed (and her body!), she wondered if this was truly the end.

NO. It couldn't be. Not before she made it to Paris! Not before she opened her own little bakery in town! Not before, not before, not before . . .

Rain lashed down and lightning lit up the sky. A flurry of footsteps hurried up the creaking stairs. The door to her bedroom flew open, and her three younger sisters scrambled inside, followed by their stricken father.

"Nidhi!" Dad rushed over to her. "Are you okay, honey? I can't believe—"

He looked a little faint, his face ashen with the thought of what could have happened. It snapped Nidhi out of her macabre musings, because she had no intention of leaving her twice-widowed father. They'd lost their mom when Nidhi was just four years old. Then Dad had fallen in love with Pop, only to lose him to a stroke nearly three years ago. He'd been through enough.

"I'm fine," Nidhi called. "I'm just . . . stuck."

As the eldest of the Singh siblings, Nidhi wouldn't let a silly thing like being pinned beneath a giant Douglas fir stop her from taking charge of the situation. Taking in the damaged walls and ceiling, the shattered window, and the enormous branch across her body, Nidhi realized that it wasn't just a broken tree limb that had crashed in: The trunk of an entire fifty-foot fallen tree was just inches from her, resting against her carved white headboard. That headboard was the only thing protecting her from being smashed flat as the potato paratha she'd had for lunch.

The sheer indiscriminate luck of it threatened to knock the breath out of her. Nidhi had always believed good planning would save her from anything life could throw her way. Yet there wasn't a single thing she could have done to prevent this.

Still, there was no use in dwelling on what could have happened.

"I'm absolutely fine!" she yelled again above her squawking sisters. Her legs were going numb beneath the weight, pine needles were poking her everywhere, and one particularly sharp twig dug right into her side. "Dad, why don't you find a tarp? My things are getting soaked. Sirisha, put my laptop somewhere dry. Rani and Avani, come pull me free. It looks worse than it is."

When you had a firm, let's-do-this tone, people tended to listen. Everyone jumped into action at once.

"Yes, of course, a tarp! Probably more than one." Dad hustled out, looking grateful to have a task.

"Your laptop!" Sirisha fished it out from under a nest of pine needles.

"Come on, Rani, pull harder!" Avani said as she and Rani each took one of Nidhi's arms.

"I am pulling hard!" Rani complained. "But the branch is too heavy! And the pine needles are poking me! Can't we call your prince charming to help with this?"

"Seriously?" Nidhi grumbled. "Matt's not here, so can you please help?" She wasn't in the mood for one of Rani's over-the-top knight-in-shining-armor fantasies right now.

"Okay, okay." Rani sucked on her finger, then grabbed the branch again, managing to heave it up to give Avani better leverage. With a bit of uncomfortable maneuvering, they eventually managed to yank the branch high enough for Nidhi to escape.

"Thanks." Nidhi gingerly stood up, her legs reawakening rather painfully. Placing a hand on the dresser, she cautiously stretched her toes and fingers, checking once, twice, thrice that everything was working properly.

"That was close!" Avani said, surveying the damage.

It certainly had been. With half a wall and a good chunk of the ceiling gone, her bedroom was more like an outdoor patio at this point. A very messy one. Her window was completely shattered, her shelves toppled over, the rain falling fast and hard.

"Ahh! My pictures!" She grabbed her corkboard from the still-intact south wall. The rain had already ruined several of the photos pinned on it, including the one from last year's Father's Day camping trip and another one with Matt at the new French bistro in town.

As Nidhi placed the board carefully in the closet, Sirisha started haphazardly tossing in everything from the desk and shelves: textbooks and recipe cards and homework assignments. Dad returned with the tarps, and the twins clamored to help him nail them up, though the hole in the attic was huge, the length of half the ceiling. To cover it, they had to affix three of them together. There was more shouting and the tarps fell down twice and the nails had to be redone and they couldn't seal everything completely anyway because they'd need a crane to remove the tree.

Everyone was getting very cold and very cranky. One thing about the Singh sisters: Despite their lifelong PNW status, they did not like to be cold or wet. They had a closet full of waterproof rain gear to prevent such things.

As soon as her most important things were safe, Nidhi sank to the floor.

"You okay?" Sirisha settled beside her, resting a head on her shoulder. "That must have been terrifying."

Nidhi's youngest sister always seemed to guess her thoughts when she herself couldn't quite articulate them—wouldn't articulate them, even if she could. Because big sisters stayed strong, even when they were quivering inside.

Nidhi's phone buzzed.

Matt, of course. Was it 8 p.m. already? He always called on the dot, unless they were together, and normally she was always ready. She pushed her damp, frizzy, pine-needle-filled hair out of her face and pasted on a sunny smile before answering the video call.

"Hi!" Nidhi hoped she sounded like her usual self, confident and in control. Firstly, because sounding confident and in control was half the battle to actually feeling that way. But also because she didn't want Matt to worry. She was fine, completely fine. A mere near-death experience wasn't going to rattle her.

"Hey!" Matt's dark hair was ruffled as always, and his easy grin soothed Nidhi. Then his brows furrowed in confusion. "Are you outside? What's with the pine needles in your hair?"

"Well, *outside* is a relative term. I mean, there is rain and there is a tree, but . . ." No use hiding it, Nidhi realized. She arced the phone around the room to show him the damage, cringing a bit at the sad state of her once beautiful turret room.

Matt whistled from the other side. "Um, so half your walls . . . no longer exist?"

"Right."

"Whoa. At least you weren't on your bed when that tree crashed on it."

"Oh, she definitely was!" Rani shouted.

"What! Nidhi? Is she serious?" His cute brow furrow was back.

Nidhi mouthed, *Be quiet*, at her little sister. Matt knew that she was no damsel in distress, but still. "As you can see, I escaped unscathed. And even more importantly, so did my laptop!"

"Well, that's a relief!" Matt laughed. "How would you know what to eat for breakfast without your planning app? Or when to brush your teeth?"

"Hilarious." He may have had her pinned, but she just wasn't in the mood.

Her hands felt clammy. And her breathing was coming a little fast. And perhaps her heart was racing a tad, even though it made no sense. The danger was over.

A corner of a tarp came loose again, flapping audibly in the breeze. Dad and her sisters were on it—more or less. Nidhi itched to take charge of the situation, but she also really needed to know that her and Matt's plans for the summer were going to work out. She fled the hammering and chaos of the room to find some quiet. She tried to will her heart to calm, her breath to slow, her body to pull out of panic mode.

"So did you hear from Lulu?" she asked him out in the hallway. "Can you come with me to Paris?"

"Are you sure that's what you want to talk about?"

"Yes. I promise." She gestured toward Dad and the twins. "They've got it under control."

Matt grinned. "Well, she just got back to me—I got the job! I'll be scooping ice cream the whole year round, but it'll be worth it to come to France with you."

"That's fantastic! Tell Lulu I'm so grateful!"

Something settled inside Nidhi. Neither she nor Matt could afford to take a trip abroad for granted. She'd only accepted the residency after they'd offered her a scholarship, and Matt needed the ice cream parlor job to pay his way. But that was one of the things that made them such a great couple: They both knew how to go after what they wanted, and they worked hard to make it happen.

It was all about having a road map and following through.

Later that night, Nidhi lay awake in the trundle bed in Sirisha's room, listening with envy to her sister's even breathing. In the darkness, the roaring crunch of a tree hurtling toward her replayed in her mind over and over again. It had missed her, she reminded herself. She was fine.

But why did her heart keep racing? Why did her hands stay so clammy?

Instead of counting sheep, she counted out Paris attractions. The Louvre. The Left Bank. The Arc de Triomphe. Surely she could banish the memories of that tiny, insignificant near-death experience that had stilled time and rewound it and fast-forwarded it at once.

Outside the wind howled and the squall blew on, tipping boats and felling telephone lines, uncaring that it had already wreaked so much havoc.

Chapter Two

On Saturday morning, Nidhi and her sisters watched one long-lashed darling of a three-month-old wail as her head was shaved. The baby's mother cradled the tiny but mighty set of lungs against her, wrapping the baby in the folds of her burnt-orange sari as if she were a hatchling awakening in a nest of autumn leaves.

The sisters stood at the edge of a circle of trees crowned with tinges of gold and fiery red. Embroidered blankets and pillows had been spread over the ground for the guests to convene on, leaving piles of shoes and elegant sandals studded with pearls out on the grass. Soft sunshine dappled their happy faces, and a few leaves fluttered in lazy circles downward in search of the perfect spot to rest.

"The ritual is meant to signify letting go of a past life and beginning anew," Dad murmured, placing a hand on Nidhi's shoulder. "Each of you had the same ceremony."

The baby's father gently swiped away the last few curly tendrils, as if letting remnants of a life forgotten fall to the ground. And then each of several dozen family members took turns pressing a thumb of yellow powder and another thumb of red powder onto the baby's forehead to welcome her into this world, this life, this family.

"I don't remember it at all," Nidhi said. "Not even Sirisha's."

"We have pictures somewhere," Dad replied, tearing up a bit. "Your mother wore a gold sari for hers, a green one for the twins', and a red one for yours. She always looked radiant. I can see a bit of her in each of you."

Nidhi glanced at Dad in surprise. He rarely dwelled in the past for long—or at all—probably because of all he had lost. All *they* had lost, actually. She knew that they each handled their grief differently, but in that moment the five of them were one, tumbling into one another for a group hug, to remind each other that they were all there.

Despite that Douglas fir that had so nearly ripped her from them.

Nidhi was a strange mess of emotions that morning, and she didn't particularly like it. Her hands would suddenly get shaky and her heart would palpitate wildly for no reason at all. She did her best to shake away the lingering shadows of that night, as well as this sudden ache for long-forgotten moments. After all, she had to help with the special luncheon, and the four-tiered cake she'd planned wasn't going to bake itself.

At 11 a.m. sharp, exactly on schedule according to Nidhi's planner app, the drool-worthy scent of Dad's crackling tandoori fish flooded the north porch and the grassy field behind the inn. A few years ago, Dad had special-ordered an industrial-size tandoor oven from India. Now he and his sous chefs—Josie and Armand—were hard at work on the enormous outdoor grill.

Nidhi's cake layers were cooling, so it was an excellent time to sneak a piece of perfectly charred fish.

"Here." Dad chuckled and piled up a plate for her, with a fish-and-veggie skewer and a piece of soft and fragrant naan. It smelled like heaven. "How's the baking coming along?"

"I've got it under control," Nidhi assured him. "I just need to stack the layers and ice them."

He kissed her forehead. "You're so talented."

"It just takes practice," Nidhi answered.

The porch steps creaked as Avani darted up to sneak her own skewer off the tandoor.

"Those are for the guests!" Dad grumbled even as he assembled another plate. "At least *some* of my daughters are helping."

He nodded approvingly at Rani and Sirisha, who were setting up tables and chairs on the grass, dressing them with linen tablecloths and fishbowls of dahlias. Of course, Nidhi and her sisters had always lent a hand at the inn, from as far back as she could remember. Dad's staff handled most of the day-to-day goings-on, but he relied on their help to make the ledgers work out in the black. Enough to stow away a bit for the future, and for unexpected emergencies—like wayward Douglas firs.

"I'm very helpful," Avani said. "I'm totally helping Nidhi with the cake."

"You mean you'll lick the mixing bowl?" Nidhi arched her brows.

"Somebody's gotta do it."

Nidhi chuckled. "Well, I suppose you can tell me if the frosting's too sweet."

The Songbird's kitchen was beautiful: sunny yellow walls, checkered tile floors, long butcher block counters, and a view of ancient pines and the neighboring lavender farm just beyond. Nidhi always felt perfectly at home there, ready to while away the hours creating delicious concoctions. It was hard to imagine cooking elsewhere, though the kitchens at Siècles du Sucre just might be acceptable. Not home, though.

With an angled spatula, Nidhi spread a lemon-lavender filling over the first layer of the bottom tier. Then she carefully slid the next layer on top of the first and repeated, until she had three filling layers between the moist blue velvet cake.

Only three more tiers to go:

• chocolate with salted caramel filling

• lemon with raspberry cream cheese filling

• strawberry with Bavarian vanilla filling

As Nidhi worked, Avani chattered a mile a minute about her classes, a guy she kinda sorta thought was cute, the enigmatic San Juan Island street artist called the Skull, and thirty other topics. Nidhi had to admit that she, too, wondered who had been putting up those gorgeous chalk murals all over Friday Harbor on various holidays, starting with Easter last spring. Apparently, the artist worked in secret at night, and though most residents thought it was a fun little surprise to wake up to, others were more cantankerous about it. She and Matt had spotted dozens of the Skull's murals when they'd visited San Juan Island over Labor Day weekend, and Nidhi had been oddly captivated by them.

But before she had a chance to dwell on the matter, Avani had moved on to discussing the novel she'd recently started working on, and why it was better than the last three ideas she'd abandoned. The sisters were so different: Avani had multitudes of interests that changed almost daily, while Nidhi had set her sights on her own bakery after decorating her first cupcake with rainbow stripes at the age of eight.

Nidhi wondered sometimes if her little sister would ever focus on anything. After all, the twins were only a year off from being seniors themselves, and then they would have to make some real decisions about college and careers, just as she had. Life wasn't all half-finished novels and fleeting crushes and new hobbies you'd drop a few weeks later.

Sometimes, you needed to be serious. Sometimes, you needed a plan.

"So Matt's officially coming with you to Paris next summer?" Avani swiftly stole a taste of lemon-lavender filling.

Nidhi swatted her sister's hand with the spatula. "Yep! The whole trip is such a dream."

And just as importantly, part of said necessary plan, but Nidhi knew that Avani would hardly understand that.

"Totally," Avani agreed. "Think of all the pastries you'll be able to eat. The amazing wine you'll be able to try. You can drink there, you know."

"I've heard that," Nidhi said. To be honest, those little differences made her kind of nervous. "Having Matt there beside me will make everything easier."

Avani gave her a funny look.

"What?" Nidhi asked. "Did I get frosting in my hair?"

"No, you're fine. It's just that I thought you wanted Matt there because it's *romantic*. Not because it's *easier*."

"Oh. Well, that, too, of course." Nidhi didn't understand what Avani was getting at (as usual). Having Matt in the city to make it feel more welcoming *was* romantic—the final piece in a puzzle coming beautifully together.

"Whatever you say." Avani sampled one of the tiny chocolate fondant banners for Nidhi's castle design. "Personally, I think being with just one person is like only ever having one flavor of cake."

"Now that would be a true tragedy," Nidhi agreed. "Help me carry this out, will you?"

Even with two of them, it was no easy task navigating the towering cake through the kitchen doors—which thankfully they'd remembered to prop open—to the main hall. The cake was heavy, and Nidhi kept picturing the tiers toppling over in a mess of frosting and flavored fillings and crumbs. Especially since she was still feeling a bit shaky from that crashing tree, the moment when time had twisted itself in a knot. It also didn't help that at that moment, a stream of construction workers in orange vests was filtering through the inn, heading up the winding staircase to Nidhi's room.

Initially, Dad had warned her that it might take weeks just to hire someone, but then he ended up getting scheduled in right away. This company had been able to put enough people on the project that she'd only have to wait three weeks from project start—today—to get her room back. Not too bad, considering they would have to completely rebuild the damaged walls and ceiling, then deal with replacing the window and woodwork and repainting. On the bright side, business at the Songbird could continue as usual, since all thirty guest rooms on the second and third floors were just fine. Only the turret bedroom on the fourth floor had been affected. (Lucky Nidhi.)

She and Avani waited for the crew to ascend the stairs before carefully proceeding with the cake on a tray between them. However, they had not remembered to prop open the north doors, and they didn't have a free hand.

"Can I get that for you?" A young, sandy-haired construction guy offered Nidhi a wide, dimpled grin. "That is one impressive cake, by the way."

He nodded at the towering pink frosted castle, complete with chocolate flags and banners encircling each perfectly sculpted tier. It had turned out just as she'd pictured it, evoking glittering fairy tales with trapped princesses and the kind of absurdly rosy endings that Nidhi would never admit to liking.

"It's an in-house creation," Avani bragged. "This girl was the mastermind, but I helped!"

Nidhi rolled her eyes. "Questionable."

The construction worker raised his brows. "You're a true artist."

"Thanks, but it's no *Mona Lisa*," Nidhi replied lightly.

He shrugged and held the door for them. "Art is art. It doesn't have to hang in a museum to count."

Despite the towering four-tiered cake in her arms, something about the way he spoke made her pause. It almost sounded as if he was telling himself as much as he was telling her.

"Oh yeah? Are you a baker, too?" she couldn't help but ask.

"Not at all, though I make a mean Cobb salad." He looked at his feet. "But I do like to sketch a little."

Was it just her, or were his cheeks turning a little pink?

"Aha! I thought there must be something," Nidhi said gently.

Avani cleared her throat. "This cake is getting kind of heavy."

"Oh, sorry," the guy said. "Go ahead."

As they started to scoot past, he pretended to take a bite.

"Don't you dare!" Nidhi warned, though her lips twitched in amusement. She tried not to notice how his white T-shirt fit across his shoulders or the way his hair caught the morning light.

He just laughed and waved them through.

With the cake safely on the buffet table, Avani winked at Nidhi. "What a hunk, am I right?"

Nidhi hid a smile. "I guess he wasn't terrible to look at."

The reunion members gathered around, oohing and ahhing as Nidhi added candles for the three birthdays and one anniversary. When the slices were served, the hidden layers of chocolate caramel, raspberry cream cheese, lemon-lavender, and Bavarian vanilla delighted everyone, including the pickiest of picky eaters. As Nidhi handed a second piece to a toddler (with his mother's permission, of course), she beamed, completely in her element.

This was the joy she wanted to spread when she ran her own bakery someday. Just like chocolate fondant flags spiraling to the top of a four-tiered multi-flavored castle cake, her life plan was falling perfectly into place.

Chapter Three

The next morning, Nidhi decided it was time to officially update the coffee bar menu for autumn. In the built-in nook where they'd set up the espresso station in the restaurant, she tied on her frilly apron and then carefully wrote up the new offerings in cursive on the chalkboard: Flavors of hazelnut and cinnamon apple and delicata squash were ready for consumption.

"Can I get a nonfat pumpkin latte, please?" a girl in a knit cap asked.

And pumpkin, of course. Tourists always wanted pumpkin, no matter how overdone it was. Nidhi couldn't really blame them; there was comfort in the familiar. Yet for some reason a restlessness had burrowed into her skin, and she found herself itching to break free from the same old menu, the same leaf-and-pinecone decorations, the same pumpkin-filled samosas they made every year.

"Sure, it'll be out in a few minutes." She offered a practiced, perky smile.

As the girl found a seat with her family, Nidhi turned back to her conversation with Matt. He'd stopped by the inn to help out, as he often did on weekends. He was in slept-in-till-the-last-minute mode with a rumpled navy T-shirt that succeeded in bringing out his olive-toned Italian complexion. His dark hair was also sticking up in odd places, as it so often did. Nidhi resisted the urge to brush it down for him.

"This is going to be the year of the delicata squash." She stirred her new homemade syrup vigorously. "If I have anything to say about it."

"Totally different than pumpkin," he teased.

"It is!" Nidhi poured the maple-and-squash concoction carefully into a cappuccino, and paired it with a white chocolate biscotti. Sweet perfection. "Could you—"

She didn't even have to finish: Matt grabbed the saucer and swept it to a table, where a yawning middle-aged couple smiled gratefully beneath coffered ceilings. Soft fall light streamed through the nearby large bay windows, a half-moon that seemed to jut out right over the sea. It was the only part of the inn where the porch and deck didn't wrap around, leaving the views unimpeded. The other three walls were similarly lined with windows, looking out at the inn's grounds and gardens and the refurbished barn where they held weddings and other special events.

When Matt was back, she had his gingerbread mocha ready for him.

"Working for you is real tough," he joked, flopping into the seat across the bar. "At least you don't pay me."

"Your consumption of cookies will probably put us out of business."

"Nom, nom, nom." He stuffed what had to be his third snickerdoodle into his mouth. "Me need sustenance."

She chuckled at his same old bit and deftly churned out the next orders in her queue:

- the girl in the knit hat's pumpkin latte

- two traditional cappuccinos for a sleepy honeymooning couple

- three lavender nonfat lattes and three regular nonfat lattes for the table of stretching cyclists anxious to hit the island roads

She and Matt had the morning routine down to a science, including the inevitable jokes about his sweet tooth.

Members of the reunion family started to trickle into the restaurant, and Nidhi took their orders as Matt chatted easily at the table of cyclists, probably recommending his favorite routes. At another table, two middle-aged women visiting from Olympia browsed a visitor's pamphlet. Nidhi smiled as she noticed that the Skull's murals from the Fourth of July had made it onto the brochure. Apparently, the street artist's surprises were now considered a tourist attraction.

As Nidhi wandered back to the counter, the sandy-haired construction worker who'd been impressed with her castle cake waved cheerfully at her.

"Good morning!" He offered her another wide, dimpled smile.

"Morning." Nidhi's stomach fluttered a bit. Perhaps those three lattes she'd already ingested had been a mistake. "What can I get you?"

He scanned the chalkboard. "Honestly, I'll settle for straight caffeine injected into my veins. We've all been up since four in the morning. Do you maybe have a coffee pot I can share with the crew?"

Nidhi glanced at the station. They had single pour and cold brew and a dozen different espresso options, but no coffee pot. Drip just wasn't the Songbird's style.

"Tell you what, give my masala chai a chance." She smiled winningly. "House specialty, made the way they do it in India. I even promise not to add lavender."

"Good! We manly construction guys can't stand the stuff." He wrinkled his nose in mock disgust. "But if you have any extra drywall dust, you can sprinkle that on."

She laughed. "They'll be up in a minute."

"Thanks. I'm Grayson, by the way." He stuck out his hand.

She took it, admiring the way he said his name. As if he knew exactly who he was and where he wanted to be. Not a hint of that bashfulness he'd exhibited yesterday when he'd mentioned he liked to sketch—though that had been kind of sweet.

"I'm Nidhi."

Of course, she mumbled it too quickly, and as Grayson headed back to work, she wondered if she'd ever be able to say her name with the simple acceptance he had. She liked the way Dad pronounced it, with a gentle accent and properly aspirated, but it didn't sound the same coming off her tongue. And she absolutely hated it when people hardened the *D*. "Ni-thee," she would then be forced to explain. As in the sonnet "How Do I Love Thee?"

"That scent is familiar." A senior member of the reunion family approached the counter, a tall man with distinguished gray hair and a gentle smile. "Reminds me of my office in Bombay. The chai-walas there knew how to steep it so strong I'd fly through the day. And the milk was frothy and just sweet enough."

Nidhi smiled. "You were there back when it was still called Bombay?"

"It seems like yesterday, my dear."

She poured a cup for him. Dad and Pop used to drink chai by the fire at 11 p.m. as the inn settled into quiet hours, apparently immune to the caffeine. That was before Pop's stroke. Nidhi stirred the sugar a little faster than necessary, pushing aside the memory.

After arranging a steaming pot of chai and assorted baked goods on a serving platter, Nidhi took the first step up the old winding stairs. The platter wobbled, but Matt was there in a flash to steady her. She gave him a grateful look. As they carefully inched their way up the stairs, his two arms were like a handy extension of her body.

"Room service!" Nidhi announced on the other side of her own bedroom.

It felt strange to have a man open her door, and she tried not to wince at all the dust and debris inside. Tried not to feel naked either, as seven people worked in her girly sanctuary. Their equipment took over the space as if it had never been hers.

Loud beeping blared, and the foreman gestured for everyone to step all the way out of the room. From outside, a crane came swooping down like a giraffe bending its neck, and Nidhi stared in fascination as it lifted the great Douglas fir away. She should be glad to see the thing that nearly killed her gone, though with the remaining wreckage, it wasn't as satisfying as she'd hoped.

But this crew was here to fix all that, put everything back to how it was. And the unsettled feeling that had been plaguing Nidhi the last few days was sure to recede. After all, it was only natural she'd feel out of sorts when her room was such a disaster.

When the foreman motioned that it was safe to come all the way in, Matt took the tray from her hands and set it on her desk, which had been pushed to a corner and covered in plastic. The crew descended eagerly, pouring tea and thanking them both.

"Okay, I might be addicted to this chai," Grayson said. He lifted his cup in a toast. "As I said, you're an artist."

"I'm glad you approve." Nidhi smiled tentatively.

As they tore through the pastries and croissants, she wandered over to the bed on the other side of the room and noticed a small rip in her mother's rose-dotted duvet. Considering the huge tree that had been lying over it moments before, the damage was minimal. And Nidhi was alive, which was what counted. Yet the rip felt like a cut in her own skin, fresh and stinging and seeping with more blood than expected.

Decades ago, Dad and her mom had an arranged marriage, a custom in India that bore little resemblance to what most people in the US thought. Dad had told Nidhi about the carefully arranged dates: a potential groom-to-be nervously wondering if the sari-clad bride-to-be would be a good fit, while their parents nibbled on samosas and pakoras. There'd been no anger or runaway attempts or forcing of their hands. Just a tradition of falling in love after the ceremony.

Dad had truly loved her, but after she'd passed, he'd loved someone else. Pop. But even though her mother had only existed in a distant life with Dad, Nidhi's heart constricted at the thought of anything happening to this remaining piece of her.

Most of the crew started to wander back toward their tools, leaving behind only crumbs and empty teacups on the tray. But Grayson poured himself a second cup.

And came over to Nidhi's side.

"I'm actually going to India next summer," he said. "I'll let you know how this compares!"

Nidhi glanced up. "You are?"

"Yep. I have forty-two countries on my list." He grinned. "I've been saving up, and I'm ready to see the world."

"Oh wow." Envy flooded through Nidhi's body, a visceral, mean thing. It surprised her with its intensity, as she'd never really thought much about going to India before. She'd been born in Portland, a child of the Pacific Northwest. And she had fabulous plans of her own—Parisian ones.

Yet it suddenly seemed terribly unfair that Grayson would set foot in her parents' homeland before she did.

"The storm really did a number here." Matt strolled over from the damaged walls, holding out a hand to Grayson. "I'm Matt. Thanks for all your help."

"All in a day's work," Grayson said, shaking it. "I'm Grayson. I was just telling your sister I'm going to India next summer. What part is your family from? Maybe I can say hi."

Nidhi blinked. Wait, had he just called her Matt's *sister*?

"Huh?" Matt squinted at Grayson. "Oh, I'm not related . . . That is . . . I'm Italian. Not Indian . . ."

"Oh, sorry, I thought . . ." A slight pink blossomed across Grayson's cheeks.

Nidhi flushed. "He's my boyfriend."

Matt chuckled, taking her hand. "I'm just here to hang with my girl. And the free snickerdoodles help, too."

"Right, of course. That makes sense." Grayson looked sheepish. "I guess you can tell I need this trip to broaden my horizons."

"No problem," Matt replied. "It could happen to anyone."

"Yeah." Nidhi suddenly needed to move her hands, so she resumed busy barista mode, fingers nimbly gathering empty cups and crumpled napkins.

Matt was of course too easygoing to even think twice about it.

"Hey, I'm heading out," Matt said. "Promised to keep Anita occupied today. Mom's trying to sell the last of her blackberry jams at the farmer's market."

He was always babysitting his little sister to help out. They'd bonded over their single parents more than once, but Matt had it a lot harder than she did. Her sisters were old enough to take care of themselves. Anita, on the other hand, was only four years old, a boundless explosion of playful energy. Part of the appeal of his job at Lulu's was their tots play area, which Anita loved.

"You're a good one." Nidhi popped a quick peck on his chin, feeling a bit self-conscious. But that was silly; he wasn't really her brother.

"You too." He tugged gently on one of her braids.

For some reason, the act grated on her. That strange disquiet she'd been feeling stirred, that niggling sense that something wasn't right. But Matt had done it a million times before, and she'd always sort of liked the silly, affectionate gesture.

The door creaked, and Dad stuck his head in. "I was about to ask you all if you wanted anything from the kitchen, but I see Nidhi and Matt have got you covered."

As Matt headed home, Nidhi trailed Dad down to the kitchen.

"What can I help with for lunch prep?" she asked.

"Nothing," Dad said, setting the tray at the dish station. "You're free to enjoy the day."

Nidhi watched as his sous chefs easily presided over the details. With Josie and Armand chopping and sautéing away, there really was nothing for her to do. Her fingers twitched for more coffee orders, but the place had cleared out. Nidhi poured herself a delicata squash cappuccino.

Unfortunately, it did sort of taste like pumpkin.

Chapter Four

The sounds of crickets chirping and waves crashing filled the night. Nidhi and her sisters trundled down the path to the small beach cove below the inn, carrying lanterns and pulling wagons loaded with camp chairs and blankets and food. They'd planned the perfect send-off for the family reunion, a bonfire night under the stars.

"Do you ever wonder why Dad hasn't taken us to India?"

Nidhi's question hung in the evening air, slowing her sisters, who shuffled to a surprised stop behind her.

After a long pause, Sirisha spoke. "I don't think his family approved of Pop."

"What?" Avani demanded. "Why not?"

"You *know* why not," Rani said.

"But he made Dad happy!"

Unspoken questions swirled inside Nidhi, fleeting musings on what it all meant: traditions and a culture that was theirs and yet not theirs, relatives they had never known, a motherland that they had yet to see. She wanted to dig into it all, but there never seemed to be a good time. "Come on, Dad's waiting for us."

It was only a five-minute walk to the cove, thick hanging branches and mossy logs soon giving way to grassy banks and sand and driftwood. At the bottom, a sweet medley of Hindi and English greeted them. On the last night of their stay, the family's chatter had slowed its rhythm, giddiness fading into comfortable familiarity.

Dad and some of the other inn staff already had one fire pit going, but the plan was to light two more. Nidhi and her sisters unloaded the supplies, spreading out blankets and unfolding camp chairs, passing out s'mores ingredients and Dad's spicy snack mix of chickpeas and fried onions. Scanning the group, Nidhi searched for anyone in need of anything. She spotted a familiar face—the man from Bombay.

"Would you like a seat?" She unfolded one of the camp chairs for him.

His eyebrows shot up. "What, do I look so old that I can't stand on my own two feet?"

"No, of course not." She bit her lip. "Um, snack mix?"

"Thank you." He accepted the cone of rolled-up newspaper that held the mix, tossing a few bites in his mouth and crunching with approval. Then he winked and sat down anyway. "Just until I work up the energy for late-night wakeboarding."

"Oh, is that something you enjoy?" Nidhi smiled at the thought of the old man gliding over a moonlit sea. Despite his age, he wasn't yet frail.

"I believe in balance in all things." He chuckled, the fire crackling with a merry golden glow, the scent of smoke mingling with sand and ocean air. "Especially when you're being towed across the water, feet strapped to a hunk of fiberglass."

"Sounds terrifying," she said, quivering at the mere thought. "I'm not super sporty."

"You might surprise yourself, beti."

Beti. It meant daughter. A lump formed in Nidhi's throat. Suddenly, she wanted to cry with love for this family that she barely knew, this family that spoke the soft consonants and musical notes of her father's language. This family that was leaving tomorrow.

The man's grandkids came, demanding he play a game of cards with them. He invited Nidhi to join, but she shook her head and let him have time with those who were truly his.

Click. Click. Click.

Sirisha hid behind her camera, as usual. But the lens was directed at Nidhi.

"Shouldn't you be taking pictures of the *guests*?" Nidhi placed a hand on her hip. She was doing that thing that she hated. The snotty practical eldest sister thing. It came naturally to her, but she knew it drove her sisters up the wall. Still, she couldn't help it. Someone had to be organized, or chaos would reign.

Sirisha smiled softly, as if she had a secret. "Look."

Her younger sis pointed to the photo on her screen. Nidhi wasn't one to obsess about her looks, but even she had to admit it was good. She'd decided that she'd had enough of braids and had attempted a topknot. In the photo, wispy curls had escaped just so, her skin glowed gold in the firelight, and her eyes were huge and black and faraway.

Rani peeked over Nidhi's shoulder. "Oooh, sexy!"

Nidhi punched Rani lightly. "Shut up."

"You should send it to Matt."

"No."

"Why not?"

"Because."

The truth was, there wasn't a good answer. Why shouldn't she send a photo she liked of herself to her own boyfriend? But something about it felt too forward, too "look at me, look at me!" She didn't need to fish for compliments; Matt had told her she was beautiful plenty of times. Of course, she couldn't exactly remember the last time he had . . .

"Whatever. Come on, Sirisha. I actually appreciate your talents." Rani tugged on her sleeve. "And I need to update my profile photo."

"Already?" Sirisha asked. "I thought you loved the last one we took."

"I can't stick with the summer aesthetic now!" Rani dragged Sirisha to the edge of the cove. "All those floral strapless dresses make no sense once school's started!"

So Sirisha got to work, somehow managing to find light in the darkness and shape the shadows into natural frames. Rani posed in a thinker position on a fallen driftwood log, laid out flat in the sand, spread her arms to the stars—a total ham to the camera.

"Take some of me and Avani, too," Rani insisted, grabbing her twin.

Avani was sitting in the sand, absorbed in some app on her phone. "Huh?"

"Earth to Avani!" Rani said. "We're doing a photoshoot now."

"Do I have to?" Avani made a face. "I was just about to get the Golden Badge!"

"Come on, pleeeease?"

"Okay, okay." Avani laughed and gamely put her phone away.

Sirisha tapped her camera softly. "All right, how about here with the waves behind you? The lighting is perfect. But can you stand up a little straighter? Your posture is terrible."

Avani rolled her eyes, but the truth was that the youngest Singh sister wielded some serious magic with her camera.

That picture of Nidhi had truly been gorgeous, transforming her into some kind of mysterious nymph out on an untamed sea. Yet that version of herself wasn't real, just a trick of light and shadows. Tomorrow, in the light of day, Nidhi would still be the same grounded girl who geeked out over spreadsheets and schedules and her precious planning app.

After a long and silly photo shoot, the twins eventually calmed down, and the sisters huddled together on a blanket, crossing their ankles over one another like twigs in a fire.

Rani nudged her. "Aren't you going to tell us to get back to work?"

Nidhi glanced around. The reunion guests were happy and occupied, helping themselves to drinks and snacks from the table they'd set up near the trailhead. Still, part of running an inn was being a good host, and she and her sisters *could* be:

- gathering empty cups and abandoned plates

- checking if the hot cocoa station had enough marshmallows and hot water

- asking if anyone needed anything else

Yet a quiet kind of feeling had crept into the night along with the stars, and somehow she couldn't even bring herself to move, to do anything besides bask in the old Hindi ballad playing in the background.

"I think we're okay for now," she said cautiously.

Rani raised her brows but knew better than to ask for more chores. Nidhi roused herself enough to bring them each steaming mugs of her special peppermint hot chocolate with pecan-flavored marshmallows. The dark nutty flavor combined with mint was cozy and crisp at once, like a leaf falling outside the window on a brisk autumn day.

A message popped onto her phone. Sirisha had sent the photo to her, adding simply, *For you. No need to share with anyone if you don't want to.*

Yes, exactly. Sirisha understood that Nidhi didn't need Matt's approval. She was a confident, independent person, after all!

But, then again, should she send it? Would he like the way she'd done her hair? And when exactly had he last really looked at her? He used to treat her as if she were a piece of rare sea glass from a sunken treasure. But things changed when you were together for a long time. And in high school, two years was practically marriage. She sighed.

"So, you do like it!" Rani crowed, catching Nidhi staring at the pic.

Nidhi rolled her eyes. "It's not terrible. So what?"

"You know, if you don't want to send it to Matt, there's someone *else* who might appreciate it."

Nidhi wondered if she meant someone from the reunion. But the party didn't have any teenagers or college kids, only young children or parents or grandparents.

"I'm talking about Grayson!" Rani said. "The hot construction guy? He likes you!"

"What?" Nidhi's cheeks heated. "No, he doesn't."

"I saw him watching you when they were leaving. You, of course, had your nose stuck in your laptop." Rani sighed dramatically. "Just saying. What a waste! He's so cute."

Nidhi listed out the reasons why nothing could happen with him: "A) I have a boyfriend. B) Matt is the sweetest. And C) Grayson's too old for me."

Rani arched a brow. "Don't get me wrong; Matt is great. He's like a brother to me. And who am I to tell you he's not your one true love? Only you can decide that. But I think you should know . . ."

Her sister dangled her sentence invitingly, and against Nidhi's will, she bit. "What?"

Rani's grin was like the Cheshire Cat's. All Nidhi could see in the darkness.

"Oh no," Avani said. "Here she goes."

"Grayson's actually only eighteen!" Rani exclaimed. "He graduated high school last year—from Friday Harbor."

"How do you know all this?" Sirisha asked.

Rani shrugged. "I can't just let eligible men wander into the inn without researching them."

"Did you google him?" Nidhi accused.

"Chill. I asked his buddies about him since he's by far the cutest guy in the crew."

Nidhi rolled her eyes, tucked her phone out of sight, and tilted her head to the sky. Out there, in the vast reaches of the universe, there were no boyfriends to worry about, no plans upon plans, no road map to follow. The immensity of the infinite unknown was formidable, but for that brief moment, she did not feel small. With her sisters and a warm drink and flickering firelight, she only felt . . .

Possibility.

Chapter Five

It had been ten days since the reunion family had left, and Nidhi found herself missing the murmur of Hindi in the dining room, the influx of brown faces and dark hair, the reflection of silky salwar kameez in the fall light. An ache settled into her heart, one that wouldn't leave even when she busied herself with variations on croissant recipes for the inn's espresso bar:

- cranberry almond

- peanut butter cup

- raspberry lemon jam

- sour tangerine

The last one had been a surprising hit with the guests, actually, but it still seemed too easy, too done . . . lacking a certain je ne sais quoi, as the French said.

Nidhi had always been great at distracting herself, at tamping out stray thoughts and leaving them in a neat little box to be examined later. (Or better yet, never.) But this time, she just couldn't escape those restless feelings. She was searching for something, though she didn't quite know what.

Nidhi gave in to her yearning to spend the afternoon paging through old photo books in the fourth-floor library, a cozy space in the Songbird where she and her sisters and Dad gathered to watch movies or study or just hang out. Though it wasn't off-limits to guests, the doors were usually left closed and nobody really ever wandered up to this floor. The furniture was well-worn, the TV a relic from a decade past. And the shelves lining the walls were overflowing.

Curled up on the shabby-chic loveseat, she came across the mundan pictures, she and her sisters' faces like tiny brown cherubs, red-and-yellow tikka pressed upon their foreheads. Their mother's gently smiling face, scarlet sindoor in her hair, her sari perfectly pleated. The elaborate folds of silk looked complicated, and Nidhi realized that she had no idea how to put one on.

And no one to teach her.

She sighed and placed the photo album back on the shelves next to the cookbooks. They had a huge variety of the latter, everything from Italian to Malaysian, hearty stews to delicate amuse-bouches. But the ones that drew Nidhi's eye were from South Asia. There were so many culinary traditions from all over the subcontinent.

Nidhi didn't know how to cook food from the motherland either. That had always been Dad's thing.

She pulled out one of the guides to North Indian cuisine, the pages yellowed with turmeric. It had Dad's handwriting in the margins, changes and substitutions. Another cookbook, even older, had notes in her mother's elegant print. Grazing her finger across the words, Nidhi missed her fiercely. Mom was gone, the reunion family was gone, but Nidhi was still here. Brown skinned and dark haired, an Indian girl who owned too much rain gear and baked too many croissants.

An hour later, Nidhi inhaled the heady fragrance of onions simmering in hot oil, tossing in veggies, tender meat, spices, and yogurt for silky texture and thickness. A few freshly diced chilies to give it a bite. She wiped the sweat from her forehead as the smells became richer and more complex, sweet and tangy and spicy all at once. This food was home, it was family, it was her father and her mother and a country far away.

It was only four o'clock, well before the sous chefs would start prepping for dinner in the restaurant, so she had the kitchen to herself. The family usually dined late, but perhaps the scent would tempt her sisters. She made up a small sampler plate and excitedly banged on Sirisha's door.

No answer. She poked her head in, but it was disappointingly empty. In the twins' room, Rani was stretched on her bed, reading a romance novel with a bare-chested man on the cover.

"Hey, want to try some very authentic Indian food?" Nidhi brought the plate forward with a flourish.

Rani poked at a piece of misshapen stuffed flatbread. "What is that thing?"

"Aloo paratha, of course."

"It looks like roadkill."

Nidhi frowned. Sure, some of her red curry was bleeding onto it. And the charred bits could be mistaken for tire tracks. And okay, maybe the potato stuffing was oozing out in a way that was not entirely unlike pus. But still. Did Rani have to be so critical of the presentation?

"C'mon, taste it," Nidhi wheedled.

"I was in the middle of a really good scene!"

"A sex scene?"

"Please. If they were finally doing it, do you think I'd stop to talk to you?" Rani shook her head and clutched the book to her chest. "It's so romantic, Nidhi, you don't understand! It's about this Scottish highlander who lost his first wife, and he meets this woman who keeps stealing his clan's goats, and *then*—"

"She steals his heart?"

"Exactly!" Rani flopped dramatically back on her bed. "It's the best."

Nidhi ripped a piece of paratha, used it to scoop a bit of meat and sauce, and held it out. "Please, just try one bite."

"I'm not hungry. Why are you bothering me?"

Nidhi wasn't exactly sure why this meant so much to her. She knew she wanted *something*, but she was afraid that Rani would laugh if she made a big deal about it. It was just paratha, after all. A funny-looking one, at that.

"It's for a school project," she lied.

Rani rolled her eyes and obediently opened her mouth, letting Nidhi hand-feed her. After a few thoughtful chews, she shrugged. "It's not terrible."

"That's it?" Nidhi's stomach plummeted.

"It's not the way Dad makes it," Rani said simply. "Now leave me alone!"

Rani's brush-off stung. Nidhi couldn't remember the last time something she'd made *hadn't* been met with overwhelming approval.

"Where are Avani and Sirisha?" she asked. Maybe they'd have a different opinion.

"Sirisha went to some art show in town and Avani had soccer practice."

"Avani plays soccer now?"

"Apparently?"

"What about Dad?"

"He was meeting some guy." Rani's eyes were glued to the page.

So much for her fabulous family meal.

Nidhi wandered down the stairway, munching on roadkill paratha and trying to contain her disappointment. She'd been picturing the Singhs sharing a family meal for once, one without any leftovers from the restaurant and everyone waxing poetic over what a natural she was at Indian cooking. Obviously, it wasn't going to happen tonight.

She couldn't let it all go to waste, though.

A banging sounded from upstairs. Of course—the ever-hungry construction crew would appreciate her meal! They'd been coming around for snacks and coffee on a regular basis, and they never left so much as a crumb on the tray. None of *them* would liken her cooking to roadkill. Probably.

Nidhi climbed the stairs toward the attic, her mind on spices and sauces, on tender fall-off-the-bone meat and the pressure cooker Dad loved to use . . .

And she did not see the pile of wood trim until it was far too late.

"Ackkkkk!" She tripped right over it, grasping in vain for something to hold on to. There was nothing, and the hot curry went sailing all over the place. Mostly onto Grayson, who had just opened her bedroom door.

"Oops!" Nidhi said, her eyes wide as she scrambled back up.

His shirt was pretty much ruined. Once turmeric got on anything white, it was over.

"Are you okay? I told Tommy not to leave these here." Grayson scowled at the stack of trim, even as he very casually—as if it were no big deal—pulled off his shirt.

OH.

He was, um, very nice looking.

And Nidhi had no business staring at him like some Scottish goat-stealing wench! What was wrong with her?

But then he did a little stretch.

Whoa.

His biceps were quite . . . well formed. She had the feeling he could totally pull off a kilt, too.

But that was not relevant!

"I'd better move these out of the way before someone breaks their neck," Grayson said.

"Good idea." Nidhi looked at her feet, the wall, anywhere but him. "I'll, uh, get the curry cleaned up."

"Tommy can do that, considering this is his fault," the foreman said, coming up behind Grayson.

"Okay." Nidhi wasn't quite certain what to say, especially since now the rest of the crew was gathering around and surveying her curry damage.

"Good grief, stop showing off and put your clothes back on, Grayson!" someone said. "You're embarrassing the poor girl."

Nidhi's face felt too hot. His pecs were indecent. Gorgeous but indecent.

And she should probably go do something instead of just standing there. Get it together, girl. "Um, do you want to borrow one of my dad's shirts?"

"Thanks, but I have a spare down in the truck."

"Great! I'll grab it for you!" she chirped, then cursed herself for sounding so eager. "Keys?"

"Um, okay." He fished a key ring out of his pocket and tossed it to her.

Nidhi mumbled something incoherent and booked it out of there as fast as she could.

"It's in the green duffel!" he called after her.

Was she just imagining it, or was the crew's laughter echoing after her? She couldn't believe how flustered she'd gotten. After all:

- It was just a bare chest, a part of human anatomy. No big deal.

- This was all Rani's fault, all that talk of Grayson the hot construction worker making eyes at her and being eighteen. But Rani was always seeing romance where there wasn't any.

- Nidhi had a boyfriend. One that she was quite happy with, thank you very much.

The construction company truck wasn't parked in the guest parking lot, but in the grass by the barn. Grayson and the rest of the crew brought it on the ferry from San Juan Island every morning. It was a long day for them, but she supposed it was paying for Grayson's grand trip to India and forty-one other countries.

There was that ugly jealousy again, a part of herself Nidhi didn't care for. After all, she was no slouch at big plans herself. Getting into the residency program in Paris was a huge deal, not to mention the scholarship that let her pay for it. Nidhi had poured her heart and soul into the application, baking elaborate desserts for every inn event, asking Sirisha to photograph them for her portfolio.

But Grayson was going to India.

Her homeland. *Her* birthright.

Ugh, could she let it go already? It wasn't his fault she'd never been there. Nidhi yanked open the back doors to the cargo area. Near the front of the truck, she spotted the crew's bags nestled behind a mess of equipment. It felt strangely intimate opening Grayson's. Inside, there was rain gear, spare clothes, sunscreen, and a few other personal items. She smiled at a soft hoodie with Chewbacca growling on the front. Maybe Grayson had a geeky side, too. As she pulled out a plain white T-shirt, a leather-bound journal fell out of the bag and landed on the floor, the pages open.

Ocean colors swirled around the silhouette of a man looking out at the horizon, an endless sky and sea. Nidhi picked it up, captured by the depth of the colors and the detail and the yearning that came through so powerfully in the picture. Grayson had mentioned that he liked to sketch that first day they'd met, but this drawing was so much more than she could have imagined. And she knew, she just knew, that she held a piece of his soul here in her hands.

A part of her wanted to snoop through all the pages, but another part wanted Grayson to be the one to show them to her. And not just because of his bare chest. He was clearly talented, and she wondered whether he planned to go to art school. Carefully, she tucked the journal back into the duffel. But she couldn't get that picture out of her head as she locked up the truck. She was at the inn door when Labor Day weekend in Friday Harbor suddenly came back to her.

She and Matt had been doing some shopping and snacking and wandering, enjoying the last free days before the chaos of senior year. The islands had been buzzing with tourists for the holiday, and the line for ice cream had wrapped around the block, the scent of fresh-made waffle cones too strong to resist. Two elderly ladies in front of them were arguing about the Skull. One of the women thought the street artist's chalk murals were all quite dashing and harmless, while the other was upset that the church across the street had been defaced.

Intrigued, Nidhi had glanced across the street and there it was on the side of the high steeple: her very first in-person sighting of the Skull's work. It was the most incredible portrait, the silhouette of a woman carrying a pick-axe, her back straight, her arms rigid and ready for work. Swirls of red, white, and blue circled her like dust and clouds. In a small corner, Nidhi spotted the artist's insignia: a little pirate flag with a skull and crossbones. But the skull was smiling and winking, and the flag was also red, white, and blue. A patriotic pirate?

After she and Matt got their ice cream cones, Nidhi had insisted they search for more of the Skull's murals. All of a sudden, she noticed them everywhere. Behind the library, a man in a hard hat. On the side of the grocery store, a woman fixing a car. At the visitor's center, a factory worker. A fisherman. A seamstress. A teacher.

Labor Day had never meant much to Nidhi, just another long weekend. But the Skull's artwork brought out the spirit of it. The pride in hard work, the celebration of all classes of people and the jobs they took on to feed their families, to raise their kids, to make a life for themselves.

Nidhi had been completely enthralled.

As they'd scoured every corner, Matt seemed to enjoy the game of it, but she'd wanted to study each mural like a specimen from an ancient civilization. How could anyone have created all of them in a single night? Though rule-breaking wasn't Nidhi at all, she guessed it must be rather exhilarating to sneak about in the darkness, racing against dawn armed with so much joy and creativity.

Now she realized Grayson's journal had the same joy and creativity. That prideful silhouette, those swirling colors, that sense there was something more over the horizon. It was all in the same style as the chalk murals that had lit up her Labor Day. As Nidhi crept up the staircase, she grinned.

She'd discovered the secret of the Skull.

Chapter Six

When Nidhi returned to her room with the shirt, Tommy was cleaning up the spilled curry as the rest of the construction crew wrapped up for the day. She approached Grayson with a mischievous glint in her eye and a grin she couldn't hide. In fact, she was so amused with the little secret that she hardly noticed his still-bare chest.

"What's so funny?" Grayson demanded.

"Oh, nothing. Nothing at all."

He searched her face as he put the new shirt on.

Thank goodness. Okay, so maybe she had noticed.

Nidhi turned quickly to the others. "Hey, I have a whole Indian meal waiting downstairs, if any of you are hungry!"

She was used to gently herding people around for inn events, but there was no need to coax and cajole this bunch; they practically sprinted down to the kitchen. Nidhi set out the curry and parathas and plates and napkins and utensils in the staff break room off of the kitchen, counting on them not having Rani's exacting expectations.

"Dig in!" she called.

"Thanks, Nidhi!" Tommy said from the front of the line. "Oh, and sorry about that mess earlier. Hope you're okay."

"No broken bones this time, but please do be more careful," she said sternly.

"Yes, ma'am."

She internally forgave him as he piled his plate high and dug in with gusto. In fact, the entire crew was devouring her lumpy, charred parathas with such enthusiasm that Nidhi couldn't help but feel somewhat heartened. A weight lifted from her shoulders, and a giddy and playful mood took hold of her.

Because now Nidhi had a mission: to get Grayson alone so they could discuss his late-night excursions. She had a history test to study for, a Comp Sci program to perfect, and kitchen inventory to review. But all that could wait.

When he went back to the line for seconds, she cornered him.

"So . . ." she started. Unfortunately, the conversation in the kitchen dropped to a lull at that moment. Her heart pounding, she barreled through. "Um, there's a gutter that's been overflowing outside. Would you mind helping me with it? I know it's not part of your job and all, but—"

"Sure, no problem. Your parathas need some work, by the way." Grayson's dimple flashed as he held up a severely burnt piece.

Nidhi made a face. "I know, I know. It was my first try."

Grayson grabbed a glass of water. "Just gotta wash out the taste of charred paper here."

She swatted him. "Don't be rude."

He chuckled. "Will it make you feel better if I tell you I burn my toast most mornings?"

"Slightly."

"Actually, I'm surprised you're not a pro already."

"Why? Because I'm Indian? So I should automatically know how to make parathas?" Something stuck in Nidhi's throat. She'd only decided to make the parathas on a whim, but now it felt like so much more than that.

Grayson held up his hands. "No, of course not! It's just that I saw that cake you made, so I figured you could pull off anything. I mean, aren't you headed to some fancy culinary school in Paris?"

Nidhi tried not to tear up, though it wasn't Grayson's fault. She just felt strangely emotional about the parathas. It was silly, but she was starting to understand why he'd been so self-conscious when he'd mentioned his sketching. She supposed food really was her art form. And even though you were supposed to take risks, it could still feel pretty disappointing when the results weren't anywhere near what you'd been hoping.

"It's a pastry school, actually," she finally answered.

"Right, pastry school." Grayson grinned. "And I bet it was super hard to get into."

"It was," she agreed.

Rationally, Nidhi knew she wasn't a failure at all; Siècles du Sucre had picked her baking artistry, her recipes and methods for their program. For some reason, though, it all felt strangely hollow at the moment.

"Let me show you those gutters," she said, ready to talk about something else. Anything else. She led him out to the north porch, where there really was a gutter overstuffed with orange and gold leaves, more falling as the wind picked up.

Grayson squinted upward. "Okay, I'll grab a ladder—"

"I know your secret," Nidhi blurted out. She'd meant to come up with something more clever than that, but the charred parathas still had her off-kilter.

"What secret? That you need a ladder to get up there?"

Nidhi squared her shoulders. "I know you're the Skull."

His mouth hung comically open like a dead fish, and his shock was honestly the best thing she'd seen in a while. She—Nidhi—had managed to surprise him. A grin spread across her face, one she couldn't contain no matter how she tried.

"How'd you figure it out?"

She told him about the journal, that she'd recognized his signature style. "I swear, I wasn't snooping! I only looked at the one page. But, Grayson, you're really gifted. I was in Friday Harbor on Labor Day, and I searched all over town to find every last mural you drew. They were just so amazing and powerful, I didn't want to miss a single one."

"Thank you. That means a lot." He nodded sheepishly, a watercolor blush creeping across his cheeks. "Promise not to tell anyone?"

"Of course. But why all the secrecy? Are you worried what other people will think?"

Grayson shrugged. "Maybe a little. But that's not the only reason. It's also just really fun. Seriously, every time I've done it, it's an unbelievable rush."

Nidhi tried to picture creating those inspiring images under a dark, starry sky. Magic and markers and moonlight.

"I'm sure it's fun," she said, "but don't you want to use your talent to go to art school or something?"

He shook his head. "Nope. Not thinking that far ahead right now."

"I guess planning your trip must keep you busy—deciding everything you want to see and do."

"Nah, I figure I'll have plenty of long plane rides to look at guidebooks. Then again, it might be cool to just land in a new place and do whatever." He cheerfully went to work on the gutter, paying no attention to Nidhi's befuddled wonder.

She and Matt were meeting up the next day to go over their sightseeing musts in France. Neither of them wanted to miss anything significant. And Grayson was really just going to drop into cities all over the world with no plan?

A fierce gust of wind roared through the trees, making it rain with leaves of fire. As they fluttered around her in a whirlwind, crisp with the scent of change, Nidhi held the ladder steady. She had her way, and Grayson had his.

Nidhi's true culinary calling had always been sprinkled with sugar and cream. The following afternoon, she decided to lean into those strengths. Her own kind of art. Of course, Dad's gulab jamun was far too legendary to compete with, so she needed another classic Indian treat to try. She landed on burfi, and ever the ambitious pastry chef, she made not one batch, but six:

- creamy rose

- coconut with bits of mango

- dark chocolate

- silver leaf pistachio

- milk cardamom

- a triple-layered version featuring the orange, white, and green of India's flag

Every guest in the restaurant that night could be offered a complimentary piece. As she cut the burfi into diamonds and arranged the pieces artfully on a large platter, Matt arrived in the kitchen, his dark hair ruffled and his canvas messenger bag bulging.

"Impressive," he said, kissing her on the cheek. Then he reached out to tug on one of her usual braids . . . but she wasn't wearing them. Instead, his fingers only caught a few wispy curls loosened from her topknot.

"Hey, you changed your hair!" he exclaimed.

"Yeah, what do you think?" Nidhi touched the bun.

She'd been hoping he'd notice. After the bonfire night, she'd returned to her usual hairstyle, but then earlier today at school, a friend had teased her about the ever-present twin braids. Actually, her friends had been teasing her about them since middle school, but she'd never thought much of it. They were easy and practical and framed her face nicely.

But today, it had finally sunk in: She was a *senior*. About to be a genuine adult. She couldn't go to Paris like that. The topknot felt so much more sophisticated. Maybe even a little—dare she think it—sexy? She glanced up at Matt, unsure but hopeful.

"I don't know." He reached out, then let his hand fall away. "I really like your braids—they're cute. I feel like I can't even touch that thing without ruining it."

"Maybe that's okay?" she said.

He shrugged. "I guess you do look really pretty."

"Thanks, I think?" Nidhi sighed, then offered him a diamond-shaped piece of milk cardamom burfi.

"Hmmm." He sniffed it first, then took a suspicious bite, chewing thoughtfully. "Not a texture I'm used to, but it's not bad. I might have to taste a few more just to be sure, though."

She laughed, though it felt a little forced. "Go for it, there's plenty."

"Conquering French desserts isn't enough for you, huh? You have to take over the rest of the world, too?"

"Something like that." Nidhi didn't know exactly what she'd been expecting. To be literally swept off her feet in a fit of passion? That was ridiculous. Still, she couldn't help but feel a bit deflated at his underwhelming interest in both her hair and the dessert. "How was ice cream scooping?"

Matt made a face. "The constant smell of waffle and vanilla is actually starting to get old."

"Never!" Nidhi declared.

"I guess you'll find out how much you really love sugar this summer," Matt returned. "Guess what, though! I have a surprise for you!"

"Oh yeah?" She touched his arm tentatively, still feeling off her usual game.

He pulled up a confirmation receipt on his phone.

It was a tour for Versailles—dated for the last weekend in July. "The woman who does these is *the* expert on Louis XIV. And we'll get to go into parts of the palace that aren't usually open to the public!"

"Wait, what?" Nidhi held up her sugar-dusted hands. "You're already booking things for our trip?"

"Well, yeah. Her tours fill up." Matt devoured another burfi, a chocolate one this time. Apparently, working at the ice cream parlor hadn't completely diminished his appetite. "Look, she wrote this. Want to borrow it?"

He pulled a huge textbook out of his bag, and Nidhi flipped through the twelve-hundred-page tome. Did she care about Louis XIV that much? She'd already learned a ton about France and its kings in school, and yet she hadn't taken one class covering Indian history. Sure, they'd touched on the Indus Valley civilization in World History, but if their curriculum were to be believed, absolutely nothing of interest had happened in her motherland in the several thousand years since.

She handed the book back to Matt. "Maybe you can summarize it for me."

"Oh . . . okay, I guess." He continued scrolling on his phone, where he'd noted down ideas for their trip. "I was also thinking we could take a train to Italy. See the little village my mom's family was from."

"Oh." It *was* a lovely idea.

Yet Nidhi suddenly felt the trip was slipping away from her, taking on a shape she hadn't anticipated. Of course, she'd been the one to invite Matt, had desperately wanted his company beside her as she stepped foot on another continent for the first time. It wasn't fair for her to feel he was intruding; Paris was their trip now, not just hers.

Still, as much as Nidhi loved filling in the dates on her planning app, she didn't want them to box themselves in. What if she wanted to hop over to Prague or Scotland or Croatia on a whim? They'd have so much in reach from Paris.

As she considered what to say, if anything, Matt reached across the platter of burfi for the jar of snickerdoodles. His weakness above all weaknesses. His messenger bag clipped the edge of the platter, and Nidhi watched in horror as all of the burfi scattered across the checkerboard tiles.

Matt put a hand to his mouth. "I'm so sorry!"

"It's okay." Nidhi blinked rapidly, trying not to let tears start falling.

It was just food after all, and accidents happened. In fact, the last one—the flying curry incident with Grayson—had led to her learning the truth about the Skull. Yet as she and Matt swept up the six types of burfi spread across the floor like multicolored confetti, Nidhi ached with a loss that had nothing to do with desserts at all.

Her mind whirled with unobtainable expectations, a motherland she'd never known, and the unsettling feeling that she was stuck in a place she wasn't sure she wanted to be, just as she had been when that tree had fallen down. Only this time, her sisters couldn't come to her rescue. Nidhi had to find her own way out.

Chapter Seven

- It rained on Monday, but Nidhi was in school during the day and then working at reception all evening, so it didn't matter much.

- It rained on Tuesday, and they had to cancel their after-school biology outing to catalog local marine life.

- It rained on Wednesday, but her bio teacher decided they were going tide pooling anyway, so they took their raincoats and boots and splashed around like happy-go-lucky preschoolers and had a fabulous time.

- It rained on Thursday, and Nidhi's boots were still wet from the day before, and her other pair was not at all comfortable.

- It rained on Friday, and the temperature dropped to forty degrees. Rani announced with certainty that the nice part of the fall was over. This would be it until April.

- It rained on Saturday, and Nidhi thought that perhaps Rani was right.

Early Sunday morning, Nidhi awoke to a steady patter on the window and a now familiar sense of restlessness and disquiet gnawing at her. Ever since the fateful fall of the Douglas fir, it seemed to have seeped into her very bones.

Perhaps it would finally recede after she reclaimed her room today. Somehow, three weeks had disappeared since they'd begun work on it. Of course, it had been fun bunking with Sirisha, staying up late chatting about the many wonders in the world they each wanted to see: ice caves and volcanoes and thousand-year-old palaces and sunken cities. But all things considered, Nidhi's back was just about done with sleeping on a trundle bed with a hard mattress.

The only downside was that the construction crew would be gone. And with them, the Skull. Nidhi wished she'd gotten to know him better, even fantasized about helping out on one of his late-night adventures. Could he possibly need an assistant, someone to help carry equipment or be a lookout? Someone to laugh with as they made their moonlit getaway?

Maybe she should ask for his number so they could keep in touch. But then again, what if he got completely the wrong idea?

She imagined herself saying, "Hey, I like you for your art only. Got it, bud?"

But she didn't think she could actually pull that off. Wandering down to the kitchen, she found Dad stirring rice in his huge steel karahi, humming along to a Bollywood soundtrack from his latest favorite film. It was 6 a.m., still dark out, the inn's lights illuminating drizzle and mist and lonely pines through the window. The restaurant would open for brunch in a few hours, but for now, the place was theirs.

"Good morning!" Dad sang.

"You seem perky."

"Do I?" He laughed. "It's foggy and wet outside, and there aren't any birds singing, but oh, what a beautiful day!"

His energy was infectious, and Nidhi couldn't help but smile as she watched him make khichdi, a rice dish convenient for using up leftovers. He tossed in yesterday's daal and veggies, added a few eggs to give it that breakfasty feel, frying everything together until it was soft comfort food. It never came out exactly the same twice, which he said was part of the fun. He took a quick taste, then spooned in a bit more ghee and a sprinkling of gray sea salt. On another burner, sweet chai simmered.

Nidhi inhaled the sweet and spicy scents. "How am I supposed to follow your recipes when you never measure anything?"

"Instinct," Dad said, filling two bowls high. "When I was studying hotel management and culinary arts back in Delhi, we were often given a table full of ingredients and then challenged to make something incredible. No recipes, no cookbooks. We just had to create."

"Oh yeah?" Nidhi wondered if Siècles du Sucre would have challenges like that.

It sounded intriguing. She itched to prove herself, yet another part of her wanted nothing more than to spend the rest of her life here, right in this kitchen. No decisions to make, no sights to see. Just sunny yellow walls and an industrial-size oven. Home.

But that wasn't the plan—and Nidhi always stuck to her plans.

As Dad poured them two cups of chai, she tried to picture him as a student, skinny and nervous, way back in another land. And suddenly she wanted to know everything about it, every detail of his life. "How did you decide this was what you wanted to do?"

Dad's gaze was faraway, someplace she'd never been.

"I always enjoyed cooking," he said, "but it was considered a distinctly feminine calling. My parents suggested hotel management, and I knew I'd get to do a bit of both. I dreamt of having my own little inn and restaurant."

"And now you do." She gestured around them. "You got your wish."

"Beti, you make it sound so easy. As if it all happened in a straight line." Dad grabbed the bowls in one arm, and Nidhi commandeered the chai.

The two of them settled at the best table in the empty dining room, the one right in the center of the large bay window. There was no view that morning, thick fog making it seem as if the inn rested on the edge of a great void.

"Did you know I worked as a bellboy?" Dad asked. "A night manager? A driver? But I couldn't raise the capital I needed to start my own business. Your mother was the one who suggested we apply for visas to come here."

"Really?"

Dad smiled, looking at once young and old, at peace with a life well-lived. "To be honest, it wasn't just economics. We both had an itch to have a new adventure, to leave everything behind and trek into the unknown. America was practically another galaxy to us, so foreign and a little scary and yet full of opportunity."

"Yeah, makes sense." Nidhi hid behind her chai. India was another galaxy to her. Foreign and a lot scary and yet . . . also hers? Would she ever get a chance to go there, though?

"You probably had the same feeling when you decided to go to Paris for the summer."

"I guess so." She'd been so thrilled about France at first, but the more she planned the trip, the more hollow she was starting to feel. The mundan ceremony and the man from Bombay had awakened a mess of emotions and wanting, all tossed together like leftovers in khichdi. "It's just that . . ."

"Yes?"

"Sometimes I don't feel Desi enough." She stuck gooey rice into her mouth, heat rising up her cheeks.

Dad's eyes pierced hers, as if he could see straight into all those confusing mushy thoughts. "You'll always be Indian, Nidhi. And you don't have to wear a sari or make burfi to prove it. You don't even have to drink chai."

Was that true? Even with all the time and distance between her and the motherland?

"You know," Dad continued, "I think my alma mater has summer programs, too."

Nidhi suddenly felt a longing deep in her bones. "But I'm already going to France, remember?"

"I just want you to know that you have options." Dad patted Nidhi's shoulder, the sound of pots rattling in the kitchen drawing his attention. Josie and Armand had arrived to start prepping.

But Nidhi wasn't ready to let go of Dad quite yet. "But—"

A tap on the window on the other side of the dining room interrupted her. It was Fernando Gutiérrez, one of the twins' fellow juniors from school. His family's farm had an exclusive agreement with the inn, and Nidhi had never tasted a tomato as juicy or flavorful as one of theirs. A true restaurant staple.

Wearing a stylish navy trench coat and his hair mussed with product just so, Fernando waved cheerfully from the north porch, pushing a dolly stacked with several crates of produce. Dressing down for delivery apparently wasn't his thing.

Nidhi waved back. "I'll help him."

"Thanks, honey." Dad gathered their empty bowls.

Nidhi paused. "About summer—I accepted the scholarship, I made all these plans with Matt. I couldn't possibly change it all now. . . ."

But Dad only did the Desi head bobble, a sideways tilting that signified neither complete agreement nor disagreement.

Later that morning, Nidhi stood outside the attic door, balancing a tray full of croissants and coffee. Nervous for no reason at all. "Can someone get the door?"

It swung open, and Grayson grinned. "It's ready for you!"

He stepped back, gesturing at the bedroom. The rest of the crew had already cleared out, and except for a can of paint in the corner, all their stuff was gone, too.

"Oh, I didn't realize you were finished painting already." She set the tray of coffee and goodies down on the desk. "I guess I missed everyone."

"Yep, but it's their loss." Grayson sniffed. "Do I smell drip coffee?"

Nidhi poured him a mug from the steel pot. "French press, actually."

As he accepted the cup, she decided not to mention that she'd bought the press thinking of him. They were just friends after all, even if she was a little too intrigued by his artwork and his secret identity.

This was perfect; she had Grayson all to herself for a moment. Now she just had to find the courage to ask him for his number. But seriously, how could she do that without sounding like she had a thing for him? She knew this whole problem sounded terribly middle school, but then again, she'd only just recently gotten rid of her braids. It occurred to her that all her overachieving had left her a little behind in the realm of social interaction.

Nidhi inhaled the scent of fresh paint as she took in her new old room. The hexagonal walls and ceiling were whole once again, the shattered window replaced with a much larger one. More light flooded the attic turret than she'd ever had before, the sun finally poking out from the clouds. Crisp new wallpaper in a vintage polka-dot pattern adorned the walls, and the wainscoting along the perimeter was a lovely bright ivory. Her bed was back in its place, a new coat of white paint over the carved headboard that had saved her life.

She ran a hand over the rose-dotted duvet folded neatly at the foot of the bed. The rip in the corner had been carefully sewn back together.

"Who did this?" she asked aloud, her heart in her throat.

"I think it was Sirisha," Grayson said. "I saw her put it back on your bed earlier this morning."

Nidhi held the duvet close to her, sniffing it. Freshly washed. A fragrant vase of flowers greeted her from the nightstand. Everything was perfect, ready for her to move back in. And she wanted to, she really did, but at the same time she yearned for so much more than just a new coat of paint. Would this unsettled feeling never leave her?

"Thank you." She turned to Grayson. "You did a beautiful job."

He wandered to the desk, not looking at her. "Of course, I'll let the team know you're happy with it."

So that was it, then? She wasn't going to see him again? Everything would go back to how it had been before that fallen Douglas fir had brought Grayson to the Songbird. Unless she did something about it. As her mind raced for a way to draw out the moment, she spotted it: a small winking chalk skull sketched in a corner by the closet door.

She knelt down to take a closer look at the swirling colors. "Is this for me?"

He bent next to her. "I thought I'd leave my mark. Since you're a fan and all."

"I love it."

"I'm glad." He smiled that dimpled smile again.

Nidhi shivered, brushing a stray lock of hair out of her eyes. Today, she'd opted to leave it down with her curls roaming unrestrained. Experimenting was fun, and she was utterly sick of braids. But then again, who knew how it looked? It might be a complete frizzy mess.

Also, why didn't guys have to think about these things? It really wasn't fair.

"So how's the cooking going?" he asked. "Tried anything new and exciting?"

She nodded with probably a bit too much fervor and pointed to the corner of the tray, where she'd stacked four different types of burfi. "I'm still perfecting my recipes, but I like to make a few different flavors at once."

"Oh wow. They're almost too beautiful to eat."

"Don't say that. They're meant to taste good, too."

He gamely tried a triple-colored one. "This is a winner—so crumbly and creamy. And wait—are the colors for the Indian flag?"

"Yeah, exactly." She scrambled for something more to say. Anything, really. "I can't believe the sun actually came out. I was worried we wouldn't see it again until April."

Yep, talk about the weather, Nidhi. That's riveting.

Blue eyes searched her brown ones now, suddenly, intensely. As if he too didn't want the moment to end. "Actually, it's supposed to warm up to almost seventy today. It could be the last really nice day of the season. I feel like we should take advantage of it."

"We?"

He paused. "How do you feel about wakeboarding?"

Chapter Eight

The marina was buzzing with activity, boaters anxious to hit the water with this unexpected windfall of warm weather in October. After being holed up indoors from a week of relentless rain, everyone was itching to get out, to do something, to stock up on some vitamin D and fresh air before the next rain came. As Nidhi and Grayson wandered down the dock, soft autumn light shimmered over the sea like tiny mirrors dotting a cerulean silk sari.

Nidhi had texted Matt to see if he could join them, and her phone pinged now with his response.

Wakeboarding? Seriously?

Even if I wanted to, I couldn't. Mom's got the flu and I've got a shift at Lulu's and Anita's being a handful. Wish me luck.

Normally, she would have offered to stop by the ice cream shop to hang with them, but Grayson's friend—the one with the boat and the gear—was waiting on them. Besides, after the gentle encouragement from the man from Bombay, the offer to go wakeboarding—yes, seriously—seemed like pure kismet.

Especially since Sirisha was saving for a new lens and had happily taken Nidhi's spot at the espresso bar for some extra tip money. Nidhi did her best to brush away the bit of guilt that touched her. Matt had to work today, and she didn't. That was fine.

"There's Rita!" Grayson waved to a sporty redhead standing at the far end of the pier. "We were good friends all through high school. Now she's at UW Seattle."

"I'm applying to their business school," Nidhi said. "Maybe we'll be there together next fall. Is she just here for the weekend?"

"Yeah," Grayson said "She doesn't have Monday classes, so she'll head back tomorrow. That's her parents' boat. One of their boats, I should say. They also have a forty-footer."

"Fancy."

"Yeah, but Rita's cool. Not stuck-up at all."

She certainly didn't seem stuck-up; not when she helped Nidhi on board and then hugged her tightly as if they were old friends. "It's so good to meet you! I hear it's your first time on a wakeboard?"

"You too. And . . . yes. I hope that's okay."

"No problem at all. We'll get you standing in no time!" A bit of friendly mischief glinted in Rita's eyes. "Though there might be a few falls along the way."

Oh dear. What had she gotten herself into?

Rita took the helm and swung the sleek speedboat easily off the dock. She didn't offer a warning before gunning the motor, and then they were off, the wind pressing fiercely against their faces, the roar of the engine too loud to hear one another talk. Around them, sailboats and yachts and ferries and kayaks abounded, but Rita maneuvered expertly through the good-weather mayhem. Nidhi couldn't help flicking her eyes toward the wakeboard sprawled casually in the backseat next to her.

She messed with her hair, pulling it into a ponytail, then a bun, then a ponytail again. She wanted to relax into the ride, but the windshield in the front wasn't doing much to protect her and it felt like she couldn't breathe with so much wind flattening her face. And the thought of strapping herself to the wakeboard suddenly seemed a very, very foolish idea. Her wetsuit became sticky with fear, her heart racing so fast that it would probably tunnel right out of her chest. This wasn't her at all; why had she listened to that man?

Grayson leaned close to her. "You doing okay?"

Nidhi gulped. "A little nervous."

"Don't be." He offered her his wide dimpled smile. "You'll be great, Nidhi."

Nice of him to say, but he didn't know her. She'd never been a natural at athletics, taking longer than the other kids her age to learn to bike, to swim, to kick a soccer ball with any force. Reasoning and meticulous planning helped her with most things, but not those.

After a while, Rita slowed the boat into a protected channel between islands, a place where the water was flat and glistening like sapphire. It was much quieter here, a double kayak the only other vessel in sight. As the couple in it paddled past, the small pup perched up front wagged its tail happily, safe in its adorable doggie life vest. Nidhi breathed, took in the sea and sky, the tranquil stillness of the afternoon.

A part of her was ready to break that stillness, shatter it into a thousand pieces. (The other part was petrified.)

"Let's do this!" Rita idled the engine. Zipping her life vest in one quick movement, she jumped off the back of the boat with a splash.

"How's the water?" Grayson called.

"Absolute perfection!" she shouted, strapping on the wakeboard. "I can't believe we got this lucky."

Grayson tossed her the tow rope, then turned to Nidhi. "Thanks for coming along. It's good to have a third when you're wakeboarding. I'll drive forward real slow, and you let me know how she's doing."

"Ah, so that's why you invited me," Nidhi said lightly. "You needed a spotter."

He chuckled. "Yep, I was just using you. But hey, you get a free wakeboard lesson out of it, so don't complain."

Nidhi rolled her eyes. "Thanks, I guess?"

In a way, she was relieved. They were just friends, of course, but in the back of her mind, Rani's theory about Grayson liking her made her nervous. As if she was doing something wrong by coming out here with him. Though, she absolutely wasn't.

Sure, they'd bantered a bit, but he'd never even really flirted with her. Then again, Grayson didn't seem like the kind of guy who would flirt with a girl who had a boyfriend. She liked that about him.

"Let's go!" Rita shouted from the water.

As Grayson accelerated, Nidhi thought that perhaps the fact that they needed her was a good thing. She could be a very excellent spotter without getting wet, and watching from the backseat was pretty fun. Rita was a pro wakeboarder, showing off with cool turns and jumps and other tricks on the water. Grayson wasn't bad either, though his jumps were slightly less elegant. On his third leap, he fell splat on his face.

Taking her duties seriously, Nidhi quickly signaled for Rita to turn the boat around.

"That looked painful," Nidhi shouted.

"Don't worry, I'm fine. Just a little water up my nose!" He gave a thumbs-up.

That wasn't the last time Grayson fell and looked ridiculous, and Nidhi kind of loved how he wasn't too macho to fail in front of them. He was fully aware that Rita was better than him, and he was fine with it.

Rita grinned wickedly after Grayson climbed back in. "Your turn, Nidhi!"

Nidhi trembled. And it had nothing to do with Grayson brushing past her, the scent of salt water in his hair, his chest filling out his wetsuit a little too nicely, the way he seemed as if he were made for the sea.

Could she face them if she chickened out? Could she face herself?

"You're enjoying this a little too much," Nidhi protested.

"Yep!"

"You promise I'll live, right?" She forced a smile. "I mean, there are things I still need to do in my life."

"Oh yeah? Like what?" Rita asked.

Nidhi thought about it—really thought about it. She'd thought she had her life in order: the program at Siècles du Sucre, business major next year, opening her own bakery. But doubts were starting to take hold, something inside her shifting indelibly. Were those really her dreams anymore, or were they the dreams of an eight-year-old with an Easy-Bake oven?

"Well, I hope I get to see India someday," Nidhi finally answered. "I've been secretly jealous of Grayson's plans to go there."

Rita nodded. "Me too! He's so ambitious, and it's awesome."

The funny thing was, Nidhi hadn't thought of it that way. She was so caught up in the world of internships and college applications that his travel plans seemed almost self-indulgent. But she supposed they really were ambitious in their scope, even if they weren't a road map toward a specific career.

"Yeah, he thinks big," she agreed. "With his art, too."

"He's into art?" Rita asked. "News to me."

Grayson shrugged with an enigmatic smile. "It's more of a hobby."

Nidhi winked at Grayson. It was fun to have this little secret between them. She really did wish she could go with him on one of his adventures, stay up all night to create a gorgeous surprise for Friday Harbor's residents. Not that she had any talent for either the art or the kind of playful mischief it entailed.

And, of course, what if they got caught?

Yet something about this boy made her want to chase wild dreams like kites in a vast blue sky. And when he reached over to adjust her life vest, Nidhi's breath caught. He was close, so close she could smell the mint and coffee on his breath, so close all she could see was his Adam's apple and his collarbone and his muscles through the wetsuit . . .

Why did he affect her this way? After all:

- She had a boyfriend.

- Matt was cute and sweet and fantastic.

- She. Had. A. Boyfriend.

Thankfully, Rita motioned for Grayson to take the wheel. "Come on, Nidhi, I'll show you how it's done."

Nidhi balanced carefully on the edge of the boat. As she contemplated the wakeboard and the waves and whether she *really* had it in her to try this, Rita patted her shoulder kindly.

Then firmly pushed her overboard.

Nidhi plummeted into the water, which was actually *freezing* even with the wetsuit. The life jacket pulled her quickly back to the surface, and she came up laughing. Rita was right there beside her, grinning like a maniac.

"How dare you!" Nidhi splashed her in the face.

"Were you ever going to get in if I didn't?"

"Er . . ."

"Exactly."

They swam a few meters behind the speedboat as Grayson watched from his spot at the wheel. Rita helped Nidhi get her feet strapped into the wakeboard and showed her how to lean back in the water holding the triangle-shaped handle of the tow rope.

"Bend your knees and keep your arms straight," Rita instructed. "Not that straight! Loosen your muscles a bit. That's good. Don't try too hard to stand up right away. If you do, you'll end up face planting. It's best to let the rope do the work of pulling you up."

Nidhi nodded, her palms wet and slippery and numb from the cold. Great. How was she supposed to hold on?

Rita climbed back into the boat, chuckling. "You look like you've been sentenced to ten years hard labor."

Nidhi stuck out her tongue. "I'm fine."

Grayson peered back. "Are you sure? I'm not going to drive until you're ready."

Would she ever really be ready? This felt like one of those moments in life where you just had to close your eyes and hope for the best, the way you did when you leaned into a kiss for the first time with someone new.

Of course, it had been a while since she'd taken that kind of chance, too. "Just go!" she shouted.

Grayson offered her a sharp salute of a nod, the kind that guys share when they respect one another. The tiny vote of confidence was enough for Nidhi to actually keep her eyes open while he carefully picked up speed.

Here she went.

As Rita had instructed, she hung backward, the board angled in front of her, her hands gripping the tow rope as tightly as she could. She had no idea how, but she did miraculously manage to keep her head, allowing the rope to tug her slowly, slowly, slowly upright.

And then she was standing! On a wakeboard! And the wind was on her face, and she was terrified to turn or do anything fancy like Rita, but she was gliding across the water. The sun winked down at her and she leaned back in exhilaration.

This moment.

There were no words.

Only sea and sky and the board beneath her feet.

And Nidhi knew then what it meant to fly, to soar so high that she might touch the sun, clasp it in her fingers, and tuck it in her pocket like a wish.

Chapter Nine

That evening, twilight filtered through the trees as Nidhi and Matt drove the island roads in the hopes that Matt's sister would stop crying and fall asleep.

So far, it was *not* working.

Nidhi had called Matt after taking a very long and very hot shower, eager to share her exploits on the water. But even though Matt's shift at Lulu's was over, he'd sounded incredibly weary with Anita shouting crankily in the background. So Nidhi had offered to pick the two of them up in the car she shared with her sisters. The twisty roads that wound along the shoreline and through forests and past farms usually did the trick of soothing Anita into peaceful slumber.

"Try changing the music," Nidhi said. "The Bert and Ernie album."

Matt rubbed his forehead. "Ugh."

Nidhi squeezed his hand sympathetically as the familiar notes of Anita's favorite song came on. They'd heard it a thousand times, and they'd probably hear it a thousand more. But the kid loved it, immediately bopping happily in her car seat.

The thing about four-year-olds is that it only took sixty seconds for their emotions to one-eighty, so Nidhi and Matt let the jaunty songs fill the car, not attempting even a word between them lest they disrupt Anita's sudden calm. Three songs later, Anita's head started drooping. By the end of the fourth, she was out.

"Thank you," Matt said, but he sounded a little begrudging.

Or maybe Nidhi was imagining it. "Of course. Sorry you had such a rough day."

"Not your fault." He paused. "So you really went wakeboarding? You can't even bike straight enough to stay on a path."

She laughed. "I know, it's so not me. But it was actually awesome—I can't believe I managed to stand up! I'm really glad Grayson invited me."

"Grayson?"

"He's part of the construction crew that worked on my room. Remember?"

Matt paused. "You didn't say you were out with some guy."

Nidhi bit her lip. "I thought I mentioned him?"

"I would have noticed."

"We're just friends, Matt." Nidhi pushed aside those uncomfortable moments of Grayson with his shirt off, Grayson standing so close in his wetsuit. . . .

She squeezed his hand. "We should all go together sometime."

"Not likely." He snorted. "It's such a bro sport."

"Rita obviously isn't a bro. And Grayson's not like that, either."

Matt shrugged. "I just thought you had better things to do than trying to impress the cool crowd. Shouldn't you have been working on your biology project for next week?"

"Well, A) It's not due till Thursday," she answered slowly. "B) Grayson and Rita are really nice. And C) I wasn't trying to impress them. I actually wanted to try wakeboarding for myself. Why are you being so down about this?"

"I don't know, Nidhi!" Matt bit out. "Maybe because I was working and taking care of a four-year-old while you were off having the time of your life with some random guy."

They neared his house, a cute little cabin tucked within a grove of giant pines. It was dark now, starlight and a gibbous moon peeking through the branches.

Maybe he had a point. Grayson did get under her skin sometimes, and maybe something could have happened between them—in an alternate world where she didn't have a boyfriend. But she did, and she wouldn't do anything to hurt Matt. Besides, why couldn't he understand how much wakeboarding had meant to her?

"He's just a friend," Nidhi repeated. "And I wanted to try something new. That's all."

Annoyance prickled through her. If Matt would give it a chance, he would have understood how incredible it had been, how the feel of gliding across the water had been so freeing that she'd almost wished land didn't exist.

"Look, I'm sorry. I trust you, of course." He sighed, running a hand through his hair. "I just feel like we've always been, you know, nerdy intellectual types. And suddenly you're into water sports and you changed your hair and you're more interested in perfecting your burfi recipe than reading about Versailles—which we have plans to visit really soon!"

She pulled into his drive, her heart fluttering faintly, a butterfly trapped in a jar. "Sorry I didn't read your book, Matt." But even as she said it, she knew this was about more than just Versailles or wakeboarding or even Grayson. "Maybe I'm acting differently because I feel different." As the words tumbled out, they grew stronger, more forceful. "That tree nearly killing me—it was kind of a big deal. A lot more than I originally thought. It changed me somehow. I'm still figuring it out."

It was true. The strange disquiet had started soon after that, the racing feeling that *something was not right*. But without the full conviction of what exactly it was. She'd tried new recipes, she'd tried wakeboarding, she'd tried a new look.

But even now, a storm rustled inside her, threatening violence if it wasn't appeased.

"Okay, I guess that's understandable," he mumbled. "I hope the wakeboarding helped."

Nidhi waited for him to say more, to ask more. She was bursting with so many feelings she wanted to share with him, but he didn't seem to get that at all. Matt only kissed her lips briefly and opened the car door. Then he gathered up Anita from the back, who immediately wrapped around him like a koala bear. After he carried her inside, Nidhi sat alone in the car for a long time, listening to the buzz of insects and the swaying of pines and waiting, waiting, waiting to simply exhale.

Chapter Ten

*N*idhi and Matt had always been like puzzle pieces that fit perfectly together. But in the week that followed, they couldn't even find a good time to talk anymore.

Nidhi kept telling herself they were both just busy. Besides helping set up for the inn's elaborate Halloween theme, she'd also started apprenticing with Dad in the kitchen in the evenings, hoping to get a better handle on Indian cooking. Meanwhile, Matt was usually working at Lulu's or running around after Anita. They saw each other in class, of course, but Nidhi had been spending her lunch hours working on her biology project. They'd even missed their 8 p.m. video call three days in a row.

On Thursday, the night before Halloween, they finally managed to get their schedules to coincide. Matt agreed to help her bake cookies for the inn's festivities after her evening shift at the front desk. She was just finishing up her homework when the bell dinged, announcing the arrival of the last family expected for the night. Their three kids went wild for the entryway jack-o'-lanterns that Sirisha had carved into various animated characters, and were even more intrigued when Nidhi offered them a map of the "haunted inn."

"It's a scavenger hunt!" she said. "Whenever you see a ghost or ghoul or other Halloween creature, mark it on your map. There will be prizes at our party tomorrow."

The maps were eagerly snatched out of her hands and the kids were running off in seconds, racing toward the faux-cobweb-covered staircase where a large rubber spider lurked, their parents thanking her as they chased after them.

The bell dinged once more. Matt shuffled in on a blast of chilly wind, his boots caked in thick mud, brown leaves stuck to the heels.

"Whoa, should I add swamp monster to the scavenger hunt?" Nidhi joked.

But Matt didn't even chuckle, just pulled off his dirty footwear. "I'll clean it up."

Nidhi handed him a rag. "What's Anita dressing as for Halloween this year?"

"A bumblebee." He wiped up the mess without looking at her.

"That sounds adorable." Nidhi smiled.

"Yeah."

And so it went as they moved to the kitchen to make cookies for the inn's party. Both of them asking each other questions. Both of them answering politely, but not giving much more:

- Matt's essay on the Civil War was "almost done."

- Nidhi thought the pilot of a new streaming comedy was "decent."

- Neither was particularly worried about tomorrow's math test.

Even talking about their Paris trip had lost its appeal; they'd already planned most of their weekends, including leaving a few free for impulse sightseeing. What else was there to say?

As Matt hunted down the witch- and pumpkin-shaped cookie cutters, Nidhi rolled out the dough. She hated that fight they'd had, hated that she'd confessed her innermost feelings to him and he'd barely responded. But she was afraid to bring it up now, scared of what might happen—what she might lose—if she let down the veneer of being happy.

She carefully punched the spooky shapes into the dough while Matt scraped off the extra. Of course, he scarfed it right up.

She cracked a smile. "Hungry?"

"Raw cookie dough! Nom, nom, nom!" Matt stuffed more in his face, then grinned at her hopefully.

His standby joke. Nidhi laughed, as she always did, and for the first time that night, that week, that month . . . things felt slightly normal. She'd missed this, she'd missed them.

She placed the trays in the oven and set the timer, then popped a quick kiss on his chin.

He, in turn, tugged gently on her braid. "Glad to see my two old pals are back."

She smiled, but it felt a little forced. Deep in her stomach she felt the tiniest hot coil of—was it resentment? She'd braided her hair that morning since he'd made such a big deal about it. But was that really what she had to do to make this work? Never change?

Tonight would be the final appearance of the twin braids, she decided. And Matt would just have to get used to it, or . . .

Inside her apron pocket, her phone buzzed. It was a text from Grayson. They'd finally exchanged numbers, and it hadn't been as awkward as she'd feared; he had such a casual way about him.

I need your help. Skullduggery! You in?

A tingle traveled down Nidhi's spine. It *was* the night before Halloween: Of course the Skull would be out tonight.

And he needed her help.

It was her secret wish come true! Naturally, she'd deny till the end of her days how many times she'd lain awake in bed imagining running off with Grayson to claim the wild darkness of the night. But now it was actually happening—now it was *real*.

Nidhi took the baking sheet out of the oven while her phone buzzed two more times. Her heart hammered in her chest. Matt didn't ask what the alerts were; he was used to her sisters texting all the time. Should she tell him, though? She'd promised Grayson she'd keep his secret, but this was *Matt*. She always told him everything.

Or she had until now. After so much angst the past few weeks over falling trees and burnt parathas and being Desi enough and working up the courage to wakeboard while also trying to be the person Matt wanted her to be . . . maybe she deserved a break.

She straightened her shoulders. "Listen, thanks for your help. I know you're tired—all that ice cream scooping and everything. You should get home."

"Are you sure? What about the icing?"

For a moment, she faltered. Should she really be ditching him? But she found herself saying, "We'll have to wait for them to cool anyway. Might as well do it in the morning."

"The candy bags?"

"Rani and Avani can handle those."

"Okay. Nidhi, I . . ." His brow furrowed, the little cute sign of worry she'd always loved.

Only tonight, she felt irrationally annoyed by it. What was the point in worrying if he wasn't going to do anything about it—especially when it mattered most?

"Yes?" She held her breath, hoping he'd come through, prove her wrong. That strange dark space between them seemed impassible this evening, but perhaps he knew the way across.

But he only shook his head. "Nothing. You're right, I'm beat. See you at school tomorrow."

Nidhi swallowed her disappointment. When his car was out of sight, she hurried back to her room for warm layers. She would sort out her complicated feelings tomorrow. Tonight, adventure was calling, and she refused to miss it.

A pack of gray clouds crept across the horizon like wolves on the hunt, obscuring the moon. As Nidhi hiked down to the cove to meet Grayson, she spotted his silhouette in the shadows, the sea behind him churning with smoke and dragons and night whispers. A thrill raced through her veins, the drug of endless possibilities. The evening was hers to claim, and claim it she would.

A small, sturdy schooner was anchored just offshore, the kind that looked as if it were made for cruising through rough weather. Grayson started when she tapped his shoulder, his gaze lost in the horizon.

"It's just me." Nidhi smiled. "Thanks for coming all the way out here to pick me up."

His shoulders relaxed. "Well, my buddy who usually helps me couldn't make it. And my parents said no freaking way were either of them staying up all night. No one else knows I'm the Skull except you."

She chuckled. "Just like when you needed a spotter for wakeboarding, huh? Thanks, I feel so special."

He laughed. "I know, I'm the absolute worst. Ready?"

He gestured toward an inflatable dinghy that had been obscured in the darkness.

"Definitely." Nidhi shivered.

She did feel weird about the way she'd left things with Matt, so much unspoken between them. And of course, there was that math test tomorrow. Yet a spell, a midnight enchantment, compelled her to shed those lingering worries, murmuring in her ear that if she didn't embrace tonight, she would regret it for the rest of her life.

The magic engulfed them like fog as they drifted across the water in the dinghy, climbed the ladder, and set foot on the gently rocking schooner. Nidhi leaned against the side, searching for her sea legs, letting the rhythm of the Salish Sea become a part of her.

"Is this your boat?" she asked.

"My mom's." Grayson secured the dinghy and pulled up the anchor. "She's a marine biologist. Runs an eco-tourism company to help pay for her research."

"She must really trust you to let you take it out alone at night." It started to drizzle, but the cold and damp invigorated her. It made her *feel*, and tonight that's what she wanted to do.

"Oh, I had to negotiate," Grayson said. "Let's just say I've got plenty of hull scraping in my future."

She smiled. "Then I'm flattered you thought I was worth it. Even if I was your last choice."

He grinned. "Which you definitely were. The very last."

When Grayson started the engine, Nidhi joined him in the warm enclosed cabin area. She felt safe, comfortable. This was a vessel that could handle a few good rollers and a bit of storm, or perhaps she just liked the thought of Grayson wearing an old-fashioned captain's hat and saying things like "Dar she blows!" as the boat bounced ferociously in a cursed gale.

Maybe she was letting her imagination run away with her, but he *was* the Skull, after all.

Grayson offered her a cup of coffee and a baguette stuffed with ham and cheese, and Nidhi thought there was nothing better than eating and drinking and speeding across the water in the chill black night. He navigated steadily through the islands, past anchored vessels and a late ferry. They didn't talk much, let the song of the engine fill the space between them. The sense of enchantment stayed with Nidhi, and they arrived at Friday Harbor all too soon. A thick mist shrouded the town, and it felt wrong to speak, to even whisper.

"It's the witching hour!" She giggled, slightly delirious as they made their way down the dock. It was past her bedtime by far, and caffeine rocketed wildly through her veins.

Under a glowing streetlight a block from the marina, he smiled. Slowly, wickedly. "I hope you're up for some shady shenanigans, Ms. Singh."

"More than you know." She zipped up her raincoat all the way to her throat. The drizzle and mist were seeping into her bones, an icy potion that she embraced wholeheartedly. "But, um, what about the rain? Won't that ruin your murals?"

"This?" He scoffed. "You call this rain? This is the PNW, and we call this NOTHING."

"So . . . the chalk won't wash off?"

"It's waterproof. It would take a pretty heavy storm to wash it off."

She bit her lip. "You really are a vandal, then."

He chuckled. "You don't have to look so worried. If the murals don't come off by themselves within a week or two, I'll spend another night cleaning them myself."

"Ah, so the Skull is a good citizen, after all." She hoped she sounded appropriately lighthearted and not overly relieved.

"Don't tell anyone, though. It would ruin my image."

"Not a soul, I swear." She tightened a hairpin in her topknot.

Before heading down to the cove, she'd ditched the braids, but she'd been in a hurry, and now her hair was definitely about to unravel around her. She wrestled with a few more pins, feeling increasingly ridiculous as several locks came tumbling out. Especially since Grayson was watching her.

"What?" she asked.

A smile played across his lips. "Nothing. Just that your hair looks nice all messy like that."

"Are you sure?" Nidhi kept fussing with the pins. "I mean, braids are more practical, but I've been trying to get away from them. Look more grown up, you know? But I guess I still need practice to make it stay up and not . . ."

She was babbling now. Grayson couldn't possibly care about all this.

But his eyes held hers. "No, it's perfect. Gorgeous."

Nidhi's fingers stilled.

"Not that I should be saying that to you," Grayson added hurriedly. "Since you have a boyfriend and all."

And yet, he couldn't exactly unsay it, now could he? Nidhi held his gaze, and the night took on another dimension. She suddenly wished she'd stayed quiet about her silly hair.

"I made that awkward, didn't I?" He scuffed his boot in the dirt.

"Er . . ."

"I'm sorry. Forget I said it. Besides, we have work to do." He held out a fist for her to bump. "We're in this together, right?"

She brushed her knuckles against his. "Together."

She took a deep breath, trying to reorient herself.

But all of a sudden, it seemed like a lot. Could she really spend the entire night alone with Grayson, a veil of fog and secrecy and art cloaking them from the demands of the outside world? Could she truly disappear into the wild darkness so completely, and if so, what about tomorrow?

But Grayson was already leading her around the corner, where a pickup truck waited. He opened up the back and started lifting out his equipment: two ladders, flashlights, chalk marker and spray, a duffel of random other gear. It was time to get to work. The next few hours flew by in a heady whirlwind. Nidhi had suspected that there were too many murals to create in a single night, and she was right. They were basically racing against dawn the entire time. Oh, but the art they created! It took her breath away.

They came to a rhythm faster than Nidhi would have believed: Grayson outlined each piece, then she swept in with hues from his sketches, and meanwhile he would refine and add texture and detail. Perched on rolling ladders, they flew across walls, streaking swirling colors and shadows across rough stone and brick and wood. Over windows and in alleys and across slanted rooftops. They needed to reach past each other so many times, and Nidhi had to admit that she didn't mind when they bumped into each other, his warmth like a lantern, his scent like an oncoming storm.

The witching hour indeed.

Their first project was the cowering silhouette of a furry horned monster chased into a corner by a throng of tiny humans. Then a ghost woman peering wearily at her sleeping family through a window. A squadron of fierce girls with brooms and pointy hats readying for battle. A skeleton curled up in a sleeping bag on a lonely sidewalk.

Grayson's monsters and ghouls were angry, they were defeated, they were scared, they were even kind and sometimes gentle. They were beautiful and haunting, and in the darkness, they came alive. Each mural told a story, and Nidhi loved playing a part in it.

But too quickly, they came to the final pages of Grayson's journal.

"This has to be the last mural," Grayson said. "Or we'll turn into pumpkins."

"Wouldn't want to be a pumpkin," Nidhi said. "How about a delicata squash, though? They have a more unique flavor."

She giggled at her own joke, sliding down against the sidewalk next to the chalk skeleton.

"Hey, Sleeping Beauty, is someone ready for bed?"

"Bed good. Pillows good. Ground hard and cold and wet." Nidhi made a face.

"Come on, we're nearly done. You can take a nap on the ride back, I promise."

He offered her his hand, helping her up with an icy but firm grip. A confusing tiny spark passed between them, waking her right up. But then he was pulling away to pick up the ladders, and she had no choice but to keep going.

"You really do all of this just for fun?" she said.

"That's not enough for you?"

Nidhi's arms ached from lugging the ladder around. Her fingers were caked in waterproof chalk. And the cold was no longer invigorating, just horrible. But still, this escapade was the most alive she could remember feeling in a long time. Maybe ever.

At a bodega on the edge of town, he flipped through his journal, coming to the last piece he'd planned. Nidhi barely had a glance at it before he pulled out the page and crumpled it up.

"Why'd you do that?"

"It was all wrong," he answered. "I've got a better idea."

On the wall, he sketched out something entirely new. He had to rework it a few times, wiping off chalk with a damp rag to make adjustments. But Nidhi's throat caught at the scene that emerged: a spider sheltering a lost boy from a storm, even as a larger, twisted creature emerged from the shadows. Grayson had managed to imbue the spider with a deep, glistening courage in the face of certain disaster.

The first warning "woof" came as Nidhi filled in the storm clouds.

Grayson was perfecting the boy's expression when the woof became a growl.

Then furious barking pierced the quiet of the night as they hurried to finish up.

"Betsy! What are you going on about?" came a woman's surly voice from the neighboring house.

The lights went on inside, and through the window, Betsy—a tiny Pomeranian with perfectly tufted long hair—snarled at them. All six pounds of her.

"Crap!" Nidhi muttered.

Grayson motioned for her to hustle down the ladder. They hid behind a corner, huddling close together as Betsy howled to protect her home from the worst criminal in all of the San Juans. Was she—responsible, sensible Nidhi—about to get in real-life trouble? She who always finished her homework on time and liked to write her college essays months before they were due?

"I know that dog." Grayson grabbed her hand again. "And we do *not* want her owner to catch us."

Sure enough, the door to the house creaked open. Nidhi let out a soft gasp as she recognized the woman who emerged in a pink nightgown. It was the lady from the Labor Day ice cream line who had grouched that the Skull was a menace to society. That he had no respect for the church or the town or anything else.

"What is *that*?" the woman shrieked, noticing the giant spider looming near her home.

"Let's go," Grayson whispered urgently.

Nidhi whirled around. "What about all your stuff?"

"Leave it. I'll come back."

They ran for it, their hands still clasped tightly. His lips were tight with concentration, but then he caught her eye and offered a mischievous, dimpled grin, and Nidhi felt her heart catch in her throat as they flew.

The street lamps gleamed golden in the thick fog, the mist and drizzle perfect for losing themselves into, but Nidhi couldn't help but picture the town waking up in the ruckus and chasing after them with pitchforks. A part of her wanted to dissolve into a fit of giggles because that pampered Pomeranian was just too much, but she managed to hold it in. Barely.

The sound of their feet slapping against the streets was like a clanging bell, and Nidhi was running out of breath in the damp cold. But Grayson's hand stayed tight against hers, that confusing spark between them crackling as they sprinted onto the dock, the sea a wall of gray and silver. More smoke and dragons and night whispers.

As they fumbled onto the boat, footsteps sounded in the marina.

"Who's there?" a low, gruff voice called from shore.

Nidhi jumped, and Grayson cursed and started the motor. The song of the engine was loud and operatic, and they sped off into a fantastical, uncharted sea. Laughing so hard that they couldn't breathe, clutching their stomachs in pain, and yet they just could not stop.

"Betsy is the best!"

"The most ferocious dog in the world!"

"She deserves a juicy bone!"

"I love her so much!"

They hooted and howled and snorted and died several times over, hysterical from how close they'd come to getting caught. When Nidhi finally wiped the tears from her eyes, the clouds had cleared and the full moon shone, the enchantment of the night sweeping them into a fanciful dream. A kaleidoscope of night and sea and a boy who fancied himself a pirate and a girl who maybe, maybe, maybe fancied him, too. They meandered through the glittering pieces of a star-tossed sea until they spotted the Songbird over the cove, bright as a lighthouse in the evaporating mist.

Grayson pulled in next to the beach, killed the engine, and dropped anchor. They stepped out of the cabin into the chill night air. The full moon had chased off the last of the fog and drizzle, and Nidhi breathed in the sudden silence as the dream wore off into reality.

She was suddenly aware of every inch of skin on her body. Every toe and every finger. Everything in between.

"Thanks," she said quietly. "This was so fun and so different from anything I've ever done before and I needed it and you're really great and talented and fun and did I already say that? Well, the thing is"—her words came faster, a rising tide—"I was kind of running on autopilot and I just couldn't break away from my plans and then you came along and I just—I don't know—I am so glad I met you!"

Her cheeks flushed at the admission. An admission she probably shouldn't be making in the moonlight alone with a boy who was definitely not her boyfriend.

"I'm glad I met you, too," Grayson said, his voice soft and gruff. "Tonight was amazing. *You* were amazing. Totally fearless."

She shook her head. It was only the spell of the night, the caffeine, the adrenaline. She wasn't really this carefree, brave girl he thought she was, the girl who took risks and created magic with a good-looking artist boy late into the witching hour and beyond. But then she remembered tonight wasn't just a one-time fluke. She recalled the feel of the wakeboard gliding beneath her feet. She'd done that, she'd figured it out with nothing more than a hope and a wish. And for a few precious seconds, she'd flown.

There are a few moments in your life when you truly see yourself, see the essence of you that exists outside time and space.

This was one of those moments for Nidhi. She saw her past and her future at once: her life as it was, as it could be, and how it would be if she didn't seize it with all of her passion and soul. And she understood. *Nothing is too much to ask for because time is so precious and fleeting and because anyone who has ever truly loved you should want the most for you and because you should want the most for yourself, too.*

And what Nidhi wanted right now, in this moment, was to kiss Grayson.

He leaned toward her; she stepped closer to him. Her breath hitched.

But at the last second, he pulled away.

"We should get you home, Nidhi."

His eyes held hers, and she knew that he didn't hold back because he didn't want to touch his lips against hers. He held back because he was waiting for something deeper than just one spellbound night.

And she was, too.

Chapter Eleven

Nidhi snuck back into the Songbird with no one the wiser, up the creaky staircase and into the quiet stillness of her turret bedroom. Her princess tower. And for maybe the first time, she actually felt like one of those storybook girls, the ones who fell into magical and dangerous adventures. Her vintage clock ticked as she lay in her bed, snuggling into her mother's rose-dotted duvet and dozing for perhaps an hour.

The days had been getting shorter, the nights colder, the sun rising later, and it was still dark out when her alarm went off. Time to get ready for school to face that math test. To face Matt.

She groaned.

The day passed in a tired haze. Even so, she crushed the test. But

Matt was another story. She knew what she had to do, but it broke her heart to even think of it. So she ignored his texts, ducked out of sight in the school hallways, even pretended to miss his wave from the school bus window as she and her sisters pulled out of the parking lot.

Saturday morning, she busied herself with crafting autumnal lattes and cappuccinos, perfecting her maple leaf designs in the steamed milk. She even finally figured out the best way to draw out the subtle flavors of delicata squash, forgoing all the hype of cinnamon and nutmeg and instead adding a touch of lavender and honey. In the end, the recipe was like coming home, a nod to the lavender farm neighboring the inn and Dad's gulab jamun.

Eventually, the morning crowd drifted out, and her busy barista fingers were left with no orders to complete. She sat at the empty coffee bar, an oversize rosy pink cardigan wrapped snugly around her. She should probably catch up on those missed hours of sleep from Thursday that she was *still* recovering from. Instead she just watched the rain patter on the bay window, a ferry passing by on the waters below. A foghorn echoed in the distance.

"Ugh. I hate November!" Rani took the stool across from her on the bar, wrinkling her nose. "So dark and dreary and horrible. Want to watch a movie?"

"Um, sure." Of course, the dark and dreary on the night of skullduggery had actually been quite lovely. She couldn't get it out of her mind.

"What's with that goofy grin?" Rani peered at her suspiciously.

"Grin? There's no grin." Nidhi tried to control her facial muscles, forcing them into her best serious big sister face. But she couldn't hold it. The grin was determined to slip out, like an errant lock of hair from her topknot. And she felt so, so incredibly guilty about it. Even though she and Grayson hadn't actually kissed . . . even so. And then suddenly she wasn't grinning anymore. She was tearing up.

Rani peered up at her. "Nidhi?"

"I think"—sniffle—"that maybe"—sniffle, sniffle—"I need to break up with . . ." Nidhi couldn't bring herself to finish the sentence.

How could she do this to Matt? Her first boyfriend, her first love? It was eating her up. Rani looked completely shocked, which made it worse.

"I know, I'm being ridiculous," she blathered, wiping at her wet face, thankful the dining room was deserted. "I'm supposed to be the one who mends *your* broken heart, not the other way around."

Rani chuckled. "Nidhi—you're allowed to be a human being."

"Hey!" Nidhi protested. "Don't laugh at me!"

"I'm not laughing!" Rani said, but then a smirk spread across her face. "Okay, so it does feel kind of good to be on the other end of things. But don't worry, there's nothing that can't be cured with a sister huddle in the library. I'll grab Avani and Sirisha."

Nidhi had to admit it was sort of nice to have someone else tell her what to do for once, so she wandered into their fourth-floor hideout, collapsing into the faded stripes of the loveseat and grabbing another one of the old photo books. This one she hadn't seen in a while, the photos beginning in the years just after Mom had passed when they were still in Portland. There weren't many pictures from that period, just a few birthday parties that Dad had felt obligated to document.

But then their photographic family history moved on to the early days when Dad had first bought the Songbird, ten years ago. It looked so different—dark and falling apart, a run-down gamble that Dad had put all their savings into. But he'd found an investment partner to help him spruce the place up, a man named Jonathan. The two of them had transformed the inn into a perfect cozy getaway perched on the edge of the Salish Sea. And somewhere along the way, they'd fallen in love, and Jonathan had become their beloved Pop.

Until a little less than three years ago, when he too had passed. Their bad luck was truly uncanny.

"That's a great picture of them," Avani said softly, plopping down beside her and resting her chin on Nidhi's shoulder.

"It really is," Nidhi replied. "Did Sirisha take it?"

"Did I take what?" Sirisha asked as she and Rani carefully brought in a tray piled with biscotti, croissants, and mugs of steaming warm drinks.

They settled it onto the coffee table, and Nidhi showed her the picture, a sepia close-up shot of Pop and Dad wearing handsome grins.

"Ah yes, my sepia phase." Sirisha chuckled as she flipped on the gas fireplace. "I was obsessed."

"Look, here's one from the Winter Ball!" Avani's voice trembled a bit.

Nidhi glanced at Avani, who sniffled and pointed. Of course Nidhi missed Pop, too, desperately at times, but this family portrait still made her smile. They were all gathered—Pop, Dad, Nidhi, and her sisters—dancing under a disco ball and a zillion hand-painted snowflakes. Pop used to spend more than six months planning the Winter Ball every year, and it always turned out to be quite the extravaganza. Though the years and balls had blurred together, Nidhi guessed she was about twelve in this one. Probably too old to be wearing matching dresses with her sisters, yet they'd done it anyway per tradition, each Singh sister donning soft gray velvet with silver ribbons.

"Here, just for you, big sis!" Rani beamed as she handed Nidhi the freshly made cappuccino. Then she caught sight of the picture. "Oh, wow—we're adorable. Avani twirling with Pop—remember that time you spun right into the buffet and knocked over his precious cheese tray?"

"Oh yeah." Nidhi giggled. "Classic Avani."

"Yep," Rani said, taking a sip of her own cappuccino.

"Whatever. I was having fun. You should try it some time." Avani sniffled again, loudly, then got up to turn on the speaker system. She fiddled with her phone for a moment before soft warm tones resonated around the library. A blues album that Nidhi didn't know but found achingly beautiful. Avani's exuberant dancing may have been typical, but so was her impeccable taste in music.

"I have fun," Nidhi replied. Thursday night hadn't been a complete aberration. Or had it?

"Sure you do." Rani took the photo book from her, shutting it. "Anyway, we're all here for you, remember? Spill it."

"Yeah," Avani said, "what's the big emergency?"

"It's not an emergency," Nidhi replied, "and please sit down. I can't think with you pacing around like that."

"I can't think *without* pacing like this," Avani returned.

Still, she sighed, grabbed a chocolate croissant from the tray, and plopped down on the beanbag next to the loveseat. Rani and Sirisha huddled on either side of Nidhi, warm drinks and pastries in hand. Nidhi wanted to tell them to be careful not to get crumbs everywhere, but somehow she managed to hold that nagging urge in. At least the scent of baked goods soothed her.

"You were saying?" Sirisha nudged her gently.

Nidhi shrugged, a little embarrassed from all the attention. But maybe she needed it. "Well, speaking of fun, did you know I was out all night on Thursday?"

Avani looked skeptical. "All night?"

"You?" Rani added, equally skeptical.

Sirisha swatted them. "Come on, let Nidhi talk for once. Where did you go?"

"Yes, do tell!" Avani munched her croissant, a few errant flakes dropping on her lap.

Crumbs.

Vacuuming can wait, Nidhi reminded herself. She channeled that other Nidhi, the braver, wilder one from the evening before Halloween. The one who didn't let all the untidy details get in the way. And she began her tale. "You've all heard about the Skull, right? Well . . ."

As she dished to her sisters, Nidhi was right back there with Grayson on a schooner in the dead of night, racing through Friday Harbor with chalk markers and ladders and flashlights in the mist. His warmth like a lantern, his scent like an oncoming storm. The pure electrical wanting that had crackled between them.

And Betsy. Dear yappy Betsy.

"Whoa, Nidhi." Rani's eyes were wide. "That is so romantic. How dare you not tell us until now!"

"We had school yesterday, remember? And the Halloween party?" Nidhi protested.

Avani poked her knee. "So what else have you been keeping from us?"

Nidhi laughed. "Um, nothing."

Sirisha's eyes twinkled. "Come on, Nidhi. All of this didn't happen out of nowhere. What's going on with you and Matt?"

Nidhi sighed. "He's great in so many ways. But . . ." How could she put it? All of the things that had been irking her—his obsession with her braids, his twelve-hundred-page Louis XIV tome—seemed kind of small, especially when compared to her spending a whole night with Grayson. Her cheeks heated at the thought.

"Maybe you've outgrown that relationship?" Sirisha guessed. "Maybe you don't need to spend your whole life with someone just because they were the first person you ever kissed?"

As usual, her youngest sister had articulated what she couldn't bring herself to say.

Avani shuddered. "Besides, who would only want to kiss one person anyway?"

Nidhi chuckled at that. Though bittersweet, it felt good to finally talk about it, to have the words said out loud. "The thing is . . . I don't even know if I want to go to France anymore. I love baking, but I don't know if I want it to be my whole life."

Avani shrugged. "So don't go."

"But A) I got the scholarship, B) I bought the tickets . . ."

"Tickets that can still be refunded, probably," Sirisha said. "If it's not what you really want, why waste your whole summer on it?"

Dad had said something similar in the kitchen. That she had options.

Rani winked knowingly. "We get it. You want to visit forty-two countries with Grayson. I'd drop all my plans for that hunk, too."

Nidhi laughed, then shook her head. "That's not it at all. I mean, Grayson is a lot of fun. . . ." She took a sip of Rani's cappuccino. It was too sweet and too foamy and had too much bite at once. But who cared? It had been made with love. "There's really only one country I'm interested in visiting right now. India."

How she longed to see the white marble of the Taj Mahal, hear the heady mix of dozens of languages, sniff spicy street food in the air, and taste those famous Kolkata egg rolls she'd heard so much about.

"You know what?" Sirisha said. "I really want to go there some-day, too."

Avani glanced at both of them. "Me too!"

Rani giggled. "I heard that Shah Rukh Khan will sometimes come out of his Mumbai bungalow and mingle with the fans waiting adoringly outside. We could see him in real life! I could, like, touch him. How do we make this happen?"

Nidhi smiled, taking another sip of the perfectly imperfect cappuccino. The blues singer's throaty voice reached a crescendo, reverberating with big dreams just out of reach. With her sisters tucked around her, telling her everything would be okay, that she could figure it all out, Nidhi had the sense that all her star-tossed wishes might actually come true.

The next afternoon, Nidhi waited for Matt at the trailhead where she'd asked him to meet her, pretending to study the map of the short hike they'd done a million times before. He was coming straight from his shift at work, but he was late. Most businesses on the island tended to slow down considerably during the winter, but not Lulu's. Everyone wanted the ingenious flavors, local dairy, and freshly made waffle cones, even in the November chill. Nidhi had actually seen a hiring sign in the window when she'd last dropped by.

Which, honestly, had been a while ago.

A frigid gale blustered, sending Nidhi's loose curls flying, and she huddled into her hunter-green waterproof parka, her uniform from here till spring. At last, she spotted Matt jogging up the road, in his own navy parka. They both wore the same brand; when they'd bought them last year, they'd joked about how they'd make the perfect REI catalog couple.

It was surprisingly hard to let go of that image.

Today, the fierce winds had ruffled his dark hair so he looked like one of Anita's favorite Muppet characters. He kissed her on the cheek, and offered her one of the two milk shakes he was carrying.

"Shakes in forty-five degrees, yum!" Nidhi accepted hers with a quick sip. Brrr. At least it was her favorite—cookies and goat cream.

"I'll keep you warm." Matt put his arms around her, drawing her close. He smelled like waffle cones, vanilla, and sugar.

It was so tempting to let him keep on holding her. To let everything stay the same as it had been. But Nidhi knew that wouldn't be fair to either of them—not when she wasn't fully in it anymore.

She smiled sadly. "Let's walk and talk, okay?"

Matt nodded, leaving an arm draped around her shoulders. "I'm glad you called me. Too bad we didn't come earlier, though. Some of the trees are already starting to look bare."

"Yeah," Nidhi said softly, her boots rustling the crunchy gold and russet leaves that blanketed the trail.

There were still plenty of gorgeous autumn hues surrounding them, fiery reds and golds and oranges, but probably not for much longer. She took another fortifying sip of her milk shake. Her fingers felt like they would freeze from holding it, even with her favorite lambswool gloves.

Matt kept up a steady stream of chatter, as if he were determined to make up for the awkward night of cookie baking. He confessed his mediocre grade on the math test, waxed poetic about the incredible pastrami sandwich he'd tried from a new café, and fondly imitated Anita's latest favorite phrase, *booty shakin' good*, which she apparently used for any and all occasions.

Nidhi had to laugh. "That's so cute."

"Right?" He shook his head. "I don't know what Mom's going to do with her while we're in France all summer."

This was her opening, and she had to take it. It was now or never.

Her breath fogged up the air. "About that. I've decided not to go."

"What? Why?"

The trail had been climbing upward steadily, and Nidhi was a little out of breath. She paused at a fallen log and turned to look at him. "I've changed my mind about Siècles du Sucre. It's a great program, but it's not really what I want right now. . . ."

"Well, that's fine. More time to see the sights. We could maybe even take a bit longer in Italy." Matt scrambled over the log, then turned and helped her, milk shakes and all. "There's tons to do in Europe."

As they approached the big rock at the viewpoint, Matt continued rattling off other ideas. This time Nidhi scrambled up first, then turned to take his milk shake so he could hop up beside her. She sat atop the rock, hugging her knees, frigid sea gusts blowing her hair into her face again. She pulled out a hairband from her purse and tugged the curly mess into a ponytail.

Matt sat down, too, taking her hand, gazing at the water below.

She squeezed his fingers, her heart thudding inside her chest.

She had to say the words.

She opened her mouth.

Closed it.

Opened it again.

And then tentatively, she spoke. "Matt, it's not just the trip. I think we should break up."

He stilled. "What?"

"I'm so sorry." Nidhi choked up. "I really care about you, but I just don't think it's working out between us. Do you?"

His face was a mask, eerie and distant. "I guess not."

And then he was grabbing his empty milk shake cup, scrambling off the rock, and stalking back down the trail. Nidhi blinked at how fast it had all happened. Should she go after him? Had she made a terrible mistake? Tears slipped down her cheeks, and everything inside her ached.

Another cold and furious November gust blew in the slate-gray skies. Below, a seaplane was landing in the water, gliding gracefully over silvery waves. It started to rain, the stinging drops mingling with Nidhi's tears. She stayed like that for a long while, until her toes were numb with a bone-deep cold that even her winter boots couldn't keep out.

Chapter Twelve

At school on Monday, everything felt strange and awkward, especially since Nidhi shared so many classes with Matt. All 135 students across four grades in the high school seemed to have heard about the breakup, and perhaps she was imagining it, but everyone seemed to think *she* was the bad guy.

Nidhi had never meant to break any hearts.

"It'll blow over soon," her friend Kendrick assured her at lunch.

"I hope so," Nidhi said, twisting an errant lock that had escaped from her topknot.

For the first time in two years, Matt sat at another table in the cafeteria. He was surrounded by a bunch of guys who kept shooting her dark looks before turning back to their food and jokes. Yep. She was definitely the bad guy.

By AP English, her last class of the day, she couldn't wait to hand in her essay and head back to the Songbird. The bell finally rang to dismiss them, but she needed to correct one small spelling mistake. As she rummaged through her backpack for an eraser, someone tapped her shoulder. She turned to find Matt, his hands in the pockets of his parka.

"I'm sorry for the way I reacted yesterday." His eyes were big and brown, his brow furrowed in its signature adorable way.

Old Nidhi would have grazed her fingers across those brows, smoothing them with a kiss perhaps. But it was too late for all that. Her sisters had been right. She knew because going back to before still sounded worse than this. And though it was faint, there was a loosening inside of her. She'd been racing toward the edge of *something* these past few weeks, but now she felt close to figuring out what was out there beyond it. What was waiting for her on the other side.

She touched his arm, that big silly doofus who loved snickerdoodles. "It's okay. I know it came as a surprise."

Matt held her gaze, and she realized that it had been a while since they'd really looked at each other, since they'd really seen the other person as who they were instead of who they had been. It had taken a breakup to make that happen.

"Not a total surprise," Matt conceded. "I guess I just wanted to keep pretending everything was okay."

"Me too. Until I couldn't anymore."

He shrugged, hands still in pockets. "For what it's worth, I'm sorry about giving you a hard time about wakeboarding. Just because it's not my thing doesn't mean you can't be into it. I guess we both need to grow up and try new stuff."

"And I'm sorry that I changed all our plans on you," Nidhi said gently.

"I'll get over it." Matt gave her a weak smile. "Still friends?"

"Always." Nidhi hugged him, inhaling the faint fragrance of vanilla and waffle cones from the job he'd worked so they could travel to Paris together. "Thanks for understanding."

Then she handed in her uncorrected essay and walked away from the first boy she'd ever really loved.

On Saturday, the PNW's ubiquitous drizzle and gray skies were on full display as Nidhi took the ferry out to Friday Harbor. She was beginning to accept that winter was on its way, and she'd have to deal with it, just as she'd have to deal with the restless storm inside her. It hadn't settled, and maybe it never would, but she was okay with that, too. Because perhaps the bittersweet ache of goodbyes and hellos was like a hit of espresso, a vital jolt to the system that could be tempered with milk and lavender and honey.

A soccer team from school was headed for a game on San Juan Island as well, so Nidhi felt compelled to at least mingle in the passenger lounge a little bit, even though she would have preferred quietly soaking in the gray. Over the ferry speakers, the captain announced a rare sighting of a breaching humpback whale on the starboard side. Nidhi and some of the soccer kids left the warmth of the inner deck to take a closer look. The railing was crowded with tourists and flashing cameras, but she managed to catch a glimpse of the mesmerizing spray of the enormous humpback.

It was a magical thing, almost a portent, though she didn't believe in that kind of thing.

That morning, she'd officially canceled her trip to Paris, and the release of it had felt as free and full of flight as the moment she'd stood up on the wakeboard. She'd been hanging on to this image of herself as a baker for so long, but suddenly she could see so many different futures in front of her. She didn't know which one she wanted yet; in fact, she yearned for them all. Every experience she could have, she wanted it, ached for it, with a ferocity that surprised her.

The storm inside her was one of possibility.

Eventually, the humpback swam away, oblivious to the ferry it had delayed—not that anyone aboard minded. When they docked at Friday Harbor, the soccer team left for the car deck to drive to their game, while Nidhi alighted with the other foot passengers.

She texted Grayson playfully:

> I'm in your neighborhood . . . in case you need a spotter for wakeboarding or someone to hold a ladder for you while you vandalize buildings or anything.

There was no immediate response, and the old Nidhi would have been impatient or nervous. It felt strange to simply decide not to worry, but even the dreariness of the weather felt like sunshine to Nidhi right then. Her steps were light. Would she look back fondly on today when she was old and gray? Would she remember it at all, or would it be like a cresting wave: lost in a vast and endless ocean?

She took a deliberately roundabout walk, passing:

- the skeleton sleeping on a lonely sidewalk

- the witches readying for battle

- the scared monster fleeing from humans

Some of the murals had already begun to smear from island weather, but they were mostly still intact. She was surprised nobody in town had hosed any of them down. Then she came to the spider protecting the small boy on the side of the bodega on the edge of town. The one they'd abandoned when Betsy the doggie PI had caught them in their nefarious act.

A woman in a crimson scarf smiled at Nidhi. "Fan of the Skull?"

"How do you know I didn't make these?" she challenged.

"Did you?"

"Nah," Nidhi said. "But I can sculpt sugar roses on a cake that look so real you won't want to eat them!"

The woman patted her shoulder. "And I dabble in poetry now and then. It seems like everyone on these islands is an artist." She wrapped her scarf more tightly around her and meandered into the bodega, holding the door open for Nidhi, who also ducked inside. The place sold artisan sandwiches that looked pretty tempting.

Her phone beeped. Grayson had finally responded.

> Actually, could you change my tire? Just joking.
> Where are you?

She dropped a pin for him and took a leap and bought two sandwiches and two iced teas. Just as the cashier handed her back the change, Grayson came through the doors looking rugged and very Northwest lumberjack in a thick plaid wool coat and jeans. Nidhi waved and offered him the baguette and iced tea.

"Thanks!" He flashed that dimpled grin of his. "Ham and cheese is my favorite."

"You said that before." She didn't add that it had been the other night, *that* night. The one that had changed everything for her.

"So about that tire . . . got your tools handy?"

Nidhi nudged him gently with her elbow. "Hilarious. Looks like it stopped raining. Want to find a spot outside to eat?"

"Let's do it."

They walked along the street, waving at Betsy as they passed by. A small woof and a couple of piercing barks echoed after them as they headed down to the marina, where pleasure boats awaited better weather. They eyed a picnic table overlooking the water.

Nidhi wrinkled her nose. "It's wet."

"And getting wetter," Grayson observed.

Naturally, it was sprinkling again. Nidhi dashed back to the shops, ducking under the awning of a closed-for-the-season cruise business. The space was small, and when Grayson squeezed next to her, she could feel the heat of him. He certainly filled out that plaid jacket quite nicely.

And this time she had no reason to feel guilty about noticing.

From across the street, a chalk mural mummy winked at her with what seemed like an eerily knowing look. Even the mummy knew what she was up to, and a little bit of old Nidhi crept in to heat her cheeks.

Grayson leaned against the shop door. "What's Matt up to today?"

They both knew what he was asking, and Nidhi didn't feel like playing games.

"We broke up." Now her face was completely aflame. Did he really feel what she thought he did? Or had she imagined everything?

Grayson's tone was cautious. "Want to talk about it?"

"Not really."

He nodded sympathetically, then took a huge bite of a slightly damp sandwich. "Mmm . . . perfection."

Nidhi laughed, only a little nervously, and bit into her own. "You know, it's not bad, even with a bit of rain soaked in."

"PNW seasoning, am I right?"

"You got it."

Soon they were wiping off the crumbs, but the rain hadn't stopped. Nidhi wondered exactly how frizzy her curls had gotten. She ran her fingers through her hair, trying to smooth it out. Grayson was watching, quiet.

She cleared her throat. "So . . . did you know Diwali is coming up?"

"Oh yeah?"

"Next week." Nidhi started to fluff her hair again, then stopped herself. "I don't suppose the Skull has any ideas for it."

"Hmm, good question." Grayson took a swig of his tea. "Maybe if there's someone who can help give it some authenticity."

"That can probably be arranged." She stepped out from under the awning, letting the rain wash over her face. It was coming down hard now, but it felt amazing, cool and recharging. She turned and gave Grayson a wicked grin. "Race you to the mummy?"

Without waiting, she ran for it. Her boots splashed in puddles on the street, and Grayson was chuckling as he pounded after her. He caught her around the waist just as she slapped her palms on the mummy. Her hands came away streaked with gray and black chalk, the rain quickly washing off the rest.

Her lashes were wet, her breathing heavy, her veins thrumming. Grayson's eyes were smoke and dragons and night whispers. He leaned in; she put her chalk-covered hands behind his neck. The seconds were agony as they searched each other for something they couldn't really define.

"Can I kiss you?" Grayson whispered.

She nodded. A list of all those restless, wild yearnings paraded through her head. But she let them go, like wished-upon dandelion seeds in the wind, and instead pressed her lips against Grayson's. Melted into him. He was an anchor, and she was adrift in a swirling uncharted sea, but in that moment they clung together as a storm raged overhead.

Chapter Thirteen

Sumptuous smells flooded the kitchen as Dad readied the Diwali feast. The restaurant was closed in observance of the holiday, and this meal was just for the family. Nidhi helped Dad roll out the bhature, and he dropped them into hot oil. Since they ate vegetarian for Diwali, they'd also prepared chole, aloo gobi, and mattar paneer. And of course, Dad's gulab jamun and Nidhi's burfi were waiting in the fridge.

She helped Dad carry out the food to the dining room, where Rani was arranging a bouquet of red and gold maple leaves and painted ceramic diyas at the table at the center of the bay window. Outside, the stars were twinkling over a shadow-dark sea. The squall inside Nidhi raged on, impervious to the changing seasons. She didn't know where she was going next summer, didn't even know where things were going with Grayson.

Yet somehow she found contentment in her heart, mingled with the endless yearning.

Sirisha had carefully lit candles in votives throughout the restaurant to celebrate the Festival of Lights. Now, she was adding more on each table, while Avani flipped through songs on her phone in rapid succession. When she found the right one, an energetic ballad sung a cappella, she nodded to herself and started scribbling in her journal.

Grayson took the bowl of chole off Dad's hands. "That smells amazing, sir."

"Thank you. An old family recipe." Dad gestured to the food. "You can all start digging in! We've just a few more dishes to bring out."

Grayson kissed Nidhi on the cheek. "Why don't you sit down? I'll help your dad. You look gorgeous, by the way."

"Thanks." Nidhi smoothed the silk of her midnight-blue salwar kameez and adjusted the chiffon dupatta wrapped loosely around her neck. It had been her mother's.

A few weeks ago, she, Avani, and Rani had taken some of Mom's old things to get tailored in preparation for their celebration. Now, they were decked out in Indian finery, each of their shimmering salwar kameez embroidered with gold-threaded patterns, mirrors, and glittering crystals. Avani looked stunning in black, Rani in hot pink, and Sirisha in a deep emerald green. Even Dad had donned a simple light blue kurta.

Grayson looked handsome in a white collared shirt and black jeans. Nidhi eyed the way he fit those jeans as he walked toward the kitchen, her pulse racing just a tiny bit. They were taking things slowly, she reminded herself.

Eventually, all the food was on the table, and her sisters were talking, laughing, interrupting one another. Grayson chuckled as Rani waxed poetic about Shah Rukh Khan. She'd recently found Dad's stash of old Hindi movies from the '90s and early 2000s, and SRK featured prominently in the collection. Nidhi was content to hang back and listen.

Tired of course. She and the Skull had been at work the eve before, another night of swirling colors across bricks and under eaves and a breathless race against dawn as they left sweeping chalk mandalas all over Friday Harbor and even here on Orcas in Eastsound. Plus one extra-large mural featuring four little girls twirling sparklers in front of a light-strewn home (or maybe even an inn).

While the sisters chattered, Dad's phone beeped. He scanned the text discreetly, his phone held under the table, and chuckled quietly to himself before texting furtively back.

"Who're you talking to, Dad?" Nidhi whispered.

Dad shrugged, a small smile playing across his lips. "Oh, just someone."

With only the glow of candlelight it was hard to tell, but Nidhi realized there was a tinge of red across Dad's cheeks.

She leaned close. "Are you blushing, Dad?"

"Me? No, of course not." He tried hard to contain his smile but couldn't quite manage it.

It reminded her of her own glee the day she'd found out about the Skull, the way she'd tried to contain it when she'd come back inside but Grayson had noticed her goofy grin anyway.

"Are you seeing someone new?" Nidhi tried to make it sound like no big deal.

"I'm not really sure," Dad confessed. "What is it you kids say? *We're just texting right now.*"

He'd had a few casual dates since Pop's passing, but nothing serious. Obviously, smiling while texting didn't mean a whole lot. But something tingled inside Nidhi. She'd learned how quickly things could change. For her, all it had taken was an unexpected storm, a felled tree, and someone new walking into her life.

Before she could ask more, Sirisha tugged at Nidhi's sleeve. "Hey, are you paying attention? Family photo time!"

They crowded around the table, and Sirisha snapped pic after pic of them laughing, making goofy faces, and raising their glasses in a toast. Grayson offered to take some of just the Singh family. After a brief tug-of-war with Sirisha over the camera, they gathered for a final shot in the living room in front of the mantel. Nidhi leaned against Dad, and her sisters stood in a row by age (Rani reminding Avani that she was seven minutes older). Avani fiddled with her phone until Grayson called her out, and Sirisha offered him a slew of technical tips that was the most she'd ever said to him.

Outside, not a single rain cloud dared to come out that evening. The sky was a vast obsidian sentinel, glittering with an abundance of stars on the night of the new moon. The luminous Songbird shone in the darkness with twinkle lights strung along its eaves, a beacon on a not-so-lonely cliffside. As the Singhs dug into dessert, an owl hooted and a bald eagle landed and sea otters napped down on the water near the cove. And somewhere in the woods behind the inn, some of the last autumn leaves feathered down in lazy circles in the shadows, settling into a new season on the damp earth.

Part Two: Winter Avani

Chapter One

*S*nowfall was never guaranteed in the San Juans—winter was mostly a lot of dreary rain—but even with half an inch on the ground, the island was transformed.

Avani pedaled hard, huffing up the curve of the drive, avoiding patches of ice and regretting overloading her bicycle's saddlebags with too many textbooks and granola bars and a pair of snowshoes (backup transportation in case the storm got under way early). Though her sisters drove to school, Avani tended to use the hour-long bike ride to expel the excess of energy she'd had her whole life. However, despite all the gear, she had the niggling feeling that she was forgetting something. Probably several somethings.

But who cared when snowflakes corkscrewed dizzily in the air, dusting the inn's roof and grounds until the Songbird resembled a swan soaring over a bed of clouds? Who cared when the kitten-gray sky glimmered with lucky silver, when the merry scent of pine and snow wrapped around her, when the ice-cold air circled her in a fairy dance?

> Sometimes a single moment
> is just too pure and
> consuming to escape from.

The problem was that Avani felt those moments far too often, regularly getting lost in a tangent when her presence was needed elsewhere. But the knowledge didn't stop her from hitting the brakes. She rooted through her bags for a pen and a notebook, sketching the scene and scribbling a little poem on the spot. Of course, she was late—chronically late, Nidhi said—but this feeling, this magical wintry feeling . . .

> it was the edge of
> something profound,
> a memory just around the corner—

Her phone buzzed with a barrage of frantic text messages: Her friend Kiera was having a party to celebrate the start of February break, but she was nervous that no one would show.

Avani pushed her notebook back into her bag and texted back:

> Don't worry, people will want to party after that precalc test. I'll be there in an hour to help set up.

That estimate was a stretch, but she preferred to be optimistic about her inn chores. She yawned—exhausted from staying up late cramming—and slowly worked her way up the drive to the bike shed.

"Where have you been?" Rani exclaimed as Avani trundled past reception and dropped her bags in the inn's spacious living room, with classic Craftsman wood detailing, gleaming hardwood floors, and brown leather furniture clustered intimately into groups. Floor-to-ceiling windows looked out onto the snowy south deck and the swirling sea beyond.

Right now, it was just Rani and Sirisha huddled on an oversize Chesterfield in front of a roaring fire, a mess of cellophane and ribbons and fruit and nuts and crackers all around them. Ah, that was what she'd forgotten. Welcome baskets for an impending wedding party.

Avani eyed the paraphernalia. "Who would want these? There isn't even any chocolate."

"The bride and groom are paleo." Rani popped an almond in her mouth, crunched it for a moment, then shrugged. "Also, we're using biodegradable cellophane and ribbons made from recycled paper. I saw a video from this adorable, *super* hunky activist about how recycling is a lie, and I figured the couple would approve."

Avani grabbed a cracker packet and scanned the ingredients. Made with tapioca flour. Hmm. "Don't tell me—they're wearing hiking boots to the wedding."

Sirisha fiddled with a bow. "With the snowstorm coming, they might have to ski down the aisle."

The image made Avani smile. "The wedding pics will be epic."

As much as she and her sisters joked, they actually loved the specific quirkiness of the Pacific Northwest. Hiking and camping and even the occasional odd health food were a part of their souls, inescapable and indelible.

Rani whistled as Dad came down the main stairs, looking unusually dapper in gray wool slacks, a lavender button down, and a pinstriped vest.

"Wow." Sirisha grabbed her camera and clicked away. "We need proof of this. Dad on a hot date."

"It's not a hot date." Dad flushed.

"Right." Rani offered an outrageously overwrought wink. "Just dinner . . ."

"With a single dude," added Sirisha.

"That you like," Rani finished.

Her sisters had been teasing Dad about his "friend," a man he'd met back in the fall, for a while now. He and Dad had gone for coffees and drinks, but now they'd upgraded to dinners? Avani's head suddenly felt light—and not just from too much midnight math homework. She wanted to see Dad happy, of course. But sometimes it felt like everyone else had moved on from Pop's death, while her grief was just as fresh as ever.

As if she'd had open heart surgery and
    nobody had bothered to stitch her skin back together.
Had it really been three years since they'd lost him?

"Seriously, it's not a big deal!" Dad laughed and hurried away. "Call if you need anything! I'll be back by ten."

As the north door shut behind him, a few stray snowflakes swirled inside before selecting a spot to rest on the hardwood floors. And there they melted, transforming in seconds while Avani was still struggling to process the whole Dad-on-a-hot-date business. Her phone buzzed from an anxious Kiera again, while her twin shoved a basket in her lap. Avani muffled her sniffle with the crunch of a salted almond, sans chocolate, realizing too late that she hadn't been paying any attention to Sirisha's demonstration on how to curl the ribbons just so.

She'd been caught up in an inescapable moment once again.

Forty mind-numbing minutes later, the ding of the reception bell roused Avani from the tedium of making yet another fruit-and-nuts welcome basket. Hers were all a bit sad looking compared to Sirisha's photograph-ready artisanal masterpieces. Even Rani's had their own signature style: exploding with fireworks of sparkly (recycled) ribbons that worked surpassingly well—convincing you bigger really was better.

"I'll get it!" Avani flounced to the front desk, antsy for a distraction.

And a distraction was exactly what she received. In the form of twenty guys—laughing, good-looking, rugged guys. Crowded around the front desk, lounging against the windows, rummaging through camp backpacks and duffel bags.

Well.

"Hello, hello." She offered a grin. Too bad she was still a little sweaty from biking home, but at least she was wearing her good jeans. Hopefully none of them would get close enough to sniff her. "What can I help you guys with?"

A man stepped forward, pushing through the others and holding up a printed reservation receipt. "Hi, I'm Jonas, one of the lucky chaperones for this bunch. You're Nidhi, right? We've met before, but you were only about yea tall." He held his hand up to his waist.

"Actually, I'm Avani—Nidhi's my older sister."

"Oops. I guess it's been even longer than I realized!" He held out a hand. "Good to see you again. Seems you girls are practically running this place now."

"I guess we are." Avani smiled, used to strangers mixing up her and her sisters. Not that she looked anything like them. "What brings you out to Orcas this time?"

"We're here for the Grizzly Drizzly on Sunday."

Ah, she'd forgotten the first race was this weekend—too much going on during midwinter break. Avani considered herself athletic—she biked everywhere, kayaked everywhere else, and enjoyed a pickup basketball game now and then—but she wasn't so sure about the concept of the Grizzly Drizzly. Only the most hard-core outdoor nuts were into it.

"Is the race still on?" she asked. "You're going to crawl around under barbed wire in the snow?" Not that crawling around in the mud sounded particularly appealing either.

"There's no barbed wire!" one of the guys protested.

"My mistake. They don't really electrocute you, either?" Avani teased.

"We're competing in an obstacle course, not training as Navy SEALs," said another guy.

"Too bad." She shrugged. "Gotta love a man in a uniform."

A third guy smiled winningly. "I wear a uniform sometimes."

"What, for the high school crew team?" she returned. He had the look—broad-shouldered and lean. "Doesn't count."

He hung his head. "Come on! Throw a guy a bone."

Avani laughed. The guys were nice, and she enjoyed flirting a bit now and then, as long as it wasn't too serious. She got bored way too easily to spend all her time with just one person. She preferred options, and plenty of them.

Jonas the chaperone cleared his throat. "The reservations?"

Right. She scanned the computer. The bookings were there, only each kid had been entered into the system separately, and now she'd have to check them in one at a time. It was going to take F.O.R.E.V.E.R. and they were already getting restless. So was she. Someone had taken out a football and of course it bounced off someone else's arm and onto the wall, rattling framed pictures and memorabilia.

"Not in here, please!" Jonas scolded.

The Most Romantic Inn award banged onto the tile behind the desk. As she knelt to pick it up, a hand caught her favorite family portrait just in time to prevent the glass from shattering.

"Thanks," she breathed, only to find herself in front of Fernando Gutiérrez.

Oh boy. Super awkward.

He was wearing a gorgeous charcoal wool coat and a creamy cashmere scarf and his hair looked a little too perfectly mussed. Behind him, a dolly was stacked with three crates of produce from his family's farm. The Songbird's partnership with the Gutiérrez farm meant Avani really had to go out of her way to avoid him.

About a month ago, the extremely tall and rather cute Mexican American boy had asked her to a concert in town. She'd said yes, but then she'd mixed up the dates and not shown up and had been too embarrassed to explain and now he totally hated her. Up until now she'd managed to keep a low profile, begging Sirisha to trade chores with her so she could miss his morning delivery. She should probably just apologize to him for what happened, but how could she admit she'd overscheduled herself as usual? He'd think she was a total flake! Just like her sisters did.

And maybe she was a little, but it was part of her charm, right? Right? Okay no, she couldn't possibly explain herself.

"Running a little behind today?" she asked instead.

"Yeah, sorry about that." Fernando pushed his shaggy hair out of his eyes. "Where should I put them?"

Avani wasn't sure—it was the kind of thing Nidhi would know, but she wasn't home yet.

"I'll find out, just give me a minute to check these guys in." She nodded to the adventure seekers.

But the computer froze three times and she couldn't find the room keys and some of the guys wanted to switch rooms anyway. Others wanted to know where they kept the kayaks—while it was snowing, really?!—and others still wanted to know what she was doing later.

"So what do you say? Tonight?" an earnest kid asked.

Yikes. Too many cute boys on the loose.

Avani rubbed her forehead, wishing she could just run away. "Well, I'm supposed to help set up for a party, but I forgot about these welcome baskets I promised to help make for the wedding tomorrow. . . ."

Ugh. Why were there so many obligations today? She just wanted to take a nap.

"I can help with the baskets," he offered. "Tell me about this party. Do you think mud-crawling weirdos would be welcome?"

She chuckled nervously. Fernando was RIGHT THERE. What a mess.

"Oh, you're starting to set up for the Winter Ball?" Jonas asked. "Is it soon? Jonathan always goes way overboard in the best possible way! I'd love to come."

"Actually, he . . ." Avani paused. She'd told plenty of people about Pop's death, so it wasn't hard for her to say. It was their reaction that she dreaded, though there was no way around it. She swallowed. "He passed away. We don't have the ball anymore."

And there it was. That flash of shock in Jonas's eyes and then . . . pity. As natural as it was, Avani hated it. She hated the way an acquaintance's feelings about Pop's death would suddenly take precedence over her own.

"Oh my gosh, I had no idea. I'm so sorry." He clapped a hand over his mouth, but then seemed to get ahold of himself. "He was wonderful, just the kindest heart. . . ."

She was glad he didn't make it too awkward, as some people did. That he didn't just change the subject and run away. Regardless,

> there was that grief again,
>> like an icepick had been shoved through her heart,
>>> infecting it,
>>>> freezing it,
>>>>> and freezing the rest of her along with it.
> Moments came back to her,
>> perfect moments encased in crystal—

Pop debating the theme and ordering way too much tinsel and fancy cheese, Dad trying out new recipes for hors d'oeuvres, she and her sisters wearing adorably matching velvet dresses. Pop had always been the center of it all, the consummate party planner and bubbly social diva. He was the perfect foil to Dad's reserved nature, somehow enticing the entire San Juans to brave the cold and wet and descend on the Songbird for a night of winter enchantment with promises only he could keep.

When she'd biked up the drive earlier, she'd been on the edge of a thought—déjà vu from something poignant and ephemeral and joyful. She knew what it was now: The Songbird blanketed in snow had reminded her of Pop, of the party he would lovingly spend half the year planning.

Avani ducked her head and returned to the computer, trying her best to focus on checking the club in. But her mind was back on the Winter Ball, the year she and Pop had been the very last ones still up. The two of them had danced the night away, every song a deeply felt favorite. The stars had shone and frost had dusted the windows and she'd sworn that Pop whirled and shook and breakdanced with unearthly magic.

And when she was with him, she did, too.

"Why is everyone waiting around here?"

Avani had found some—not all—of the room keys when Nidhi came flying through the door, a whirlwind of snowflakes and rosy cheeks and excitement. Grayson at her side, of course. That girl had it bad, even if they still weren't actually calling themselves official.

But all thoughts of how cute their romance was disappeared when Nidhi came around the back of the front desk with The Look. Her patented Concerned Sister™ look. Which was sure to be followed by absolutely nothing good.

"Hello, Avani? Why is everyone waiting around here?" Nidhi asked again. "And why did I catch Fernando wandering outside in the cold?"

Oh man. Fernando had left? "Well, the computer wasn't working, and I couldn't find all the keys. . . ."

"The computer works just fine." Nidhi nudged Avani aside, and in a few efficient clicks she checked in the whole Grizzly crew at once. "You have to search for the group name, not individual last names."

Then she dug out a shiny new lockbox, which apparently was the correct place to look because it actually had all the room keys, neatly organized into their own tiny cubby holes. The ones Avani had dug up were just the spares.

Nidhi was kinda making Avani look bad. Why couldn't she just explain how the outdated software worked without being so annoying? Avani narrowed her eyes, vowing that she would memorize every detail of this process and totally kill it the next time.

But as usual, instead of paying attention to Nidhi's string of instructions, her thoughts were racing ahead like dogsleds on ice. She had other ways to make her mark on the inn. The Winter Ball, for one.

Bursting back into the living room, she squeezed herself ungracefully between Rani and Sirisha on the sofa. They didn't mind.

"How convenient, you're back right when we're finishing the last basket." Rani tied a neat little silver bow with a flourish of about a zillion curling ribbons.

"You try dealing with twenty guests at once!"

"Twenty *cute* guests." Sirisha handed her a cup of hot cocoa. "It didn't seem like you were having such a bad time."

Avani shrugged coyly. "Well, one of them did ask to come to Kiera's party with me."

"Oooh, tell me everything!" Rani popped an almond in her mouth as if it were popcorn and she was expecting a real-life rom-com in the making.

But before Avani could begin the story, Nidhi wandered in, and Sirisha made room for her on the sofa. They were all four squeezed cozily together, but Avani had the sense that she was about to get lectured big time about the check-in process, which she absolutely did not want to hear.

So she leapt up fast. "Welp, Kiera's expecting me to help set up for her party."

Party. As she said it, she remembered what she'd meant to bring up before Nidhi showed up. The Winter Ball, of course. Well, it was now or never.

"Speaking of celebrations," Avani said slowly, "I was talking to the chaperone of that Grizzly Drizzly crew, and it turns out he'd been to Pop's Winter Ball back in the day. He was going on about how fantastic it was . . . and, well—it was pretty great, wasn't it? We should bring it back."

Nidhi smiled kindly. And maybe a little patronizingly. "I think it's a little late for this year, don't you? Pop used to start planning it during the summer, remember?"

Of course Nidhi would overthink it.

"Okay, but he was kind of excessive," Avani countered. "If we scaled it down, I think we could throw a nice event—"

"I don't want people to expect Pop's Winter Ball and get something totally different," Nidhi interrupted. "I mean, he would rent professional lighting, hire extra kitchen staff, send out gold-trimmed invites. It was huge. Remember when the four of us spent an entire fall painting those giant snowflakes?"

Avani did not in fact remember it, but she wasn't about to admit it. "Whatever. We don't need to hand-paint all the decorations! I'll order some online and dig a few lights out of the storage room."

"It's more work than you think."

There's a certain "big sister" tone that sends younger siblings right up the wall, and Nidhi had it nailed. But Avani would not be driven to violence. At least not this time. Her sisters were always telling her to focus more, and for once she actually had something she wanted to focus on.

Her heart clicked onto the project, this party that once upon a time had meant the world to her.

"I'm throwing the Winter Ball," Avani said—quietly but with determination. "You don't have to worry about a thing—I'll handle every detail."

Nidhi shook her head. "Seriously? No. You don't know what you'd be getting into."

"Don't be so pessimistic!" Avani threw a beseeching look to her other sisters for backup.

Sirisha leaned forward thoughtfully. "It *is* a lot to take on. But I think it would be nice, too. I'm willing to help."

Rani looked dreamy. "Oooh, this is perfect: a beautiful, romantic ball! Count me in, too. Music and dancing and gorgeous people . . . maybe a visiting dignitary, a few royals . . ."

Avani, Rani, and Sirisha all raised their brows at Nidhi expectantly. It was three against one, but the truth was that very little happened in the Songbird without their eldest sister's blessing.

Nidhi sighed loudly. "Fine, but first you have to ask Dad. And even if he okays it, you're in charge. No flaking out because you suddenly remembered you joined a traveling theater troupe and need to rehearse for Spring Fest or whatever it is you're suddenly interested in out of the blue."

"That's kind of harsh," Avani said. "I told you I really want to do this."

"I'm not trying to be harsh, just realistic," Nidhi answered. "You *know* that sometimes you can be kind of scatterbrained, and I have a ton of other obligations, so you can't just hand everything off to me the way you did at reception just now. Agreed?"

"Agreed," Avani returned between clenched teeth.

Sure, she didn't have the best track record for being organized. But despite what know-it-all Nidhi thought, Avani was perfectly capable of pulling together a fabulous event. All she had to do was focus and make a few of those neurotic little lists other people liked.

But right now, she was overdue at Kiera's—except hadn't she promised to bring something? Was it napkins or cups?

It was definitely napkins, of course.

Unless it was cups?

Chapter Two

Grayson offered to drop Avani and her Grizzly Drizzly semi-date at the party, since Nidhi was busy with more wedding prep for the next day and he was meeting a friend in town anyway. As they pulled down the long driveway that led to Kiera's parents' big waterfront property in Grayson's rickety white pickup, the tires skidded a little on a patch of ice.

"Whoa." Jake—the eager Grizzly Drizzly guy who'd pleaded to come along—clutched Avani's arm.

"Don't worry, this baby's got four-wheel drive," Grayson said, patting the steering wheel as they successfully rolled to a stop. "Just text me when you're ready to go."

"Thanks, Grayson!" Avani jumped out.

Jake trailed after her like an eager puppy, but her mind was still on Nidhi's infuriating words about the Winter Ball.

No flaking out . . .

You know that sometimes you can be kind of scatterbrained . . .

Scatterbrained? Seriously? Being multitalented did *not* mean she was scatterbrained.

Nidhi thought Avani was still the same nine-year-old girl who'd knocked over a lamp when jumping on the bed, the girl who'd once cartwheeled right into a patch of nettles. Yes, she had done those things, but they were long past. She'd show Nidhi that her seventeen-and-one-month-old self was totally capable of being responsible when it was something she cared about—by throwing the most beautiful Winter Ball ever. She could picture it now: The living room would be converted into an old-fashioned dancing hall, strung with lights and hanging stars and snowflakes. Lanterns and candles and a string band . . .

Or maybe it would be more fun to have a DJ? And strobe lights? Really get everyone's heart thumping with the beat? So many decisions to make.

Also, brrrrr. It was freezing, and Avani's fur-lined snow boots left prints in the inch of snow. The weather reports were predicting several more inches by morning. In fact, they were expecting a snowpocalypse in the next few weeks—one of those years where the island was dumped with way more snow than the half an inch they usually got. Everyone would get in a tizzy over it and things would get shut down (although hopefully just school). The San Juans transit department had a plow or two, but Avani recalled it taking a long time for the roads to be cleared in the last snowmageddon four years ago.

"Aren't you forgetting something?" Grayson called over the music blaring from inside Kiera's house. Even though Avani was incredibly late (which was not her fault, at all), it sounded as if the festivities had kicked off just fine.

"I am?" she asked.

He pointed to the giant stack of napkins left on the seat.

"Oh yeah." Avani grabbed them. "Thanks!"

Inside, Kiera's sleekly modern place was swarming with almost every junior, half the sophomores, and a smattering of seniors from Orcas Island High School. They were the kids Avani and her sisters had grown up with, the kids they saw way too much of. Island life was beautiful and charming—but social options were few and far between in their school of a hundred thirty-ish students.

Rani, of course, had decided that staying home to read a romance novel was her top priority. She wasn't interested in any of the "miscreants" at school, as she characterized them. Avani didn't always understand her twin's criteria for love (nor did she really understand her own). But she agreed that finding it here was unlikely; most of the teens on the island were either already paired up or desperately restless for new prospects. They'd probably go wild over the Grizzly Drizzlies—in fact, she should have brought more of them.

Spirits seemed high as Avani made the rounds, Jake following after her like a second shadow and gallantly carrying the napkins for her. Avani immediately relaxed as the catchy R&B playing over the speakers enveloped her. She shook her hips and wiggled her shoulders while stopping to slap hands and exchange inside jokes with various classmates.

"Ugh, so glad we're on break." JJ Doherty downed their drink in a single gulp. "That precalc test was brutal!"

"Agreed." Avani shuddered. "If I have to deal with complex numbers one more time, I can't account for my actions. There might be blood."

At her elbow, Jake laughed. He always laughed, even when her jokes weren't super funny. Good thing he was cute—nice broad shoulders, scruffy brown hair that he mostly covered with an old baseball cap—and Avani supposed spending one evening with him wouldn't be too much torture. Especially if she could somehow get him to do some push-ups . . . um, yes, push-ups would definitely be welcome.

Sara Goldstein obviously agreed, mouthing, *He's hot!* as Avani and Jake worked their way to the open-layout kitchen laden with party offerings. (Jake was, in fact, hot, but both Sara and Avani knew his true appeal was that they hadn't known him since elementary school.)

As Jake put the napkins down on the enormous island, Avani realized there was already a towering stack of them—and only, like, three remaining red Solo cups. Oops. Maybe she had gotten it wrong after all.

She opened the well-stocked fridge and grabbed a can of sparkling water. "What'll you have?"

Jake grinned. "Whatever you're having."

She chuckled. "You don't have to do exactly what I do, you know."

He shrugged sheepishly. "I'm bad at making decisions."

"That makes two of us." She started to toss him the can just as one more cute boy walked into the kitchen. Oof. Another problem with island life was the impossibility of avoiding Fernando. Distracted, Avani threw the can with a little too much force, and it nearly smacked Jake right in the face.

Luckily, he was an athlete with quick reflexes and managed to catch it. "That's quite an arm you have."

"I play softball. . . ." Avani lost her train of thought as she took in Fernando, who was looking a little too adorable in a tight-fitting green sweater. She'd known him forever and a day, but when he'd asked her out, she'd been forced to see him anew. Suddenly, she couldn't help but notice the fact that he had really nice cheekbones. And eyelashes.

Not that she was into him. She just felt bad about what had happened, that was all.

Fernando found an empty spot on the counter for the queso he was carrying—which smelled absolutely *divine*—along with the chips he'd brought. And cups. Dang, how had he known about the dire cup situation? Just that kind of guy, she supposed.

"Hey, man!" Jake held out his hand. "Aren't you the vegetable guy from earlier? I'm Jake."

"I'm Fernando." He shook Jake's hand, but his eyes darted to Avani.

Meanwhile, the aroma of melted cheese was drawing a crowd. Thankfully, she spotted Kiera, who was just coming in from the deck. Perfect timing for Avani to make her getaway from awkward chitchat with Fernando and Jake at the same time (yikes!).

"Kiera! Sorry I'm late!" Avani swept her friend in for a huge hug.

"You jerk, you said you'd help set up!" Kiera squeezed her back. "But I'm so glad you made it! I was afraid the snow was going to keep everyone away."

A chorus of jock guys vehemently disagreed: "NO WAY!" "We need to PARTY!" "WOOOO!"

Avani laughed. "See? I told you not to worry."

Kiera glanced at the pack of cups that now graced the island. "And you remembered the cups! Yes! I didn't want people going for my parents' crystal or I'd be . . ." She made a slicing motion across her throat.

"Oh, well I didn't—"

"At least they're at some fundraiser tonight and they'll be out late. OH WHAT IS THAT HEAVENLY SMELL?" Kiera grabbed Avani's hand, bringing her right back square in Fernando's path.

That freaking queso. Avani gave in and plunged a chip into the gooey and admittedly delicious dip.

"THIS IS FIRE!" Kiera exclaimed, inhaling several chips.

"Fab," Georgina Brooks chimed in. "Fernando, is this a *special family recipe*? From the region of Mexico you're from—remind me where?"

"Nah, it's Tex-Mex." Fernando shrugged. "I got the recipe online."

"Oh." Georgina looked befuddled by the very idea.

Fernando and Avani exchanged a look. Orcas was a pretty progressive place, but it was also mostly white and sometimes that could be a bit much. Avani still recalled when a kid in the fourth grade had asked her if she lived in a teepee. Avani hadn't known where to begin with that question, but Fernando had artfully intervened by accidentally-on-purpose spilling the kid's chocolate milk. She'd decided he was all right after that and had even invited him for a game of kickball with some classmates (where she'd beaten his team mercilessly). They'd stayed friendly over the years. Until he'd wanted something more than that.

Avani abruptly broke eye contact and scouted out escape routes with the urgency of a secret agent. The door to the game room was open. Bingo.

As Avani ducked into the game room, Jake stayed firmly by her side, detailing his hopes and dreams for the competition on Sunday.

"I'm awesome at rope-climbing," he was saying, "but I'm nervous about the balance beams. . . ."

She didn't hear the rest because a rowdy game of beer pong was under way, with about fifteen kids surrounding the table, some playing, some just watching.

As soon as Derek Moskowitz saw Avani, he ushered her to join them. "Avani! We need you!"

"Hey, who says she's on your team?"

"I invited her first!"

Avani glanced at Jake. "What do you think?"

"I'm down," he said.

The squabble over Avani continued as they approached. She had a reputation as a master at beer pong—she had killer aim and could take down the other team with barely a drink. Ultimately, she decided it was fair for her to join the underdogs and give them a fighting chance.

"Game ON," she said, tossing her first ball, which found its target easily.

"AH-VUN-NEE! AH-VUN-NEE!" her (rather uncoordinated) team cheered.

Avani had a seriously competitive side, and soon she got caught up in the game. Several rounds later Jake was looking at her like she was a beer pong goddess.

"I think I'm in love," he said fervently.

Avani laughed. "That's all it takes?"

Jake nodded, leaning closer—just as Fernando wandered into the game room.

Uh-oh.

"Who wants to hot tub?" Kiera hollered through the door in the nick of time.

Avani jetted out of there.

Despite the literal snowstorm that was forecasted, she'd worn a bathing suit under her jeans and sweater just in case, because hot tubbing was a time-honored tradition at Kiera's. Soon the tub was packed. And whoa, did Jake look good shirtless. Of course, now other girls were fawning over him, which was completely unsurprising. Avani didn't mind though—let Sara Goldstein have him; it wasn't as if Avani took any of it seriously.

She tilted her head back
    let the falling snowflakes gather
        feathering her nose
           her chin
                her hair
                    her lips
she was in her own place
    a quiet haven
        amongst the laughter and chatter
where she could dream
    of magical winter nights
        past and present

Someone slipped in beside her, but she paid them no mind, just dreaming of Pop's infectious energy, of lights too beautiful to look at and music too beautiful to listen to and food too beautiful to eat.

Until that someone spoke. "Hey."

Ack! Fernando again. So much for avoiding him. Suddenly, she noticed that the hot tub had mostly cleared out, making it impossible to pretend she couldn't hear him. He was here, right in front of her. Even Jake had disappeared, probably off with Sara.

And Avani's breath caught as she noticed
    his moth-brown eyes aglow
        cheekbones sculpted with shadows and snow
           golden shoulders
                a dusting of chest hair
                    just visible above the steamy water

He was looking at her just as he had at another one of Kiera's parties, right before he'd asked her to that concert. When something in his soft, earnest eyes had scared her. But she'd thought that she could handle it anyway, and she'd given him a breezy, "Sure, let's do it!" And she'd been so busy pretending to be breezy that she'd *marked the wrong date* in her calendar.

(Information that should never, ever reach Nidhi.)

She knew she could tell Fernando it was all just a mistake, but the truth was that she didn't *want* him to ask her out again. Didn't want to see that open earnest look of his, the one that made her want to promise him things she didn't feel ready to promise. Better to let him think that she'd changed her mind about it all. Which she sort of had.

"Hey," Avani replied warily. Unable to soften herself the way girls were so often expected to.

"So you and this Jake dude, huh?" There was an edge in his voice as he grazed a finger over the water in a half circle.

Maybe it would be better to let him think that Jake was the issue, instead of something fragile inside her.

"Yeah, Jake's great," she said casually, hoping he wasn't inside making out with Sara right at that moment. She searched for something more to say about the Grizzly Drizzly who had proclaimed his love for her over beer pong, but luckily her phone beeped and she was saved.

"Hang on a sec." Avani hopped up to check it. Oops, she'd already missed several texts from Grayson when she'd been in a daze of snowflakes and party planning. "Umm . . . apparently the storm is coming early, so I have to go. See you later!"

"Oh, okay . . . do you have a ride?"

It was just like him to be concerned even though she'd made it clear that nothing was happening between them.

"Yeah, my sister's boyfriend will pick us up. I'm gonna go find Jake." Avani knew she should probably dig into all those swirling feelings that made her freeze up and run away around Fernando. Maybe when she was journaling in bed tonight . . .

She scurried from the deck, searching for Jake—who had actually started doing push-ups in the living room for an audience of cooing fans (how had Avani predicted that?)—and then Grayson was texting that he was outside, and others were also getting the news about the snowpocalypse and the party was obviously over, and Kiera was freaking out because her parents were headed home and someone had spilled beer on the rug, and Avani was hurriedly helping her scrub and then she and Jake were piling into the old truck (with four-wheel drive!), cruising along treacherous island roads and the snow was almost a wall and Avani just hoped everyone made it home safe.

As Avani, Grayson, and Jake pulled into the inn's parking lot, they saw headlights just behind them. It was Dad. Avani felt a surge of relief that he was home early from his date, then immediately felt bad about it.

All

    the

        mixed

            feelings.

They barreled into reception, dripping with wet snow, powder caked on their boots.

Luckily, Sirisha was ready with a mop. "Oh no, Dad! You had to leave your date early!"

"It's okay. It was short but sweet." Dad patted her shoulder. "At least everyone got home safely. Grayson, you'd better stay the night. I'll figure out which room is free."

Grayson glanced at the blizzard outside and nodded. "Thanks, I'll just call my parents and let them know."

In the living room, Nidhi had thoughtfully put out a self-serve hot cocoa station. Some of the wedding guests were hanging out around the fireplace, and Jake immediately rejoined a few of his fellow Grizzly Drizzlies horsing around on another cluster of sofas. Despite them, it was surprisingly quiet for such a full house, as if the impending snowstorm had cast a spell. There really was little to do but cozy up.

Yet Avani's mind was swarming with too many hot tub feels. It was all a bit overwhelming to comb through, so when Rani suggested a movie in the library, she agreed. The distraction would help settle her.

"How was the party?" Rani nudged Avani, her eyes on the Grizzly boys.

"Well, I rocked at beer pong . . . er, don't tell Dad, obviously. And"—Avani arched her brows—"Jake did push-ups."

Rani's mouth dropped. "I can't believe I missed that!"

"How was the romance novel?"

"I cried. Like, a lot. My HEART!" Rani clutched her chest dramatically.

"A masterpiece, huh?"

"Truly."

In the library, they found Nidhi hunched over her laptop on the beanbag. Muttering to herself.

"What's up?" Avani asked as she flipped on the gas fireplace. Ooh, that felt nice.

When Nidhi didn't immediately answer, Avani plopped down next to her, nosily looking over her elder sister's shoulder. The browser was open to the site of a culinary institute in India.

"So you've decided on something?" Avani asked.

Over the last few months, Nidhi had been researching scholarships, UW's policy on studying abroad, and programs all over India.

"Nothing is exactly what I want!" Nidhi sounded grumpy and frustrated. "Most culinary programs seem to be combined with hotel management, and I'm more interested in a deep dive into cooking and food culture. And a lot of the programs don't really fit with UW's calendar, so I might have to apply for two terms abroad instead of just one. Also, I really want to be able to take classes on Indian history and things like that, too. I'm just . . . ugh . . . overwhelmed!"

"Too many options?" Avani guessed. Even though she'd barely started planning the party, she was already having trouble deciding between a live band and a DJ.

"And none that are just right," Nidhi agreed.

"Maybe you're making this too hard on yourself," Avani said. "Why do you need to combine your trip to India with school at all? You could just go visit for a few weeks in the summer. Or if you wanted to take a whole term off, you could probably get permission for that. Then you could just explore on your own—you'd learn a ton of history by going to the museums. You might be able to sit in on different classes and dabble more."

Nidhi shook her head. "I wish. The only way I can afford this trip is if I get a scholarship, and the only way I can get a scholarship is if it's a proper study abroad program."

Avani had the feeling UW would allow Nidhi to design her own program, but her elder sister wasn't listening anymore—already googling away. Even though Avani was used to being dismissed, it still hurt. Nobody took her seriously. All the more reason that she had to throw the Winter Ball. The "flaky" and "scatterbrained" labels were getting super old.

Avani retreated to the loveseat, where Sirisha was already curled up.

Rani clapped her hands and plopped down next to them. "You're all gonna love this movie!"

At least it was the kind of thing that would get her mind off her problems. Hopefully. The opening credits began to play with a catchy song, and a girl and a boy met cute. Both leads were white and blond (ah, the '80s, when nobody else apparently existed). Dad and Grayson wandered in as zany hijinks ensued. They'd left Dad's favorite spot on the armchair open for him, and Nidhi scooted to make room on the beanbag for Grayson.

"I've seen this one before," Grayson said, hanging an arm around Nidhi. "My mom and I watched it together a long time ago. It was pretty cute."

Nidhi chuckled. "You and your mom watch rom-coms together? *You're* cute."

They made googly eyes at each other. Meanwhile, Dad was slyly texting again, a goofy grin on his face as he typed. Ugh. Everyone was just so happy and cozy, weren't they?

She should have told Rani she wasn't in the mood for romance. But then again, arguing with Rani on that front was generally useless. Rani always picked the movie. And the movie was always a romance. Sometimes tragic romance, sometimes wild romance, sometimes a romance with vampires. (If the vampires were hot, Avani could deal.)

Actually, this movie wasn't terrible—it had a great soundtrack and several laugh-out-loud jokes. The best scene was at the end, when everyone came together at prom. That was the magic that Avani wanted to create with the Winter Ball: the moments that everyone would remember for years to come. Just as she could never forget staying up late dancing with Pop.

After the credits rolled, Avani slid off the loveseat, anxious to ask Dad about bringing back the ball. But he and Nidhi were already huddled together, intently discussing study abroad options—which they'd already discussed about a zillion times before.

Avani's stomach sank as they talked and talked . . . and talked.

It was always the same—Nidhi's needs were the most important. Sure, her eldest sister was a senior, she was starting college next year, her future was on the line. All stuff that Avani was actually glad she didn't have to worry about yet because she had no clue how anyone could narrow down their passions to just one career. Was there such a thing as a writer/radio host/pop star who also played professional beer pong?

For as long as Avani could remember, Nidhi had always been on a single-minded track to own a bakery. And then for some reason, she'd suddenly changed all her plans (which Avani could empathize with) and therefore needed to hog Dad's attention (which wasn't cool at all). Avani only needed two minutes of Dad's time to get permission for the Winter Ball, but they were talking for so long that she eventually slunk off to the room she shared with Rani.

Typical.

Curled up in bed with her pajamas on, Avani stayed up late with her journal, working out her first lists for the Winter Ball on paper. She'd need a guest list, invitations, food, drinks, decorations, music—was there anything else? She tapped her pen against the journal, then started doodling what it would all look like: a big bash with her sisters and Dad and Kiera and the Songbird staff and friends from school. Fernando.

Even her own traitorous brain wouldn't allow her to avoid him, and she found herself drawing him as he'd looked with his arms draped over the side of the hot tub. She wasn't that great of a sketch artist, but somehow she got the curve of his lips just right. A little too right—she scribbled over the whole thing, pretending she'd meant to draw an angry rain cloud instead.

Yet that night she dreamt of moth-brown eyes glowing under the deck lights.

Chapter Three

The next morning, the Songbird grounds were coated in fresh powder, enough for cross-country skiing through the hills and trees of the island. Avani and Dad had a tradition of going out together after a rare snowfall like this, but the inn was way too busy this weekend. Hungry wedding guests and Grizzly Drizzlies had taken over the dining room for breakfast, and there wouldn't be time to savor the cold and the stillness the way she'd like to.

As Avani worked the dining room, she mentally put together the perfect playlist for the Winter Ball. She already had over forty songs picked out: some early mingling music, followed by some you-totally-need-to-dance numbers, then a steady mixture of ballads and slow songs and the fun stuff. Pop's absolute favorite song would be the last one of the night.

"Hey!" a hottie in a cable knit sweater interrupted her thoughts. "I didn't ask for salmon on my eggs Benedict. I wanted bacon."

"Oh, sorry!" Avani quickly exchanged the plate with another.

"No, this isn't mine either. I asked for no Hollandaise sauce."

Arggghhhhhh.

There had been far too many orders of eggs Benedict that morning, a brunch obsession Avani didn't really get. She'd take a ham-and-cheese croissant any day of the week.

"I'll check on that for you in the kitchen," she managed—though she was internally far more concerned with whether "YMCA" was too cheesy to add to the list or not.

Of course, as distracted as she was while weaving between the crowded tables, she bumped the tray Rani was carrying. Drinks splashed out of their mugs, splattering one another, though luckily Rani recovered well enough not to drop the whole thing.

"Oh no! Nidhi will have to remake all these," Rani said in dismay.

"Sorry!" Avani winced at the mess.

The look on Nidhi's face when Rani broke the news to her was S.C.A.R.Y.—horror movie scary, serial-killers-with-machetes scary—and Avani slinked out of the line of sight. Ugh. Did she have to keep messing up in front of Nidhi? Then again, maybe big sis should just chill. The occasional spilled drink was inevitable.

She found Sirisha working on an English essay at reception, which was nice and quiet at the moment.

"Hey, will you swap with me?" Avani begged. "I don't have the right headspace for the restaurant right now."

Sirisha looked up from her homework. "I'll trade you . . . for a favor."

That sounded insidious. (Also, "YMCA" was definitely too cheesy.)

"I was kind of hoping that my sweet little sis would just do this out of the goodness of her heart," Avani said.

Said sweet little sister only grinned. "It's only a small favor."

"Like my firstborn child?"

"I need a model for a photography club project," Sirisha said.

"Why don't you ask Rani?" Avani asked. "She loves the camera."

Sirisha tapped her pen on her essay. "This is supposed to be candid, and Rani hates candid. I could ask someone at school, but . . ."

"You're too shy?" Avani guessed.

Sirisha ducked her head, shrugging. She was open and relaxed with her sisters, but she had a really hard time at school. She could barely get two words out, though they'd grown up with most of their classmates. Avani didn't totally get it, since random banter had always seemed to flow a little too easily from her own lips. But she knew Sirisha had always been more comfortable in the background.

Besides, Avani had to escape the restaurant—and Nidhi. "Deal."

"Cool." Sirisha gamely put away her homework in her backpack and hopped off.

Perfect. Working the front desk was far more conducive to finishing the most amazing playlist ever. ("YMCA" was definitely in.) Pulling out her phone, Avani tapped her mental playlist into her music app, then downloaded a party planning app. Who needed Nidhi's advice for organization anyway? Once Avani had planned and executed the most *it* event of the year, Nidhi would have to admit that she was wrong about her. Ah, it would be so satisfying—but Avani wouldn't gloat, of course. That would make it seem like she'd been worried she couldn't pull it off.

Which she absolutely wasn't.

She did have another one of those faint suspicions brewing that she was forgetting something else she'd promised. But she was sure it would come to her, just as soon as she added five more vital songs to her playlist.

RING.

RING.

RING.

So much for quiet. Avani answered the phone again and again: The entire PNW had suddenly decided that the snowstorm under way meant that they should plan their summer vacations. Avani rubbed her temples. Not exactly living in the moment, were they?

RING.

Omg, it was the Chaudary family—*the* Chaudary family, of the big bike app company. Avani only knew this because the rich parents had been featured on the cover of a copy of *Wired* that someone had left behind in the living room. She took down their details excitedly, three rooms for three weeks in the summer. Ooh la la, what fancy clientele. Wait till she told Rani.

RING.

At least Dad would be happy with all these bookings. And right—she was supposed to ask him for permission—

RING.

The last call was from the rental company that was providing the chairs for the wedding ceremony that evening. Apparently, the trail down to the cove was too icy to transport the chairs, and also probably not the best idea for the guests to traverse anyway.

Normally, she would have asked Dad or Nidhi what to tell the rental company. But if she wanted Dad's permission to throw the Winter Ball, she should really learn to handle a few things herself. And although weddings down at the cove were a Songbird specialty, Avani had a perfect spot in mind for a backup.

In fact, should she even throw the Winter Ball indoors? Maybe it should be out in the fresh air, under lush evergreen boughs dappled with snow . . .

RING.

RING.

RING.

Avani sighed, picking up the phone once more.

An hour before sunset, the last touches for the wedding ceremony were under way. The spot at the top of a gently sloping hill was surrounded by elegant, towering pines and even offered peekaboo views of the sea—at a safe distance. No worries here that any kids would wander off a cliffside.

"Nice save," Dad said, draping silver garlands across the branches of two blue cedars. The trees leaned into each other, creating a natural archway for the bride and groom to exchange vows under. "This is a great spot."

Nidhi surveyed the area, a clipboard in hand. "A bit of reshuffling, but it worked out. How did you know this trail wouldn't be too icy?"

Avani hadn't known, but she was hardly going to admit that. "I guess I just have a natural gift for planning events."

She tied a recycled-paper bow on the holly garlands Rani and Sirisha had strung across the rows of chairs. She had another surprise up her sleeve, a fun end to the ceremony. If everything went smoothly, Dad would be super impressed at her event skills and then—and only then—she'd finally leap in and ask him about the Winter Ball! Avani did her best to contain a secret smile.

"What's so funny?" Nidhi asked.

"Oh, nothing . . ." She spotted the bridesmaids and groomsmen coming up the slope. And among them—was that Fernando in a wintry blue suit? No.

Yes.

"Did you know that he was in the ceremony?" she whisper-shouted.

"Yeah, why?" Nidhi looked bemused at her tone.

Of course the delicate situation between Avani and Fernando would be one of the few things Nidhi *didn't* know about under the roof of the Songbird Inn. She probably had in her head the exact number of onions in the pantry, yet she was completely oblivious to Avani's wild excuses not to be around for morning produce delivery. It was simultaneously infuriating and useful—if Nidhi found out about the missed date, she'd probably start lecturing Avani on proper use of a calendar. Ugh.

Rani, on the other hand, was clearly on high alert. She pulled Avani a little away from the others. "Spill it. What's up between you and Fernando?"

Her twin was generally less judgmental about Avani's laissez-faire nature, so Avani quickly (and quietly) filled her in on the concert she'd flaked out on. Of course, Rani would probably have a heart attack at the very thought of not remembering a romantic engagement. But then again . . . "Why are you smiling like that?"

It was Rani's matchmaking grin—a formidable grin indeed. Oh boy.

"True love is always tested," Rani said in mystic tones. "This is the obstacle you must overcome before your happy ending."

Avani rolled her eyes. "You read too many romance novels."

"I read exactly the right number of romance novels," Rani returned. "You'll see. This family needs me."

"Did it ever occur to you that I might not be interested in him?"

"Oh please, you two have had chemistry since elementary school."

"We have not."

"Uh-huh."

There was no arguing with her. Rani just didn't get that Avani wasn't looking for some fake happy ending with a guy. Winning a basketball championship or finishing writing that sci-fi short story she'd started or learning to kickbox were all higher priorities. Sometimes, clipping her toenails was honestly a higher priority. She liked boys well enough—even swooned over the right set of cheekbones—but too often, kisses came with promises she couldn't be expected to keep.

Of course, now Fernando had spotted them under the trees. Instead of lining up with the other groomsmen, he was waving and coming her way and looking really hot in his wintry blue suit.

Yikes.

"Hey!" Fernando said, clearing his throat and stumbling slightly over the snow. His hair looked all disheveled, as if he'd run his hands through it a lot.

"Hey," Avani said brightly, gearing up for her escape. "So you're part of the wedding? Cool. Good to see you! I gotta go help my dad—"

She started power-walking away.

Unfortunately, Fernando was right on her heels. "My cousin was relieved they could still have an outdoor wedding and—"

"Your cousin?" Avani muttered. Now that she thought about it, he and the groom did share a similar nose, the same skin tone . . . and cheekbones so prominent they probably should be outlawed.

"Yeah, Manuel's my cuz. He was kinda nervous about the snow

ruining everything, and the family had a bit of a breakdown over the situation earlier." Fernando ran a hand through his usually perfectly mussed hair again. "It was a little rough, to be honest."

"Yeah, people can get a bit heated about weddings." Yet another reason romance was overrated.

"You said it." Fernando rolled his eyes. "At least the main roads were plowed so everyone could make it out to the inn."

"Yeah, thankfully." Avani braced herself for the other shoe to drop, excuses for missing the date running through her mind. She'd been sick! No, her grandma had been sick (not that she had any living grandparents)! Okay, it was their neighbor's second cousin, but she'd been very worried! Anything sounded better than admitting she'd just plain forgotten. It sounded cruel, like she hadn't cared.

She did care. Just about too many things at once. Besides, all the excuses in the world weren't going to get to the heart of the matter: that she did *not* want a boyfriend. It was better not to bring it up at all.

Classical strings began to play, and the groomsmen called Fernando to their side.

"Talk later?" Fernando asked.

"Sure!" Avani lied.

The bridesmaids lined up with bouquets of holly and berries (the wedding couple was far too eco-minded for out-of-season flowers). Wind instruments joined in as the groom took his place, and then the delicate notes of a harp drifted in the chilly February air as the bride walked in gray suede snow boots along the aisle, the lacy train of her gown dusted with snow behind her, new flurries swishing down to crown her hair.

"You gotta admit, Fernando does look good in a suit," Rani whispered in her ear. "Why don't you just apologize and ask for a do-over?"

"I don't *want* to," Avani said, her insides like the island's slushy roads.

Rani shook Avani's shoulders dramatically. "Do not allow your pride to chase away true love!"

Avani couldn't help but chuckle. "Right, whatever! Now hush!"

As the officiant warmed up the crowd with a few jokes about frosty weddings, Avani's eyes kept wandering to Fernando. A bright orange butterfly with dark-edged wings landed on his shoulder. She hadn't known that butterflies could live in the winter, especially after a snowstorm.

It was obviously the butterfly that captured her attention, nothing else.

As the guests lined up to congratulate the couple, Rani poked Avani. Avani poked her back. After a few more undignified pokes—which only a few guests happened to notice, and perhaps Dad—Avani gave in.

"What do you want now?" she whispered.

Rani clutched Avani's hand. "A misunderstanding can't keep love apart. You need to go to him. You need to tell him!"

"I told you that I'm not interested—"

"Be true to thine own heart, dear sister!"

Oh boy. Her twin was such a character—and probably seriously mangling Shakespeare. But Avani couldn't be bothered by all that nonsense now because it was time for the surprise finale to the ceremony. As she grabbed the cross-country skis she'd hidden in the trees, she stopped quickly to check her phone for any additional wedding chores. She'd set up an alert to remind her of each task.

Oops—unfortunately, she'd missed one. Delivering the welcome baskets.

Oh well. Thanks-for-coming baskets would be even better.

Avani hadn't told anyone but the bride and groom the real reason she'd picked this spot for the ceremony. The couple—who'd absolutely loved Avani's idea for a sendoff—accepted the skis and boots as the guests murmured with delight. Avani had tracked down boots in their sizes from the inn's storage room, which luckily was filled with far more sports equipment than strictly necessary. In moments, Ariana had pinned up her gown's train, and she and Manuel were speeding off down the hill on smooth powder, weaving expertly over a white carpet through the maze of pines. The crowd cheered as the couple's giddy laughter echoed after them in the wintry air.

Fortunately, the reception was much warmer than the ceremony. The refurbished and well-heated barn, where so many Songbird receptions were held, had an understated chic. People loved to come to Orcas for simple, rustic weddings like the one Manuel and Ariana had planned, with driftwood centerpieces and candles in mason jars, the ceiling strung with twinkle lights and silvery garlands.

Since the snow had stopped, the live band had been able to arrive by ferry just in time. They played covers of just about anything, from mariachi to classic pop. Dinner began with a romantic ballad. To get people on the dance floor, they turned to a fast-paced salsa.

As Avani was gathering empty glasses, she caught Fernando twirling a pretty girl with dyed red hair and, admittedly, a few decent moves. (Not as good as Avani's of course.) The sight of them dancing brought Avani back to the eighth grade, when she and Fernando had ended up as partners for the salsa unit in gym class. Or maybe they'd picked each other—Avani couldn't remember. But she did recall how they'd shown up most of their classmates, how they'd kicked and spun and how Fernando's hips had moved in ways that shouldn't be possible.

Of course, now those hips were moving in ways that shouldn't be possible with this *other* girl, and Avani felt a pang that definitely wasn't jealousy. She was only staring at them because they were so technically good—in fact tons of people were cheering them on. Yes, that was it.

As the song came to its last few notes, Fernando happened to catch Avani's gaze . . . and she realized she was still holding the same couple of empty glasses, frozen in place like a zombie. He made his way through the crowd toward her.

"You used to have some moves," he said. "But you've probably forgotten them."

"Better go back to your partner," Avani retorted, "since you couldn't possibly keep up with *me*."

He raised his eyebrows at the challenge and held out his hand. "Try me."

Avani's competitive spirit warred with her desire to stay away from him. But her hips never could resist a good beat and that pang inside her had morphed into pure heat and soon they were moving together and it felt so natural and there was even more cheering and hooting as their dancing got frenzied and fast. With just a small press of his fingers on her lower back, she knew when to turn. With barely a flick of her ankle, he knew where she was headed. They anticipated each other's moves,

and he was leading
  but so was she
    it was what had always been
  between them
a give and a take
  a flash of a grin

a swish of hair
an understanding without words
a silence between beats
a song that pulsed
like the ember of their friendship
a flame lit from so many twigs
gathered over the years . . .
But another memory flashed—
Pop offering to help her practice
the perfect excuse
to turn the music loud
and twirl . . .

Avani stumbled, the rhythm inside her broken.

"You okay?" Fernando asked.

"Yeah, I . . ." Her heart was racing, and not just from the dance. "I need to get back to work."

"Okay," Fernando said softly. "Take it easy."

"Thanks."

Of course, Avani made sure he didn't find her again that night. Soon the guests were gone, and it was time to clean up. Dad's staff was handling the endless dishes, Rani and Dad were sweeping the floor, Sirisha was stacking chairs, and Avani and Nidhi were taking down the decorations.

"Ooh." Avani wrapped a silver garland around her neck as if it were a mink stole. "We could definitely reuse these for the Winter Ball!"

Nidhi rolled her eyes. "Have you even asked Dad about it yet?"

"I'm going to." Avani had been waiting all day for the right moment. She glanced over to where he and Rani were goofing around, playing an impromptu game of shuffle hockey with their brooms. Rani had terrible aim and slammed their crumpled napkin hockey puck right on Nidhi's forehead.

"Hey!" Nidhi cried.

Another one came sailing their way, but Avani caught it easily.

"Nice!" Dad said, giving her a thumbs-up. "Hey, girls, could all of you come here for a second? I want to talk to you."

They huddled around him, and Avani noticed Dad kept rubbing the stubble along his jaw. He only did that when he was nervous. Uh-oh. Her muscles always clenched up whenever there was "news" (because wasn't it always bad?). With Mom lost to a car accident and Pop's sudden stroke, she braced herself.

But Dad smiled.

He *smiled*.

Her pulse slowed.

"As you already know," Dad said, "I've been seeing more of Amir. He's . . ." He paused, his face warring with itself as he tried to articulate his feelings. "He's really wonderful and funny and kind. And I want you to meet him. I asked him to come by for the wine-and-cheese event we have scheduled for Wednesday."

Sirisha squealed, attacking Dad with a hug. "Of course! I can't wait!"

"Ahh, Dad's in love!!!" Rani shrieked, piling into the hug. "I knew this was going to happen!"

Dad laughed. "Okay, we're not *that* serious yet. . . ."

"It's useless arguing with her," Sirisha said.

"It really is," Nidhi agreed, hugging Dad, too.

"I was right about you and Grayson. . . ." Rani huffed.

"We're keeping things casual," Nidhi reminded her.

They gestured for Avani to join them, but she felt very much on the outside, not just of them . . .

outside herself
    outside her head
if only she could
    banish that heaviness
that sensation of falling
    and just hug her father
like a good daughter would.
      "Happy for you, too," she said softly
as her heart
    squeezed and slushed—
a snowball thrown
    an icicle broken
powder pressed
    with footsteps.

When they pulled apart, her sisters asked Dad all sorts of questions about Amir, what he did and why he liked him and if Amir preferred samosas or pakoras (because that told you a lot about a person). Dad happily answered—though Avani hardly heard his responses as her own thoughts swirled and enveloped her, as they so often did. She was positive, absolutely certain that someday she could be happy—really, truly happy—for her father. But why did all this have to come now,

when her
    unstitched skin

was still hanging open

an unhealed wound?

Eventually all her sisters' excited talk about Amir and Dad died down, and Avani touched Dad's arm. She swallowed, nervous and aching.

"What's going on, Avani?" Dad waited patiently.

Maybe this wasn't the right time to ask. But she only had a couple of weeks to make it happen.

"I want to throw Pop's Winter Ball again," she blurted, then hurried into an explanation of the hows and the whys and her thoughts on playlists and decor and invitations. "And even though we need to have it soon, like in a couple of weeks, I can definitely handle every detail. You won't have to lift a finger, I promise. In fact, I'll even—" She knew she was rambling, and Dad was already nodding, so she came to a sudden stop.

"The Winter Ball, huh?" Dad said. "Well, I suppose we're due for something fun. It'll be a lot of work, of course, but you did a great job helping with the wedding today."

"What did you think of the ski sendoff?" Avani asked hopefully.

He chuckled. "It was perfect. Sirisha got some beautiful shots of them in the snow so they'll be able to look back on it fondly. You have Pop's gift for flair, and I know you'll do a great job planning the Winter Ball, too. I'll help however I can. And oh, oh, oh!" He bounced on his heels excitedly.

"What is it?"

He grinned. "I just remembered—I saved Pop's original menu from the very first Winter Ball ten years ago. Would you like it?"

Avani teared up. "That would be amazing."

Chapter Four

*S*unday afternoon gleamed sunny and bright, and the Grizzly Drizzly guys returned from their competition howling like happy wolves after a successful hunt. They were dripping mud and snow all over the place, though Avani could hardly complain because when they threw off their parkas, their shirts were clinging to them in all the right ways. . . .

She'd been working on the Winter Ball guest list (still reeling from the fact that Dad had okayed it, that it was *actually* happening), but she had to admit that as far as interruptions went, twenty guys tumbling into the Songbird looking all rugged and handsome wasn't the worst.

Some ran up to their rooms, but others were dropping onto the living room Chesterfield sofas, moaning loudly about their injured knees or elbows while glancing around to see if any pretty girls were noticing. Of course, only Avani was there, near the fire with her laptop—so apparently much of the show was just for her.

"Guys, you're making a mess!" Jonas scolded.

"Well, we have to wait our turns for showering!" someone returned.

"Hooligans." Jonas looked worried. "Don't worry, we'll clean all this up ourselves."

"Thanks. Luckily, the leather wipes down easily," Avani said. "You may as well wait till they've all cleaned themselves up."

"Thanks for understanding." Jonas sighed and headed upstairs.

Avani turned back to her spreadsheet. The boys were cute and all, but she really did have work to do. She'd divided up the guests into different categories: Songbird staff, suppliers and other business acquaintances, Dad's friends, friends from school, her sisters' friends. Old friends of Pop's. She was planning to put up general invites on social media, but she also wanted to send out handwritten invites.

"You should have seen it, Avani." Jake plopped down on the sofa right next to her. "The wall they made us climb was like fifty feet high—"

"Probably higher!" another guy chimed in. "And we were trying to run in snow up to our chests—"

"It was so cold, I thought my toes would literally fall off. . . . " someone else said.

"Can't believe we have to do it all again next week, though."

Avani perked up. "You'll be back?"

"Yep!" Jake exclaimed. "There's three more races—we'll be here for the next few weekends." He batted his eyelashes flirtatiously.

He was definitely a looker. But Avani was excited for a completely different reason. "That's fabulous! You can make it to the Winter Ball then! It'll be two weeks from now."

The guys exploded in enthusiasm: "PARTY!" "WOOO!" "Oh man, I'll get to show off my dance moves!" "Like you have any . . ."

Avani added the Grizzly Drizzly team to her list. Perfect, they were going to have a great crowd.

Jake leaned close. "Oh, and it turned out that you were right about the barbed wire. Look." He pointed to his parka, which had several huge rips on the back.

Avani grazed her finger over it, laughing. "You didn't believe me!"

"I didn't remember reading that on the website," Jake returned sheepishly.

"As punishment for doubting me," Avani said, "you all have to do a hundred push-ups."

To her surprise and delight, they got to work!

As they showed off, Rani happened to be coming down the steps. The girl was all eyes—although she managed to quickly shoot Avani a glare in there, too. They were twins, so of course Avani knew exactly what Rani was saying: *How dare you not tell me about these hunky guys doing push-ups?*

Avani shrugged: *You weren't here. Am I supposed to let you know telepathically?*

Rani raised her brows: *Yes. Yes you are.*

Twins! They always expected so much from you—including mind melds. As the guys raced past the hundred that she had asked of them and things got kind of sweaty in a really hot way, Avani leaned her elbows on her laptop's keyboard. She was entranced—those biceps!—but when they'd finally ended their manly displays, she glanced back at her spreadsheet.

Where her entire guest list had accidentally been deleted.

She scrambled to recover it, but it was no use. It was gone. As Dad was fond of saying (she was pretty sure it was an Indian thing, but she'd only heard him say it): Uff-oh!

Wednesday evening, Avani and Sirisha braved the mess that was the Songbird's storage room. Somewhere, among the kayaks and the folding chairs, Avani was certain she'd find the perfect decor for the Winter Ball. Unfortunately, she didn't quite understand Dad's organizational system—or if he had one. On the other hand, it was gratifying to know that Dad had a slight penchant for chaos, even if he kept it hidden.

Click. Click. Click.

Sirisha was at it again with her camera.

Avani groaned. "Why are you taking pictures in here? It's a mess."

"Yeah, but these are little pieces of our lives. Our tents"—*click*—"and our picnic basket"—*click*—"and even some of our old toys."

Sirisha took some pictures of an old wooden train set, a giant stuffed pumpkin with a jolly smile, and a doll whose face had been scribbled over with marker. Then she pointed the lens at Avani. The flash was blinding in the dimly lit room, and Avani had to put up her hands in defense.

"Hey, I'm not some old memorabilia."

"You promised me some candid shots, remember?"

"Right now? You're supposed to be helping me with the Winter Ball."

"I will. Two birds and all that." Sirisha smiled. "Is that okay? I really need to get this project done."

Avani could never turn Sirisha down for anything—mainly because she always asked so nicely. Nothing like the way certain bossy elder sisters acted. Although it really would be nice if Sirisha could find some other candidates from school for her project. Sigh. Avani wished she could help Sirisha gain just a smidgen of social confidence. Maybe she should drag her to one of Kiera's parties sometime? In the meantime, she did her best to ignore the camera as she rooted through boxes of twinkle lights.

"Ooh, I love those. What do you think?" Sirisha gestured at a set of gold egg-shaped bulbs.

"They're nice. . . ." Perfectly lovely, but Avani wasn't sure if they were quite what she wanted. She didn't know what she wanted exactly—except that it had to remind her of Pop.

Her memories
    were a warm impressionistic glow
        the taste of winterberry she'd never tried
  a song that hadn't actually played
    a feeling she'd never told a soul

"Ooh, I just had the best idea!" Sirisha said as she rummaged through their staple wedding decor, most of which was completely wrong for the Winter Ball. (Rustic barn look wasn't what Avani wanted—she was certain of that.)

"What?" Avani asked wearily.

"A photo booth!" Sirisha said. "We had one at the fall festival this year, remember? Actually, Bethany's dad was the one who got it for the school. Do you want me to find out if he can get us one?"

Was Sirisha actually volunteering to interact with Bethany—a perfectly nice sophomore? The idea did strike a chord with Avani, solidifying in her mind the kind of event she wanted. It was just the right touch of whimsy, a relic of things past. A playful spirit. "Actually . . . yeah. That would be really cool. I can ask her, if you want." She rifled through a box of costumes with a greater sense of purpose, then triumphantly held up a sparkling tiara. "We could provide accessories like this for the booth. Very ice queen, don't you think?"

"Totally," Sirisha said. "And I know you've got a lot on your plate, so don't worry about it. I'll contact Bethany. And make sure the photo booth is here and set up on time."

Avani raised her brows. "You'll actually talk to Bethany?"

Sirisha shrugged. "I mean, I'll email her."

Ah. So much for social interaction. Still, Sirisha was seriously the best just for taking it on.

Click.

Even though she took too many photos.

Not long later, Avani squealed as she came across the exact perfect item: a disco ball, complete with strobe lights. It was in its original box, with lots of tissue paper to keep it intact. She gently lifted it out.

"Do you remember this?" Avani whispered.

Sirisha touched the small star-shaped mirrors on the ball reverently. Pop had bought it on a whim, and that very night they'd had an impromptu dance party in the library. She and her sisters had been small then, and he'd easily twirled them in the air, one by one.

> She wished she could
> > bottle in a jar
> > > the feeling of floating
> > > > of flying

and return to it whenever
the fierce missing came
like a sudden rain.

The door burst open just then, Nidhi dragging in a folding table. It was the one they'd set outside the barn for the wedding reception, to hold the guestbook for all the attendees to sign.

"You were supposed to bring this in, remember?" Nidhi admonished. "It can rust."

"Sorry, I'll grab some rags and wipe it down," Avani said. "Sirisha, can you find a good spot to set aside the stuff we're using for the ball?"

"On it, boss!" Sirisha saluted.

As Avani headed toward the cleaning supply closet, there was a rather pungent aroma in the air. It didn't smell bad or anything, but it definitely assaulted the senses. Soft voices floated from the living room, and Avani heard Dad's laughter.

It sounded different from his normal laugh.
Smokier.
Flirtier.

Wait, how had she forgotten? He'd said that Amir was going to drop by for the wine and cheese event on Wednesday. Which was today. Her heart thudded.

Amir. Was. Here.

Amir. Was. *Here.*

Ugh. She had to get out of there, stat—even if it meant she was a coward. She hustled to grab the towels and cleaner—

"Avani!" Dad popped into the hallway. "I thought I heard someone out here. Come on, there's someone I want you to meet."

"Okay . . ." Avani left the towels in the closet, since she didn't particularly want to meet Amir with a bunch of rags in her hand like some kind of sad fairy-tale orphan.

She followed Dad out to the living area, where adults were mingling, talking in soft tones, lounging with legs primly crossed—a completely different scene from when the raucous Grizzly Drizzly guys had taken over the place. Not a sexy push-up in sight.

Dad led her to a corner near the bar, where a good-looking South Asian man about Dad's age was waiting. He had short hair with only a flash of silver near each temple, a trim beard, and a nice smile.

Also, for some reason, Fernando was there, arranging a bunch of fancy cheeses (the cause of the pungent aroma she'd noticed). He wore a black turtleneck and black jeans, which was exactly what Dad was wearing, too.

"Wait—did you two plan your outfits together?" Avani asked.

"You know it!" Fernando high-fived Dad.

Dad laughed. "Yeah, we decided on a coordinated look. The Gutiérrez farm is starting a new artisan cheese venture. You have to try the queso panela—you'll die! The gouda is also excellent. But first, I want you to meet"—he patted the other man's shoulder—"Amir."

So this was it
    this was *him*
        a new man
            beautiful and smiling
                squeezing her hand
                kind eyes

> perfectly lovely
>
> with no idea
>
> how her loosely stitched heart
>
> unraveled.

Amir was attentive, heartily asking her questions about herself, about the Winter Ball, which she answered in a blur. He mentioned something about his own business—he was a doctor of some sort? But she couldn't focus. And then Dad and Amir went in search of the other sisters while Avani tried to remember everything she'd said, and whether she'd disappointed Dad, and . . .

"It's in less than two weeks, right?" Fernando asked.

"Huh?"

"Um . . . the Winter Ball? Your dad was telling me about it." Fernando's moth-brown eyes flickered in the light.

"Uh, yeah."

Awkward silence as she failed to elaborate. But her thoughts were still on Amir . . .

Fernando cleared his throat. "Do you want to order some cheese for it? We've been making all kinds—Mexican, French, Spanish. You name it, we've probably got it."

At least he was talking about cheese, and not about the missed date. Something inside Avani eased. Maybe they could return to just being friends. Maybe she didn't have to run away and hide for twenty whole years. (Maybe seventeen or eighteen would do.)

She had to admit he looked good in black. That turtleneck. Those jeans . . .

"Thanks," she said, not referring to the cheese. "This is really amazing." Again, not about cheese. "But actually, I've already placed an order. It's real Camembert—from Camembert, France. Pop had ordered it and paired it with a very particular jam at the very first Winter Ball." Okay, that part was actually about cheese.

Fernando nodded. "Sounds cool—I can't wait to try it. I hope my invitation doesn't get lost in the mail!"

Oh boy. His cheekbones were really too much.

"It won't," she promised.

But then it did.

Or rather, Fernando's invitation was returned to the inn. They *all* were.

Avani started sobbing when Nidhi handed her the huge stack of slightly battered envelopes, each stamped with *insufficient postage*. She'd worked so hard on them, crafting them by hand on heavy ivory and silver card stock and embellishing them with ribbons.

"You won't have time to resend them now," Nidhi said (as if it wasn't obvious).

Avani snatched the stack and stuffed them in her backpack. She'd been curled up in the library, finishing up an essay on *Little Women*—ah, four sisters!—because it was the last Saturday of midwinter break, and on Monday, she'd be back in school with even less time to work on the last-minute details of the Winter Ball.

"We could hand-deliver the ones on Orcas, so they won't be wasted. Since the roads are still a bit icy, we can use Grayson's truck; he's coming over later," Nidhi said. "And maybe make an online invite for the rest? I can help you design it, if you want."

No lecture?

"Really?" Avani brightened. "It would be nice not to have to waste all of these." She patted her backpack with the silver invitations.

"Yeah, let me grab my laptop," Nidhi said. "We'll send out the online ones first."

"Okay, I'll get us some hot cocoa," Avani said. "We can't think clearly without hot cocoa, can we?"

"Definitely not. Get the mint marshmallows, please!"

Honestly, Avani was surprised that Nidhi wasn't insisting on making the cocoa herself. She'd always been finicky about how it was made—actually she'd been finicky about how anything was made, really. But her sister had chilled out a lot about certain things in recent months. If only her new chill would apply to inn chores.

Oh well. Baby steps, right?

Avani felt lighter as she dropped the requested marshmallows into two oversize mugs. She even stirred in a dash of hazelnut syrup—not too much, because Nidhi didn't like overly sweet drinks. When she returned to the library, Nidhi was typing away, her face alight.

"What's up?" Avani asked. "Did Grayson ask you to marry him or something?"

Nidhi laughed. "Of course not. We're not that serious."

"Good girl," Avani said approvingly. "Keep your options open, I always say."

Her big sis looked at her with gentle eyes. "You're right—at our age, options are good. As long as you can recognize when something is too perfect to let slip away."

Avani shrugged. "If it's slipping away, maybe it's not perfect. Maybe the timing just wasn't right."

"Maybe," Nidhi conceded. "As long as it's not your indecision making the choice for you. I can't wait forever to decide about next year, or nothing will happen. Luckily, Dad asked his cousin—our phua—to help me. Look, she just emailed. She wants to get to know me. Isn't that cool?"

Avani scanned the email, a lively and chatty note from Lalita Phua, who asked lots of questions about Nidhi and her plans.

"Yeah, cool," Avani said, though she noticed that Lalita Phua hadn't asked anything about the rest of them.

But why would she? Nidhi was the eldest, Nidhi was first at everything. Whether Avani was interested in traveling to India or reconnecting with any long-lost relatives didn't matter, at least not until Nidhi had done it all already. It was just the way of things.

Nidhi took a sip of the cocoa. "Hey, this is really good."

But then she was typing away to Lalita Phua. A jolt of yearning flashed through Avani. She was intensely curious about this aunt she'd never met. Dad was always so reticent when it came to his relatives, to everything about that motherland they'd never stepped foot in. She didn't blame him, not when she knew that the family had faded away like mist in the horizon after he'd gotten together with Pop.

They were probably all jerks anyway, she told herself.

She waited a few minutes, but Nidhi was completely engrossed in her email. Who knew how long she would take? The invitations needed to go out as soon as humanly possible. Grabbing the backpack, Avani retreated to her room. It looked like she'd be designing the online invites on her own.

Chapter Five

The next morning, Avani's inbox was already singing the sweet melody of RSVPs pinging. She'd sent out the online invites, Grayson had helped her hand-deliver the ones for people on Orcas, and now people were actually coming to her Winter Ball! It was real, it was happening, and she just had to make it the biggest and best bash of the year. She lay back in her bed, stretching out in her fleece peppermint-candy pajamas.

Only six days to go.

Of course, the thought made her immediately break out into a sweat—why, oh why had she committed to something so big? She hated committing to things. She wasn't the committing type; she liked to come and go as she pleased. But obviously, she couldn't just roll into the Winter Ball an hour and a half late like she had to Kiera's party. On top of that, local weather experts were predicting a lot more snow in the following week—truly a snowpocalypse by San Juans standards—and it certainly wouldn't be a party if no one could even make it to the Songbird.

Well, perhaps a few stalwart citizens who decided to ski in. Maybe they could also organize a shuttle? Actually, that wasn't a bad idea. She quickly added the task to her party planning app. She looked over her Winter Ball to-do list for the day, which surprisingly wasn't that long. Only a few last hors d'oeuvres to hunt down.

She pulled out the original Winter Ball menu, which she kept tucked safely under her journal on her nightstand. Just seeing Pop's handwriting made her heart twinge: His angular cursive was accompanied by plenty of excited exclamations and underlining, notes added in about exactly which venue or brand he wanted. It was an eclectic mix of foods, all meant to be consumed easily on tiny snowflake plates before returning to the dance floor. Pakoras with spicy chutney, crab rangoons, chanterelle mini quiches, patisseries, and of course a crust of bread topped with a particular kind of local fig jam and the very fancy French Camembert. (He'd underlined the boutique cheesemaker's name, Zélie Toussaint-Blanchet, three times, so he'd definitely been set on her fromagerie in particular.)

Mmm, figs and cheese. Heaven.

Avani flopped back on her bed. There was a ton of P.R.E.S.S.U.R.E. riding on this party. If it wasn't completely flawless, it just wouldn't be the same as Pop's bashes. His exclamations and underlinings said it all—he'd been meticulous, and she'd feel like she was letting him down if she messed it up. Not to mention, everyone would think it was all an inevitable consequence of her flakiness.

Rani plopped down beside her, sneaking a look at the RSVPs in her email (privacy was not a thing with twins, clearly). "The Grizzly Drizzly guys are coming? SWOON!"

She grabbed Avani's arm—twirling her around the room, dancing to a waltz that she hummed rather badly. Rani never seemed weighed down by silly trivialities like being in tune. They laughed and pranced in their pajamas, and Avani forgot all about those pesky things called responsibilities.

Until her email pinged once more. The subject line read: ORDER DELAYED.

"Oh no! No, no, no, no, no, no, no!!!" Avani yelped as she scanned the email. Zélie's Camembert was now supposed to arrive three days AFTER the date of the party. Completely useless.

"Shipping delay, huh?" Rani put her chin on Avani's shoulder, reading the email along with her (no privacy indeed).

"I really wanted to re-create the menu just as it was!" Avani moaned, picking up Pop's original Winter Ball menu again from her nightstand. She scanned the list for the zillionth time. Unfortunately, Zélie Toussaint-Blanchet was still underlined exactly three times.

"Camembert, eh?" Rani grinned mischievously. "Methinks that perhaps fate is afoot."

That afternoon, while Avani was obsessing over the menu—trying to come to grips with the fact that the special Camembert from Camembert was not happening—Dad suggested taking a break from party planning for their traditional snowy day cross-country skiing.

"I don't know," Avani hedged. "I have a lot to do."

"Come on, we never get this kind of snow," Dad said with a hopeful look on his face.

"We got it four years ago."

"It's been ages. Besides, we might lose our reputation around here if we don't. The Jocks passing up fresh powder? It wouldn't look good."

Avani laughed. Her sisters and Pop used to call them the Jocks because they were the only ones decent at recreational activities that required an ounce of balance. She had to admit that there wasn't anything she could do about French cheese at the moment, plus Dad was right—it would be truly tragic to pass up this fresh snow. Soon they were outside,

zigzagging
over puffed clouds
through evergreens
it was the kind of cold
that was actually warm
the kind of blustery cold
that made warm possible

As they weaved expertly through a particularly narrow opening between trees, Avani smiled. "Remember last time, when we dragged Pop with us? And he crashed into one of those snowbanks around a tree?"

Dad laughed. "His skis were pointing straight up, like in a cartoon."

Avani giggled. "He complained so much the whole time."

"The boots were too tight, his ankles hurt. . . ." Dad rolled his eyes, rounding a tree.

"It was too cold, his fingers were going to fall off. . . ." Avani added, showboating a little as she swerved deftly through three in a row.

"The trees were too close together. . . ." Dad topped her with a jump off a slope.

"The hill was too curved. . . ." Avani took the same jump, landing right next to him.

They laughed, and it felt so good. It was the same way they would have teased Pop if he were actually here. Sometimes, it felt like Pop had been reduced to his death,

to the memories of sirens
blaring as the EMT took him away
but he'd been so much more.

"I miss him," Dad said.

Avani let that sink in for a minute. She realized she'd been waiting for someone to finally say it out loud. To admit that he was still on their minds, just as he was on hers. "Me too."

"Not just the idea of him either, you know," Dad said. "Him, the real him, the way he was with people and how he could make us laugh even when he was whining about skiing."

"About how his mittens weren't the right kind . . . whatever the right kind actually is." A lump formed in Avani's throat.

"I even miss the way he would nag me about preparing for the Winter Ball." Dad laughed. "Even though he was the one who messed up the first year!"

"Messed up? I thought it always went without a hitch," Avani said.

Dad shook his head. "I suppose you were too little to remember the first one. Pop wanted everything to be so perfect that he had trouble settling on anything. He took too long to choose the invitation designs, so no one got their invitations! We ended up just calling everyone and begging them to come at the last minute."

"Calling them? On the PHONE?" Avani was horrified at the very idea. "Why didn't you just text or email?"

Dad laughed. "We were old-fashioned, I guess."

It made her feel better about her own screw-up with the invitations. And she always had trouble deciding on things, too—maybe that was one of the reasons she and Pop had been so close. They thought alike, and they always, always, always liked to keep their options open.

As she thought back through the many Winter Balls, she started to remember some of the other imperfections. The time the power went out in the middle. The time Rani had a stomach bug. And of course, the time Avani had spun so hard she'd knocked over a table full of food. But despite the myriad of mishaps over the years, her strongest memories were always of pure magic—twinkling lights and the strains of song and dancing the night away.

"Slow down for an old man!" Dad called.

Avani realized she'd been furiously weaving through trees as memories flooded over her. That inevitable frantic energy that always enveloped her when she was lost in her thoughts. Now Dad was huffing to keep up.

"Since when are you old?" Avani scoffed, but she did stop to lean against a tree.

"Look at all these gray hairs!" Dad said, pointing. His helmet covered what was on top of his head, but for the first time, Avani noticed that his whiskers were definitely getting more silver than black.

"Whoa, Dad." The thought of Dad aging made her really uncomfortable. "Whoa."

He shrugged. "It had to happen sometime. Amir says I look distinguished."

"I guess he does have good taste."

"Better taste than me, probably." Dad wrinkled his nose as they paused on a hill. "He watches artsy films with sad endings."

Avani laughed. Dad notoriously couldn't stand anything besides happily ever afters. He and Rani had that in common. "Maybe we can have a film night together," she suggested.

As soon as she said it, she kind of regretted it. But Dad looked so excited that she obviously couldn't take it back. Still, Dad dating was hard. Harder than she'd realized it would be.

They reached a curve, and he went sailing past her.

"Try to keep up, will ya?" he joked.

"Oh, it's on!"

Apparently, Dad had gotten a second wind, and they raced over gently rolling slopes, the birds chirping and the sun shining. Honestly, Avani never understood how anyone could be cold when you were flying like this, your heart pumping warmth all over.

A silence settled between them, a silence that was part of the snow and trees and the island itself. Eventually, he slowed under a particularly impressive silver fir. Its canopy of branches cast shadows all around him but not on him. In a sunlit spot, he looked at peace.

Avani wasn't there yet, not at the place where she could miss Pop and also move on. But Dad was—and she wanted that for him. She wanted the world on a platter of fancy cheeses for him, she wanted twirling to an infectious beat with a sexy partner for him, she wanted snow and sky and cold that was actually warm for him.

She wanted it all
    for him
        and perhaps even
    for herself
too.

Fernando came into reception with another produce delivery the next evening as Avani was working the front desk. He looked as cozy as a present in his light gray wool coat, a thick indigo scarf wrapped around him, his forehead glistening with a few beads of perspiration. (Okay, was it weird that Avani always found sweaty guys kinda sexy? Not that she was planning to do anything about it, but . . .)

"Hey," he said.

"Hey," she answered far too perkily. No, just the right amount of perk. Because they were just friends. "How's it going?"

Awkward pause. It was the norm for them now, apparently. How could she fix that?

Luckily, a bunch of loose onions bounced off the cart, breaking the silence with a *thump, thump, thump* as they hit the floor and rolled along the tiles. Avani and Fernando scrambled to get them back in place, their hands brushing as they wedged them into a box.

"Thanks." He was looking at her in a way that made her want to run away.

Or maybe grab him and kiss him. Oops, that thought had come out of nowhere. It definitely wasn't a possibility, not with Fernando, not when she was determined to keep her options open and not get tied down. Somehow, she knew that whatever would blossom between them if they dated could never be casual.

RING.

Avani yanked the landline phone in a hurry. "Hi, you've reached the Songbird Inn. How can I help you this fine day?"

A woman's voice responded. "Hello, I'm Samantha Kim from *West Coast Travels*."

"Oh, hi?!"

"I'm a travel writer and I'd like to cover the Songbird Inn in our next issue. I have to see the Most Romantic Inn in America for myself. I know they announced it months ago, but congratulations on the award. That's quite an honor."

Oh right, that award they'd won. Avani scanned the wall behind the reception desk in search of that shiny plaque. Hmm, strange—it wasn't where it was supposed to be. "Um . . . thank you. We were very honored."

"I've also heard you're planning the event of the season next weekend. The Winter Ball, I believe you call it?"

Whoa. How in the world had some travel writer heard about the Winter Ball? (Also, where was that plaque?)

"Yeah, it's on Saturday," Avani managed to confirm.

"Great, I'll be there. I'll need one queen room."

The travel writer was coming to the ball? Avani's ball? Ack!

In a daze, she let herself
    just stop
        for one glorious moment—
she didn't believe in signs
    just the kind of magic
        that people brought
            to themselves.

"Hello? Are you still there?" Samantha asked.

"Um, yes, of course," Avani said quickly, "I was just opening up our reservations. Yes, we do have a queen room available. . . ."

After taking Samantha's information and hanging up, Avani scanned the wall again. Nope, no plaque. Something tickled the back of her mind—hadn't she seen it recently? She couldn't quite remember. Ah well, it would turn up again at some point or another, as lost things usually did at the Songbird.

Meanwhile, Fernando was watching her, his eyes inscrutable. Her cheeks immediately burned; he'd caught her spacing out completely.

"Sorry, do you need me to sign for the delivery?" Avani said.

"Um . . . yeah, sure," Fernando said, and passed her the order slip.

Actually, they almost never bothered to sign for the deliveries, so Avani wondered why he'd come to reception at all. He'd been doing more evening runs, but they'd worked out a routine where he left the produce on the north porch and the staff would take it all into the kitchen. So maybe he'd come here . . . to see her?

"Exciting guest on the phone?" he asked. "You looked really happy."

Avani nodded. "Yeah, actually. It was a travel writer. She wants to cover the Ball!"

"That's awesome. In that case . . ." He reached behind the onions and pulled out a small red cardboard box. A delicious aroma emanated from within, and he opened it to expose a wheel of cheese and a small rounded knife. "You'll definitely need some camembert for the occasion. It's a must."

He put the box down on the reception desk and sliced into the wheel. Gooey soft yellow cheese spilled out, and it smelled even more amazing than it looked. As Avani gaped, Fernando produced some crusty bread and fig jam (wait, had he hunted down *the* fig jam?), and then handed her a small square with everything on it.

"Okay, try this."

Avani's eyes nearly rolled back in her head as she let the flavors of the fig and cheese mingle in her mouth, complemented by the crusty soft bread.

"Um, this is to die for."

He raised his brows, his expression serious. "I think it's really similar to the Camembert you were ordering. And not that I would know—but *just in case* your shipment was delayed or something—I could probably get you enough for your party. I mean obviously ours isn't actually made in Camembert, France, so I guess it's technically *camembert* with a lowercase c."

She blinked. "Rani told you, didn't she?"

Fernando shrugged and smiled slightly in a way that brought those cheekbones into full display. Ah, twins! They were some kind of wonderful. Avani was suddenly so emotional she didn't know what to do. It wasn't from Zélie Toussaint-Blanchet (underlined three times), but something told her Pop would approve.

It was just cheese . . . but it was also so much more than cheese.

"The Winter Ball is saved!" She threw herself in his arms, laughing and sniffling and breathing in the scent of him.

In a completely platonic thank-you-for-the-cheese way, mind you.

Chapter Six

The cheese was gone.

Fernando's special camembert.

The camembert!

Avani tried her best not to completely freak out, checking and rechecking the extra-large secondary fridge in the kitchen. It was filled with things Dad and his sous chefs would need to cater the Winter Ball (she'd been wrong that she could do all this without help since her cooking skills were pretty much nonexistent). In a frenzy, she rifled through ingredients for extra spicy pakoras, the crab rangoons, the chanterelle mini quiches, the shrimp cocktail, samosas, tartlets—everything she'd painstakingly planned from Pop's original menu . . . except for the cheese!

Maybe she'd accidentally placed it in the main fridge? She rooted past eggs and milk and produce, taking everything out and putting it back in, but the fact of the matter was that the cheese was gone.

Her heart pounded. Her face felt hot. Beads of perspiration formed on her forehead.

The Winter Ball was TODAY.

She needed everything to go smoothly. People were counting on her. Her friends were all coming, the staff, the Grizzly Drizzlies. Samantha Kim from *West Coast Travels*!

Then, the distinct smell of camembert—and not just any camembert, *her* camembert—wafted past her. Avani ran after Rani, who was carrying a tray of crepes out to the restaurant.

"Stop!" Avani commanded, then took a whiff. "WHO USED MY CAMEMBERT IN THE CREPES?"

"What?" Rani looked confused at first, but then she winced. "Um . . . I don't want to say. Gotta go!"

And then she ran off with the tray to the dining room. Avani whirled around. Nidhi and Grayson were chatting by the big kitchen island while Dad readied his crepe pan for another order. Since the kitchen staff would be working hard on the Winter Ball later, Dad had given them the morning off.

Avani stormed toward them.

"Why?" she said between gritted teeth.

Dad paused. "What's the matter, honey?"

She spotted the camembert box in the recycling, the cheese completely gone. She pulled it out. "*Why* did you use the Gutiérrez Farm camembert in the crepes?"

Dad looked shocked. "Nidhi, I told you to grab the brie in the fridge."

Nidhi bit her lip. "Yeah, I thought this was it."

"This isn't brie!" Avani pointed to the box, which had the Gutiérrez Farm logo on it, plus a handwritten inscription labeling it as camembert.

"Sorry, I didn't see that!"

"All the stuff in the second fridge is for the party!" Avani tried not to raise her voice—and failed. "YOU KNOW THAT!"

"Well, this box was in the main fridge," Nidhi argued. "So I thought it was the one Dad wanted. You should have put it with the other party stuff."

"Yeah right . . . how convenient," Avani said, waving the box around. "You've wanted me to fail this whole time, haven't you?"

"Of course not!" Nidhi folded her arms.

"Avani, that isn't fair," Dad said. "Nidhi didn't do this on purpose—"

She felt her rage spiraling out of control. "Yeah, but it happened—because she just doesn't care. If something doesn't revolve around *her*, Nidhi thinks it has no point. She said she'd help me with the invitations, but she got too busy. Obviously, she wouldn't remember that I've been talking about this camembert for a week straight!" Tears were streaking Avani's cheeks. "If it's not about her, it's not . . ."

She sobbed, couldn't finish the words.

Nidhi looked stricken, as if Avani had hurt her. Good. Maybe she'd think twice about what it meant to support someone. Maybe she'd think twice about what it meant to be a big sister. Maybe she'd think twice about being her usual infuriating self!

"Avani . . ." Dad said. "There's another issue. There's a storm coming this afternoon. The roads will be a mess. I'm not sure if we can get it cleared in time."

"It's just snow, Dad!" Avani fumed. "We've already planned for the shuttle! It will have chains."

"Yes, but . . ."

Avani didn't want to hear it. She ran out of the kitchen, out of the inn in a blur of tears.

Her heart was pounding so fast, bursting with fury and panic and something else—something she couldn't quite put her finger on. Nidhi had obviously deserved her harsh words, and besides, she was always scolding Avani for messing up. Well, this time Nidhi was the one who had messed up!

And the snow . . . it was just a little snow, wasn't it? Why was Dad making a big deal about it? Avani had planned and planned, had even managed to arrange for the shuttle. Besides, plenty of guests had already arrived at the Songbird, making a weekend of it. The Grizzly Drizzlies were here. And—though Avani hadn't seen her yet—Samantha Kim from *West Coast Travels*.

She couldn't let them down.

Avani kept racing, her breath coming out in quick gray puffs in the cold, until she was surrounded by a grove of snow-tipped pines. She bent over, head in hands, panting. She wasn't wearing winter boots or even a coat. Her extremities were going to fall off if she kept going.

The camembert . . . She absolutely, positively needed that camembert! The fig and camembert was an essential part of the menu, the semi-sweet snack that balanced out all the spicy pakoras and samosas and mini quiche. Pop would have agreed it was vital, if he were here.

She pulled out her phone.

Texted Fernando.

> SOS.
> Winter Ball emergency.

Chapter Seven

*I*f Fernando wasn't going to answer any of her texts (she'd sent about seventeen at this point), then she was just going to have to find him. Avani had a feeling that Dad wouldn't let her take the car with snow on the forecast, though. Besides, she couldn't bear to look him in the face—not after the way she'd blown up in the kitchen.

But she *wasn't* sorry.

Anyway, Avani had cross-country skis, the Gutiérrez Farm wasn't that far, and she had plenty of furious energy to burn off.

the white covering the hills and trees
was all she could see
swallowing

                    her grief and heartache
                        pressing it
                            under the powder
        a lost girl
            who only wanted
                to recapture
                    a bit of magic

By the time Avani arrived at the Gutiérrez farm, she was numb, both
with cold and from too many emotions—about cheese, of all things. At
this point, she was starting to feel a bit sheepish that she'd made such
a big deal about camembert, that she'd come all the way out here just
to get every last item on the menu. What would Fernando think of her
obsession?

Maaah. Maaah. Maaah.

An adorable black-and-white baby goat came running out across the
snow, and Avani swerved at the last second to avoid the rascally thing.

"Frida!" someone called in the distance. "Get back here!"

Of course, since Avani's attention was on the goat, she slipped on a
patch of ice and fell into a well of snow gathered around a tree. And then
she was the one with her feet sticking up like a cartoon character.

"Oomph!" She tried to wriggle free, her head smooshed up in snow,
her torso twisted in a strange angle, the skis heavy on her legs flailing in
the air.

"Are you okay?" Fernando asked, trying to pull her up.

"Mmm-hmm . . ." Avani pushed and wriggled as he tugged, and
snow went flying as she struggled to escape the snow well. It felt like
quicksand.

"I've got you!" Fernando yanked hard, and Avani pushed with all her might, and finally she went tumbling backward on top of Fernando.

She twisted, and then they were face-to-face, her torso against his chest, her ankles throbbing, snow in her hair and on her lashes and all around them. His eyes were soft and warm and slightly bemused, his cheekbones still cheekboning (as cheekbones will do).

"Hi," she breathed.

Maaah.

The goat nosed her cheek with its nubby little horns.

"Quick," Fernando whispered urgently. "Grab Frida."

Avani tried, she really did, but the little rascal was too quick for her, galloping off into the trees. With a heave, Avani scrambled up, skiing after Frida, Fernando just behind them.

"She escaped from our barn," he explained, "and I need to get her back in."

Frida the baby goat led them on a merry chase, through trees and over hills. At last, they caught her sniffing a patch of tall grass that was poking out from the snow at the top of a hill.

Fernando held a finger up. Avani nodded. She quietly took off her skis, leaving them behind a tree. Then, she approached the goat. Seeing her, Frida tried to make a getaway, but Fernando was already in position to grab her.

He jumped. "Finally! You've been a very bad goat!"

Frida nuzzled him, pretending that she'd never been trying to run away all along. Fernando grunted as he picked her up like a baby. She wriggled uncomfortably, bleating sadly. Avani rubbed Frida's stubby black horns, then slowly petted her behind the ears, under the chin, and over her back until she calmed. Her black-and-white fur was soft as cashmere.

"Here, maybe she'll be more comfortable in this." Avani took off her parka and wrapped it around the goat.

"You'll freeze!" Fernando said.

"I've got this thick fleece, and it won't take me long to ski to the barn. Meet you there?"

"Sure—and thanks!" He glanced at her. "By the way, what brought you here?"

"Didn't you get my texts?"

He shook his head. "Sorry, must have missed them."

"A bit of a cheese emergency"—*maaah*—"actually, let's go before Frida gets too restless. I'll tell you everything in the barn. See you in a few."

Avani whipped her skis back on, and then it was through the trees and hills again. She stayed close to the road so she wouldn't get lost, especially since it had started snowing again. She was pretty wet and cold by the time she reached the barn; thankfully, it was heated.

Inside, there was an open space in the front, one wall lined with haystacks, the other fitted with a supply shelf. Avani wandered back to where pens were lined up in two rows with a center aisle. She found a few other baby goats calmly suckling their mother, a couple of pigs, some chickens, and a chocolate-colored pony. After she petted her mane and offered her some oats from a barrel, Avani peered out the open doors. The snow was really coming down now. She hoped Fernando would get back okay. Maybe she shouldn't have left him with the goat.

But then she made out his silhouette in the trees. He stumbled in the snow—rascally Frida was wriggling in his arms again—and Avani ran out to help him.

"She napped for a few minutes . . ." Fernando shook his head.

Maaah.

Avani helped him wrangle the silly goat back into the barn. They put her down in her pen as the wind howled behind them. A furious banshee of a gust screamed—a lot louder than any baby goat—and the barn door slammed.

Then a *FLOOMP* as they heard the sound of snow falling from the roof.

"Ummm . . ." Avani pushed against the door. "It's stuck!"

Fernando pushed with his shoulder. "Ugh, the snow must have hit the latch on the other side. We're locked in!"

"No way!" Avani slammed against the door. He just had to be wrong.

Baby goats bleated, the chickens pecked for food, the pigs paid them no mind, and the pony harrumphed. But it was no use—the door was indeed stuck.

The Winter Ball was only a few hours away, and Avani was trapped in a barn. And not a rustic wedding barn, like the one they had at the Songbird. Nope, this one was filled with smelly animals.

And, of course, *Fernando*.

(!) Not delivered.

No matter how many times she tried to send a text for help, it just wouldn't work. She had zero bars on her phone and waving it around wasn't changing that fact.

"Is this barn made of lead or something?" she muttered.

"Maybe it's the storm." Fernando grabbed a couple of lanterns and blankets from a tall shelf, which also held animal feed and various other supplies. "Don't worry. I'm sure someone will come looking for us soon."

Avani's stomach rumbled. She hadn't eaten breakfast—and she also hadn't told anyone where she was going. Dad would be worried, especially since from the sound of it, the snow was continuing to fall steadily. If she didn't get home soon, would the Winter Ball even happen? Even though she knew she should focus on staying safe, a part of her wanted to go screaming out into the wilds.

Avani gestured desperately to a shuttered window high up near the pointed roof of the barn. "Can we crawl out of that?"

"We have a ladder." Fernando grabbed it from the back of the barn. "But how'll we get down from the outside?"

"Let me take a look—maybe there's a way to scramble down." Avani removed her ski boots and climbed up in her socks, rung by rung, determination pushing through her. The Winter Ball needed her. If it didn't happen—well, she couldn't bear to think of it not happening. It would be like losing Pop all over again,

> a raw cold emptiness,
> a void.

Her head nearly banged on the rafters as she tugged at the shutters, which didn't budge.

"Ugh, this thing is stuck!" Avani pulled harder, forcing them open. A gust of snow came barreling in, knocking her off-balance.

"Careful!" Fernando said as she wobbled on the ladder.

Her foot slipped on the wet snowy step, and she went

> tumbling
>   down
>   down
>   down

into the sturdy arms
    of a farm boy
        with moth-brown eyes

Oomph.

"Got you," he said.

And he certainly did. Snow was still blowing down from the window, flurries falling like diamonds in his hair, on his eyelashes. He looked a little too kissable in that moment, and moths fluttered inside her as she reached up to brush his hair from his eyes.

He cleared his throat. "I guess we better close that window. We don't have a way to get down the other side anyway. Unless you still want to try jumping?"

"It was higher up than I thought," she admitted, "and you can't see a thing out there."

"Probably better to wait the storm out a bit," Fernando agreed, not letting go of her. "I'll go up this time, okay?"

"Sure," she replied just a little breathlessly.

And then all too soon she was on her own two feet again, away from his warmth, his arms. (They weren't bad arms, okay?) She held the ladder as he climbed up and shoved the shutters closed.

"I guess we're stuck together," Fernando said, putting the ladder back.

"I guess we are. Now what?"

He shrugged. "We've got time to kill. What was the big cheese emergency, anyway? Was something off with the camembert I brought over yesterday?"

"No, not exactly." Avani paced the room, her mind frenzied again with the fight she'd had with Nidhi. Fernando would probably judge her for it, and she wasn't in the mood. "I don't feel like talking about it."

"Okay . . ."

Another one of those awkward pauses. What was life without awkward pauses?

Then suddenly, Fernando grinned, handing her a broom and kicking an empty tin can her way. "The door is the goal. I'll be the goalie."

A game? Avani did have a weak spot for them, and it could also help with that frantic feeling building inside her. Besides, Fernando was a bit too cute for her taste—clearly she needed to take him down a peg. Without warning, she whipped the tin can past him with a force worthy of the NHL.

"Hey, hey, hey, I need my goalie gloves!" He grabbed a pair of work gloves and a horse-riding helmet from the shelf, then crouched with knees bent slightly, loose arms, hands at the ready in front of the barn door. "Bring it."

Avani narrowed her eyes fiercely. That door was her archnemesis. That door was keeping her from the Winter Ball that she'd spent the last two weeks toiling over.

That door was most definitely getting its butt handed to it.

She positioned the tin can carefully in the center of the open barn space outside the line of stalls. She nodded to Fernando. He nodded back.

And then she was furiously sprinting forward, her broom whacking and—*swoosh!*—the tin can was flying and Fernando was leaping to stop it, but that was pure folly because it was clanging onto the door.

"Point," she called, setting the can back in the center.

Fernando wasn't bothered, just nodded at her to come at him once again. And she did—oh boy did she. She had so much pent-up energy, so many frustrations and emotions she couldn't quite name yet.

And the tin can was Nidhi
    telling her she couldn't do it.
The tin can was Dad
    preoccupied with other things.
The tin can was Fernando
    for no reason besides being a distracting boy.
It was Sirisha and her camera,
    it was Rani and her romance novels,
      it was her teachers, her friends, her enemies,
        it was even Pop . . .
Oh yes: It was definitely Pop,
    who had left her.
      He'd *left* her.

Sometimes, Fernando managed to stop her explosive tin can. Most times he didn't.

"Is that all you got?" he asked, smirking.

"Oh, I've got plenty." She smirked back.

Whoosh.

"Come on, Singh, that was weak!" More smirking.

"Your forehead's about to bleed, Gutiérrez." Narrowed eyes.

Clang.

"Nice try." Smug grin.

Kablonk.

"Who's weak now?" An exceptionally wicked grin.

Whiz.

Soon, the air in the barn was thick and warm with their panting and their sweat, and Avani had scored thirty-three points and Fernando had managed to block a paltry seventeen shots. Avani grinned, feeling for the first time in a while like maybe they could go back to their childhood friendship. They swapped places, and then Avani was on the defense, but Fernando only scored twenty-one out of fifty shots.

"You win!" he declared, collapsing to the floor, his chest heaving. They'd both thrown their parkas in the corner in the heat of the game.

"Don't tell me I tired you out?" Avani teased, breathing just as hard as him.

He found a blanket and gestured for her to sit. Then he rummaged through a small shelf on the side of the barn that she hadn't noticed before. But clearly—judging from the mouthwatering scents coming from a plastic container he'd just opened—it was where they were aging their cheeses.

"You keep the cheese in the barn?" she asked—just as her stomach let out the loudest, most embarrassing, mama-bear-protecting-her-cubs-level growl.

Fernando almost fell over laughing. "Luckily for you, we do. We're looking for a better place, but it does stay roughly the right temperature."

Another growl erupted from her stomach, and this time he actually did fall over laughing.

"I haven't eaten yet today!" she protested.

"Or for the past three weeks, apparently?"

"Hush, you." She surveyed the spread of delicious-looking cheese plus an array of crackers, trying to control herself from stuffing them into her face. "What are all these?"

Fernando pointed to the different varieties. "They're all made with goat dairy. This is an asiago. Here's a queso blanco. A traditional chèvre. And a gouda."

Avani closed her eyes, enjoying the mouth-melting queso blanco. "This is amazing. When word gets out, business will boom!"

"Well, there's only so much cheese my family can actually produce. But I hope so."

They chewed in comfortable silence for a while, and then Avani asked the question that had brought her all the way out to the farm. "Do you have any more of that special camembert you made for the party?" Her voice hitched noticeably.

"Actually, we do." His eyebrows raised in concern. "You ready to talk about what happened?"

Avani bit her lip. "I guess so." She quickly filled him in on Nidhi and the crepes—and the fight. The accusations she'd thrown at Nidhi. She didn't *need* to tell him so many details about it, but she couldn't stop herself.

"I probably overreacted," she admitted sheepishly when she'd finished.

Fernando leaned back against a pile of hay. "No. I mean, yes, a little. But it makes sense. The Winter Ball means a lot to you."

Avani nudged his foot with hers. "Yeah, I guess it does."

She didn't say anything more about it, and Fernando didn't press. Instead, he nudged her foot back with his own. She answered with a slight push. Soon they were full-on foot wrestling and giggling.

Hanging with Fernando was so easy, like sinking into a cozy beanbag. And he'd never even bothered her about that missed date—

"So, about that concert we were supposed to meet at . . ." Fernando nudged her foot again, very gently. "Why didn't you show?"

Shoot.

There wasn't anywhere to run to.

Avani raised her eyes, taking in the farm boy, with his beautiful cheek-bones, the shaggy mussed-just-so hair half-covering his golden eyes. He'd come through for her with the camembert. He'd managed to make being trapped in a barn together *fun*. He deserved better than her evasiveness.

She screwed up her courage. "I'm really sorry about that." She hung her head. "I actually mixed up the date for it—I had it wrong in my cal-endar. And I didn't see your texts because I was having"—gulp, this was embarrassing—"a really intense dance party with Rani in our room and it was too loud for the alerts."

"That's okay," he said. "You could have just told me later. I thought I'd done something wrong."

He really was too good to her.

"You're right, I know I should have explained." She swallowed. "First of all, I was just mad at myself. Nidhi's always calling me a flake—and she's right. I do tend to get distracted about a lot of things. I try not to, but even when I'm using all the apps to help me remember, I still make mistakes."

"That's natural," said Fernando. "Everyone does."

"Yeah, I guess so. But she makes me feel really insecure about it. But there's something else, too, something that has nothing to do with all that."

"Okay . . ." He waited.

And waited some more.

Finally, she spoke. "I kind of realized that I wasn't ready for us to be something more than friends. I mean, don't get me wrong . . . it's tempt-ing. *You're* tempting."

His lips curved into a smile, showing off those cheekbones. "That's good to hear."

Moments came back to her
   snowflakes in hot tubs
     a give and a take
    a silence between beats
 a song that pulsed
   the ember of their friendship
     a flame lit from so many twigs
   gathered over the years . . .

"But what if it didn't work out? I wouldn't want to lose your friendship either. We've always been really good together."

"Sometimes you have to take a risk."

"I guess I didn't feel ready to." It was hard to explain everything swirling inside her, the wanting mixed with the fear of losing too much. Tears threatened to come, but she desperately didn't want to cry in front of Fernando.

THUMP. BUMP.

Maaah. Maaah. Maaah.

As Avani struggled with her feelings, Fernando went to go check on the goats. "Frida, you are a naughty girl!"

Avani shakily followed him as more thumps and bumps sounded. "Aww, she wants to come out!"

"She doesn't deserve to come out," he grumbled—even as he opened the pen.

Frida immediately trotted right up to Avani, who petted the silly little adorable thing. "Good thing you're cute."

"Want to see some chicks, too?" Fernando asked.

"Um, yeah I do!"

Soon there were a few fuzzy yellow balls of floof wandering around, pecking at her. She picked one up, and the baby goat was immediately jealous.

"You like having all the attention, don't you?" she chided.

Maaah, the goat responded.

"Lucky goat," Fernando muttered.

Now Avani's cheeks were burning, and she couldn't help but look right into Fernando's eyes, which glowed again in the lantern light, taking her to someplace warm and cozy. Actually, she already was someplace warm and cozy—with Fernando.

For some reason that pit of fear she'd felt before was gone. Right now, she was too exhausted to be scared about potential heartbreaks in hypothetical futures. She leaned back against a haystack, snuggling with Frida. Fernando settled close to her, petting one of the chicks. He had long, elegant fingers. Her eyelids drooped as she watched them stroke its feathers. Suddenly, she was so tired—from the skiing, from chasing naughty Frida, from staying up late party planning. The game of tin can hockey had taken the last of her energy and now she was so . . . sleepy. . . .

Maaah.

Chapter Eight

A goat was licking Avani's forehead. She was warm and comfortable, her face against something soft and fuzzy. A hunter-green-and-gray argyle sweater.

Who would wear this sweater?

And then she remembered.

Fernando.

Avani sat up with a start—oh no, they'd fallen asleep together! He had his arms around her, and she'd had her face pressed up against his chest. It was nice, but they were *still* in the barn. She scrambled for her phone, which was dead and refusing to turn on.

Clutching the useless thing, she let out a frustrated moan.

"Wha . . ." Fernando's eyes blinked sleepily (which was really cute—but not the point at the moment).

Avani shook his shoulders. "I need to get out of here! The Winter Ball! We'll be late! I'll miss the whole thing!"

And then
    tears fell
        faster and harder
            than the snow outside
everything was slipping
    and sliding
        like runaway skates on ice
            headed for a crash

"It's okay," Fernando said, his eyes worried. He patted her back. "We'll get out of here . . . we just have to be patient . . . we just have to—"

"No, you don't understand." Sobs barreled out of her like a train on a track to nowhere. "POP!!!" she screamed.

She didn't see Fernando anymore. Didn't see the barn anymore. All she saw was him, her beloved Pop. He was waiting for her at the Winter Ball, waiting for her back at the inn, but she was here, stuck in a barn, stuck in limbo without him—a failure who couldn't even manage to plan a party in his honor, a girl who couldn't get anything right.

"Hey, hey, hey," Fernando whispered, pulling her close. "It's gonna be okay."

"No it's not!" she bawled. "It never will be. Because Pop's never coming back!"

Fernando swept her hair back, his palms cupping her cheek. "You're right. He's not."

She couldn't face it, couldn't face reality, couldn't face this horrible world that had chosen to take away someone who had been so full of life and laughter and goodness, the last person who deserved to go.

But Fernando was holding her
    letting her be
        letting her *hurt*
and it did hurt
    it *hurt*
        it HURT
and for the first time
    someone was there
        listening
quiet enough to
        let Avani feel
    every icicle
        digging into her organs.
Every cut
    every sting—
        they were *her* cuts
        to feel
    her blood
    to drip.
The sadness was hers
    a white blanket of snow
        muffling every sound—

it had been three years
and the powder just as fresh
as the day she'd lost him
because grief comes in winter storms
covering everything once again
sometimes only a dusting
and sometimes several feet deep
it hurt
it *hurt*
it HURT

Fernando kept on holding her, and somehow the bleeding slowed, clotting just a little bit. But Avani knew that the grief could bleed out again at any moment, that this wound would never fully close. That Pop had left a hole in her life, a crack in the ice. Her heartbeat thumped against Fernando's, her face still buried against him.

"I'm a mess." She wiped at her eyes, which were probably covered in mascara.

"It's okay to be a mess sometimes," he said. "I know that I'll never stop missing my tía or my abuela. At least my grandmother lived a full life, but my aunt was only thirty-seven when she passed."

"I'm so sorry," Avani said. "That's terrible."

"It is. But losing a parent is just . . . I can't even imagine." He brushed a hand through his hair. "And you've lost two."

"Yeah," she said. "But grief isn't a contest."

"No, it's not."

They were quiet again. She stayed in his arms, and he just let her think. Let her feel. And she was glad to know that he understood where she was coming from, how she'd never get over it, not completely. She didn't even want that. He seemed to get that, too.

Avani looked up. His eyes were warm and bright and kind, like an ornament atop a tree. And she realized those beautiful golden eyes were always the same—always flickering with warmth and kindness. Even after she'd hurt him with her carelessness.

Avani winced. Carelessness, just like Nidhi and the cheese—

The thought of Nidhi tickled her memory. Her older sis had said something the other day that was relevant, something annoying but probably true: *Options are good. As long as you can recognize when something is too perfect to let slip away.* And it dawned on Avani that even though Pop had trouble settling on decisions just as she did, even though he liked to keep his options open, even though he loved living moment to moment: Pop hadn't hesitated in falling in love with Dad.

Avani obviously wasn't ready for forever (she was only seventeen!). But maybe, maybe, just maybe . . . she was ready for right now.

"Fernando," she whispered, "I'm so sorry that I didn't call you after I'd realized I missed the concert. Maybe I wasn't ready to take a risk then. But I'm starting to feel ready now."

She was staring in his moth-brown eyes, as little moths fluttered inside her. She couldn't look away from him, not his cheekbones, not his shaggy hair flopping forward. Not his lips.

He had nice lips.

"What about Jake?" Fernando asked.

"Oh, him." Avani rolled her eyes. "We aren't really an item. He's just a friend."

"That's not what you said."

"I say a lot of things when I'm scared."

"How about right now?" His lips were so close. Avani inhaled, taking in the (slightly goaty) scent of him. "Are you scared?"

She shook her head, traced her finger along his eyebrow. "Not right now, no."

They were already as close as they could be. Fernando could pull away if he wanted to—she was a mess and she wouldn't blame him if he did—but he stayed put. She leaned her face toward his. Paused. Millimeter by millimeter, she gave him a chance to decide if this was still what he wanted.

And when their lips finally met, soft and firm at once, they were in complete agreement. The kiss was rose petals and snowflakes. It was salsa twirls and wedding cake. It was candles and a cozy barn. It was a moth fluttering in the lamplight.

It

    was

        magic

            in a

                mason

                    jar.

Chapter Nine

Avani grabbed Fernando, scooted onto his lap, wanting to devour him. Frida bleated, always hungry for attention. But for the moment Avani was focused only on one person. She'd never felt this way before—

THUMP. CREAK. FWOOSH.

Voices and frigid air suddenly swirled around them as the barn door burst open.

"Avani!"

"Fernando?"

"Avaniiiii!" squealed Rani.

Suddenly, everyone was there. Dad, Rani, Sirisha, Nidhi, Fernando's parents. Jonas and several Grizzly Drizzlies. A stylish East Asian woman with a camera around her neck—could it be Samantha Kim the travel writer?

And Avani was on Fernando's *lap.*

Caught in flagrante delicto, as Rani's romance novels would say.

A few of the Grizzly Drizzlies hooted their approval, which drove Rani to burst into a fit of giggles.

"Apparently, she's alive and well," Nidhi said.

Rani raised her eyebrows. In twin speak: *You kissed him! You kissed him! You kissed him!*

Avani's face was completely aflame as she untangled herself from Fernando. *Yeah, maybe a little bit.*

Another smirk from Rani: *I told you that a misunderstanding can't keep love apart.*

So you did. Avani couldn't stop smiling as she and Fernando slowly stood up as one. He reached over to brush hay out of her hair—just as she did the same for him.

Maaah. Frida head-butted their knees insistently.

The Gutiérrezes burst into hearty guffaws—and then Sirisha, Dad, and even Nidhi joined them. Samantha Kim snorted behind a gloved hand. Fernando chuckled sheepishly. And then Avani couldn't stop laughing either, clutching her stomach, gasping for breath.

Finally, after they'd calmed a bit, Dad ran over and embraced her. "We were so worried—most of the inn came out to look for you. Luckily, Nidhi managed to follow your ski tracks."

Nidhi grabbed her tearfully. "Don't ever run away like that again!"

"I wasn't running away—" Avani protested.

"You were!" Nidhi scolded while simultaneously crying. "And I'm sorry about the cheese, but that's no excuse. OW!" Her big sis looked down to find Frida head-butting her.

Avani scooped the goat up. "It's all her fault!"

"It's definitely Frida's fault," Fernando agreed.

"Hey! Chicks, come back here!" his mom yelled.

Indeed, the yellow floofs were wandering out into the snow, so everyone got to business wrangling the chicks and baby goats all back into their pens, laughing as Avani and Fernando caught them up on the runaway goat, the barn doors, and the storm. No need to mention

the kiss

the *kiss*

the KISS.

Avani stood in the center of an empty ballroom in a silver satin dress, her hair done up in an elaborate coif, sparkling earrings swishing from her ears. Ready to let the wintry night take hold. She and her sisters had pushed aside the living room furniture to leave a grand dance floor, and it looked fantastic—the wood floors freshly polished for a sheen. Rainbow stars hovered and danced around the room, reflected from Pop's disco ball. Strings of icicle lights glowed along the edges. The fireplace was blazing. Best of all, every item on Pop's original Winter Ball menu was included in the spread in the dining room, and Dad's staff was circulating with the hors d'oeuvres.

Guests staying at the inn were already popping in, clad in their finest. The main roads had been cleared (thank you, San Juan County Public Works). She'd heard from some friends that they were snowshoeing or skiing from their steep, treacherous driveways to get to the shuttle Avani and Dad had arranged. Now, that was dedication, and Avani was so grateful for the good vibes coming her way.

She could hardly believe it. She'd actually pulled it off. All the planning, all the stress, chasing down cheese in a blizzard—it had all come together

for
    this
        perfect
            moment
and whoever came
    or didn't come
        didn't really matter
because Avani
    had planned the night
        for Pop
    and for herself too.

Avani had just stuffed her mouth with a triangle of crusty bread dressed with fig jam and Gutiérrez Farm camembert (amazing!), when Fernando himself sauntered in.

Fernando in a black tux.

Whoa.

He looked *good*.

And Avani had a mouthful of cheese that she was desperately trying to swallow as he strode toward her. She ended up choking on it and coughing, and then Fernando was patting her on the back as she struggled to speak. Sirisha swept in with a flute of sparkling cider, thankfully. Avani took a swallow, her face burning, and then finally managed to say, "Hi."

"Hi back," Fernando said, amused. "Didn't realize the camembert would literally kill."

She punched him lightly in the shoulder. "It's really good—I just—"

"Couples! Good evening!" called JJ Doherty, the DJ and emcee for the night. They mixed a bit of rap in with a slower jazz number, creating a beat gorgeous and infectious at once. "Get out here and get the party started!"

Avani didn't bother to finish her sentence—Fernando knew what she meant anyway. Instead, she grinned at him. He grinned right back.

The dance floor was mostly empty when they took their first steps, but by the last chorus it was completely packed. Grizzly Drizzlies busted out some breakdancing moves, Sara Goldstein twisted and turned with Jake, Dad's friends pretended they were still young, and DJ JJ easily transitioned to the next song, keeping the energy alive.

After the party had officially warmed up, Avani worked her way toward where she'd spotted Amir hovering at the edge of the dance floor, snacking on a samosa with Dad. People were everywhere—from school, friends of the Songbird, Pop's old besties, and they all shouted their thanks that she had brought the party back—but Avani focused now on the future.

"Hi, Amir," she said. "It's good to see you again."

"Good to see you, too."

"How's business going?" Avani asked. He'd mentioned something about a business, hadn't he?

"Pretty good, since I'm the only ophthalmologist on the island," he answered. "My patients say they're really happy not to have to get on a ferry to get their prescriptions updated."

Ophthalmologist. Right. She'd have to remember that.

Dad patted her shoulder, murmuring something about checking on the kitchen staff, and Avani understood he was giving them a chance to get to know each other. This time, she didn't let the newness of Amir scare her away. They chatted for a long while—trays of scrumptious finger foods keeping them afloat—and she learned the basics about Dad's new beau. Firstly, Amir preferred samosas to pakoras (she was a pakora girl herself, but she wouldn't hold it against him). Born in Pakistan, he and his family had immigrated to the US when he was ten years old. His accent was beautiful, a mix of the places he'd lived growing up: a hint of Pakistan but also a bit of Texas and Minnesota thrown in there.

He'd never been married before, taking on the "bachelor life" before finally coming out to his family. They'd been supportive, he said.

"I'm glad to hear that," she said. "Are you close?"

Amir nodded. "Yeah, pretty close. I have a sister in Boston—also a doctor—and a brother in Minneapolis who's a teacher. We talk all the time, though. You have to make an effort when you don't live under the same roof."

Avani was *almost* going to mumble something about needing space sometimes, but then she spotted her sisters dancing together. Rani in a curve-fitting little black dress that was drawing plenty of attention from the Grizzly Drizzlies, quiet Sirisha speaking volumes with just the swishing of her flirty scarlet A-line skirt and the graceful sweep of her arms. Even Nidhi looked relaxed and happy, her long, flowing ankle-length navy dress shimmering and her hair piled high—and Avani found her resentment drifting away. Grayson worked his way to join them with some decent rhythm, and when they noticed Avani with Amir, her sisters gestured for them to come to the circle.

"You go ahead," Amir said. "I'm going to grab some water. Be right back."

Avani waved at her sisters, but her attention caught on a couple exiting the photo booth that Sirisha had managed to procure after all—even if only via email. "Wait, can we do a quick photo sesh first?"

Amir smiled. "Sure, that would be fun."

"Cool."

Soon they were laughing at the printed photos, Avani in oversize sunglasses and a feathered hat, Amir posing with a '20s style mob hat and a finger gun. Then a thumping classic brought even more people onto the crowded dance floor, including Avani. It was a crush, the reflections of stars whizzing above like shooting stars. She danced, feeling as free as the bubbles JJ was now releasing into the air (yes, Avani and Sirisha had found a bubble machine in the storage room, too).

"There you are!" Dad called over the music a few songs later.

The travel writer Samantha Kim was at his elbow in a corner just off the dance floor. They both had drinks in hand, and Samantha was wearing a stunning black number, her long dark hair shiny, her lips pink, pink, pink. A camera hung around her neck.

"Hi," Avani said, shyly working her way over to them.

"Looks like the event of the year!" Samantha said. "I had no idea that the Songbird could turn into an amazing lounge and nightclub like this. This isn't your usual B&B birdwatching event."

"Birdwatching is an art!" Dad protested. "But, I have to admit, this transformation is all Avani's."

"Aww, thanks, Dad," Avani said, looking at her feet.

He kissed her forehead. "It's true. Want to dance?"

"You? Dance?" Avani teased.

"Hey, I can dance!"

He shook his shoulders a little. Avani laughed and twirled with him—though actually he was a little awkward on his feet, unlike Pop. Not that it mattered in the least, since Avani was just glad to have a moment of his full attention.

"Proud of you," he said as the song slowed. He leaned his chin on her head as they swayed. "Everything is beautiful. Perfect."

She glanced up at him. It was obvious that they were both remembering the balls of winters past, the huge presence of Pop shining over them. They missed him so much, and they'd never stop.

But the song
          came to an end
                    as all songs do.

After Dad disappeared to find Amir, Avani shook it with her sisters, sang along to rowdy favorites with her school friends, twirled round and round with Fernando until she was dizzy, and when Pop's all-time favorite came on, a rock ballad filled with nostalgia and regrets and new hopes, she knew the night was at an end.

She'd always teased Pop about this song—she wasn't a rock ballad fan—but he'd always played it at the end of the night at almost every party, not just the Winter Ball. Nidhi teared up, recognizing the first chords; Avani put her arms around her shoulders. Sirisha joined them, then Rani. They pulled in Fernando and Grayson and Dad and Amir.

They swayed as one
          shouting the words

jumping with fervor
together in the
right here
and the
right now.
Pop's disco ball
shone with stars
and song
and Avani felt full
with
love and light.

Chapter Ten

A good after-party was essential—or at least Pop had always thought so, though Dad had opted for bed. But the sisters continued the hallowed tradition, gathering in the library with the fireplace running, a carefully selected playlist, and plenty of food and drinks. Freshly brewed chai was a must (caffeine was necessary to stay up later) as well as leftover appetizers (they were S.T.A.R.V.I.N.G. after all the dancing).

"Best party ever!" Rani declared, inhaling a samosa on the loveseat. "I danced with at least seven certified hotties."

Avani gobbled a pakora. "You were the belle of the ball!"

"Only because *some of us* left the field wide open." Her twin winked. "Did you even dance with anyone besides Fernando?"

"Um . . ." Avani's cheeks heated. "Does Dad count?"

"No. No he doesn't." Rani grabbed Avani in a bear hug. "I'm so happy for you two. You're so adorable together!"

"Can't. Breathe." Avani looked to Sirisha for help from Romancezilla. Her little sister only smiled secretively and picked up her camera. "You do look great together. See for yourself!"

Obviously, there was no such thing as an after-party that didn't involve reliving the whole evening via the photos. Avani, Rani, and Sirisha squished together on the loveseat while Nidhi leaned over its back as they all peered at the camera. Sirisha had tons of shots of happy guests eating and dancing (success!), but she flipped quickly ahead to one of Fernando and Avani dancing cheek to cheek.

"This is sweet," Sirisha said, "but I have one that's even better."

Again, she flipped quickly through her photos, some with Rani and various Grizzly Drizzlies, some with Grayson and Nidhi, some of Dad and Amir, and then stopped on Fernando and Avani again.

"Oh, I love it!" Avani said.

They were both spinning with abandon in a crush on the dance floor, Avani's hair swishing across her face—hairpins gone—and Fernando's shaggy mane with a mind of its own. A moment caught in a whirlwind, a moment of movement and unearthly magic.

"It's so you," Nidhi agreed. "Right in the center of the party that you so flawlessly put together."

Wait, was that . . . *approval* in Nidhi's voice?

"Um, say that again?" Avani asked. "Did you say I put it together *flawlessly*?"

"I did. Don't let it go to your head, though." Nidhi grinned, then cleared her throat. "And for the record, I'm sorry I was so hard on you about the ball. And that I messed up the camembert. You're right that I was being careless. Forgive me?"

Avani stared up at her big sister. Perfect Nidhi, apologizing? She should probably just accept it and move on gracefully. But she didn't feel that graceful, not yet. "You knew how much it meant to me. You know how much I've missed"—her voice cracked—"Pop."

"I'm sorry," Nidhi said again, her own voice wobbling. "I guess I didn't know, exactly. I miss him, too, of course. It was really wonderful to have this Winter Ball for him. I think he would feel very loved if he knew that we remembered him this way. You do things your own way, but somehow it works. You did really good, little sis."

"Thanks." Avani's heart was in her throat. There was a long silence.

"Remember when he planned that surprise fancy picnic?" Sirisha said suddenly. "He told us to get dressed up, then dragged us on a long hike. We all wondered where in the world he was taking us!"

"Yes!" Rani squealed. "And then we came to the viewpoint where he'd set out sparkling cider and chocolate-dipped strawberries! It was epic. Also, remember that time we thought he and Dad forgot our birthday? I was so mad because they said they'd signed up for an all-day hospitality seminar! But really they'd planned a sailing trip to Sucia for us."

Avani nodded, crying a little. "Best birthday ever!"

"Remember all the stuff he'd do whenever we were sick?" Nidhi chimed in. "He'd make us toast and tomato soup and then perform those hilarious sock puppet shows for us?" And then even she was crying.

"Ernie the sock puppet!" Rani wiped away more tears. "How could I forget?"

Nidhi joined them on the too-small loveseat and the four of them cuddled together, knees and elbows tangled up, but no one wanted to move. Instead, the sisters each told more stories about Pop—memories that came out in a flood—and it was so good to share them, to celebrate him, to just know that he had truly been there. He wasn't gone completely, and he never would be.

Something inside Avani started to settle as they talked. And when they finally quieted again, she leaned her head against Nidhi's shoulder. Said the thing she knew she had to. "I'm sorry, too, you know. About yelling at you in the kitchen. I may have overreacted."

Admitting to acting like a jerk was hard, but if Nidhi could do it, Avani could, too.

"It's seriously okay." Nidhi patted her shoulder. "I do get caught up in my own stuff."

"I suppose what you're doing next year is *sort of* important," Avani said, nudging her gently. "It's just not the *only* thing that's important."

"You're right," Nidhi agreed. "Definitely not the only thing. The good news is, I have it all figured out now."

"Wait, you do?" Avani asked.

"Tell us!" Rani demanded.

"Exciting!" Sirisha clapped her hands.

Nidhi smiled. "Yeah, it is exciting! Lalita Phua said I can stay with her in New Delhi and train with her personal chef. Apparently, he's very highly regarded. I checked with UW, and since Lalita Phua has degrees in history and philosophy, I can get credit for independent study with her, as long as I turn in some research papers!"

"Wow." Avani squeezed Nidhi. "I'm so happy for you."

Jealous, too, but she didn't have to let that ugly part of her take over. Maybe she'd always be a little jealous of Nidhi, who got all the firsts through no fault of her own. She was the eldest—that was life. And anyone could see that this was Nidhi's dream, the thing she'd been hungering for, the thing she needed to feed her soul.

Just as Avani had needed the Winter Ball.

Rani poked Nidhi. "You better tell us right away if you have any Shah Rukh Khan sightings."

"I will," Nidhi promised.

Sirisha reached out to hug Nidhi as well. "Staying with a relative sounds really nice."

"Yeah, I think so, too," Nidhi agreed. "It almost feels like coming home."

Home.

Obviously, nothing could be home to them the way the Songbird was. Still, it had a nice ring to it. Another home, one that Avani too would explore someday. But for now, she was right where she wanted to be, with the people she wanted to be with.

Flopping into bed in her favorite fleece peppermint-candy pajamas, Avani reached for her journal. She noted down a few important thoughts—such as "YMCA" turning out to be a real hit, and that maybe eldest sisters had redeeming qualities—when her phone pinged with a text.

Fernando:
Epic party tonight.

Avani:
Only because of the camembert.

Fernando:

And your silver dress. Wow.

Avani:

Your tux wasn't too bad either.

Fernando:

Gotta thank my second cousin who let me borrow it then.

Avani:

Hey—do you want to maybe come over for breakfast tomorrow?

Yikes! What was she doing? They'd just been trapped in a barn for many hours together, then they'd danced forever that night. He probably needed a break from her. Was there an unsend button?

Fernando:

I'd love to.

She stopped her fidgeting and smiled. He truly was a pearl among a sea of options. The only one worth considering, really.

Avani:

It's a date.

Turning off her lamp and snuggling into her pillow, she set her alarm for the morning. Actually, she could easily sleep through one alarm.

Better
make it
two.

Part Three: Spring

Sirisha

Chapter One

*J*agged cliffs. Raging waves. A gust of gulls.

An unexpected downpour, a short fall, a skinned knee. A busted tripod, a missing lens cap. Hair wild and tangled. Nose red from the spring damp. Sirisha was a mess, but she had the shots she needed. Her head churned with diffused light and exposure lengths and unexpected focal points. In black and white, they'd be stark and ethereal, a collection of macro imagery that would hopefully win her the prize in the San Juan Snaps photography contest.

Last year, she'd spent hours capturing lovely landscapes, but then she'd seen the shots others were submitting. Far more visually intriguing than her own. So she hadn't entered. This year, though, she was really pushing herself to create a portfolio that stood on its own. And then maybe she'd actually send it in this time.

Maybe.

Win or lose, at least she was outside. By herself, with her own thoughts. Three sisters and an inn full of guests made her nerves skitter like a faulty camera shutter. Armed with her DSLR, Sirisha lost herself to the seashore lupines and chocolate lilies starting to bud in the brush.

The sun peeked out, and warmth spread across her cheeks. The first sleeveless weather she could remember since October. Sirisha stuffed her cardigan in her bag, eager to reshoot some of her work with the changed lighting. But her viewfinder focused on an unexpected subject.

A girl, just about her age. A flowing, floral dress. Dark cedar skin that glistened in the sun, eyes big and bright, a cloud of curly natural Black hair.

A wry half-smile that made Sirisha's heart skip.

"Excuse me, I'm looking for the inn's barn? I followed the trail, but I think I went the wrong way." The girl gestured ruefully around them. It was nothing but cliffs and sea on one side. Grass and rocks and a few bunnies on the other.

Sirisha let out a nervous laugh, trying to push her knotted hair out of her face. Her knee was a ghastly sight, her leggings shredded. Why couldn't she ever look right when it counted?

What she wanted to say: "Got a bit turned around, huh? I was heading back to the inn anyway."

What she actually said: "Turned around? I—[incoherent mumble]—inn."

Lovely. Sirisha hung her head, wishing she could physically suck the words right back inside her. If only they could be conveniently caught in one of those bubble clouds in graphic novels.

The girl let out an easy, tinkling laugh. "Yes, the inn! I'm Brie, by the way. I'm with the theater troupe performing in the barn for Spring Fest."

Sirisha's eyes widened. The Thousand Shores act meant so, so much to her. Lifting a loneliness deep inside her. She saw herself centered on stage: queer girls, dark-skinned girls, girls who were both brown and queer.

She yearned to tell Brie all this yet now the words stuck in her throat. Pieces of unused sentences. Phrases without enough meaning.

She was better with images. Frozen ephemera, still and silent.

"Are you all right?" Brie gaped at her bloody knee.

Sirisha moved her lips, practicing creating sound. "It's okay, I'llcleanitupattheinn."

Her face burning, Sirisha trotted forward, gesturing for the other girl to follow behind her.

Brie didn't seem to mind her lack of eloquence. "I've always had a terrible sense of direction," she confessed. "Last month, we were doing a show on Whidbey, and I'd just gotten my license, so I'd volunteered to drive the van with all the costumes for a quick errand between performances. Except I somehow ended up in Seattle? How do you even do that when you're on an island?"

There was a bridge, Sirisha remembered, but Brie continued on before she could quite mention that fact. Which was actually perfect.

"In my defense, it was dark. And I was hungry. I can't think when I'm hungry." From there, Brie unraveled another tale or three as Sirisha led the way back along the craggy cliffside.

Breakups after performances, scenes behind the scenes, ticket sales and forgotten lines. She was a talker, a natural storyteller, a comedian. Her words flowed like a creek swollen with April rain, her descriptions high-resolution, her slices of life perfectly focused. And she was so pretty, her lips full and rosy, her smile wide and infectious.

Sirisha nodded along, wishing she had even half of Brie's confidence, as they ambled through a thicket of trees, past a stream and a chicken coop and a wine barrel and a bed of freshly budding tulips.

When they arrived at the barn, Brie finally took a breath, her lively travel stories hanging in the air like musical notes on a scale. "Excellent, we've made it. You're probably ready for me to shut up by now."

"Oh, no, I . . ." Sirisha faltered once again.

"It's okay, I know I'm way too into the monologue." Brie patted her bare arm. "Thank you for indulging me. Next time, you do the talking and I'll practice not interrupting. I'd love to see your shots, by the way. The San Juans are amazing in the spring."

Ack! Her heart fluttered frantically, panicked and yearning all at once.

What she wanted to say: "Sounds good."

What she actually said: ". . ."

How cool was she?

But Brie only laughed and bowed, as if onstage, then pirouetted through the barn doors. Lights and painted sets and costumes waiting.

Sirisha sighed, overheated and shivering at once. She'd had crushes before, but they'd never gone anywhere. Mostly because she usually preferred to interact with people through the safety of a zoom lens. But this time, she wondered if she could possibly make something happen? Make it real?

Oof. Sirisha had a lot to learn about dating. And her sisters had better help.

◆◆◆

Roti and daal. Mattar paneer and aloo ghobi. A rainbow of vegetarian dishes.

Dad and Amir laughing. Her sisters chattering. Sirisha's head swirled, her skin tingled, her heart thumped too fast. She felt feverish, but not from any ordinary sickness. From a crush. It was strange to think that she'd only met Brie once, and yet she was so restless and wild to see her again. Brie, who was so magnetic. Witty. Smart. Talented. Beautiful, too.

And Sirisha would never work up the nerve to talk to her.

The Singh family had congregated for their recent tradition of a weekly Sunday dinner at their favorite spot in the Songbird dining room, the big table by the bay window. Rain lashed against it and the ocean roared in the darkness. It was 9:30 p.m.; Dad's new commitment to "work-life balance" didn't include closing the restaurant before nine. By now, they'd learned Amir didn't mind eating late, though. "A familiar part of Desi life," he'd said.

Not picking at leftovers in the library in front of the TV was nice. Amir was not a strict vegetarian, but he preferred less meat in general and also liked relatively mild flavors—which Dad was happy to accommodate with his cooking. Sirisha liked the change, too. She let her tongue sit with the flavor of the lentils, the slightly crumbly texture. Turmeric and salt and just a hint of paprika.

Dad had another Sunday evening rule, though: no devices. And that included Sirisha's camera. No snapping shots while everyone was chatting. She had to "participate." Luckily, the lively conversation usually went on without too much input from her. Just the way she liked it.

Today she had something to say, though.

Something to ask.

But how to tilt the conversation her way?

"You wouldn't believe what one of my patients told me yesterday," Amir was saying. "She's convinced that her cats can see spirits of the dead—but only when it rains."

Dad snorted. "She must see a lot of ghosts around here, then."

"She moved here from California for that reason," Amir said. "She wanted to spend more time with her dearly departed mother. And a few great-aunts."

"Hmmm," Avani said. "Speaking of eccentric old ladies and haunted places, Rani and I watched a documentary last night about this doll shop in Seattle—"

"I can't believe you made me watch that!" Rani cried. "Dolls already give me the creeps with their dead eyes. And that place was definitely haunted. I couldn't sleep!"

"You couldn't sleep because you were staying up reading another romance novel."

"I had to! To erase the image of those creepy doll eyes."

"Creepy like this?" Avani turned her head for a moment, and then whipped back around with her eyelids flipped up and a disconcertingly dead stare.

"Ahhhhh!" Rani spit out her food, sending bits of roti and daal flying everywhere.

"Yuck." Nidhi wrinkled her nose as she wiped at her shirt. "Thanks, Avani."

"Hey, why are you blaming me?" Avani complained. "Rani was the one who—"

"It's not my fault. Avani—"

"Please, you just—"

This was going to go on forever. Meanwhile, Sirisha couldn't hold in her feelings any longer.

"How do you talk to someone you like?" she cut in.

Everyone turned to stare at her. Oops. Not exactly the smoothest transition to a new topic. But she'd been waiting patiently for her chance to speak. Besides, nobody wanted to listen to her sisters bicker all night.

Unfortunately, everyone was suddenly far too interested in her. She shrank back in her chair. She was going to die if they asked too many questions. Just die.

Dad smiled fondly. "Honey, just be yourself! You're a lovely girl—so creative and inventive. Anyone would want to talk to you!"

Sirisha's face burned. Of course her own father would say that. That didn't mean anyone else would think she was remotely interesting. Especially since she could barely get two words out with most people.

"One thing I love about you," Nidhi added, "is that you're so easy to talk to! You're a fantastic listener."

Yes, she was good at listening. But eventually people expected you to speak. And not just in squeaks like a mouse.

"Also," Rani said, "you take the best pictures! You make us look good."

Hmm. Could she start a relationship based on being a great photographer? Did that even make sense?

Avani patted her shoulder. "Any girl would be lucky to have you. You're so sweet and helpful! Always trading chores when I ask you to."

"In exchange for favors." Sirisha winked. If only she could feel comfortable enough to wink at Brie. Her sisters were one thing. She was one person with them—quiet but relatively composed.

But with Brie, she was completely pathetic. Her face burned as she remembered the day before, the way she'd stumbled over her sentences.

"Speaking of favors," Avani said, "Dad, can I borrow your car after school tomorrow? Nidhi needs ours for *yet another* event for the seniors. OI High School is obsessed with seniors. . . ."

"I *am* graduating," Nidhi said mildly. "It's kind of a big deal."

Avani rolled her eyes. "So, Dad, the car?"

"Of course, honey."

The subject shifted to Avani and Fernando, and their new joint venture in chicken raising. The two of them were so happy. So were Dad and Amir. Nidhi and Grayson. And Rani and . . . her romance novels? If Rani ever actually met her dreamboat, she'd be ready, at least. A little too ready perhaps, but ready.

As the conversation again darted away from Sirisha, she sighed with both relief and frustration. Their words were sweet, but not exactly the practical advice she'd hoped for.

Hey, Brie! Do you have any problems you need a good listener for? I don't have any solutions, mind you, but if you need someone to silently sit next to you while you figure things out yourself, I'm your girl.

No? Okay, then, how about any photographic needs? A new social media profile pic? Not right now?

Well, I'm also really helpful. Need any favors? I could—um—do your laundry?

Sigh. She was better off staying silent.

Chapter Two

Tuesday afternoon photography club was usually the highlight of Sirisha's week. The place where words gave way to pictures. Where images and lighting and composition told their own poignant story.

Today, Ms. Jones had them studying past winners of the San Juan Snaps contest. Passengers unloading off a ferry, sneakers left on a basketball court, an eagle soaring over a cliff. They were varied enough that Sirisha wasn't sure what brought them together. What earned a collection that coveted blue ribbon while others faded away into the background?

Sirisha gathered her cardigan around her, the room a little too chilly. Outside, sunshine was beckoning. It had been a long and dreary winter, wet and awful except for those brief couple of weeks of snowy excitement. Early spring had been fairly damp and cold, as well. But this week was gorgeous. She itched to roam around out there, sneaking up on the world with her camera lens.

Yet she was apprehensive, too. Afraid her photos were no different from anyone else's. Afraid that she'd fall away into obscurity along with her pictures if she didn't win. Sometimes, she felt like the blurred edges of a bokeh effect.

"The use of light and shadow here is just phenomenal," Ms. Jones said, stopping at a self-portrait. "Obviously, the judges agreed, since she placed first last year."

The girl in the photo was at a distance, posing in black and white in her bedroom, her gaze outside the window. She was mostly silhouetted, but somehow she'd managed to make her pensive eyes stand out.

"Did she use a secondary light source?" Paola asked.

Sirisha wanted to answer but took too long working herself up to it, her words tumbling under the weight of her tongue.

"Maybe she had a ring light?" Mark suggested.

"Or a reflector?" Genevieve squinted at the picture.

"What do you think, Sirisha?" Ms. Jones crossed her arms. Her teacher knew by now that she wasn't going to speak up on her own, not when the others were so quick to answer for her.

Sirisha worked her mouth as best she could: "There's . . . um . . . nutherwindow."

"Great observation," Ms. Jones said. "There is another window in the room. Can you make it out in the reflection?"

"Oooh, now I see it!"

"Rad!"

"Good catch!"

What Sirisha wanted to say: "The use of light is amazing, but I think

what I like the best in this shot is the sense that she—the photographer—
is expecting something or someone. She's looking out, but not in a dreamy
way. It looks more like someone is coming, someone she's ready for. In
fact, with the dress she's wearing and her makeup, she might be waiting
on a date."

What she actually said: ". . ."

And then Ms. Jones was moving on. Her teachers were always moving
on while words tumbled and dried in her mouth. It was time for each of
the club members to share their work on their portfolios so far. All four
of them were planning to enter the San Juan Snaps contest. But it was a
supportive group, not competitive.

Ms. Jones asked for volunteers, her eyes on Sirisha. Sirisha gave a brief
but frantic shake of her head. Not ready.

"I'll go!" Paola jumped up and fitted her USB drive into the laptop,
taking over the slide show.

Paola had focused on farms and farm-to-table culture in the San
Juans. She had shots from various farmer's markets from September,
which would start back up in May. Self-help produce stands with honor
system lockboxes. Backyard chickens. The year-round school plot where
students grew the produce used for lunch.

"I love this shot of the girl pulling the asparagus out of the earth,"
Ms. Jones said. "The camera's perspective is low to the ground, so it really
makes the asparagus larger than life, and it brings out a sense of human
triumph as she holds it in the air. Did you lie down to take it?"

Paola nodded.

"Nicely done."

Then Mark showed off his sailing shots, and Ms. Jones commented on
the way wind played a central role, a unifying motif. Next was Genevieve's

portfolio, bursting with wildlife shots from around the islands. Orca whales, seals, otters, deer. A bunny that seemed to tell an entire story with its twitching nose.

Finally, Sirisha was up.

She was nervous. A little excited, too. Here, she didn't have to speak. Only show. She started with wildflowers. Blue violets. Fairy slippers. Seashore lupines. Worked her way up to larger flora. Thistles. Fiddleheads. Ferns. The emphasis on the dewy freshness of spring sunshine after a rain. Finally, a madrone on a windswept bluff. Gnarled branches, peeling bark, orangish-red twigs like fingers. A sense of movement and yearning.

"They're pretty," Paola said. But she didn't say anything else.

"Very pretty," Genevieve agreed, then became silent.

"Plants are cool," Mark said, in a way that made it obvious he didn't think they were very cool.

Sirisha flushed. Was her work really so boring? Why didn't they comment on the yearning in the madrone branches? The sense of things bigger than themselves?

Ms. Jones cleared her throat. "Sirisha, your technical work is masterful. The use of light, perspective, and composition is all excellent."

"Thank you." Sirisha gulped, bracing herself.

"But . . ."

There it was. Why did Sirisha always think she wouldn't get feedback? She was there to get feedback. Yet there remained a part of her that hoped everyone would say it was perfect. And not in a slightly bored and overly polite voice.

"What is the story you're trying to tell with your collection?" Ms. Jones asked.

Sirisha had thought the pictures spoke for themselves. Obviously, they didn't.

She wished she could articulate extremely brilliant thoughts about yearning and reaching. Themes of wilderness, freshness, hope.

What she actually said: "Um . . . spring?"

"Spring is a season. We experience it every year. But why did you choose it as your focus? What do you want us to know about it? What does it mean to you?"

Her thoughts were dust particles in a ray of sunshine. Tiny. Transient. Trifling.

"The judges will be looking for more than beautiful pictures," Ms. Jones said. "They'll be searching for a portfolio that enlightens us about some aspect of the world or ourselves. This isn't just advice for Sirisha—I urge all of you to dig deep into what drew you to your choices. What are you trying to say? What makes you intensely passionate about it? Why should a judge pick your collection above all others?"

Fingers trembling, Sirisha took her USB drive. Shoved it back into her backpack. Tears threatened to erupt. No, no, no. She couldn't cry in front of everyone. She'd look like a baby. She already felt like one most of the time. Her three older sisters were so worldly, so breezily cool. So in command of what it was they wanted. Sirisha had thought photography was her one skill, the one place where she could be confident. But Ms. Jones still wanted more from her.

She *had* a story. It was etched into her photos. The lines, the composition, the light.

The shadows.

Why couldn't anyone read it?

The Songbird Inn's barn bustled that week. The Thousand Shores theater troupe arrived early each morning, stayed till six each evening. With them came set pieces and costumes. Light and sound equipment. Headsets and scripts. The troupe had one month before opening day as part of Spring Fest, a joint celebration of the performing arts. Plays and musicals and ballet recitals performed in venues across the San Juans.

This was the first year the Thousand Shores was using the Songbird's barn, but Sirisha had seen them perform the previous year in Eastsound, and they'd been fabulous. They were a variety show, each act unique as a fingerprint. Sketches and monologues. Poetry and dancing and even acrobatics.

They told so many stories, and Sirisha couldn't even tell one.

On Wednesday after school, she squatted on an old tree stump, inside Fernando and Avani's fenced chicken pasture, fiddling with the settings on her camera and replaying that horrible photography club meeting from the previous day in her head. All those polite but unimpressed responses to her portfolio. How could she change that? She felt like she'd given so much of herself to her photography, and yet it wasn't enough.

Meanwhile, Avani danced nearby like the Pied Piper, leaving a trail of seeds behind her in the grass. The chicks followed in a line.

Click. Click. Click.

Avani gave her an annoyed look. "Could you not right now? I'm a mess." She blew her hair out of her face.

Sirisha protested. "But. The chicks. In a perfect line. So cute!"

Avani rolled her eyes. "Photograph the chicks then."

"Okay, okay!"

"I think you look adorable, Avani." Fernando put his arm around her shoulders, grinning straight at the camera. "Say cheese!"

Avani scrunched her nose at him. Then nodded her assent at Sirisha. Not exactly a candid, but Sirisha adjusted her lens to focus on them.

Fernando said, "Queso panela!" while Avani shouted, "Camembert!"

The look they gave each other was great; a mixture of surprise and delight that they'd both made the same joke.

Click. Click. Click.

Avani swatted Fernando. "Hey, you know camembert brought us together!"

He nudged her shoulder with his own. "Too on the nose, obviously."

As they play-bickered, Sirisha clicked away. The truth was, she had about a million photos of Avani and Fernando at this point. She'd even gotten one of the kiss in the barn when the family had found them after the snowstorm. She hadn't told Avani though. Just imagining the fuss her sis would make over a photo of that private moment . . .

Too scary.

Maybe it could be a wedding gift in the distant future, if they stayed together.

Sirisha had been documenting their whole lives. But she doubted any of the Singhs wanted her to put all their private moments out there for everyone to see. Ms. Jones wanted a story, but Sirisha needed to find the perfect balance: something personal but not too personal.

Sigh. She'd thought her spring flora were perfect. Turned out they were perfectly boring.

She clicked away, gathering more shots of the chicks, the barn, the afternoon sky. Avani with her long hair frizzing and her jeans covered in mud. She'd hate it, but Sirisha didn't. Somehow her sister looked beautiful anyway. Her frizz was just right. Unlike Sirisha's bird's nest.

Then Brie wandered into Sirisha's viewfinder once more. Flouncing into the barn with a medieval purple dress on a hanger thrown over her shoulder. Sirisha's breath caught, her heart fluttered. All the signs of the crush she'd tumbled into so quickly.

Maybe she could offer to help out with something. The crew might use an extra hand. But she didn't move.

Couldn't move.

Avani put an arm around Sirisha's shoulders. "Hey, don't look so glum. I think Ms. Jones was being way too hard on you—your shots are totally brilliant! My favorite was the one of that ring of mushrooms—the fairy ring? It's so cool—maybe you could go for a fairy tale theme? And the mossy logs by the creek? Super creepy! Ooh, maybe it should be a fairy-tale-turns-to-horror theme?"

Sirisha laughed. "Yep, fairy tale horror. Totally my style."

"You never know till you try!" Avani shrugged. "Fernando and I are going for a hike. Want to come? You might get some inspiration."

"Yeah, sure," Sirisha said. "Let me just change into my hiking boots."

"Okay, but be quick."

As Sirisha headed past the barn, she wished, hoped, prayed. That Brie would come out and she'd have no choice but to say something. No choice but to suddenly be cool.

Unfortunately, there was no sign of her.

Chapter Three

The scent of cedar pines. Salty sea air. The hint of lavender from the neighboring farm that always lingered like a bird's wing skimming the water. Hikes on Orcas never disappointed, even if they'd explored every trail many times over. The views of ferries gliding across shimmering water. A flock of sandpipers circling as one in the air. Purple sea stars clinging to an old pier.

As they walked, Sirisha spotted a hollowed-out tree stump. The opening resembled a dark, shadowed heart. A vision of what might happen to hers if she never opened up. Sirisha snapped a photo, as a reminder. A warning. A cautionary tale.

Hearts popped up all around her, an invasive species. There was a heart in the shape of a spotted mushroom's cap. The petals of wildflowers. A cloud in the sky. Hearts, hearts, hearts.

As the three of them headed back down the trail, a heart winked into existence in the space between Fernando and Avani, formed by their legs and entwined elbows. It disappeared as they playfully bumped hips and joked, but always seemed to come back. A peekaboo game.

The loop was about six miles, and when they returned to the Songbird, they were all a bit peckish. Avani suggested raiding the kitchen. Within its sunny yellow walls, they found Nidhi adding a dollop of strawberry jam to *heart-shaped* cookies. There—it wasn't all in Sirisha's imagination. Hearts truly were haunting her, insistent and fierce.

"Oooh, those look good!" Avani said, snatching a cookie.

"Hey, those are for the theater troupe!" Nidhi protested.

"Mmhmmm." Avani of course swiped another cookie and a pile of finger sandwiches with a wink at Fernando. He shrugged helplessly at Nidhi as Avani raced out, clutching his hand.

"Those two!" Nidhi harrumphed, but she was smiling.

"I'll help you put together more sandwiches if you need," Sirisha offered.

"Thanks. How was the hike, anyway?" Nidhi grabbed smoked salmon and cream cheese from the fridge. Pear and brie. Cucumber and avocado.

Sirisha shrugged. Confusing thoughts swirled for attention, tripping on her tongue. Ms. Jones, her portfolio, her boring spring flora. All she had from this afternoon was a portfolio of hearts. The judges would laugh her out of the room.

As they worked on the snacks, Sirisha caught Nidhi smiling at a text from Grayson. She was used to her sisters and their various romantic interests, but right then it was a bit of a gut punch.

Sirisha had never even been kissed.

She'd never let bits of her soul mingle with tongue and teeth and lips.

She wanted to pretend she didn't care. That she and her camera and the spring flora were enough. But the glaring message behind today's excursion was too obvious to pretend otherwise. She was full of a feverish longing, her heart itself a madrone reaching out over a windswept bluff. Hoping to be caught by someone.

Nidhi looked up from her phone. "What's going on?"

"Nothing. What do you mean?"

"You just had a faraway look on your face."

"Oh." *Caught.*

Nidhi raised an eyebrow. "Well?"

"It's nothing."

"Fine, don't tell me." Nidhi tucked a lock of Sirisha's hair behind her ear.

Sirisha flushed. Should she confess? That she'd never been kissed and suddenly an ache had taken over and she wanted it more than anything? Longed for all those experiences that everyone talked about, those feelings of wanting and floating and fervor?

She opened her mouth. Closed it. Opened it again.

What came out: "I can take the snacks to the barn for you."

"Okay, if you're sure?" Nidhi asked.

Did her big sis guess? She couldn't have guessed. None of her sisters had seen her with Brie the other day. And they'd barely reacted when she'd asked about talking to someone you like at dinner Sunday night. Besides, Nidhi was busy with her own things.

"You still have a funny look on your face," Nidhi said. "And you've been hovering around the barn these last couple of days. And why were you asking about how to talk to someone you like the other night?"

Oops. Maybe Nidhi wasn't as busy as she'd thought. In fact, for as long as she could remember, her elder sister always seemed to guess Sirisha's thoughts when no one else could.

Sirisha wiped her forehead. She was perspiring a little. A warmth prickled in her toes. She really wanted to see Brie again. She took the tray and literally ran out before Nidhi could ask her more questions.

Yes, it was cowardly.

Yes, she was a dork.

Yes, she caught Nidhi's look of amused bafflement.

Yes, yes, yes.

"Just be yourself!" Nidhi called after her.

Just be herself. But herself was boring. A mouse. A wallflower. A blurry background. She needed to borrow someone else's personality. If only she, too, could learn to become an actress, to fake it until she could make it.

She imagined herself walking up to the other girl, cool and collected. *Hey, Brie, want to share a sandwich? Also, remember when you said you were interested in my photography? Actually, I could use some help with it. Apparently, my collection needs to tell a story. I know, right? I thought it just had to be visually intriguing, too.*

Ugh. Sirisha couldn't possibly say all that without messing it up. She'd tumbled over her own words too many times. They'd race each other, in a competition to leave her lips. Knock each other down in the process.

She turned around. She'd have to tell Nidhi she couldn't deliver the goodies after all. But then again, Nidhi was on to her. She'd have to face her questions if she returned.

Sirisha turned back to the barn.

To the inn.

To the barn.

To the inn.

She was about to head back to the Songbird, when she overheard hushed voices that piqued her curiosity. One of them sounded familiar, but she moved closer to hear better.

"The gown doesn't fit right, I feel awkward, the lighting stinks . . ."

"What's wrong with the lighting?"

"It's too bright. It makes me dizzy."

Sirisha peeked around the corner of the barn, where Brie sat with her legs crossed in the grass.

A girl with long pigtails and paint-stained coveralls patted Brie's shoulder. "I'm sure Loretta would be willing to listen to your concerns—"

"But they hated my ideas for tweaks to the script."

"No, they didn't, they only said they wanted to think about it more."

Brie let out a deep, long sigh. "I know I'm probably overreacting. But this is the biggest role I've ever had. And I just want people to get it. I want people to get *me*."

"They will—it's brilliant."

"But what if they don't?" asked Brie quietly, her chin trembling a little bit.

When Sirisha had caught the troupe's act last year, the production had been top-notch, from the lighting to the costumes. But then again, getting everything just right was probably a process. Also, maybe what Brie was worried about wasn't really the lighting or the costumes at all. Maybe she was simply nervous?

Or was that just what Sirisha would feel in her shoes? After all, Brie was so different from her, and it was hard to believe a girl who seemed so utterly confident and put-together would have a case of nerves. Still, Sirisha longed to plop down beside Brie and talk it out.

As if she could even get the words out.

Instead, her shoulders sagged and she shuffled into the barn, which had been transformed. She'd seen the large, open space inside decorated for plenty of weddings. But now there was a new stage built from scratch. Set pieces everywhere, in various states of completion. Theater lighting, racks of costumes, props. Chaotic disarray, but with a purpose.

The cookies and sandwiches soon drew a crowd. People came and went, thanking Sirisha.

The next thing she knew, Brie was at her side, smiling widely. Not a trace of her doubts on her face. "Hi—it's Sirisha, right? These cookies look amazing, and I don't even like jam on my cookies. In fact, I barely like cookies. Who made this? Your sister Nidhi? I heard she's into baking?"

Sirisha nodded. "Yeahshe'sgreat."

"I love your family's inn," Brie continued breezily. "It's just so charming, seriously. Historic, tasteful, the right amount of coziness but totally updated and fresh, too. And the views! Amazing. I'm from Lopez, but we don't live on shoreline. Not even remotely affordable."

So Brie understood island life then, all the little things that were different in the San Juans than on the mainland. It was an opening.

So, island life, huh?

Can you imagine going to a school where you don't know the name of every student?

Also, what even is a Target?

There was a drawn-out pause as Brie waited for Sirisha to fill in the silence. She tried—she really did—but she didn't know if she was actually funny or insightful. Eventually, Brie let her off the hook, sharing more about her home on Lopez and how her mom homeschooled her, an arrangement that allowed her to travel for her theater work.

Sirisha was so intensely curious that words came tumbling out, a question unbidden. "Whydoyoulikeit?" She gulped. That sounded weird and rushed so she explained, as slowly as she could manage. "Going up onstage, I mean."

Brie's voice thrummed with passion. "There's so much I want to say with my acting. There are all these preconceptions about storytelling and who deserves to be heard—and I just want to shake it all up." As she spoke, she had a glow on her as if a spotlight followed her around. Only there was no spotlight; it was just Brie.

Sirisha understood, too. Wanting to shake things up, to say things with your art.

Maybe they did have a few things in common after all?

Nidhi walked in with a pitcher of lemonade and cups while Sirisha's unsaid thoughts were fluttering in her head like hummingbirds, restless and twitchy. She was entranced with Brie. Brie with rosy pink lipstick. Brie in a mauve-and-chocolate dress. Brie with eyes dark and bright, lashes long and smoky. Brie who smelled of citrus and wildflowers.

Brie, who talked a mile a minute. Brie, who possibly had secret nerves about her performance. Brie, who braved forward anyway.

Meanwhile, Nidhi lingered as she rearranged the sandwiches, pouring lemonade for anyone who came by. Glanced their way just a few too many times. Big sis totally knew. How did she always know? Nidhi patted Sirisha's arm, handed them each a cup of lemonade, and sauntered out of the barn—leaving Sirisha on her own again with Brie.

Who cleared her throat. Slowed her 120 mph words. And said, "So

I haven't spent much time on Orcas before. Maybe you could show me around sometime? Where do people our age hang out?"

Sirisha choked on her lemonade. Was Brie *asking her out*?

No, she was just being friendly, obviously. And Sirisha should respond with equal casualness.

What she wanted to say: "Of course! I'd love to show you the sights. When are you free?"

What she actually said: "Erm . . . (cough, cough, choke)."

Before she had a chance to recover, a girl approached with a clipboard. "Hey, Brie, I hear your costume needs adjusting. Want to come try it on for me?"

Brie sucked in a breath. "Yes! One sleeve is shorter than the other, and it's a little tight across the hips."

"Okay, don't worry. We'll get it right."

"Thanks." Brie bit her lip and turned to Sirisha, waiting.

But Sirisha only smiled and eked out, "Seeyoulater!"

"Oh," Brie said, sounding a little taken aback. "Okay, later."

Fantastic. Now Brie thought Sirisha *didn't* want to hang out. Brie had twice asked to spend time with her. Offering to look at her photography the day they met, and just a second ago.

But if Sirisha kept choking, Brie would stop asking.

Chapter Four

The next day after school, Sirisha curled up in the porch hammock with her laptop and textbooks, sunshine warm on her face. It had rained earlier, but the clouds had parted in the afternoon. She could get away with just a sweater, something pretty, instead of her extremely functional winter parka.

A couple of hawks cruised the skies above the Songbird, swooping and gliding in an intimate dance. Purple finches cozied up on the big rhododendron tree just off the porch. Far below on the water, geese flocked. Though they were too small to see from the Songbird, Sirisha knew they probably had plenty of fuzzy goslings among them.

The air was fresh and wild, the creatures of the island busy searching for appropriate mates and making babies. Meanwhile, Sirisha had only her homework for company. Which she could not focus on for the life of her.

It wasn't 3x + 5, it was 3 Brie + 5.

Her Spanish practice conversations weren't about el aeropuerto, they were about bellísima Brie.

And somehow, it was also Brie leading the Normans to victory in 1066.

Sirisha knew her intense feelings didn't totally make sense. But with Brie, she felt all the clichés she'd ever heard about romance: butterflies in her stomach, a fluttering heartbeat, warm toes. Actually, were warm toes a normal crush-induced reaction?

Perhaps this intensity was just part of being fifteen. If so, she was ready for that magic transformation into someone older and wiser, someone who didn't need to dream of being kissed because they'd already *been* kissed plenty of times.

Giving up on the homework, Sirisha pulled open her San Juan Snaps folder. Which was also a mess. No consistency in mood, style, or composition.

"You have it bad," Rani said, leaning over Sirisha's shoulder.

"What?" Sirisha quickly shut her laptop.

"Scoot." Rani climbed into the hammock beside Sirisha, until they were shoulder to shoulder, their legs spread out against the length of it, textbooks and homework rocking with them.

"Show me your portfolio again," Rani demanded.

Hands trembling, Sirisha reopened her laptop. The password prompt came up and Rani waited pointedly as Sirisha logged in. It took her three tries to get her password right.

And then, there it was.

Heart-shaped clouds. Heart-shaped leaves. Even a heart-shaped paratha.

"Explain this," Rani said with raised eyebrows.

"Spring flora?"

"This doesn't look like flora." Rani pointed to the paratha.

Sirisha sputtered, reaching for an explanation she didn't have: "Idon'tknow . . ."

"You have a crush, don't you?" Rani crowed, then hugged Sirisha so hard that the hammock tilted and swung wildly. Papers scattered.

"Ack—"

"I'm so excited for you!" Rani clapped her hands. "Who is it? Oh, I know."

"You do?"

Rani waggled her eyebrows. "It has to be Paola. She's gorgeous, and you're always talking about her!"

"Um . . ."

Paola was a lovely girl, but also just a friend. The two of them geeked out about their cameras sometimes. They'd gone on a few hikes together for inspiration earlier in the year. Then Paola had fallen in love, not with Sirisha, but with farm-to-table produce. And Sirisha wasn't hot and bothered about her either. Not the way she felt about Brie—where her toes tingled with a strange warmth whenever she thought of her. Seriously, should someone be able to change the temperature of your toes?

"It's definitely Paola," Rani said. "I can tell by your hesitation."

"Um . . ."

Rani was far too excited. When Rani got excited, she didn't let things go. But the evidence was there. The heart-shaped paratha was definitely *not* flora.

"So, what are you doing about it?" Rani demanded.

"Um . . ." Sirisha gulped.

She was still working up the courage to see Brie again. It was pure torture to know that the pretty thespian was probably in the barn right at that moment. Nidhi might even be preparing some snacks for the troupe. Had Brie really almost-kinda asked her out? Or had she read the whole thing wrong?

Maybe she *could* use Rani's help.

Rani seemed to read all that yearning in her face. "You really do have it bad. Don't worry, the Official Love Guru is here to help."

The Official Love Guru had plenty of ideas about romance and love. Perhaps too many. Sirisha wasn't sure what she was in for, honestly. But since she'd been stumbling for answers in a dark void, she decided to go along with whatever her sister had planned.

Until they were in the library, and Rani put on a Hindi movie.

"*DDLJ?* We've seen this before!" Sirisha protested.

Dilwale Dulhania Le Jayenge was a Bollywood megahit from the '90s. Sirisha recalled that Shah Rukh Khan and Kajol hung out in Europe and then eventually got together. But how was that going to help her?

Rani huffed. "It's one of the most popular films in India of all time. A theater in Mumbai showed it every day for about a zillion years. I can't remember if they're still showing it or not, but seriously—it's big for a reason."

"A heteronormative reason," Sirisha muttered.

"True . . ." Rani said. "But the romance! The tension! Even the title tells you what you need to know: *the one with heart will get the bride.*"

"I'm not looking for a *bride.*"

"Don't quibble with words."

Sirisha just shook her head. Another day, another romantic comedy in the library. One that seemed very far from real life. But then the movie started. The gentle rhythms of Hindi on the tongues of the stars. Kajol's haunting beauty floating off the screen as she sang. Wishing. Dreaming of someone to love.

Sirisha shivered. She'd spent an awful lot of time recently daydreaming, too.

Next, Simran (Kajol) and Raj (Shah Rukh Khan) meet and bicker; they miss trains, travel Europe's back-country roads, dance in scenic towns, have too much to drink in a barn.

And then the movie twists.

The carefree European vacation is over; Simran's heart has been thoroughly captured by Raj. But she's betrothed to another. The wedding is in days. Her father's big, angry eyes loom over her every move. Sirisha didn't relate to that part—Dad almost never got angry. And though he'd had an arranged marriage to Mom so long ago, he'd made his own path since then. Still, the urgency of Simran's situation was gripping. As wedding rituals erupt in color and song, Simran waits for Raj. He arrives but refuses to elope. Instead, he wants to win her father's blessing. He sets out to prove that he is most worthy of Simran. Prove that he has the most heart.

The one with heart gets the girl.

"I have plenty of heart," Sirisha muttered.

"Of course you do." Rani patted her arm soothingly.

But did she? If she had enough of it, she'd march down to the barn and declare her feelings, just as Raj does in the big climactic face-off with Simran's father.

Friday after school, spring break started. An entire week off—with the Official Love Guru's attention fully focused on Sirisha. Perhaps she'd made a terrible mistake. That evening, Rani ransacked Sirisha's closet in search of attire worthy of a date. She dug through leggings with holes. Dresses with grass stains. Faded T-shirts. A whole lot of yoga pants.

Hmm. Perhaps saving for new camera equipment had left Sirisha's wardrobe in a state of neglect. There was that scarlet skirt she'd bought especially for the Winter Ball, of course. Sirisha pulled it out, hoping that Rani wouldn't notice the tiny snowflake embroidery along the hem. "This is pretty, right?"

"Very pretty, just not exactly right for this season." Rani dismissed it with a flick of her wrist before holding up a pair of muddy, paint-splattered, faded overalls. "What exactly are these?"

"Um . . ." Sirisha assumed that was a rhetorical question.

"Burn them," Rani said. "These, too."

She held up Sirisha's favorite leggings.

"What?" Sirisha said. "No way. Those are super comfy."

Rani wrinkled her nose at the patterned electric blue. "You can never wear these again."

"But—"

"Oh, here's something!" Rani pulled out a red polka-dot dress.

"Um, that was my Minnie Mouse costume for Halloween a couple of years ago?"

"It's cute. Put it on."

"It's a costume. And it's probably too small for me . . ."

Rani, Official Love Guru, would not take no for an answer. The next thing Sirisha knew, she was wearing a too-tight Minnie Mouse dress, black heels that she could barely walk in, and long dangly gold earrings that were not her style at all.

She should probably just be grateful that Rani hadn't insisted on the mouse ears.

Saturday afternoon, the torture continued. The Official Love Guru gathered her nefarious instruments. Makeup case, blow dryer, hair straightener. Too many products to count. Sirisha considered climbing out the third-floor window. A swift and desperate escape.

"Sit!" Rani commanded. A drill sergeant in the making.

"Okay but you're not going to . . ."

"Don't worry, I've cut Nidhi's hair before." Rani's eyes gleamed.

"Cut?!" Sirisha squeaked. "You didn't say anything about cutting!"

Not long later, Sirisha's hair was a good six inches shorter. Shiny. Silky soft.

Sirisha swished her locks back and forth. With attitude. And she had to admit, she pulled it off. She'd never had attitude before.

Rani wielded her makeup brush like a wand.

And suddenly Sirisha had actual cheekbones. "How did you do that?" she asked, fascinated.

"I'm your fairy godmother. Now—we just need the perfect lipstick shade."

Rani rolled out her lipstick case, an arsenal of pinks and nudes and plums and wines. Sirisha eyed them, then reached for a subtle color. Something that wouldn't draw attention to itself.

Naturally, Rani batted her arm away. "That one's fine for a hike in the woods. With your sister. Not what we're looking for. We need something that can steal a heart or two."

"There's a lipstick for stealing hearts?" Sirisha asked.

Rani made her selection. Darker, silkier. A hue meant for poetry under moonlight. A shade for fireflies and candles, for roses and chocolate-dipped strawberries. For kissing.

And when Sirisha carefully put it on, pressing her lips together, she hardly recognized the girl in the mirror. Thunderstorm eyes. Midnight locks. Lips of magic and mayhem.

Rani grinned, petting her blown-out hair. "I did good, right?"

Sirisha smiled softly. "Don't let it go to your head."

Rani definitely let it go to her head.

A few hours later, the two of them stood at the edge of a jagged cliff, waves crashing below. The first pinks of the sunset just barely visible in the sky over the sea. At the Official Love Guru's insistence, she was wearing the Minnie Mouse dress. She'd barely managed to hobble her way up the trail in heels to what Rani declared the most cinematic spot.

At least her lipstick was nice.

"Say the lines again!" Rani urged.

"No! I refuse!" Sirisha protested, folding her arms. "I've already said it so many times!"

"You said it at home," Rani returned. "And it was pretty swoon-worthy, to be honest. But now I want you to try here, out in the open. After all, you can't hide behind a pillow when you talk to Paola."

Rani shoved a copy of the Shakespearean sonnet in her hands. Sirisha bit her lip. Saying it alone in her room was bad enough, but this was one of Dad's most recommended trails and several guests had already seen her in this mortifying costume dress.

Besides, this was all pointless. She wasn't planning to recite poetry to Brie. It was so over-the-top. It was written by a dead white male. It was . . .

"Come on, with fervor!" Rani insisted. "If you can say this, you can definitely ask someone to coffee. Right?"

Sirisha gulped. Maybe Rani did have the tiniest bit of a point. She screwed up her courage. Imagined Brie in front of her. Imagined that she was fighting for her love. Her voice wobbled with emotion. *"Love is not love, which alters when it alteration finds . . ."*

"Good, good," Rani said. "Keep going. With even more urgency."

Sirisha cleared her throat, raised her voice. *"Or bends with the remover to remove . . ."*

"Amazing," Rani said, clutching her heart. "You sound fantastic! Dig as deep as you can for this next part!"

Sirisha bit her lip, trying to bring all that aching and yearning inside her to the forefront. She closed her eyes. Spoke powerfully and loudly as if onstage, her voice resonating from deep in her diaphragm, quivering with a passion she hadn't known she was capable of:

"O no! it is an ever-fixed mark
That looks on tempests and is never shaken;
It is the star to every wandering bark,
Whose worth's unknown, although his height be taken."

The words hung in the air, a storm cloud of everything Sirisha had been feeling. She felt exorcised.

To her surprise, people were clapping and whistling. A crowd had gathered around her. More inn guests, holding the little trail maps Josie had made.

"Fantastic!"

"She must be here for Spring Fest!"

"Oh, yeah, the Thousand Shores. If they're this good, I'm definitely going!"

"Love that dress, by the way," a woman said. "And those earrings."

Really? The Minnie Mouse dress? Sirisha stood there, immobile under their enthusiasm, cheeks burning. After those lines, there was absolutely no way she could squeak out a single word more.

Meanwhile, Rani wiped tears from her eyes. "The best student. Now, let's practice your dance moves."

Sirisha groaned.

Chapter Five

The sunny weather was starting to feel too good to be true.

In the Pacific Northwest, spring was supposed to be dreary. Moody. A spectrum of grays. The silvery cumulonimbus lining, however, was that cloud cover could do a lot for a photograph. Soft light from all angles. No harsh shadows.

But blinding sunniness had its own merits. An experiment in overexposed photos. Not advancing a story, as Ms. Jones had urged. Just a fun technique to play with. Especially with the new lens Sirisha had recently been gifted. Sirisha followed the same cliffside trail where she'd first run into Brie, a part of her hoping that perhaps she'd show up on the path, somehow once again taking a serendipitous wrong turn.

Click. Click. Click.

The breeze ruffled Sirisha's hair, but with the length of it chopped off, she knew it wouldn't get into a wild tangle. There were uses for this bob. *Click. Click. Click.*

Sirisha worked her way back to the inn, delighting in overexposed flora. With each step, she was getting a little closer to the barn. To Brie. She started to sweat, just slightly. Her heart fluttered like the white butterfly flitting around near her. It seemed to think she smelled like nectar.

At last, she was back at the Songbird, her skin dewy with sun and wind. She wasn't wearing lipstick, but she'd at least borrowed a spring dress and a creamy cardigan from Rani. The Official Love Guru would probably approve if Sirisha took a quick peek in the barn. If she maybe just waved hi . . .

Only, when she opened the barn doors, no one was there. The place was a mess of set pieces and costumes and props. Apparently, the troupe had taken the day off. They'd worked the Sunday before, but perhaps that was only because it was their arrival day? She searched for a schedule posted up somewhere. No luck. Nidhi and Dad would know, though, since the inn had been providing light meals and snacks.

She sighed.

As she stepped back out into the sunshine, the Official Love Guru came running up to her. Waving car keys.

"There you are!" Rani said. "Ready for your next lesson?"

"Leave me alone." Sirisha focused her camera on a pot of tulips next to the barn door. "We've already established that I can't move my hips that way."

"True," Rani said, "so you clearly need to focus on other skills. Like driving. How can you go on a proper date if you have to ask us for rides all the time?"

"Dad's been teaching me."

"Yeah, but he's pretty busy. You'll never get a license if you depend on him. Nidhi helped me, and I'll help you. Come on, let's see if you can take us to Eastsound."

Driving made Sirisha anxious. But Rani was resolute. And Sirisha was terrible at saying no. And saying yes. It was something she needed to work on, but it never quite seemed worth it. A few minutes later, she was nervously adjusting the driver's seat, the mirrors.

"Ooh, I have the perfect daytime lipstick for you!" Rani fished a silver case out of her purse.

"Do I need lipstick for a driving lesson?" Sirisha asked.

"Of course!" Rani said. "What if we break down and need to seek help? What if we have a flat tire and it's raining and Paola comes to our rescue?"

Sirisha's face burned. Being rescued by a pretty girl did sound nice. So she put on the darn lipstick. It was a lovely color on her lips, a breezy raspberry pink. Just slightly pert.

After a quick prayer, her clammy hands claimed the wheel. The engine softly growled on. Oh dear. She'd probably mix up the accelerator with the brake and ram the car right into the front desk. Then the Songbird would no longer be the Most Romantic Inn in America but the Inn Most Damaged by a Bad Teen Driver. Not exactly a plaque to be proud of.

"Get moving, Grandma," Rani said.

Sirisha put the car in reverse, very gently placed pressure on the gas, and managed to pull out of the spot without hitting any of the guest cars in the lot. A small victory, but one to be savored. Of course, Rani sighed with impatience ill-fitting a driving instructor. Sirisha drove at a snail's pace along the driveway, then through twisting roads past farms and pines and beaches until they'd made it into Eastsound. When at last she managed to park, she tumbled out of the car like a dizzy bee. She'd made it. Hadn't driven off a cliff.

Small wonders.

"You're about two feet from the curb," Rani noted. "But whatever. It's a wide street."

"I need ice cream," Sirisha said. Her knees felt wobbly.

"I could go for some Lulu's right about now, too," Rani said.

With schools closed for spring break, the ice cream parlor was hopping. Mainlander tourists chattering, toddlers crashing around the play area, indecisive folks sampling upward of twenty-seven flavors. Lily, one of Sirisha's classmates, was working the counter alongside Matt. Sirisha braced herself, her tongue tangling already. Her normal awkwardness was magnified by a factor of a hundred when it came to her sister's ex.

A woman was interrogating him with the intensity of a CIA operative. ("Are you absolutely certain the vanilla was made with real vanilla beans? How do you know? Were you there when it was made?") Meanwhile, his sister Anita happily chewed on a train in the corner as a boy next to her toppled his own block tower and laughed before repeating the exercise.

"Hey," Matt said as they came to the front. "How're things at the Songbird?"

"Um . . ." Sirisha bit her lip.

Even though she'd encouraged Nidhi to follow her heart, she wasn't sure if she herself could have done it. Breaking up with someone seemed impossible. Not that she'd ever had someone to break up with. The bright side of never advancing past a distant crush.

"Pretty good," Rani answered. "Sometimes there are actually snickerdoodles left in the jar."

Sirisha winced. Not exactly the gentle comment she would have offered, but Matt chuckled.

"Ouch!" he said. "By the way, I recommend the chocolate rhubarb, our seasonal special. Want a sample?"

"Why not?" Sirisha chirped as Rani said simultaneously, "No thanks."

Matt chuckled at that, too. He seemed chill, so Sirisha let herself exhale. Love could be a transient thing, and that was okay. A good reminder that she didn't have to worry quite so much over every tongue-tied moment.

Sirisha ended up with the special, while Rani opted for mint chocolate chip. As they found an outdoor table, cones in hand, Sirisha chided her sister.

"You should be nicer to him! Nidhi broke his heart."

Rani rolled her eyes. "He's a big boy. And anyway, I heard"—she glanced around both ways, then stage-whispered—"that Kiera has a thing for him." She waited expectantly for Sirisha to gasp with surprise.

In fact, Sirisha had heard that, too. Avani wasn't exactly the best secret keeper, and besides, people tended to spill things to Sirisha. When you're quiet, people like to talk. And tell you things they didn't intend to. An introvert superpower.

People at nearby tables didn't seem overly concerned with Rani's salacious secret about two teens who liked each other, either. Probably because they were tourists.

"So tell me more about why you like Paola," Rani demanded.

After Rani had just spilled the beans about Kiera liking Matt? Sirisha didn't dare say a word about her fake crush. Instead, she licked her ice cream. Let the breeze ruffle her short hair. Inhaled the scent of spring along with chocolate and rhubarb. Sunshine warmed her, her creamy cardigan felt soft against her skin, and ice cream slid lazily down her esophagus, a river of sugar and chocolate and fruit. Bees buzzed in the lavender bushes, and two girls on bicycles rounded the corner. Sirisha recognized the musical notes of a tinkling laugh right away. Brie.

Her breath caught.

Brie, in navy shorts and a white tank showing off her long legs and silky arms. Brie, for whom she'd suffered through the Official Love Guru's torture sessions. Brie, the girl she'd watched through her camera lens far too many times.

It was time to speak. That's what all those lessons had been for, hadn't they? She'd recited a silly sonnet to strangers on a cliffside, wearing that ridiculous Minnie Mouse dress. She could do this. Quickly, she wiped ice cream from her chin. The breezy pink lipstick was probably all gone, but she couldn't worry about that now.

She waved her hand. "Bric!"

Brie startled, but when she caught sight of Sirisha, her smile was pure effervescence. She pedaled to the curb, dropped her bike.

"Hi, Sirisha! I love your haircut," Brie called, slightly out of breath.

"Ergmthnks," Sirisha replied, touching her newly shorn hair. "Rani here cut it for me."

"That's right," Rani said, preening. "Stylist extraordinaire."

"It looks fantastic, seriously." Brie beamed.

Meanwhile, her friend pointed to a coffee shop. "I'll be right back."

Brie waved her off, then pulled up a chair, beaming. "Oh my gosh, it's so nice to get away from the troupe! I mean don't get me wrong, I love everyone. But we've been practicing nonstop this week. I'd heard that it would basically be a one-month intensive, but somehow I hadn't fully processed the *intensive* part. I'm so behind on my homework—my mom's given me a ton of independent study assignments—but at least the director gave us the day off. How's your weekend going?"

Sirisha smiled shyly behind her ice cream. "Pretty good."

It was only two words, but she'd said them! And she hadn't sounded like a squeaky mouse. Progress. She could take it slow and easy. Not overdo that whole talking thing. Brie's lips, her cedar-brown skin glimmering in sharp contrast to the white tank, her hair a gorgeous thundercloud . . . it was all so electrifying, and Sirisha's toes again warmed from the insides.

"Glad to hear it." Brie nodded to Sirisha's camera, which poked out of her bag. "So what have you been shooting lately?"

This was Sirisha's chance to finally share something of herself.

Nervously, she handed Rani her ice cream cone and pulled out the camera. She stopped at her experiments in overexposure from that morning. More spring flora, insects, and butterflies. No, she couldn't possibly show Brie these. Too boring.

But Brie was already hopping to her side to take a look. "Wow. Those are absolutely gorgeous. I don't know much about photography really, but if that's what you can do with a tree stump . . ."

Seriously? Was she actually impressed? It wasn't possible.

"Oh, you should see her portrait work," Rani said, holding out her phone. "Look at this photo she took of me. And some more of my sisters."

They were the photos Sirisha had taken at the bonfire night at the cove back in September. The firelight flickered on her sisters' faces. A close-up of Nidhi with her dreamy, faraway eyes and wisps of soft curls framing her face. The twins laughing as they pranced on a log, waves glinting in starlight behind them. Four sets of legs crisscrossed in the sand like logs in a fire.

Brie nodded over the pictures. "Wow. I can't believe you were able to get these with such low lighting. You're a master."

Compliments. From Brie. Sirisha's heart skittered and fluttered and did all those silly, wild things hearts did when someone you liked said nice things about your photography.

Now if only she could ask Brie out.

"I'm really excited to see your performance," Sirisha managed. Okay, not actually asking her out. But still. Baby steps.

"Thanks! I'm excited about it, too. I know I'm biased, but the show is so good, you won't believe it. But I'm nervous, too. What if my act is the only one that's terrible? And I only have three weeks left to practice! I should probably go hide in the barn and never come out." Brie covered her face with her hands.

Sirisha was touched that Brie was sharing all this—her innermost fears. It felt like a beginning, especially since Sirisha had shared her photos, her own innermost thoughts. Something could grow between them . . . if only Sirisha would say something helpful in return. She searched for the right words. Elusive bits of speech, which when strung together in phrases created connection.

Brie's friend sauntered back, an iced coffee in hand. She nudged Brie over on the chair with her hip. "Are you freaking out again? You'll be great, hon."

Apparently, Brie didn't need Sirisha's help. She had plenty of friends already.

"If you say so," Brie said. "This is Liza, by the way—I'm staying with her until the play is over."

"Oh yeah, the Songbird sisters," Liza said, waving at them. "We've met a couple times before."

"Hi, Liza," Sirisha and Rani chorused.

It was a small island, and they'd seen Liza around, though not as often as they would have if she went to their high school. Liza and her brother were part of an alternate schooling program offered by the district.

"But seriously, my girl is amazing onstage. She's going to kill it." Liza sipped her coffee and linked arms cozily with Brie.

"If I can survive," Brie said. "My mom's really strict about me keeping up with independent study. She assigns me tons of homework—on top of all the rehearsing! She gave me an English paper this week, can you believe it? I stayed up super late last night writing." She rested her head against her arms on the table, her eyes fluttering shut as she took an exaggerated snooze.

Liza laughed, rubbing Brie's shoulder casually. "You're doing it all, babe."

Sirisha's eyes laser focused on Liza's hand on Brie's shoulder. Were they . . . together? Had she gotten it all wrong? Sirisha'd thought that maybe Brie had been flirting with her. That Brie had been asking her out when she'd said she'd wanted to see the sights of Orcas. But what did she know of love? Real love, not the kind in the movies? She hid behind her ice cream cone, letting everyone else's voices take over. There was no point in speaking, not now.

On the way home, Rani agreed to drive. Thankfully. Sirisha couldn't concentrate on the roads, not when her insides were squooshy goo.

"Liza and Brie are so cute, don't you think?" Rani said, completely oblivious to Sirisha's anguish. "The way Liza wouldn't stop talking about how great Brie is going to be in the performance was so sweet. I want that for you."

"Thanks," Sirisha answered with a sigh.

Through the window, trees and farms and the seaside rushed by. It was starting to drizzle again. She'd known the sunny weather couldn't last. Brie and Liza would be cycling home in this. It would be so romantic, their skin glistening with raindrops, their clothes clinging to their curves. . . .

"I think you're ready to talk to Paola," Rani added. "You've got the right makeup, we've figured out what to do with your hair. You recited that sonnet like a pro. So when are you going to ask her out?"

Sirisha shook her head. "Never."

"Come on, don't be like that." Rani squeezed Sirisha's shoulder. "I know you're shy, but it'll be worth it."

But it wouldn't.

Perhaps it was for the best. It wasn't as if Sirisha would've ever gotten the nerve to talk to her anyway. She'd been trying. But maybe romance wasn't for her. She couldn't flirt the way people did in the movies. When the moment came, she always froze. Her words sticky as ice cream fingers.

Rani pulled up to the Songbird as dark gray clouds menaced the sea below. Sirisha stumbled out of the car. Tears threatening to burst.

"Sorry I wasted your time, Rani," she said. "But I don't think I can talk to Paola or . . . or anyone."

"Sirisha . . ."

But Sirisha shook her head and ran inside. To hide in her room. And never, ever come out.

Chapter Six

*L*ocals loved pointing out that the San Juans actually received fewer inches of precipitation annually than New York. The PNW had a bad rep, they'd exclaim. What they were conveniently omitting: the tally of legitimately sunny days. Spoiler alert: There were very few.

Naturally, Sirisha's experimentation with flora drenched in sunshine came to an abrupt end when the sun fled the area for more suitable climes. A Monday cloudscape turned into a Tuesday drizzle that grew into a Wednesday, Thursday, and Friday of true rain. The kind that caused creeks to swell; the kind that seeped into your waterproof boots; the kind that would ruin a camera.

Not exactly the weather that most of the kids on the island had hoped for during spring break. As others in her class lamented missing out on swimming or boating or bike rides, Sirisha lamented her lack of photographic inspiration. By Friday afternoon, she still had no clue how to create a story with her photos. She lounged in the dining room, cradling a white chocolate mocha in her palms. The sound of rain lashed against the window, a lyric of heartbreak and dejection.

This was the last day she'd allowed herself to wallow. The last day to nurture the dark thoughts gathering inside her like rain clouds. Brie had a girlfriend. Brie had been charming and funny because that was simply who she was. Not because she'd returned Sirisha's squishy feelings.

"Penny for your thoughts?" Nidhi eased into the seat across from her.

Sirisha shrugged. "Just feeling kind of blah."

"I'm sorry. Anything I can do?" Nidhi glanced out the window. Instead of selecting a table with a view of the sea, Sirisha had picked one facing north. The barn.

"I don't want to talk about it." She sipped her mocha, the creamy white chocolate a balm for her slightly fractured heart.

Neither of them said anything for a minute, and her big sis didn't push. Sirisha chewed on a piece of shortbread, letting the sugary sweetness coat her tongue.

Ping. An alert on Nidhi's phone.

"Grayson?" Sirisha swallowed. She was so freaking lonely. Being an introvert didn't stop you from feeling that way.

"Actually," Nidhi said, "I've been chatting with some of our relatives in India."

"You have?" Sirisha was surprised.

First, Lalita Phua had come out of the woodwork. Now Nidhi was in contact with more of their extended family? Sirisha wasn't certain how she felt about it all. She had a fuzzy memory, one that seemed to return even as it drifted further away. Dad in the library, pacing. A phone conversation. Heated voices. Maybe even some tears.

She'd been all of seven years old.

She hadn't told her sisters about it. She hadn't told anyone.

"Apparently, our cousin Prakash built this app." Nidhi pointed to a laughing face icon on her phone. "It's called Chatterbox."

Nidhi clicked it, revealing a rushing river of GIFs and chatter from lots of Indian names Sirisha didn't recognize.

"These are our relatives?"

"Yep. Turns out we have a big family! Even though Dad doesn't have siblings, he has plenty of first and second cousins—our aunts and uncles—and they've had lots of kids of their own. Want me to send you an invite for the app?"

Did she?

Angry voices crowded her head.

Her heart.

She didn't know what the argument on the phone had been about when she was seven. But the calls and letters had fallen away after that.

"We don't really know what happened with Dad," Nidhi said, as if reading her thoughts. "I know you think it had to do with Pop, but it could have been time and distance that made us lose touch. Also, obviously he didn't lose complete contact, since he had Lalita Phua's current email address."

Nidhi was right. Sirisha was making her own assumptions.

And it wasn't as if she had to get close. She could suspend her judgment for now. "Sure, send me the invite."

A few minutes later, Chatterbox was on her phone. It was a little overwhelming. Names and relationships she didn't yet know. Family shots on cellphone cameras. A nine-month-old happily munching on mushed peas. An uncle glowing after his son was accepted to a prestigious university. A family posing in front of their bungalow. So. Many. Cousins. Fashionistas, politicos, tech geeks like Prakash. Those who liked books and art and philosophy, too.

"Well, are you going to introduce yourself?" Nidhi asked, watching her.

"Umm . . ."

Nidhi patted her shoulder. "I'm helping Dad with some dinner prep, but maybe you could show them some of your photography? They've been really interested in learning more about us."

Sirisha nodded. Soon, it was just her and a quiet dining room. A barn through a window. An app full of messages. Entering that space felt like entering a crowd. Her throat closing up. Words in a tangle.

If she wanted to introduce herself, she'd have to do it with her photography.

If.

Saturday, between helping out with breakfast in the restaurant and her late afternoon shift at the front desk, Sirisha found an hour to spare for a walk. Camera and tripod in hand, she had an idea. For a self-portrait.

It wasn't just for those relatives on Chatterbox. Ever since she'd seen the San Juan Snaps blue ribbon winner in photography club, she'd been playing with the idea of attempting a self-portrait of her own. A way to state who she was with a single photo.

Sirisha hiked along the cliffside trail again. Jagged edges. Raging waves. Wind-tossed wild hair. She stopped at the reaching madrone, with its gnarled branches yearning. At the edge of a steep precipice, only sea and sky beyond.

She set up the tripod. Selected a lens. Adjusted the manual controls. And then, she contorted herself so she was lined up with the tree and its reaching branches. Knees low. Hips thrust back. Spine bent. Stretching forward like a dancer.

Sirisha was careful, of course—uninterested in becoming one of those selfie-taking casualties reported in the news. She repeated the pose with a variety of camera settings. Hoping that one would take in edges and shadows, lighting and composition, framing and focal depth in a way that would truly tell a story. Her story.

Though a part of her was afraid, too. Afraid that she didn't really have a story to tell. Afraid that she was a boring blur in the background, that she'd never be able to take focus.

On the way back to the inn, Sirisha spotted Avani and Rani with lunch trays, heading for the barn. A chore Sirisha had explicitly been avoiding over the break. Nidhi had happened to leave her phone open to the Thousand Shores rehearsal schedule, and Sirisha had happened to memorize it. They were working this weekend and didn't have many days off—the next one was on the following Wednesday.

Her stomach rumbled as the scent of sandwiches fluttered under her nose. Pumpernickel, ciabatta, and delicious herby focaccia. Nidhi had been baking away. And Sirisha was feeling good, a little more herself. A self-portrait was something like an exercise in self-love, and it made her feel she could actually handle seeing Brie. Who was just a nice friendly girl, after all. One who wasn't single.

Plus, Sirisha wasn't allowed to wallow anymore.

"Need any help?" she asked the twins, feeling at once brave and foolish.

"Sure." Avani dumped an entire tray in Sirisha's arms, leaving herself empty-handed.

"Hey!"

"What?" Avani smiled impishly.

Inside the barn, Sirisha's skin immediately tingled with anticipation. The lighting had transformed the space. The set pieces were taking shape. Eclectic costumes shimmered on a rack.

Onstage, a modern apartment in bold colors. Two women rehearsing. An argument, filled with poetic soliloquies and lyrical insults. Beautiful swirling lethal words. No costumes or makeup yet, and there were occasional mistakes and hiccups. At one point, one of the actresses couldn't deliver her line because she was laughing too hard. But then, a moment later, she was back on track.

Yet despite its roughness, the piece stole into Sirisha's soul. It featured two queer women of color, and that was integral to who they were, of course, but the scene wasn't focused on race or queerness. Instead, it portrayed their joys and hurts. Their love and exasperation for each other. Both characters were unique, each with their own flaws and their moments of grace.

The act ended with a frantic kiss.

Ethereal and earthy at once.

Raw.

How Sirisha longed for passion like that.

The troupe had moved her when she saw them the year before, but somehow the feeling was so much more acute now that she was seeing them behind the scenes, without all the impeccable lighting and costumes.

Without their scripts rehearsed to perfection. There was something so powerful about it, about the half-finished enchantment that was still in the making.

Next to her, Avani and Rani hooted and clapped. The actresses blew kisses at them and bowed. The cast went about their work; they'd probably seen it all a thousand times before. As Sirisha walked back to the inn with her sisters, Avani and Rani raved about the troupe. Apparently, they'd seen many of the sketches while delivering snacks and treats, offering water. Sirisha realized she'd been missing out as she'd sought to avoid Brie, and that truly was a sad thing. She thirsted for more—and she was intensely curious about Brie's act, too.

That evening, Sirisha couldn't stop thinking about that snippet she'd witnessed. A story told in a fight between lovers. A slice of life painted with a few minutes, a few pages of a script. Could she tell a story with even less? With no words, only a moment frozen in time?

Diving into her self-portrait shots, she discarded the ones where her features were too crisp, the lighting far too traditional. Instead, she found herself coming back to one in which she was bathed in warm sunlight, slightly washed out. Another experiment in overexposure. She converted it to black and white, darkened the shadows of the tree framing her. The madrone anchored her. Spotlit her. The way she usually hated being centered.

It didn't reveal all. It was simply a glimmer, a yawning moment in the timeline of her life. Fifteen years under her belt and many more to go.

Everything else a secret that remained hers.

Sirisha loved it. Irrationally, wholeheartedly, perhaps a bit too much.

With some trepidation, she closed her eyes. Uploaded it to Chatterbox. Captioning it only, "Hi all, Sirisha here."

Now what? She added the waving emoji, for good measure.

In moments, there were gushing responses, from aunts, uncles, cousins. Great-aunts and great-uncles. Not that she needed validation, but her heart did swell a bit. She wasn't Boring Wallflower Sirisha; she felt mysterious and powerful. A force to be reckoned with.

A DM pinged from a cousin named Sona. *What a shot! Did you hire a professional to take it?*

The cozy warm feeling expanded in Sirisha's belly. *Actually, it was a self-portrait.*

Sona: *That's amazing. Seriously, the lighting is out of this world. What kind of camera do you have?*

It turned out sixteen-year-old Sona was also a photography geek. They chatted, discussing their dream equipment, their favorite styles, other photographers. Sona sent her shots of the streets of New Delhi. Markets, shopping centers. Busy, busy streets full of motorcycles, cars, cabs, rickshaws. And so many people. Sirisha admired Sona's skill. The way in one shot she'd homed in on a family of four piled on a motorcycle, features crisp even in motion, the dizzy lights of other cars speeding past in the background.

In return, Sirisha shared with Sona her recent love of overexposed photos, sun-drenched flora, the way it left traces and outlines of her subjects.

Sirisha: *But my teacher says I need more to win the contest. That my photos need to tell a story.*

Sona: *That makes sense. But remember, a story can be big or small. With my city shots, I wanted to tell one about the vibrancy and vitality of New*

Delhi. I know we've got all these issues—pollution, traffic, poverty. But I wanted to capture more than that. Because we ARE more than that. I started with shots of families and regular people. I think they're important. But lately, I've wanted to go beyond showing what things are—I want to portray a hint at what COULD be.

Sirisha: *What do you mean?*

Sona sent more photographs of the vibrant streets of New Delhi. But these were of protests spilling into the streets. For laborers on the brink of losing everything. For sexual assault survivors. For religious minorities. And, yes, even for LGBTQIA+ rights. Sirisha knew the government had at times cracked down hard on the protesters, that democratic norms of the free press and the right to protest had not always been upheld. That was true in the United States, too. But she could see with her own eyes from Sona's collection that—like the US—India was certainly no static place.

She didn't know what had happened with Dad and his relatives eight years ago, whether whatever had come between them had to do with Pop. But it had been so long, and things were changing. People were fighting.

And Sona was a small part of that—documenting it, boosting it.

Sirisha: *Wow. Your work is so inspiring.*

Unlike Sirisha's spring flora collection. Sigh.

But her cousin, from half a world away, somehow knew just what push to give.

Sona: *There must be something that excites you. What do you want to tell the world? What do you want to CHANGE about it?*

Chapter Seven

The idea came to Sirisha in the dead of night.

She awoke with her heart pounding. Her room grainy with darkness. The moon luminous through the delicately patterned window sheers. Her skin clammy, her cheeks flushed. Her pajamas damp with unfocused dreams.

Scenes from the Thousand Shores danced in that space between slumber and rousing. Not just their acts, but their prep. The mess of extra set pieces, the tangle of costumes, the glitz of the light board. Players running through lines, the director adjusting blocking. The sound master engrossed in the slamming of a door and the slapping splash of water.

They were individuals, but together they were creating something. Joining voices to tell a thousand different stories. Queer stories, disabled stories, Black and brown stories. Asian stories and Native stories. Stories from the unheard.

Sirisha yearned to tell a story, too. A story about them. A story that was also about her.

Early the next morning, Sirisha rushed into the twins' room. Rani was in the shower, and Avani was scribbling a poem in her journal. Sirisha tried to steal a peek.

"Excuse me!" Avani shut it closed. "Do you need something?"

Sirisha sat on the bed beside her sister, her camera strap looped around her neck, her equipment ready to go in her backpack. The troupe was working again today, and she was anxious to put her dead-of-the-night idea into action.

"The lighting is so great this morning. I just have to work on my portfolio." Sirisha deliberately left out the tidbit that most of her shoot would be indoors. "Would you mind trading chores with me? I'll take extra evenings this week."

"Yeah, sure," Avani said. "Actually, that works perfectly—you can take my afternoon shift at the front desk so I can spend time with Fernando. Although . . . I'm not looking forward to serving brunch on the last day of spring break. Seattleites thinking of going home are always kinda grouchy."

Sirisha nodded. "I owe you one."

Avani patted her shoulder with a slightly evil look. "Don't worry, I'll collect."

"Sounds ominous." Sirisha laughed, pretending to run away with her camera.

Okay, she was actually running. But when she stepped outside the Songbird in the morning light, her plans suddenly loomed a bit too large. What was she thinking? She couldn't exactly take photos of the troupe in secret. They might not want cameras in their theater. She'd have to ask for permission.

And that would require speaking.

Sirisha's throat tickled at the thought. She was squeaking even in her own head.

As she waited for the troupe to arrive, she started with preliminary shots of the barn's exterior. It was a cloudy morning, the light soft and diffused. Not long later, cars began pulling up in the lot. Sirisha pretended she was taking photos of chickens and the inn. While actually capturing the troupe's morning joie de vivre. Coffee-in-hand quips. Sleepy eyes from those who weren't natural early birds.

Then she zoomed in on Liza dropping off Brie.

Who was still beautiful.

Still taken.

And before she could hide, Brie's face was large and looming in her lens. No zoom necessary.

"Hey," Brie said cheerfully. "I haven't seen you around much. Just when you came in briefly yesterday during Justine and Kat's rehearsal, but you disappeared before I had a chance to say hi."

What Sirisha wanted to say: "Oh, you know, I've been really busy during spring break. You see, I had to . . ." (Insert mysterious and alluring spring break anecdotes.)

What she actually said: "Ermrillybusy."

"Yeah, I heard the inn was overrun with tourists on break," Brie acknowledged. "Well, I hope you come watch more of the rehearsals.

Only two weeks to showtime, and we need audience reactions. Honestly, I could also use some moral support when I'm up. We're practicing my act later this morning. Can you make it?" Her eyes were earnest.

Sirisha flushed warm, her heart doing the usual things it did around Brie. It seemed like a big deal that Brie was asking her to come. Or was any old audience reaction good enough? And of course, what about Liza?

But she didn't ask those things. Instead, managed to chirp, "Sure."

Good thing she'd asked for the morning off.

Brie hugged her enthusiastically. "Thanks!"

Again, confusing! Was Brie with Liza or not? Why didn't people write their relationship status on their foreheads? That would make things much simpler.

Sirisha hurried back inside, through the busy dining room. As Avani had predicted, the last day of spring break meant breakfast was pure chaos. Too many orders of eggs Benedict, overstuffed suitcases, ferry schedules, and long lines at the dock. Rani and Avani raced to fill orders, while Nidhi rushed to make drinks at the espresso bar.

"Want me to put together a continental breakfast for the troupe?" Sirisha asked.

Busy as she was, Nidhi paused. A smile played across her lips. "I thought Avani said she was covering morning chores."

Sirisha's face burned. "Yeah, well I just wanted to help. . . ."

Nidhi nodded gravely. "I see. Yeah, go for it." She gestured to the ridiculous amount of baked goods under the bar. "Everything's ready. It'll probably take a couple of trips."

Sirisha could feel Nidhi's knowing eyes on her as she put together a tray. She was impressed that her big sis wasn't demanding more explanation. No invasive inquisition, not even a peep.

Not that this was about Brie, of course. This was about her portfolio.

Orange juice and the aroma of dark roast French press. Bananas, blueberries, sliced honeydew. Pastries glistening with jam, almonds, or cream cheese. Organic yogurt and local-made granola. Thick-cut brioche. Plates and cups and napkins. A hungry cast.

"You're spoiling us. I don't think we've met before—I'm Loretta. The director. They/them pronouns." An imposing figure with curly brown ringlets and a bright smile stuck out a hand.

Sirisha shook it bashfully. "I'm Sirisha. She/her pronouns. And I'm . . . abigfanoftheThousandShores."

It felt good to say it aloud, even if she did rush it. She wanted to say more, about how the troupe's variety act meant the world to her. How her family had watched them during Spring Fest last year. How she'd seen herself represented for the first time. But as usual, her tongue tied itself into a knot. Those few sentences were all she'd had in her.

"This is my first year directing," Loretta said, "but I was a fan first. I was nervous about taking it over since they've been going strong for nearly seven years now. But my partner told me I had to do it."

Sirisha was dying to ask Loretta how they could be confident enough to take over directing a company that had been receiving so much critical acclaim. Sirisha wouldn't have had the nerve. Not that she'd have the nerve to direct anything.

"I know you're probably busy helping your dad at the inn," Loretta continued, "but feel free to stay for the rehearsal if you have time. And you're all invited to the main event, no charge. Your dad's discount for letting us rent this place—and providing meals on top of that—has been absolutely great for our shoestring budget."

Sirisha nodded. "Noproblem."

Loretta selected a lemon poppy seed muffin, poured a coffee with a splash of cream, and started shooting off instructions to get rehearsal started. Meanwhile, Sirisha was still standing there, in awe. But then she remembered. The awe was the reason she'd come. The reason she'd been so determined to document all this.

The good thing about being quiet as a mouse was that people didn't tend to notice you. She worked her way around the room. Took candids of the cast and crew at work. The costume assistant in a sparkly vest sewing a new Peter Pan collar on an old dress. A set designer in jeans and two long pigtails painting the starry blackness over a cityscape. Baritones and tenors serenading the chickens outside with a catchy a cappella number. The prop master with a mohawk checking inventory. A thespian with smoky makeup and gold lipstick waiting in the shadows behind the curtain for their cue.

Rehearsal continued, and the morning fell away as Sirisha worked. She wasn't focused on the performances, but the people behind them. The act of creation itself was fascinating: how they took a script and made it come alive with colors and flavors and sounds and textures.

"Hey," called a voice behind her. "What are you doing?"

Startled, Sirisha whirled to find Loretta staring at her, hands on hips. "Um . . ."

"Photos aren't allowed in here," Loretta said.

"Um . . ."

Sirisha knew she should have asked for permission. But she'd been scared. Now she scrambled for words. To explain, to convince. To beg.

Unfortunately, more eyes were on her. A lot of other eyes. One pair in particular, belonging to Brie. Who smiled encouragingly. But that only froze Sirisha further.

A lump blossomed in her throat.

A guilty silence.

"I've seen her work," Brie cut in finally. "She's an amazing photographer. Really talented."

Brie was backing her up? Brie was backing her up! They locked eyes. With just a raising of her eyebrows, Brie seemed to understand all those words tripping over each other in Sirisha's mind, the ones she couldn't yet speak.

Meanwhile, Loretta eyed her camera. "Let me see your pictures."

"Um . . ." Sirisha flipped through a few shots on the LCD screen.

It had taken her a while to find the right lens. The right settings for shutter speed and exposure that would work in the low lighting of the barn. But eventually, she'd figured out the best ways to capture the warm gold spotlight. The yellows and reds and blues from the light board. The grainy noise of the shadows only added to the atmosphere. And she was intent on making the thespians look good, to lovingly bring out their natural skin tones—gorgeous shades of tans and olives, pinks and beiges, a wide spectrum of lovely browns. They all deserved to stand out.

"These do look really professional." Loretta said, blinking at her. "What were you going to use them for?"

Okay, Sirisha couldn't let words fail her now. It was amazing that Brie believed in her work, but Sirisha needed to stick up for herself, too.

She took a breath. *Talk slow, talk slow, talk slow. Enunciate.*

Heart aflutter. Words curling like ribbons. Photos of glamour and sparkle.

Talk slow, talk slow, talk slow. Enunciate.

"Um . . . I wanted to . . . usethemfortheSanJuanSnapsPhotography-Contest." Okay, not exactly slow, but she'd gotten it out. "My photography club teacher . . . um"—*cough, choke*—". . . wantsmetotellastory."

Sirisha couldn't believe it! It was rushed, but she'd managed to tell someone what she wanted and what she needed. Someone she'd only met today. That was huge.

Brie nodded encouragingly.

"You should have asked for permission first," Loretta returned.

Truth.

"Sorry," Sirisha squeaked. There was another drawn-out silence.

But Brie didn't let it stretch. "Don't you think we need promotional photos? Our social media posts have been all text and graphics, but they say that faces get the most clicks. You said yourself that Sirisha's work looks professional."

Again, they locked eyes. Brie seemed to get how important it was to her. No words needed.

Loretta glanced back at the camera. "They really are good, and it would be a shame not to use them. Hiring someone would eat into our budget . . ."

Sirisha held her breath, hoping, hoping, hoping. Every inch of her skin tingling.

"Okay," Loretta finally said. "You can use them for your contest, but you have to get each photo approved by me first. And you have to let me pick some to use for promotional material. Deal?"

Sirisha squealed. "Thankyouthankyouthankyou!"

"And don't even think of using the flash," Loretta added sternly.

"Wouldn'tdreamofit." Sirisha's heels bounced.

After the director returned to the front row with their clipboard, Brie high-fived her. "Way to go! Loretta can be tough, but they're fair. My act is coming up. Can you stay to watch?"

Sirisha nodded. She was all out of coherent sentences, but hopefully her face said everything. She was happy. Grateful. Excited. She had her story for the portfolio, and she could help the troupe. Be a small part of this fantastical, whimsical, and absolutely thrilling world.

"Breakaleg!" she said to Brie.

A fairy tale princess. Locked in a tower. Long hair tumbling down.

An escape that Rapunzel engineers herself.

The act was still vaguely shaped. A rehearsal without costumes and makeup. Forgotten lines. Random interruptions. Sound checks. Yet even still, Brie's lead part was fun and funny, the dialogue shimmering under the stage lights. Sirisha did her best to capture that half-woven magic. The spell of something in the making, theatrical carpentry in the works.

Click. Click. Click.

Soon Brie was set to deliver her final lines. Her showdown with the queen.

She allowed a pregnant pause to hang in the air.

Expectant with power.

"You're a bully," Brie said, her voice echoing across the converted auditorium. "You're a bully because you're scared. Well, take a good look. This is me; this is who I am. A princess who is about to take you down."

Sirisha shivered. Words were a curse for her, but for Brie/Rapunzel they were a weapon that could cut. A machete that could slash open a new trail. She longed for that same power. And yet Sirisha knew she had power of her own. This time, her portfolio would tell the world what she felt. What she wanted and what she needed.

Just as she'd miraculously been able to tell Loretta.

When the act ended, Sirisha hurried out of the barn, late for lunch duty. A hand touched her shoulder. "Can I see your photos?"

It was Brie, looking glossy and glamorous as always.

What Sirisha wanted to say: "Sure, I love the ones from your act. You were so empowering and beautiful. I hope I captured some of that."

What she actually said: (unintelligible squeak)

But Brie leaned close, her scent of citrus and wildflowers tickling Sirisha's nose. Sirisha's hand trembled ever so slightly as she pulled up the shots. Brie with her long Rapunzel wig. Brie in a tower. Brie yearning for adventure and stories of her own to tell. Brie looking for love.

Or Brie's character, anyway. Sigh.

"Youwerebrilliant!" Sirisha squealed at the same time as Brie said, "These are incredible!"

They both looked at each other and laughed.

"No, really," Brie said. "I usually hate being photographed, but you've somehow managed to make me get over myself. I'm so glad we're going to use these for promo instead of just graphics and random cell phone shots." She wrinkled her nose.

"Thanks," Sirisha said shyly. "For helping me convince Loretta."

"No problem!" Brie messed with her dress. Another floral number. Soft linen. Black and cream. "I was so nervous to go up there, but then James told me about this ritual he does before going onstage . . ."

Brie hadn't seemed nervous at all, despite what she'd said—today, and back at Lulu's. Sirisha wondered if someday she, too, could hide all those skittering feelings inside her, if she could learn to act confident even when she felt the opposite.

"He got it from his father who was in the military, who would do it before going into action. The truth is when you get up there . . . Oh, listen to me! I'm just chattering away, not letting you get a word in edgewise!"

"'Sokay," Sirisha said, her face heating.

Heart pitter-pattering. Toes toasty.

Oh, those toes. Would they ever warm for anyone else the same way?

"Well, again, thank you," Brie said, breaking the silence. "Not just for making me look good. For coming to the rehearsal. I really appreciate the support."

"Ofcourse," Sirisha replied too quickly.

Brie reached out for a hug; Sirisha met her halfway. It felt good, and now she caught the even subtler scents of theater dust and old costumes, of dreams and stories and performances under glittering lights. Of standing ovations, even.

Sirisha skipped back into the Songbird.

Heart still pitter-pattering.

Toes still toasty.

Chapter Eight

With opening day approaching fast, the troupe lived and breathed theater. Rehearsals ran throughout the day and now late into the evenings, 9 or even 10 p.m. Rain or shine, they practiced. A mixture of breathless anticipation and excess energy mingled together like salt and fresh waters in the Salish Sea.

Some of the other Spring Fest productions were opening to audiences later in the week, and Loretta was determined to make the Thousand Shores performance stand out among the competition. They were so busy, Sirisha took over their social media, posting photos that hinted at the magic brewing in a barn behind an inn at the edge of the sea.

The more photos she took, the more she wanted. Kenneth the costume designer's attention to detail as he patched up a ripped blouse. Luke the lighting guy at his booth, reading a playwriting guide as he waited for a cue. Loretta's pained look when someone forgot a line. Cast members hanging out behind the barn after a performance, that moment when they took off their stage faces. The moment of exhalation.

Sirisha loved that moment.

The Monday before opening day, she caught Brie in it. In her Rapunzel costume. With stage makeup. Soft eyes. Her lips relaxed out of her usual smile.

Click. Click. Click.

Dusk fell like bits of silver and indigo confetti around Brie as she took a seat on an old tree stump, her arms crossed against the sea breeze that had meandered past the inn. Others were outside, too, chatting and laughing. Discussing anything but the play. Tired eyes and weary feet. Sirisha hid behind a tree, hoping the evening shadows would keep her from having to say anything. Hoping the opposite at the same time.

Crack.

Oops. She'd stepped on a twig.

"Sirisha?" Brie squinted. "Is that you?"

So much for remaining in the background. Sirisha stepped toward Brie. Goose bumps traveled down her arms. She gulped. "Justmoreshotsformyportfolio."

Brie laughed her tinkling bell of a laugh. "You don't have to hide in the brush."

Sirisha swallowed. "Right."

Brie patted the space beside her on the stump. "Come. Sit with me. I could use some company."

Another chance. Sirisha didn't want to blow it, so she plopped down next to Brie.

Oh, how she yearned to just *talk* to Brie, the way she did with her sisters. About everything and nothing. About hopes and dreams and TV shows and pop songs. Conversation that could splash and frolic in an April creek. Not get pulled under the unforgiving current.

But Brie didn't try to break the silence with chatter. Surprisingly, it wasn't awkward, either. Brie's face was serene, if a bit tired. They'd both seen so much of each other in the past week, and each time they locked eyes in the barn, Sirisha had felt . . . understood. Without explanation, without words.

Even now, they let the shadows around them dance and twirl, not needing more. They were alone but not alone in the glinting twilight. Everyone else fading into the surprisingly chill evening air. The whispering of the pines and maples. A ballad of crickets serenading them.

And Sirisha thought that perhaps silence had its own power, too.

Sirisha whipped fresh cream in the stand mixer. Scraped in vanilla bean seeds. Zested a little orange. She could see why Nidhi liked baking so much. It was comforting. A temporary reprieve from the ghost of flickering golden moments. She'd been at rehearsals whenever she could after school and between inn chores. Oh, how the new project had taken over her heart, so completely immersing. Invigorating. Intoxicating.

She'd also caught Brie on that stump several evenings over the week, lovely quiet moments. Sometimes Brie talked about the show or homework. Sometimes Sirisha showed her the day's photos. But often, they just sat. And Sirisha wanted to dwell in that silence, to breathe it in like the citrus scent of Brie's hair. Still, she knew that there was more to Brie, swirling depths under turquoise sunlit seas. And to reach those depths, she'd have to swim. She'd have to speak.

"You seem quiet tonight," Nidhi commented.

"Just thinking."

Friday had brought more guests to the Songbird as people flocked to Spring Fest events all over the islands. A ballet, a puppet show, several concerts. Sirisha was helping Nidhi with a chocolate cake for a wine and cheese event that included poetry readings and an open mic. The Thousand Shores would open their act tomorrow, and Sirisha's insides were squishy goo once again. They'd blow the audience away, she was certain. But a week after that, they'd scatter to the four winds.

Just as she was beginning to feel a part of something, she'd be on her own again.

"Looks great—stop the mixer," Nidhi instructed. "And thinking about what?"

"Oh, you know." Sirisha peered at the whipped cloud as if it might hold answers to her destiny. "Just about life. Next year. I still can't believe you'll be gone. A whole semester in India—it's so cool, I know, but I'm going to miss you."

Nidhi lathered the whipped cream onto her sumptuous cake. "I know it seems strange. It does to me, too. But I'm always here for you, even when I'm on the other side of the planet. I promise, I'll hop on video chat if you need anything."

What Sirisha wanted to say: "But that's not enough! I can't handle high school! Crushes! Girls! Aahhhhhh!"

What she actually said: "Thanks."

In any case, maybe now was the time to start solving her own problems. As Nidhi continued to sculpt the whipped cream over the cake, Sirisha pulled out her phone.

Typed into the search bar. *How to talk to girls.*

"HOW TO TALK TO GIRLS?" Rani exclaimed, her face suddenly appearing just over Sirisha's shoulder.

Sirisha's entire body flashed hot and cold as she quickly hid her phone. "Where did you come from?"

"Dad sent us to check on the cake," Avani said from behind Rani. "So, I guess Rani's romance lessons weren't enough, huh?"

"Excuse me!" Rani huffed. "I prepared you for any scenario. And here you are, no lipstick, wearing those ugly leggings I thought I tossed, and googling nonsense on the internet instead of asking your big sisters."

"These are my lucky leggings!" Sirisha protested. "And my lipstick . . . wore off."

Rani squinted. "Likely story."

"We just want to help." Nidhi patted Sirisha's shoulder. "It's not like I have a ton of experience—but I think it's nice if you're both into each other's passions." She carefully added the next layer of cake, then spread another layer of whipped cream. "When we met, I first fell in love with Grayson's artwork. And he said my baking was an art in itself. It meant so much to me that someone understood. On top of that, we both desperately want to travel and see the world. We always have something to talk about."

"Well, that's no problem," Rani said. "You and Paola can geek out about apertures and g-stops."

"It's f-stops," Sirisha corrected.

"Whatever." Rani rummaged through the second fridge and popped open a locally made blackberry soda.

Nidhi glanced curiously at Rani, then raised a brow at Sirisha. *Paola?*

Just as Rani and Avani had their occasional twin mind melds, Sirisha and Nidhi didn't always need words to communicate. Sirisha's lips twitched. *Come on, you know Rani would blab it to the entire troupe.*

Nidhi shrugged. *Good point.*

Meanwhile, Avani grabbed a spoon and stole some whipped cream before Nidhi could stop her. "Fresh vanilla beans? Yum. Anyway, my advice is not to force it. Things happen when you least expect it. Who knew that Fernando and I would get trapped in a barn because of a baby goat and have to huddle together for warmth in a snowstorm?"

Sirisha giggled. "It was a heated barn, I think. But it was pretty epic. Can anyone arrange to trap me somewhere with a gorgeous girl?"

Rani raised her hand. "Oh, I'll totally do it. Because all this don't-force-it stuff is terrible advice!"

"Hey!" Avani poked her twin.

"It's true." Rani poked her back. "Avani got lucky, but the rest of us have to actively pursue love. I mean, did SRK just sit around in England hoping Kajol wouldn't get married? No, he fought for her. He didn't just leave her hanging, unkissed at sunrise on a hammock—"

"Wait, are you talking about Raj/SRK from *DDLJ* or Raj Mehta from last summer?" Avani asked.

"Raj Mehta?" Rani asked. "Never heard of him."

Avani rolled her eyes. Sirisha hid a smile. They'd all heard plenty about Raj and Rani's non-kiss last summer. It was clear that Rani hadn't exactly moved on, no matter how hard she pretended.

Rani huffed. "I'm just saying, inaction is the worst. You have to fight for the person you like. You have to show them that you care. Unless you want to end up lonely *forever*."

Sirisha shivered.

Like a panther closing in on its prey, Rani leaned forward and mouthed, *Lonely forever*, again.

Avani rolled her eyes. "You're a little scary."

"Scary good at getting people together," Rani corrected. "But seriously, you're ready, Sirisha. Just say, 'Hey, girl, you're as beautiful as a new telephoto lens.'"

Avani giggled. "Hey, baby, my shots of the sunsets over the sea are nothing compared to your eyes."

"I think I broke my lens." Nidhi grinned as she grated chocolate shavings over the cake. "Because, honey, everything is a blur except for you."

Sirisha chuckled. "That's actually pretty good."

"Yo, babe," Rani said, "I've got a great idea for a horizontal landscape, if you know what I mean."

They all cracked up.

"You're terrible!"

"I'm brilliant."

Her sisters continued with more and more silly pickup lines, and Sirisha couldn't stop giggling. She even came up with one of her own: "Hey, girl, I think I know what's missing in my portfolio. It doesn't have a single picture of us in it."

She'd never say that, obviously. But possibly, just *possibly*, she'd been too focused on looking cool for Brie. Could pursuing a girl actually be fun?

Eventually, Amir popped into the kitchen. "Hey, your dad sent me to check on the dessert . . . What's so funny?"

Oops, they'd forgotten all about the cake.

"Oh, you know, we're just coming up with the world's worst pickup lines," Avani said. "Got any?"

Amir thought for a moment, scratching his short beard. "I think I need a new contact lens prescription. Because no one could look as gorgeous as you."

"Nice!" Avani high-fived him. "Is that what you used on Dad?"

"No . . . but I can try it out right now."

Rani clapped. "Oh, I've got to see this!"

Nidhi arranged the decadent chocolate affair on a beautiful glass display case, Sirisha gathered plates, and Amir helpfully grabbed forks and napkins. Together, the Singh sisters and Amir made their way to the Songbird's living room. Where people mingled, soft blues played, a fire blazed, rain pattered on the windows. Fernando had brought an elaborate display of Gutiérrez Farm cheese. Avani winked at him as Amir used his line on Dad.

Who absolutely glowed in reaction.

Later that evening, Sirisha sorted large prints of her portfolio. A laptop was fine and all, but she loved the blown-up images on matte photo paper. Her photo printer was another one of those expensive purchases that had left her wardrobe in a state of neglect. But completely worth it.

In her tiny third-floor bedroom, Sirisha pulled down her old photographs to make space for the new ones. Big, dark images from the barn-turned-auditorium contrasted nicely with her cream-colored wall. As she attempted to create a meaningful order, she pondered her sisters' advice when it came to affairs of the heart. Though they'd all said wildly different things, there was a kernel of truth in each of their points of view.

Nidhi had said how important it was to care about each other's passions. And she was right: Brie had told Sirisha that it meant a lot that she'd come to her rehearsal. And Sirisha was so excited and grateful when Brie had helped her convince Loretta to let her take photos of the troupe.

Avani had said not to force it. That things would come when you least expected it. That was true, too, like that first quiet moment they'd had on the tree stump. Neither of them had said a word, but it had been wonderful. And then it had become almost a ritual for her and Brie, something she never could have planned or forced.

Rani, of course, had said to push yourself to make love happen. And she was also right; if Sirisha never bothered to try with Brie, she'd never even have a chance. The only way to find out if Brie liked her romantically was to ask.

She'd do it tomorrow, Sirisha told herself. Opening day.

"Hi, honey," Dad said, carrying a slice of leftover cake from the event. He stopped, noticing the photos on the wall. "Wow. Those are amazing."

"What do you think?" Sirisha asked. "I'm still working on arranging the right build."

He moved closer to the wall, peering closely at each image and offering his thoughts on the lighting, the composition, the use of shadow. He noticed just the things she'd hoped he would. How the costume designer was working while the rest of the crew crowded around the lunch offerings behind him. How the lighting guy had a half-written script on his desk. Loretta dancing at the foot of the stage when everyone was focused on the actors in the spotlight.

He came to a stop at a picture of Brie. Decked out in full Rapunzel costume and makeup, including the wig, of course. One shot showed her hovering behind the curtain, waiting. And then in the next, she's onstage, leaning out of the plywood tower. Her arms spread wide, eyes sparkling. Luminous.

Dad surveyed the two images. "She's so confident onstage. But I love how you caught the moment before. Where she's nervous."

"To me, it just looks like she's waiting."

"Are you sure?"

Sirisha pored over the picture, realizing Dad had caught something she hadn't: Brie clutching the curtain, her fingers in a tight fist.

Oh wow.

She'd somehow caught that secret other side of Brie. Of course, they'd talked about her apprehension of the big day so many times, but Brie almost never outwardly showed it, at least not once she was onstage. And a part of Sirisha still hadn't really, completely believed it, couldn't fathom it in someone who seemed as together as Brie. Someone who weaved so many tales and jokes without even trying. And yet, clearly Brie had her moments of vulnerability, too.

Maybe Brie wasn't born a star.

Maybe she had to work at it, just as Sirisha had to work at speaking up.

Dad swiped a forkful of whipped cream with chocolate shavings off the top of the cake. He savored the bite with a look of pure indulgence. "Great work, honey. I think the judges will be really impressed by my brilliant daughter."

"Thanks." Sirisha smiled. "By the way, it's been really fun talking with our relatives online. We're using this app one of our cousins made called Chatterbox. Nidhi, Avani, Rani, and I are all on it now. In fact, Sona Didi was the one who gave me the idea to shoot the troupe."

"I'm glad you're getting to know them," Dad said. "Even though we lost touch, they're your family."

"And yours," Sirisha said gently. "Do you want an invite to Chatterbox?"

A noncommittal head bobble. "Maybe later. Anyway, I'm beat. Heading to bed. Don't stay up too late!"

And then he was gone. Questions played ping-pong in Sirisha's head. Exhausting questions. About a past she was too young to remember. That echoing, angry phone call. How happy Dad had been when he and Pop had gotten together.

She navigated back to Sona's pictures in the app. The one with all the protests in Delhi. They were each extraordinarily beautiful. Cinematic. And full of hope.

Chapter Nine

The day of the first performance of the Thousand Shores had finally arrived.

It was a glorious, blooming first Saturday of May, and people from all over the islands and even the mainland gathered for the 3 p.m. show, which would give them time to catch a ferry off the island afterward. Many were making a day of it, shopping at artsy boutiques, hiking, beachcombing, and then heading over to the Songbird for the show.

It was the kind of ordered chaos the Songbird handled best. Grayson and Fernando directing cars in the overflowing parking lot. Dad grilling kebabs, hot dogs, and burgers. Rani placing fishbowls of gerbera daisies and chocolate lupines on outdoor tables. Nidhi at the espresso machine,

Avani handling the register. An audience snacking and drinking and chatting in the sunshine as they waited for the barn doors to open.

Sirisha clicked away, loving the energy of the day. Crowds and people weren't usually her thing, but ever since she'd started documenting the troupe, she'd felt the thrill of a thief. Stealing into the secret lives of the cast and crew, sneaking into their souls. Smuggling out the jewels of their expressions and exhalations.

"Need any help?" Amir asked, coming up behind her in the grass.

She shook her head. "I'm sure Dad wouldn't mind an extra hand at the grill."

"Actually," said Amir, "he shooed me away after I accidentally burned a bun. I asked your sisters, too, but they all shot me down." He put his hands in the pockets of his jeans, looking just a little wistful.

Sirisha understood. They were all so used to hosting and running things, but Amir didn't want to be just another guest at the Songbird. He wanted to be a seamless part of it all. Besides, even Fernando and Grayson had been put to work in the parking lot. It was past time for them to start assigning chores to Amir, too.

Even though it wasn't particularly helpful, she couldn't stop herself from snapping a shot of him, his hair glinting in the afternoon light, his smile a bit unsure. "Sorry, you looked nice just then."

"Don't apologize," he returned. "I can't stand in the way of greatness."

She laughed lightly in surprise. "Greatness?"

"I'm serious," he said. "The photos on the Thousand Shores website are really amazing. Your dad told me that was all your doing. I think the judges for San Juan Snaps will definitely be impressed."

"Thanks." Sirisha blinked. "Funny, I'd almost forgotten that I'd started all this for the contest."

"So it's not what you're doing this for anymore?"

She shrugged. "Yeah, I'm just having fun being a part of it all, you know?"

"That makes sense. Belonging is a powerful thing." He tucked his thumbs in his pockets, wriggling his fingers and bouncing on his heels. Still at a loss of what to do with himself but relaxed at the same time. He'd been living on the island for nearly nine months now, and Sirisha thought that a bit of Orcas was spilling into his eyes, his posture. A loosening inside, the feeling in your bones that there were no truer measurements of time than the wait between ferries and the pace it took to grow backyard strawberries.

Sirisha cleared her throat. "I suppose you could pose by the barn doors with your ticket. Pretend you're really excited by the show."

There was plenty of excitement among the crowd without trying, but Amir looked thrilled to have his own task. He gamely posed for her while pretending to buy his ticket from Avani, waiting in line for a veggie dog, and faux-mingling with the waiting audience. Then she snapped a few photos of him with the chickens, just because she thought Dad would like them.

"Let's get some candids," she said. "Act like I'm not here."

"No problem." Amir let loose, twirling in the grass as the hens pecked for seed around him.

He looked perfectly at home.

Click. Click. Click.

After their photo shoot, Sirisha headed inside the barn, where things did not exactly look showtime ready. Maybe island time had seeped in a bit too much, as there were costume racks and set pieces strewn where there should have been seats. People making last-minute adjustments and hollering instructions at one another.

The doors were supposed to open in just twenty minutes, but there appeared to be a hubbub behind the curtain, concerned voices drifting out. Curious, Sirisha made her way back there.

"It's okay!"

"You'll be great!"

"Everyone gets pre-stage jitters!"

As Sirisha approached, she saw who was at the center of it all. Brie—clutching her chest, her legs dangling off the edge of the stage. Her forehead clammy. Sirisha wasn't sure she should intrude. But then their eyes met. As they had so many times before. Brie gestured for her to come closer.

People made space. Words tumbled in Sirisha's mind, but everyone had already been encouraging Brie. They'd told her that she'd be great, that everyone got nervous. Maybe this was another moment for Sirisha's greatest strength.

Not speaking.

Brie waved away everyone else and motioned for Sirisha to sit next to her. Sirisha's heart fluttered. They'd had so many quiet moments, but she still couldn't quite believe she hadn't imagined them. And now—what did it mean that Brie wanted *her* in this time of need, and no one else?

They sat together in silence for a minute. Two minutes. Three.

Brie's breathing slowed. She wiped her forehead with her sleeve. Sniffed. Got up.

"Come outside with me?" she asked Sirisha.

Sirisha nodded. They wandered out the back door. Past the chickens. Followed a small trail into the towering cedars and fir trees. Until they were away from the sounds of everyone else at the inn.

Birds chirped. Leaves rustled. A spotted doe ran past. Then three more.

"I can't do it," Brie finally said.

Sirisha didn't ask for more. Only waited.

Brie looked at her. "I can't go onstage. At first, I thought my Rapunzel bit was cute. That we'd subverted all the right tropes, that we were creating something incisive and cool."

Sirisha allowed the silence to build until Brie just had to fill it.

"But now I'm not so sure. I thought I was saying something, but what if it's all the same stuff that's been said before? I thought . . ."

More deer. A rabbit. More soft earth underfoot. More roots to climb over.

Tears from Brie. "The real problem is obvious. I'm terrible. I really am. I'm just not cut out for being a leading lady."

It was time. For Sirisha to speak. For once in her life.

She touched Brie's arm tentatively. Her warm skin. Brie blinked at her, another tear working its way slowly down her cheek.

What she wanted to say: "Brie, you're going to be amazing."

What she actually said: "Brie, you're going to be amazing."

Somehow, somehow, somehow the words actually came out—easily. Because this time she wasn't worried what Brie thought of her. This time, she was far too worried about what Brie thought of herself.

"How do you know?"

"You know you're a star, right?" Sirisha said with urgency. "Seriously.

The power you have up there when you're onstage, the power you have with your words—I'm blown away every time."

"Thank you." Brie's lips curved into a smile. Her lashes still glistened with dewy tears, but she brushed away the dampness on her cheek. "Thanks for just listening. I knew there was a reason I was drawn to you."

Sirisha's cheeks heated. Her toes warmed. No, her entire body warmed. "You were drawn to me?"

"Yes." Brie took her hand. "I mean I'm still drawn to you. As in present tense."

"As in"—Sirisha gulped—"romantically?"

Brie chuckled softly. "Yeah, I think so."

"Um, what about Liza?"

"Liza? Our moms went to high school in Spokane together, and we've known each other our whole lives. She's just a really good friend."

Just a really good friend.

And that meant . . .

It wasn't just words that tumbled around in Sirisha's mind. It was a mess of feelings, too. But Brie's lips were rosy, her cheeks brushed with lilac dust, her dark brown eyes speckled with gold embers.

It had been one of those overexposed sunny days, but somehow during their short walk things had changed, as they sometimes do. Damp mist curled around them. The kind of wet you couldn't escape with an umbrella because it wrapped all around you. A panorama of moisture.

Yet Sirisha wasn't cold. And from the looks of it, neither was Brie.

What she wanted to say: nothing.

What she actually said: also nothing.

And then Sirisha didn't know who reached for who. How it started exactly. But they were clutching each other. Brie's hands against the nape of her neck. Sirisha's cupping Brie's cheeks.

Their lips were melding. Soft silky petals. Then a little more urgently. And soon, a wildfire.

Sirisha's heart ignited. Her toes. Her very being.

Chapter Ten

*H*er first kiss ever.

Sirisha's feet no longer touched the ground. She was floating on air. But as much as she wanted to stay out in the woods with Brie, to keep her for her own, it was time to share. They rushed back to the hall, the performance about to begin. Even though Brie's act was later, Loretta gave them a displeased look as they snuck in the back door.

Sirisha shrugged. "She needed a pep talk."

Loretta sighed. Gestured for Brie to get into place. But as Sirisha walked away, she caught Loretta's quick, knowing smile. Just for a fraction of a second, too fast for a camera.

The first act opened with a poetry reading, which soon shifted into a song. Then morphed into a dance number to a rap and finally ended with more poetry. Even though Sirisha had seen every bit of the variety show, she was entranced. As the official photographer for the event, she was allowed to roam the aisles, taking shots of the actors shining bright on the stage. The audience enraptured. Loretta in the shadows, the force behind it all. Anxious. Demanding. And proud.

And so was Sirisha. She hoped that she'd do the cast and crew justice. Meanwhile, Amir, Dad, her sisters, Fernando, and Grayson all watched from the front row. Sirisha managed to snap a few candids of them sharing glances with one another. Nidhi listening deeply. Avani looking as if she had too many ideas she longed to scribble down. Dad and Amir laughing in tandem at a particularly witty bit.

Click. Click. Click.

The Thousand Shores truly did have a thousand stories. Perhaps more. So many voices, historically ignored. But not today. Today they showed the world that they mattered, too. That they would not be overlooked. As Sirisha took a moment to sit down with her family, she once again marveled at being a part of it, the photography contest she'd once been so focused on blurring into the background. Win or lose, she knew her San Juans Snaps entry would be bursting with passion.

And then Brie was there onstage. Filling up the room with her mere presence. With her voice, with her words. With her humor, with her heart.

Ethereal and earthy at once.

And as different as they were, Sirisha reveled in all the ways they were similar, too. They both wanted desperately to be heard. To be seen. To shout to the world about who they were and all the mess of ideas in their heads. They just spoke in really different ways. But Sirisha was starting to understand that her way wasn't less. That she could speak, that she could tell the world about all the passions spinning inside her like hurricanes.

When Brie's act came to an end, Sirisha found herself jumping up. Out of her chair. Whistling and hooting. Not shy or quiet at all. Her heart full of wonder and joy.

Rani glanced at Sirisha, surprise written all over her face at her suddenly loud little sister. But slowly, Rani's expression switched to a gentle understanding. "Rapunzel, huh? She was brilliant."

Sirisha sighed happily. "She *is* brilliant. And gorgeous. And the best kisser."

Rani screamed and hugged Sirisha. Around them, the audience was all on their feet by now. Cheering. Whistling. Pounding their hands together to create thunder.

In the spotlight, Brie laughed. Gave a little bow, a short pirouette. And sashayed off the stage. Just in time, Sirisha remembered to capture that moment of triumph as she disappeared into the shadows behind the curtains.

Click. Click. Click.

Shimmering water, islands in the distance, sailboats out for an evening cruise. The mist had cleared, the evening sun warm. Music thrummed at the cast party down at the cove. Jubilant dancing. Chatting on driftwood logs. Toes dipped in sand or water.

Click. Click. Click.

"Our social media is blowing up because of your photos!" Loretta said, "Seriously, good work. And thanks for getting them uploaded so fast."

Click.

Loretta shielded their face. "Okay, you can stop now. Sit back. Relax. Have a drink."

Sirisha nodded, lowering the camera. She fully intended to cover the party, but it was clear Loretta was done being a subject. Totally fair. Some people loved the camera; others merely tolerated it.

Besides, she did have a few other goals tonight. She tucked the camera momentarily away in her backpack and pulled out a wrapped gift. It was easy to spot Brie. Surrounded by awed cast and crew. Apparently, there was a lot of buzz online for her act in particular.

"They're calling you 'a star in the making,'" said a girl, scrolling on her phone.

Sirisha didn't try to push her way through the crowd to Brie. She waited for her moment. It didn't take long; Brie's eyes sought hers. A wide, wry smile. And then Brie came to Sirisha, leaving her adoring fans behind.

It felt as if a beach pebble had lodged itself in Sirisha's throat, but hopefully her gift would say everything.

Brie carefully untied the bit of string. Unfolded the butcher paper. She wasn't a present ripper, Sirisha noted. She hoped Brie would like it. People were weird when it came to photos of themselves, full of self-criticism and impossible standards.

The picture was from a dress rehearsal earlier in the week. Brie under the starry stage lights. Long hair trailing from the end of the tower. The moment Rapunzel makes the decision to save herself. And Brie had, of course, been luminous.

A star in the making.

"I love it!" Brie said, sincerity ringing like musical notes in her voice. "You really caught me, just the way I wanted to be seen. That's some kind of magic. Are you sure you aren't a witch?"

Sirisha shrugged shyly.

Brie turned the frame over in her hands. "And did you make this yourself?"

"Yeah . . . from driftwood." Taken from the very cove they stood in.

Brie was silent for a moment, her eyes on the photo, on the frame. On Sirisha. Then, after tucking it carefully in her bag, she held her hand out in invitation.

Sirisha squeezed Brie's fingers. Brie grinned. And then, together they were running into the waves. The ends of their dresses soaked. Their toes curling over rough sand.

"Ack!" Brie squealed. "It's cold!"

"It feels good." Sirisha turned her back on the horizon, so all she could see was Brie and the cove and everyone there. "So . . . you've only got another week of performances." The unspoken question: Where were they going from here?

Brie wrapped her hands around Sirisha's waist.

"Yeah . . . but Lopez is only a ferry ride away." Brie arched her brow. "We're neighbors."

The water lapped at their knees. A symphony of splashes. It felt almost warm, now that Sirisha was used to it. Her toes on fire.

"So I'll still see you plenty?" she asked.

Brie pressed her forehead against Sirisha's. "Plenty."

And then it was Sirisha's second ever kiss. And her third. And maybe her fourth and her fifth. Whistles and hoots and laughter and chatter surrounded them.

And then Sirisha didn't need to keep count anymore.

Chapter Eleven

The Thousand Shores sold out all week. Spring Fest did its job to bring people into the arts. The islands were a frenzy, but like all frenzies, things had to slow down. The evening Brie was packing up to go home, Sirisha visited her at Liza's house. The three of them hung out, got some coffee in Eastsound. Liza really was funny and nice. But then it was just Sirisha and Brie.

It was the second week of May, the first day that felt truly hot. Bare legs and linen dresses and the breeze on their skin. Sirisha realized wryly that she'd started dressing a bit more like Brie, opting for delicate floral patterns that she'd plundered from her sisters' closets. She had to admit they were the right mix of comfortable and feminine. Hopefully, Brie wouldn't mind.

The two had dinner at a little bistro. Candles and flowers and delicate flavors. Flaky, buttery halibut in a zesty lemon and rhubarb sauce. Then they walked out to Crescent Beach. Held hands. Meandered the sandy flats. Skipped a few rocks over the water.

Kissed.

Soon they'd be on different islands. There would be weekends and ferry rides, of course. But at that moment, Sirisha didn't want to let go. She was flooded yet again with yearning and a flustered fever and warm toes. Skin against skin. Breath against breath.

It was truly a golden moment that she hadn't missed—and that was a triumph. Yet far too soon Liza and Brie were headed to the ferry dock, and Rani was driving Sirisha home.

"So, your first real date!" Rani said as they cruised along the shoreline, the sea lustrous with sapphires and diamonds.

"Yep."

"Come on, you can't keep all the details to yourself."

Sirisha laughed. "Avani and Nidhi will probably want a full report, too. So I might as well save it."

"Hmmph." Rani side-eyed Sirisha. "Sure, just make me wait. Even though I so nicely offered to drive you. You really need a license, you know."

"I turn sixteen next month."

"And who exactly has been giving you all the driving lessons?"

"You."

"That's right."

Rani pretended to huff more but couldn't help breaking out into a grin. "Just a small preview?"

Sirisha chuckled, then cleared her throat:

"Brie's lips are like roses, her hair like the night.

Her laugh like the breeze, her eyes dark and bright.
When she looks at me, I feel no fear.
Now—is that what you wanted to hear?"

Rani giggled. "Basically yes. But your poetry needs work."

They pulled up the driveway of the Songbird as the sun began its descent beyond the horizon. Walking around to the porch, they found Avani and Nidhi lounging on the hammock. A pitcher of iced tea and a plate of lemon bars rested on the railing.

The Singh sisters squeezed together, marveling at the warm weather, the colors over the water to the west. Pinks, oranges, violets. A streak of violently delightful red. To the east, dark purples and blues.

Of course, the inevitable barrage of questions came hurtling. Every detail of the date up for dissection. The food. The drinks. The talk. The walk. And of course, all the feels. So many feels. Only, Sirisha didn't know how to describe them, not with words anyway. She just knew that Brie was brilliant, beautiful, bold.

Ethereal and earthy at once.

The door from reception swung open, Amir stepping out in dark jeans and a pastel polo. He looked both handsome and comfortable. There was a lightness in his step, that same island easiness that Sirisha had noticed on opening day.

"Do you know how lucky you have it, with this view?" he asked, walking over. "South facing so you get to enjoy both sunsets and sunrises?"

Nidhi pulled over a lounge chair for him. "We probably don't appreciate it enough."

Her tone was full of wonder and longing. And Sirisha knew she was thinking about how these days would soon end. These familiar, comfortable days where they were all living together under one roof.

Rani added, "Well, usually there's also front desk duty to attend to—"

"And helping out in the restaurant," Avani added.

"Not to mention our homework," Sirisha chimed in.

Amir nodded to them. "I think it's incredible the way you four care for your dad and help with the inn and still manage to have your own interests and passions. The Songbird is truly a magical place, and you're four very accomplished young women."

Sirisha and her sisters glanced at one another, flattered, embarrassed. But proud.

"Yeah." Rani grinned. "I guess we are."

Amir poured himself a glass of iced tea and took a lemon bar. Neatly, with a napkin. At their Sunday dinners, he was always kind and helpful. Never expected anyone to wait on him. Which Sirisha and her sisters appreciated, given they waited tables all the time. They had enough customers.

"Listen," he said, leaning against one of the porch columns. "I wanted to ask you four something. How would you feel . . . if I proposed to your dad?"

For a second, there was silence as they all took it in.

Surprise coursed through Sirisha. But the more she thought about it, the more she knew this was right. Just as Orcas had seeped into Amir's countenance, his presence had seeped into their lives. Until his footsteps in the hallway, his favorite foods, and even his taste in movies and music were as much a part of the Songbird as any of theirs.

It wasn't long before delighted squeals erupted from the sisters.

"Oh my gosh, that would be amazing!" Avani leapt to hug Amir.

Nidhi joined the embrace, nodding as if she had predicted Amir would one day join the family. Sooner or later.

Rani squeezed them, while simultaneously hooting. "I totally knew this was going to happen! Ever since we won the Most Romantic Inn award, I've been waiting . . . and now a wedding! Ahhhh!!!"

Sirisha felt the weight of her trusty camera in her bag. Deftly pulled it out. She wanted to be immersed in the moment, to join in on the hug. And she would. But her sisters' and Amir's faces were a flurry of emotions, full of hope and anticipation, full of buoyant joy. A story in the making. So first—

Click. Click. Click.

Part Four:
Summer
Rani

Chapter One

*P*ots and pans clanged outside the tent, her sisters were loudly going on about the dang sunrise, and Dad was humming an annoyingly jaunty Hindi tune from a Bollywood romance. Amir was exclaiming about the tame island deer while a couple of birds were tweeting as if they'd started their own symphony.

"The sun rises every friggin' day, in case you never noticed!" Rani hollered before sticking her pillow over her head and burrowing deeper into the sleeping bag.

Her sisters, Dad, and Amir only laughed and talked louder.

Camping. It always sounded romantic: sleeping under the stars, listening to the gentle lap of waves against the shore, waking up to the scent of bacon frying on the camp stove. And on Jones Island, the deer would eat right out of your hand.

But even with an air mat, a night on a pebble beach was a special form of torture. A huge rock had been poking Rani for the past eight hours, digging right into her lower back. No matter where she moved, she couldn't escape it, especially since she was sharing the same one-person tent with Avani they'd had since they were kids. It worked when they were seven. Not so much anymore.

"Breakfast is ready!" Dad announced.

She sat up guiltily. Leave it to Dad to fix his own Father's Day breakfast. Of course, he was the only one who really knew the secrets of camp cookouts, how to make everything mouthwateringly smoky and crispy. But Rani and her sisters would definitely wash the dishes and stow the camping gear. It wasn't often that he got a break from the inn—on a weekend, no less.

Inside Rani's sleeping bag, something distinctly hairy and many-legged crawled up her thigh. "Ackkk!" she yelped, standing up too quickly, only to remember the tent wasn't big enough for that. Her shoulder banged against a pole, and then she was tripping over her own sleeping bag—or rather, something beneath it.

Rani fell to the ground with an "oomph!" and maybe a few curses. Kicking aside the sleeping bag, she saw what had been keeping her up all night. It hadn't been a rock after all.

"You okay in there?" Dad asked.

"I'm fine!"

Her throbbing toe told another story, but she was preoccupied with the shiny wooden plaque staring up at her. The award from nearly a year ago, the one that proclaimed the Songbird was the Most Romantic Inn in America. How in the world? She hurried out of the tent, clasping it against her chest like long-lost treasure.

"Good morning, sunshine!" Dad said, decked out in his favorite camping outfit: hunter-green shorts, brown fleece, and an orange fishing cap that he thought screamed classic Americana—though Rani firmly believed that it should be outlawed.

Dad waved a tantalizing plate just under Rani's nose. His camp specialty: flapjacks dotted with bits of maple-glazed bacon. (When you were camping, you had to use old-timey words like *flapjacks*, obviously.)

But Rani wasn't to be distracted. She held up the plaque. "Does anyone know how this got under my sleeping bag?"

Dad's forehead crinkled. "Wasn't it hanging behind the reception desk?"

"Come to think of it, I noticed an empty spot on the wall a while back," Nidhi said.

Amir, Avani, and Sirisha shook their heads, puzzled.

Nidhi of course, had a logical explanation: It must have fallen off the wall at some point when someone careless brushed past it, and then it never got returned to its correct place.

"But how did it end up in the camping gear?" Rani challenged.

Nidhi shrugged. "You were working front desk duty before we left. It must have fallen into one of the bags."

Oh please. Rani's big sis may have graduated high school, she may even have planned an amazing study abroad trip to India, but she sometimes still showed a startling lack of imagination. Meanwhile, Rani felt a thrumming in her veins, silver and gold specks of possibility racing through them. A delicious smile crept across her face as it dawned on her: It was a Sign. A cosmic force, stronger than reason or physics.

Ever since the Songbird had received the award, romance had befallen her sisters and father. Sweet romance, exciting romance, slow-burn romance. The kind of romance that was leading to a wedding in just a few short weeks. Soon Rani would have two parental figures again. It had been truly a whirlwind courtship and engagement, just the type that she had always hoped for herself—someday. So romantic! So epic! So dreamy!

Rani had been patiently waiting all this time, knowing in her heart of hearts that romance had to be coming her way, too, that the heartbreak and unrequited yearning of last summer meant something: She was a heroine just like the girls in her favorite fictional romances. And now, at long last, it was her turn.

Destiny was on its way. (With a capital *D*.)

Rani ate her bacon-bits flapjack on the rocky beach of an uninhabited island, stretching her toes and dragging a finger over a slice of grainy sand and inhaling the salty sea air. The sunrise burst into full bloom over the Salish Sea, and it had never been so ferociously, untamably beautiful.

On the paddle back to Orcas from the campsite, Rani hummed and tried to picture the stranger headed her way. Tall, dark, and handsome? Short, sunny, and unconventionally cute? She didn't care—Rani knew beauty was in the eye of the beholder. She just wanted to be swept off her feet by a love indescribably grand.

Lately, she'd become even more addicted to Dad's stash of Bollywood films. She adored all the drama and the songs, the heroines' exquisite ensembles and the heroes' unfettered dance moves. Now, the universe was signaling that love was on its way, and Rani couldn't help but picture herself as the star of her own hit movie:

EXT. A GRASSY FIELD – DAY

RANI dances and sings in a field, decked out head to toe in gorgeous jewelry and an elaborate lehenga. Her song is replete with longing for her one true love.

Splat.

Rani was so busy daydreaming that she dropped her paddle, and the fierce morning wind pushed it halfway back to their campsite. Oops.

Amir offered to tie their kayaks together and tow her behind him. It was slightly humiliating, but not enough to dispirit her. After all, she'd soon be meeting the man of her dreams. An exuberant school of southern resident orcas escorted them to the cove below the inn, gliding over the water in great leaps and spins. Clearly, another Sign from the universe.

The moment they returned to the inn, Rani showered off the camp grime and hurried to her afternoon shift at the front desk, anxious to finally meet her prince charming. One of Dad's sous chefs, Josie, had been in charge while they were gone overnight.

Josie handed her a stack of brochures. "I'm hearing good things about Pete at Sunset Cruise Company right now, in case any of the guests need a suggestion."

"Huh?"

Rani was, of course, back in her Bollywood fantasy:

INT. INN – DAY

RANI is working in her family's cozy inn, where each of her three sisters
has found love. An astrologer and fortune-teller has assured her that
she will be next.

RANI

Can my fate truly be written in the stars?

The bell chimed, bringing Rani back to the present. She hadn't even
noticed that Josie had left! But a balmy breeze wafted in through the door,
sweeping in with it—a boy.

It was happening.

Rani knew with a thrilling certainty that he wasn't just any boy. He
was the One she'd been waiting for. He dutifully rolled in the luggage
as his parents spoke to each other in rapid Japanese with a few English
phrases thrown in.

INT. INN – DAY

A handsome stranger arrives. He is muscular, with a quick and easy
smile. Lightly tanned skin and an adorable cleft in his chin. A charmer.
RANI nearly melts in a pool of want.

He grinned at her. "Whew, it is hot! I'm ready for a swim!"

She smiled back, her heart thumping wildly. "There's a beach just a
five-minute walk down the trail."

"Excellent!" His eyes danced. "Care to join me?"

Rani laughed and couldn't help imagining him in his swim trunks. She suspected he might look film-worthy without a shirt.

"Don't mind him." His mother rolled her eyes. "He doesn't understand that some people have to work for a living."

"Sure I do," he said, "but it's too beautiful to stay indoors all day, don't you think?"

That smile could light a forest fire. Rani tingled with too many feels as he directed it fully at her. He certainly didn't waste time! Which she appreciated, since she was eager to get moving on her Destiny (capital *D*). Somehow she managed to get the Nakamuras checked into the inn—and accept an invitation with gorgeous Leo for an early evening dip.

Now that her prince had already arrived, Rani wasn't in the mood to deal with other guests. Unfortunately, she was on duty for another hour.

Then another car pulled up the drive. It was posh, it was pretty . . . it was a Porsche. Whoa.

Out stepped a South Asian family, posh and pretty themselves. And they were no ordinary Desis! Rani recognized the parents right away: Lalu and Asha Chaudary, Seattle tech wizards who had created an electric bike-sharing app and then sold it for about a zillion dollars. Now they were investing in all sorts of green tech. And their kids were brilliant, too: Eighteen-year-old Anjali had penned a best-selling series and her seventeen-year-old brother Vikram was a politico and an internet-famous activist.

INT. INN – DAY

A second gentleman arrives, nothing like the first. Medium-height with a lean build, deep voice, and closely shorn hair. He's a man of the world, prominent and respected.

RANI

This one can't possibly be my fate. He is far too worldly, his family too powerful for a simple girl like me.

FORTUNE-TELLER

Never underestimate your worth. All I can tell you now is that your destiny is on its way, and it's up to you to uncover it.

After they checked in, the elder Chaudarys left for a walk down to the cove, and Anjali muttered something about a deadline and retreated. But Vikram hung around reception, seemingly very interested in all their memorabilia hanging on the walls. The Most Romantic Inn in America plaque was back in place, gleaming in the sunlight filtering in through the windows.

"Hi," Rani said, wondering if she was a fool to even talk to someone like him. "My sisters love your channel. I mean—I do, too."

Vikram smiled—fairly modestly, considering he had four hundred thousand subscribers. "Thanks, but right now I need a break from everything broken in the world. All I want to think about is where to find the best ice cream on the island."

Rani pretended to think. "That's a tough one. Do you like lavender?"

"I do."

Right answer.

INT. INN – DAY

RANI
Which of these handsome suitors is my true destiny? Will
you read the stars for me once more?

FORTUNE-TELLER
The stars keep some secrets for themselves. Follow your
heart, and you'll know what to do.

With two dates already planned, Rani was itching to get going and hardly interested in more guests. She only had a half hour left in her shift when the bell dinged again. A tingle cruised down her spine as another family walked in. A family she knew.

Raj Mehta, with his parents and twelve-year-old sister.

Raj Mehta, the boy from the previous summer who had told her that he was really going to miss Dad's gulab jamun. The one she'd spent so many lazy hours playing board games with, the one she'd never run out of things to talk about with. The one she'd fallen for—and the one who had left her unkissed on the hammock.

Unfortunately, he looked more handsome than ever. He seemed to have had a major growth spurt in the past year. His messy black hair flopped adorably over one eye, and his T-shirt fit him well, even if it had a dorky gamer pun on it. Ah, how many times had he compared real life to video games? They were his version of a romance novel, she supposed.

Not that any of it mattered to her anymore.

INT. INN – DAY

> RANI
>
> What is this cruel twist of fate? Why did the one who broke my heart have to return to my life?

> FORTUNE-TELLER
>
> Patience, my dear. The answers you seek will soon be revealed.

> RANI
>
> Of course, of course. I'm super patient. But Raj is definitely a jerk, right? He never called me all year!

Chapter Two

*R*aj smiled hopefully at her. "Hey, remember me?"

"Hey, Raj." Rani forced a pleasant expression on her face. "Welcome back, Mehta family."

Sheetal, Raj's younger sister, waved brightly. Rani went through the motions of checking them in. Like Vikram and Leo, they were staying at the Songbird nearly three weeks, right up until the inn closed to everyone except wedding guests. Apparently, taking long vacations was in this year. Rani couldn't blame anyone; summers on Orcas were pretty amazing.

Raj never stopped looking at her, and she wondered if he, too, was remembering their lazy days together the previous summer. Picking wild blackberries on a beach you could only get to by kayaking. Playing board games on the deck. That time he'd surprised her with a moonlit picnic.

She'd thought they'd been on the edge of a timeless romance. But the weeks had gone by, and nothing. No kiss, no breathless declarations of undying love. And then that last morning on the hammock, he'd had one last chance to make a move . . . and zilch.

Plus, he hadn't even texted or written in the months between. So why in the world was he looking at her with those big brown eyes like he still cared?

Hmmph. Whatever.

Rani might be a hopeless romantic, she might believe in a love that transcended time and space, but she wasn't one to engage in needless torture. She refused to look him in the eye, ignoring him masterfully. Raj who again?

Eventually, he and his family left for their rooms. Now she could focus on her true destiny. At least, once she finished her shift.

"No, sorry, we're booked full for the weekend!" she said cheerfully into the phone, though privately she was wondering how so many people could possibly think they'd have last-minute availability in the summer season.

Be nice, be nice, be nice.

When Avani finally came to relieve her from duty, Rani hugged her. "You're my savior!"

"Um . . . okay." Avani batted her away with a laugh. "Is there a cute boy waiting for you in the living room or something?"

"There is." Rani winked, putting Raj and the Mehtas firmly from her mind.

Vikram was indeed waiting for her, heatedly typing something on his phone. He muttered to himself, a few strong words in the mix.

(Though with his rumbling deep voice, even those not-so-nice words sounded *very* nice.)

"I thought you wanted to get away from all that's broken in the world?" she said gently.

He looked up, startled at first—and then a bit sheepish. "Yeah, I did. Sorry. I have a bad habit of getting carried away with things. Seriously, if you can call me out when I get too into my phone, it would be a huge help."

Rani allowed herself to bask in the moment. This was perfect: her way to help Vikram Chaudary of *the* tech whiz Chaudarys! She could hardly believe her luck. No, it wasn't luck, she remembered. It was fate.

INT. INN – DAY

> VIKRAM
>
> Please, fair maiden, I require your assistance. My flaw is that I care too deeply about the world, even those who are rascally and undeserving. Will you help me find my way?

> RANI
>
> Darling, all you had to do was ask.

Out in the parking lot, Vikram walked straight up to the Porsche, keys in hand.

She erupted in a delighted smile. "Seriously? Your parents don't mind?"

He grinned. "I texted them and explained that it was for a really important date."

Whoa. Vikram opened the door for her, and she slipped onto the supple leather seat. So this was what the other half lived like. She could definitely get used to it. Vikram was confident behind the wheel as they zipped to Eastsound with the top down, the breezy island air bringing with it the scent of summer blossoms and new beginnings and perhaps the faintly sweet perfume of Destiny. Rani found herself in its spell.

Vikram maneuvered easily into a parallel spot next to Lulu's. The ice cream parlor was packed, though July and August would be even more hectic with travelers from all over the world. Which was great for local businesses, but not so great if you just wanted to grab a quick cone. Oh well. The line snaking out the door and around the block was the perfect excuse to learn all about each other.

Rani peppered Vikram with questions about *the* Chaudarys. Was Anjali's new book really based on something sinister that had happened at her high school? Were his parents really close to a breakthrough in plastic recycling? And most importantly . . . did Vikram's political activism include addressing the toxic masculinity and sexism that came out when people discussed romance novels?

"A compelling topic, to be sure," Vikram assured her. "Maybe you could let me interview you for a deep dive into it?"

"Oh, I could definitely do that," she said, excited for the chance. She could see it now: Rani Singh—feminist, political activist, slayer of misconceptions.

He laughed, and Rani wasn't sure if he thought she was joking or not. (She obviously wasn't.)

"More people need to get on board with the fact that relationships are a huge part of our lives," she continued. "My sisters are always rolling their eyes at me, too—but look what happened this year. My dad's getting remarried and . . ."

But as she was talking, Vikram glanced at his phone and started thumb-typing with a vengeance.

"You're doing it again." She nudged him lightly.

"You're right, sorry." He finished up his tweet—she caught the words *asylum* and *refugee* in there. And she knew those things were important, so for now she dropped her impassioned speech on the under-appreciation of romance novels. They'd get to that later.

On his web show!

At the front counter, the chalkboard featured three special seasonal flavors: strawberry cheesecake, peach cream crumble, and of course— Rani's absolute favorite—the lavender vanilla. She dreamt of this particular lavender vanilla throughout the year.

"This is going to be the best ice cream you've ever had," she declared. "Sometimes they have lavender in the spring or fall, but it's never the same as *summer* lavender vanilla."

Vikram chuckled. "I see."

"You don't see yet," Rani said, "but you will."

"Here you go." Lily, the ice cream scooper on duty, handed them each a heaping cone.

"Did Matt leave for Paris yet?" Rani asked. Lily, a soon-to-be junior, had been working alongside Matt for several months, but Rani didn't see him there today.

"Yeah, I'm so jealous." Lily wiped her hands on her apron. "Meanwhile, I'm stuck here all summer. *So* bored."

Rani understood those restless and lovelorn feelings. It had been her the previous summer, but now here she was, a woman much in demand. A woman grabbing ice cream with an internet-famous politico slash hunk with four hundred thousand subscribers. A woman with multiple suitors, even. She was still planning to go swimming with Leo later, but for now she wanted to give this date all the attention it deserved.

Feeling suddenly generous and worldly, she winked at Lily. "You'll get your turn."

EXT. VILLAGE – DAY

> VIKRAM
>
> Though I have conquered many realms and encountered many maidens, you truly are a prize. Wise, insightful, and beauteous.

> RANI
>
> Oh how you flatter me, dear sir. (But don't stop now!)

Rani and Vikram stepped out into the warm afternoon sunshine. It was a perfect eighty-two degrees, the sea air wafting up through the breeze, mingling with the scents of freshly made waffle cones and— of course—that distinct perfume of Destiny (capital *D*).

Rani waited eagerly for Vikram to take his first lick. It was seriously going to blow him away, she just knew it. Unfortunately, instead of enjoying the treat, he was muttering and checking his phone again. But obviously her fate was to be here to help him.

She cleared her throat. "Vikram, you wanted to break away, remember?"

He nodded but kept scrolling. "I'm trying, Rani. But just—ugh. You put your phone down for two seconds and then you find out the US refused to sign onto the latest UN resolution on the use of drones. . . ." He proceeded to launch into a long rant involving military overstep and the situation between several countries that Rani was pretty sure she'd heard of but couldn't quite place on a map.

Clearly, she had her work cut out for her. That was okay. Rani could be patient. She licked her own ice cream. And just like every year, it was out-of-this-world good, a paradox of heady and delicate at once. Orcas Island at its essence. Vikram was really missing out with all his talk of politics.

He finally paused, as if expecting her to respond.

Rani tried to look intelligent. "Wow, yeah. Our government needs to take this stuff more seriously! I'm glad we have people like you to hold them accountable."

He smiled. "I'm doing my best, but I wish I didn't have to."

"It's great you care so much!" She smiled encouragingly. It occurred to her that she didn't need to understand—or even listen to—every single word he was saying. All she had to do was be supportive.

He smiled. "Thanks, I appreciate your vote of confidence. You're really cool, you know that?"

"I like to think so." She beamed. She'd known reading all those romance novels would help her when she got to the real thing. Which they would discuss in that interview, whenever that happened. "So . . . are you going to try the ice cream?"

"Yep, here I go." He breathed in the scent of it. "You said it's world-famous lavender vanilla, right?"

"Yep."

He took a lick. Nodded appreciatively. "Okay, yeah, this is definitely the best ice cream I've had—in the United States. I don't think it quite beats the gelato I had in Italy, but it comes close."

Rani raised her brows. "It comes *close*? How dare you. This is the most sublime thing that exists in the universe."

Vikram grinned charmingly. "Well, maybe one day we'll go to Italy together and you can decide for yourself."

Italy? With Vikram?

She could be down with that.

Leo was already shirtless and in the water when Rani came down to the cove to meet him. Her mind was still swirling with all the things Vikram had talked so fervently about—politics and equity issues and helping people. Even though he'd said he wanted to use this time to get away from it, it was obvious he was too passionate to ever put activism completely out of his mind.

She admired that. In fact, he was inspiring her to get involved, too. Add her voice. Help spread the word about the importance of romance to those silly laypeople—

Wowza.

Leo's abs were *really* distracting. In fact, even more so than the cover of the Highland warrior on the paperback buried inside her beach bag. Especially since little droplets of water were curling their way down his impeccable muscles. He must be a swimmer. And lift weights. And, and, and . . .

EXT. VILLAGE – DAY

                LEO

Lovely maiden, I beg you to tell me that your heart is not spoken for.

                RANI

It has yet to be claimed, good sir.

RAJ

(Walking up)

That's good to know!

Wait a minute. Raj? What was he doing in her fantasies? Rani was totally over him. Her brain had obviously gotten into a confused tangle after seeing him at reception.

EXT. VILLAGE – DAY

RAJ

A sporty guy? You hate to sweat.

RANI

Hmmph. You know nothing about my depths. Get out of my fantasies!

"Want to race?" Leo started running. "Last one in the water gets splashed!"

"Not fair!" she shouted. "I'm still getting ready!"

He turned around and winked. "Okay, I'll wait."

Rani took her time laying down her towel and bag. Her romance novel peeked out at her, but she shoved it back behind her other things. No need to escape to the Highlands when she had a hottie right here in front of her. As she stripped off her tank top and shorts to reveal a black bikini underneath, Leo's rapt attention made her feel like a movie star. A tingle pulsed down her spine. Could this really be happening?

"Okay, ready?" he asked.

"Nope. I have to put on my sunscreen."

Leo fake-pouted, then sat down on the sand beside her, watching her through lowered lashes. Rani's nerves danced, and she took her time spreading sunscreen over her legs, her arms, every inch of her glistening mahogany skin. She channeled all that was sexy and beguiling—

"What's this?" Leo asked, pulling out the paperback.

"Just something I'm reading." As much as Rani loved to talk romance novels, was he paying attention to her glistening mahogany skin or not? She batted her lashes at him.

But Leo was busy studying the cover. "So *that's* the look you're into," he said, pointing at the kilt-wearing warrior.

Well, if he was actually interested, Rani couldn't resist telling him just a bit more.

"I'm into a lot of looks," she said. "But this is more than just a hot guy on the cover, you know. This is a subversive masterpiece—you'll never see the twists coming."

"Oh yeah?" He flipped through the pages. "I didn't realize romance novels had that many twists. Isn't it all just hot scenes followed by declarations of eternal love?"

"Those are there, too," she agreed. "But there's so much more than that! This one delves into issues of consent and power dynamics in a really masterful way. Romance authors tend to tackle plenty of uncomfortable topics."

"You have me intrigued." He continued scanning the pages.

She grabbed for the book, leaning in close enough to smell the salt water on his skin, to brush against those oh-so-perfect muscles. "Happy to tell you all about it."

He lifted it high out of her reach—at least so long as they were both sitting on the sand. "Oh, here's a good part . . ."

He squinted at a steamy passage, but she swiped the book from him and rolled her eyes.

"You can't just skip all the buildup," she said sternly, making a big show of putting the book carefully away in her beach bag and zipping it up. "That's cheating."

Besides, it was time to get this date moving. Talking about romance was one thing, but she wanted to experience it, too. Before he had a chance to react, she sprinted into the water.

"Beat you!" she cried as her calves hit the waves.

"Oh yeah?" With his long legs, Leo was only steps behind her. He tackled her, and they fell together through the water, which was cold but not too cold.

She came up laughing and splashed him across the face. "My prize for winning the race, remember?"

"Sure," he said with a wicked smile. "You get exactly one free splash. You're safe for ten seconds. Ten, nine, eight . . ."

Splash.

Rani squealed. "Hey, what happened to seven?"

"I got impatient."

"Oh you did, did you?"

A full-out water war ensued, furious and fun. After a bit of rough-housing, the water actually felt quite warm. Probably not like in the tropics, but a girl could pretend. Rani had to admit that being with Leo was easier than with Vikram. No need to overthink anything—he was all playful flirting and wild energy.

She usually didn't like getting her hair wet, but she dove into the water and swam as hard as she could. He was right behind her. She made it to a rock outcropping when he caught up with her, and they play-wrestled in the gentle waves some more. After they'd done way too many laps all over the protected cove, Rani was breathing hard. Leo, on the other hand, was still going strong. Had she thought it was easy being with Leo? She took it back. This was actually quite the workout.

Even now, Leo was swimming under the surface behind her. He caught her legs.

She turned to him.

He popped up.

They were face-to-face.

So close.

She was ready to end the chase. Leaned in toward him.

He smirked. "Catch me if you can!"

Seriously? Would Leo ever rest? She knew it was only their first date, but she didn't want a repeat of last summer—all that pent-up energy ending with a whole lot of nothing.

Leo noticed she wasn't following him. "Everything okay?"

Rani sighed. "I'm beat. I'm gonna go sit on the sand."

"Already? But we were having so much fun." There was that sexy pout again.

She really couldn't resist that pout. Again, she reminded herself she'd only just met Leo today. It wasn't fair to compare him to feckless Raj and that non-kiss on the hammock. Leo would show how he really felt, she was sure of it.

She took a deep breath—and dove after him.

EXT. COUNTRYSIDE – DAY

RANI and LEO run through fields and waterfalls, their clothes
wet and clinging to them, the chemistry sizzling while they sing a
romantic ballad.

> RAJ
>
> Really, this guy? I thought you had feelings about things
> deeper than abs.

> RANI
>
> I have deep feelings about plenty of things, including but
> not limited to abs. Also, didn't I tell you to go away?

Chapter Three

*R*ani was exhausted but feeling warm and fuzzy after the swim date with Leo.

Two dates in one day. She was truly a woman of international mystery, a woman who beguiled men, who captured them with her charms. A siren in the Salish Sea . . .

She was also a bit peckish after all that swimming. Even sirens had to eat.

Leo and his family had left for a late dinner in Eastsound, and Vikram and his family had gone for a sunset cruise. So after a nice hot shower, Rani wandered downstairs to the restaurant on her own. She'd probably just take a plate up to the library.

The Singhs weren't planning their usual Sunday evening dinner since they'd already spent so much time together on the camping trip, and Dad and Amir were engulfed in wedding planning. Nidhi—as the responsible eldest—had naturally taken over much of the work, but she still needed their input on things like color schemes and appetizers and what traditions they wanted to include in the ceremony.

Through the big bay window, sunset was blooming outside. The summer solstice was coming up soon, and the last rays of twilight lingered after ten. The days were long and packed—today especially. In her head, it had been just like a Hindi film rife with music and color.

She was still floating on air.

INT. INN – DAY

RANI

My heart has been cleaved in two. Please, madam, tell me who is my true destiny.

FORTUNE-TELLER

Cleaved into only two pieces? Are you certain?

Her head buzzing with daydreams, Rani crashed right into—
Raj.
Ack!
"Oh, hi, Rani." He was all smiles. "I was hoping to bump into you. Though not necessarily literally."
"Oh." Rani edged backward. "Hi."
Still riding high from her two dates with two gorgeous and charming admirers, the last thing Rani wanted to do was deal with him.

"It's good to see you again," he said.

"Yeah . . . good to see you," she said. If he could be polite and nonchalant, so could she. After all, she was completely indifferent to his dubious charms at this point. They'd had a few laughs and talked for hours, but she was certain all of that would come with Vikram and Leo, too. She was only just getting to know them.

"How've you been?" he asked.

"You would have known if you'd bothered to keep in touch." (So much for being polite and nonchalant.)

At least he had the grace to look properly abashed. Maybe this was it. Maybe he'd fight for her! Maybe it had all been a misunderstanding, the kind of twist fate threw at lovers as they struggled to find their way.

Maybe this was a test.

If so, Raj really needed to prove himself. So Rani tossed him a withering glare. "Well?"

"I—"

But then Raj's sister Sheetal came up and tugged on his sleeve. "Mom and Dad say come sit down with them. They ordered dessert."

Okay, this was his chance. Would he choose dessert or her?

"I'd better go," he said. "My parents are really into family time right now."

"Uh-huh."

He was so full of excuses, and Rani was *done*. She whipped around and sauntered to a table near the north windows. And if she was secretly hoping that Raj would follow, that he'd explain everything to her, then she was destined to be disappointed.

Raj rejoined his family at their table on the opposite side of the restaurant. His parents smiled at him, ushering him to sit as they idly sipped their wine. Sirisha dropped off their desserts, which included a fresh fruit tart and some of Dad's gulab jamun. Raj dug in, his eyes on the dessert.

So there it was. The universe had tested them, and he was still more enamored with gulab jamun than he was with her.

Well, that was just fine with Rani. She had other options.

EXT. HILLTOP – DAY

> VIKRAM
>
> Fair maiden, may I have your leave to extoll your virtues?

> RANI
>
> Extoll away, dear sir.

> VIKRAM
>
> My dearest, you are a true vision: your hair, those eyes,
> that smile. Yet it is your heart that I adore. We are both
> full of boundless passion for the world. . . .

> LEO
>
> The gentleman is far too enamored of his own voice.
> Darling, may I show you how I feel?

> RANI
>
> Oh my. How?

                    LEO
How's this?
                (Literally sweeps her off her feet)

                    RANI
Not bad at all.

                    RAJ
These two buffoons? The lady deserves better.

                    RANI
You again?

While Rani had been daydreaming about her many admirers, the place had emptied.

"Hey, sis," Sirisha said, sliding into the chair across from her. "How'd your date go?"

Rani grinned. "Which one?"

Sirisha raised her brows. "How many did you have?"

"Just two."

"Oh, *just* two," Sirisha teased lightly. "Did either of them happen to be with a certain guy from last summer? Because I saw his family is back."

"What? No! I mean, yes, they're back. . . ." Rani took a deep breath. "But it doesn't matter, because I'm so over him. Both my dates were far superior."

"Well. I'm sure the Official Love Guru knows what she's talking about."

"I do." Rani glanced over to where Raj's family had been sitting before the restaurant had cleared out. She stuck out her tongue at imaginary him, who waved.

Sirisha raised her brows again, a small smile playing across her lips.

"What?" Rani asked.

Sirisha shrugged. "It's just a really big coincidence that you suddenly have all these guys asking you out—and Raj is back!"

"There's no such thing as coincidence," Rani returned. "It's fate. The universe is reminding me about all my bad choices so I won't make the same mistakes again."

"How do you know it's fate? And not just as random as stepping in deer droppings?"

"Gross," returned Rani. "And I prefer to believe in a universe full of meaning."

"Even deer droppings?" Sirisha asked.

Rani rolled her eyes. "You're giving me a headache. Also, I'm *starving*. Leo and I were swimming at the cove. He's gorgeous and all, but now I'm exhausted."

"Tough life," Sirisha teased. "I'd like to meet the guy who could convince you to get your hair wet. I haven't eaten either. Let's see what's in the kitchen."

Josie and Armand were cleaning up, but they assured the girls that they didn't need help. Rani and Sirisha managed to score some still-crispy curly fries and a fish taco spread.

"Oh man, these are perfect," Rani said, stuffing a fry in her mouth.

"Thanks," Josie said. "Don't forget to take the tartar sauce for the tacos. It's really good."

"Oh, and your dad's gulab jamun is in the fridge, too." Armand patted his stomach and groaned. "I had a few too many myself."

"I can't believe the wedding is just three weeks away!" Rani said as they settled into their favorite table by the window with the taco, fries, and gulab jamun feast. "So exciting! I really hope my next dress fitting goes okay. And that Dad and Amir like what I picked for them."

As the person with obviously the best (or the only?) fashion taste in the family, Rani had picked out all the wedding party's attire. She was proud of it, though she'd been underwhelmed by the way her dress fit her. They'd imported the clothing from India, and now they were getting the final fittings done by a talented local dressmaker. Rani adored Beatrice and her shop, but was also a little apprehensive about whether she understood how best to handle the Indian fabrics.

Besides her dress, though, she was more than ready for the big day: ready for Amir to be a part of their lives of course, but also ready for song and dance, ready for cake and speeches, ready for the Singh sisters to look absolutely gorgeous in silk and sun. Ready even to invite the perfect someone to be her date, to dance cheek-to-cheek in the warm evening garden, to feel her heart soar . . .

"I'm sure the lehenga will come out perfectly. I love the color you picked for me, too," Sirisha said, generously adding the tartar sauce to her taco and taking a messy bite. "Did I tell you that Brie said she can make it for the wedding after all? She's going to let her understudy have the part for the weekend."

"Aww, that's sweet. Giving up fame and fortune just for you." Rani stuffed another fry in her face. "Good thing I helped you find each other."

"Um, you thought I had a thing for Paola?"

"So? Did I not hunt down the perfect shade of lipstick for you?"

Sirisha laughed. "Okay, okay. You did. I could never have won Brie over without that lipstick."

"That's right," Rani said. "And you do look fantastic in the spring-green lehenga."

They chatted more about the wedding, and the tacos and curly fries were amazing, but when it came time for the gulab jamun, Rani pushed hers away.

"Full?" Sirisha took a slow bite of her own.

"Just not in the mood."

It smelled amazing, honestly. But she could still picture Raj telling her that he'd miss the dessert instead of her. What a waste of precious August days he'd been: all those countless hours pining after him, looking at her phone and willing for there to be a call or a text from him.

"You're glaring at the gulab jamun," Sirisha told her gently.

She was right. And Rani just wanted to relax and bask in how much fun she'd had earlier. Two hot guys vying for her attention. It was a dream come true. She certainly wasn't going to let Raj ruin any of that. She took back her bowl and forked up a mouthful of dessert.

And honestly? It tasted delicious.

That night, a summer breeze rustled through the open windows as Rani eased into her nightgown, a sheer and delicate thing that she'd found in a vintage shop in Friday Harbor. It made her feel as if she was from another time, one where knights rescued princesses from evil locked towers. She knew, of course, that most old fairy tales weren't terribly feminist, yet the pure romance of them had always drawn her. The idea of someone slaying dragons for her, even if she was perfectly capable of slaying them herself. The idea that someone would battle evil witch queens and bring her back from the brink of death with a mere kiss . . .

Swoon worthy.

INT. PALACE – EVENING

RANI
(Rubs eyes sleepily)
What happened? Where am I?

PRINCE CHARMING
You slept for nearly a thousand years from that evil
queen's curse. But I battled through the thorny vines
that had wrapped themselves around this palace. When I
pressed my lips against yours, true love prevailed.

RANI
Would you like to press those lips against mine
once more?

PRINCE CHARMING
It would be my pleasure. . . .

"Spill it!" Avani bounced on the bed, cozy in a soft T-shirt-and-shorts pajama set. (Rani had actually bought them both vintage nightgowns, but Avani never seemed to wear hers.) "How does it feel to date multiple gorgeous guys in one day?"

"Pretty amazing actually." Rani laughed, giddy with the thrill of it all. The surf of the sea was still pounding in her ears. The scent of waffle cones still tickled her nose.

Her phone was also erupting with texts.

Avani grabbed it. "Whoa. They want to set up more dates! You're popular, princess."

Rani tossed her hair dramatically. "I know."

Avani scrolled. "These guys are seriously into you. Vikram's asking about sailing on his family's yacht?! What?"

"Yeah, they're *those* Chaudarys. The bike app Chaudarys."

"Oh yeah—come to think of it—I vaguely remember when they called to make their booking," Avani said.

Rani's eyes popped. "And you didn't mention this to me?"

"Hmm, guess I forgot."

What?

"How could you possibly forget to mention *the* Chaudarys?"

"I had a lot on my mind, okay?" Avani rolled her eyes and continued perusing Rani's texts. "Besides, you know about them now. Ooh, Leo's asking to go windsurfing with you. Your new admirers are so fancy!"

Rani decided to let the lack of information about *the* Chaudarys slide. All was well that ended well, she supposed. She rested her chin on Avani's shoulder so they could both see the screen. "They're pretty over-the-top, aren't they? I mean Vikram even mentioned going to Italy together. On our first date!"

"They probably have a private plane that they use to just hop over there for lunch on Saturdays."

"Isn't it like a twelve-hour flight?"

"Details." Avani waved her hand. "The point is, the world is your oyster. Enjoy it while you can."

"I plan to." Rani flopped back on her bed, a slow smile spreading across her face. *The* Chaudarys. Leo's abs. Yachts and windsurfing and lavender ice cream, oh my!

A knock sounded on the door.

"Come in!" she called, even though all she wanted to do was get lost in one of her daydreams.

"Hey." Nidhi popped her head in. She looked a little frazzled. Which was certainly unusual for their put-together eldest sister. "Can I talk to you two?"

"What's up?" Avani asked.

Nidhi sat down on the bed between Avani and Rani, putting her head in her hands. "Everything is a disaster. There's so much to coordinate with the wedding—augghh!"

Rani and Avani exchanged bemused looks.

Avani: *Big sis is feeling overwhelmed? For real?*

Rani: *Strange. Very strange.*

Avani: *I won't rub it in that party planning is surprisingly hard.*

Rani: *That's very gracious of you.*

Avani: *I know.*

Rani patted Nidhi's back. "If anyone can handle it, you can . . ."

"You don't understand. Dad's planned hundreds of weddings at the Songbird. He always makes it all look so easy." Nidhi rubbed her temples. "I was video chatting with Lalita Phua when the caterer called and said half the menu needed to be reworked because of a bad crop of asparagus. Ugh. Anyway, Lalita Phua asked me what was going on . . . and I . . . *told her about the wedding.*"

Avani and Rani were silent for a moment as Nidhi flopped back on the bed between them. Clearly, big sis was upset, but Rani wasn't totally sure why. "It's not supposed to be a secret, is it?"

"No," Nidhi agreed. "Definitely not. But the thing is . . . now the relatives on Chatterbox are asking all sorts of questions, and it's getting kind of awkward since Dad's barely spoken to them in so long."

Avani crossed her arms. "Did you mention Amir?"

"Not yet," Nidhi said.

Rani picked up her phone, glancing through her feed on Chatterbox. Nidhi was right—all their relatives were now intensely curious about the wedding, asking tons of questions about the date, the venue . . . and of course the person who Dad would be marrying.

Pronouns were studiously being avoided, which felt like a positive sign. Possibly.

She and her sisters had been using the app regularly to stay in touch with their family, but Dad had never accepted his invite. Up until now, they'd mostly tiptoed around the subject of him, given whatever had happened so long ago to make them all lose touch. The relatives had always known about Pop, of course, and he still came up in conversation now and then, so it wasn't as if there was any secret about Dad's sexuality. It's just that the relatives had never flat-out commented on it one way or another.

And the Singh sisters had noticed. But now it was time for the relatives to either support Dad or not. Be clear about where they stood.

Rani picked up her phone with determination. "Why should we wait around wondering what they think of it all? We're proud of Dad, and we love Amir. I'm posting a picture of them right now." She found one with the two lovebirds wading into the water at the beach cove, sun and sand in their hair. "They're adorable, and our relatives better agree."

Inside, of course, she was quaking. She'd loved getting to know her cousins and aunts and uncles in the past few months. It was really something knowing there were all these people all the way on the other side of the world who cared about them, who were full of never-ending love and support.

But what if that support wasn't actually never-ending?

What if it had a line?

The sisters waited.

And waited some more.

"Well, it's really early in the morning in India right now," Nidhi said.

"Oh wait, there's a message!" Avani said.

Rani was a little afraid to look at the app. But when she did, something inside her settled. Aunts and uncles and cousins were commenting away: "Congratulations!" "What a handsome couple!" "Best wishes for a happy marriage!"

The door opened, and Sirisha came stumbling in, phone in hand.

"Thanks for posting this," she said quietly.

And then the sisters were hugging, clutching each other with relief and tears and hearts swelling like the tide down at the cove when the moon loomed near and bright.

Chapter Four

*S*ummer tourism was serious business, especially with a wedding to plan (and pay for).

Every day was busy and bursting at the Songbird, and scheduling in time for dates—with both Vikram and Leo—along with all Rani's inn chores felt like a complicated algebra problem. Yet Rani couldn't possibly complain. Two hot guys wanted to shower her with attention. Two amazing, fun, romantic guys who seemed completely enraptured with her. TWO.

Okay, maybe even three. Raj had been texting her, too.

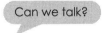

Can we talk?

But she ignored him. After all, she'd already given him so many chances.

On Thursday, she had yet another double dosing of dates planned. After the rush cleared out of the restaurant for the morning, Rani plopped down at the espresso bar where Nidhi was cleaning up. Rani's admirers had been texting her all morning, but she'd known better than to check her phone while trying to carry a tray full of varying types of eggs Benedict.

Now she grinned as she scrolled through the messages: Vikram had sent her articles about the UN and asked her opinions on Very Important Matters. Meanwhile, Leo had sent her a bunch of pics of cute baby hedgehogs and several adorable selfies. They were both peacocking in a big way, and Rani was here for it.

INT. INN — DAY

RANI
(Collapsing on an old-fashioned fainting couch)
All of this attention is too much. I can barely keep up
with it.

FORTUNE-TELLER
My dear, I'm happy for you. Just be sure to keep your
heart open.

Nidhi slid a cup of masala chai her way, which Rani accepted gratefully as she tried to come up with the appropriately earnest, flirty, and/or romantic responses to all the texts.

Yet another text from Raj popped up: another *Can we talk?* Along with some places he was going to be today. Like she was supposed to just show up and hope he was there. He was so self-absorbed, and she just wanted to move on. Time to mute.

Nidhi moved around to the other side of the bar to sit beside Rani, indicating she was officially off duty. "Hey, we have a cake tasting scheduled later, do you want to come give your opinions?"

Rani took an appreciative sip. "I wish I could, but I'm meeting Leo in a little bit."

"It's in the afternoon."

"Um, I'm meeting Vikram then?"

"Uh-huh." Nidhi looked both amused and frustrated. "Okay, you can get out of this one. But don't think for a second that you don't have to help out with the wedding."

"Of course, I'll help!" Rani said, sipping her masala chai quickly so she could get away from Ms. Responsible Spoilsport. "Definitely. Don't worry!"

Nidhi raised her eyebrows. "Planning to bring either of these eligible bachelors to the wedding?"

Rani groaned. "Nidhi, that's ages away. Let me enjoy this, please!"

"It's not ages away—it's only two and a half weeks!" Nidhi looked stressed. "There's so much to do. I keep marking things off in my planner, but the list never ends!"

"You love lists, don't you?" Rani asked.

Leo was sending her more hedgehog pics, and she couldn't help but fall in love with them. Who knew hedgehogs could be so cute?

"Right now, Avani's in charge of music and Sirisha said she'd keep track of RSVPs. So what can I assign you?"

"Uh-huh."

"Are you listening?"

Uh-oh, Nidhi was starting to get that annoyed tone. The one right before she completely freaked out. Rani knew just a little bit about survival at the Songbird, and when you heard Nidhi's patented Concerned Sister ™ tone, you didn't want to stick around.

She grabbed Nidhi's phone and scanned her list of upcoming to-dos. "How about this? I'll come to finalize the menu with the caterer on Saturday."

"That's a start." Nidhi tapped her fingers against the counter.

"Great. I have to get ready to meet Leo now. See you later!" She chugged the rest of the chai (burning the roof of her mouth in the process) and ran away. Rani fully intended to help with the wedding; she loved weddings, obviously. The union of two people, the pomp and circumstance, the flowers, the lights, the cake. Glasses clinking for another kiss from the lovebirds.

But she was beginning to think she loved the part before even better.

The part with shy glances and first kisses and tingling nerves. The butterflies in your stomach and the crush that feels like a fever. Being in that early stage of romance with both Vikram and Leo was a little overwhelming, but it was also a kind of bliss she'd never known before.

And she was determined to enjoy it.

Oh boy. Leo was running across the beach again. Shirtless. Toward her.

He carried a paddleboard under each arm, causing his muscles to flex in really—really!—nice ways, and Rani was convinced she was the luckiest girl on Orcas.

Drool.

EXT. SHORELINE – DAY

> RANI'S SISTER
>
> It is unseemly to watch a man in this manner. He will think you too bold.

> RANI
>
> I cannot help myself. He has enchanted me.

"The class is starting. Don't want to be late, do we?" Leo grinned and handed her one of the paddleboards.

Which was really bulky and had surprising heft considering it was inflatable. Oof!

Somehow, Rani managed to lug it into the water. She eyed it suspiciously as it floated on the surface. At least there was no wind today, and the sea was nice and flat and sparkling with sunshine. It looked simple enough, but a part of her was definitely wary. After all, balance sports were more Avani's lane. (Plus, would she have to get her hair wet again?)

Of course, Leo was already paddling with his arms out to where the class was starting. Rani contemplated her painted toenails, still safely dry on sand. Did she really want to give that up? And her hair! She'd spent a lot of time on this bun.

Just then, she spotted Raj and his family walking out onto the beach with a picnic basket and a blanket. Now that she thought about it, she might have seen a mention of a beach from his text that morning before she muted him. Ugh, maybe she should have paid more attention just to know which places to avoid.

Raj caught her looking at them, and waved.

Rani looked quickly down at the sand, pretending she hadn't seen them at all. No way was she going to get distracted by fickle Suitor #3.

"Rani, you coming?" Leo gestured encouragingly from the back of the class, and she couldn't resist his impish smile.

Here was a guy that was straightforward.

Here was a guy that made her nerves tingle.

Here was a guy that even encouraged her to try new things. (Which better be worth it.)

"Yeah, I'm right behind you," she shouted back. Maybe a little more enthusiastically than she would have otherwise.

She wasn't exactly graceful, and the board wobbled, but she managed to get on board with her belly flat, legs flailing. She fumbled until she got her knees beneath her. Phew. She looked almost normal! She paddled with her arms toward the rest of the class.

"We'll start with some simple breathing exercises," said the instructor, a cheery white woman with long brown hair.

Breathing exercises?

Oh no. This wasn't one of those paddleboard yoga classes, was it?

Please don't let it be a yoga class.

"Don't worry, beginners! We'll try a few sitting poses before working our way up to some harder ones."

Oh.

That explained why there were no paddles.

As the instructor guided them through a few warm-up stretches and twists, Rani pushed aside her uncomfortable thoughts on cultural appropriation and yoga, focusing for the moment on not embarrassing herself by falling off the board.

"Okay, now let's try the downward dog pose. Start by lying flat and bringing your arms forward. Now press on your hands and toes, and slowly lift your hips."

Naturally, Leo looked like a model, and Rani admired his very delectable form as she lifted her own hips. Maybe paddleboard yoga wasn't all bad.

They switched to upward-facing dog, then a plank.

Creak.

Yikes, was that her back? Maybe Rani desperately needed more yoga in her life.

"Great job, everyone," the instructor called. "Now we're going to try slowly standing up into a salute pose. Bring yourself forward. Make sure your stance is nice and wide as you rise."

Leo deftly sprang up, and soon he was showing everyone up with a perfectly balanced one-legged tree pose.

EXT. SHORELINE – DAY

LEO
Am I not a specimen to behold?

RANI
Truly.
(Swoons)

LEO

Fair maiden, you've seen naught yet.

RAJ

So now you're into yoga paddleboarding, huh?

RANI

Yeah, do you have some sort of brilliant opinion on it?

As Leo showed off with another advanced move—the revolved sugarcane—a powerboat zoomed across the other side of the sound. Despite the distance, the wake rippled across the water, and Rani quickly fell back onto her knees, holding on to her board for dear life. Meanwhile, Leo flailed and—

SPLASH!

EXT. SHORELINE – DAY

RANI

Dear sir, you need not go to such lengths to impress me.

LEO

Are you certain, fair maiden? You have many suitors.
Also, who's that guy that seems to be staring at us?

"Thanks for the ride!" Rani told Fernando and Avani as she sprinted back into the inn. She barely had ten minutes to get ready before meeting Vikram. After Leo had fallen off his board, she'd felt compelled to jump into the water to "rescue" him. And they'd played in the water as the yoga class did their best to ignore the flirting teens.

It had been so fun and sexy that she'd decided getting her hair wet was *probably* worth it.

Her heart was still skipping, but she didn't want to smell like salt water for her next date, so she scurried into the shower. Exactly nine minutes and thirty-two seconds later, she was walking down the wide spiraling staircase, determined to make an entrance. Her long hair tumbled with curls hot from the iron and her strapless summer dress flounced with tulle and lace. Again, she channeled the woman she wanted to be, the heroine from a movie who beguiled men with her beauty and wit.

From the way Vikram's jaw dropped, she knew she'd succeeded in casting a spell.

A half an hour later, she and Vikram were at a long dock, climbing the stairs up to a seaplane. With their ability to take off from and land in the water, they were ubiquitous in the San Juans. But Rani had never been on one, and she was secretly delighted at the prospect. It wasn't Italy, but honestly this was better than a twelve-hour flight.

Of course, she couldn't resist teasing Vikram, either.

"Seriously? You chartered a private plane for us?"

"It's a seaplane, not Air Force One." Vikram shrugged. "I heard it was a must-do in the San Juans."

"Oh, yes. Simply *everyone* rents their own plane." She nudged him.

He nudged her back. "Quit laughing and enjoy it!"

As the pilot went over the safety instructions, Rani clicked in her seat belt. Vikram gripped her hand, anticipation twinkling like stars in his dark brown eyes. The engine roared, the two big floats beneath them skimmed the water like skis, and then they were off. She felt something lift inside her stomach as the plane ascended into the cloudless blue skies.

She clutched Vikram's hand even more tightly.

"Beautiful," he whispered.

But his eyes weren't gazing out at the sapphire surface of the Salish Sea, nor the lush green of the islands. Not the peaks and valleys, the orchards and beaches and rocky cliffs. They didn't notice the ferries and sailboats zipping below like toy boats in a bathtub. Instead, they held hers.

EXT. VILLAGE – DAY

> VIKRAM
>
> Fair maiden, for your comfort I have procured this golden chariot of the skies.

> RANI
>
> These grand gestures are far too much for a simple lady such as I. (But please, keep them coming.)

"So, did you read that article I sent you?" Vikram prodded. "About the healthcare reform bill? What are your thoughts on rising drug costs?"

Chapter Five

riday night, Rani made her way to the garden just east of the barn. In the grass between the hollyhocks and the lilies, she spread out a red picnic blanket. She'd brought a wicker basket, a small outdoor lantern, champagne flutes and sparkling cider and chocolate. The air was warm and the Songbird glowed golden and the fragrance of summer blossoms enveloped her.

The atmosphere was perfect, and she hoped she looked appropriately enchanting. The dim light of the lantern would complement her complexion, give her a rosy glow. She'd been tempted to wear an extremely over-the-top ballgown, but Leo seemed so casual and athletic that it didn't seem quite right for him. Instead, she'd opted for a delicate lacy top and black jeans. She fluffed her hair, and stretched out as sexily as she could, a rose clamped beneath her teeth.

Hopefully, her pose whispered, "Come hither!" and not "I really like to chew on thorny plants!"

Because yuck, rose stems were not yummy.

It had been hard to decide whether to invite Leo or Vikram to a moonlit picnic—so Rani had invited both. Not on the same evening, of course. Leo tonight and Vikram tomorrow. She was more than ready for starry nights replete with poetry and intense yearning and the vast, dark sky glimmering full of possibilities.

Rani heard a rustle in the bushes.

"Leo?" she asked, tossing her hair and batting her eyelashes.

"Sorry," Raj said, appearing in the shadows. "Must have gotten the wrong moonlit picnic."

Rani sat up and crossed her arms. "You're having a moonlit picnic, too?"

He shrugged, his face in the shadows. That moonlit picnic with Raj from last summer came crashing back into her thoughts: the chirping crickets and warm summer air and Raj's nerdy sense of humor. He'd insisted the constellations looked exactly like his favorite video game characters. Obviously, she'd countered with made-up constellations of her favorite film stars. They'd giggled and sketched out their versions of the figures in the night sky on a napkin and proved that neither of them was particularly good at drawing. They'd had a perfectly lovely time, but it had ended with him yawning and telling her it was getting late.

Typical Raj.

She flushed as he gazed at her in the light of the lantern. The lacy tank suddenly felt too chilly. Too exposed. She wished she'd brought a sweater. "Well, my date will be here any moment, so if you don't mind . . ."

"Right, your date," Raj said. (Not moving.)

"Is there something you need?" she asked in a clipped voice. Those little daydreams that Raj kept intruding on felt a bit too real at the moment.

"Sorry." He shuffled his feet. "You're right. I don't know why I keep texting you when you've obviously moved on."

"I don't know why either," Rani said. It was harsh, but she couldn't help it. Was he suddenly only interested because other guys were? That wasn't good enough for her.

Raj's shoulders slumped, and he started walking away.

As he did, Leo arrived, nearly bumping into him. "Oh, hey man. Didn't see you there."

"No problem," mumbled Raj, his footsteps fading into the night.

Rani focused on pouring the sparkling cider. And definitely not on the forlorn look on Raj's face. Nor the guilty feeling that maybe she should give him more of a chance to explain. Then again, would those dragon-slaying knights have wasted this much time to reclaim a long-lost love? Would they have texted *Can we talk?* instead of just coming up to her and spitting out whatever excuse they had for never getting in touch?

Maybe the modern age wasn't all it was cracked up to be.

"This is so romantic," Leo gushed, plopping down beside her and accepting the crystal flute.

At least Leo appreciated her. And boy, she appreciated him. One good thing about the modern age was the invention of tight black shirts and sexy black jeans. Leo could probably pull off anything, but this was much better than pantaloons. (If pantaloons had been what knights wore—Rani wasn't quite sure.) In fact, he matched Rani's lacy black top and black jeans almost a little too perfectly. But dang, he looked hunky, even as the night shadows curled around him, those destiny-holding stars twinkling overhead (which definitely did not look like video game characters!). He smelled amazing, too. Whatever his aftershave was, it was making Rani's head spin.

"Did you bring your favorite book?" Rani asked, ready for the most intense conversation of her life. She'd had a lot of fun roughhousing with him in the water, but she wanted to know more about him, too. What made this Prince of Abs tick. She wanted the whole package, really.

"Yep." Leo presented her with a book of love poems, classic sonnets from Shakespeare, Elizabeth Barrett Browning, Lord Byron, and more.

"This is your favorite book?"

Even in the dim light of the lantern, she could tell it was brand-new. The back cover sported a sticker from the only bookstore on Orcas.

"Okay, I'm not much of a reader." Leo offered her a hopeful smile. "But there was a poem we read in English class that was really nice. It reminds me of you."

EXT. INN – NIGHT

RANI
A gentleman who doesn't share my love of books? Can he possibly be for me?

FORTUNE-TELLER
My dear, look inside yourself for the answers.

RANI

You're really unhelpful, you know that?

"Would you like me to read it to you?" Leo asked, flipping through the pages.

She nodded, her heart racing. So what if the book was brand-new? Leo was about to read her poetry! In the moonlight! This was an absolute dream.

EXT. GARDEN – NIGHT

LEO

She walks in beauty, like the night . . .

RANI

Oh Leo, this is the most romantic thing that ever
happened to me.

And it was, it really was. In the darkness, his voice was husky and sweet. He looked at her with dark night eyes. Leaned in close. Rani straightened, ready for the moment. Ready to feel his lips against hers, to melt into his arms, to find out if this was indeed Destiny, capital *D*.

"Ouch!" Leo said, swiping at a bug. "Ugh, I'm getting swarmed by gnats!"

Apparently, his aftershave was a little too compelling. As the tiny bugs swarmed him while he helplessly swatted, she hoped this was just the universe drawing out the sweet seconds of their fledgling love, only delaying the inevitable.

EXT. GARDEN – NIGHT

RAJ

Or could it be a sign that he's not the one for you?

RANI

Who made you the Official Love Guru?

Saturday afternoon, Rani was stuck debating tomatoes in Bella, the bistro in Doe Bay that would be catering the wedding. Apparently, there was an asparagus crisis, and the entire menu needed to be upended. Katrina, the caterer, assured them that all was not lost—the dishes would instead focus on the amazing flavors of fresh Gutiérrez Farm tomatoes. However, there was much ado about which variety to use.

She was late for yet another date with Leo. She couldn't wait—minus the bugs, the previous night had been so amazing. The moonlit garden, the scent of the hollyhocks and the lilies. Poetry and stars.

Even at 3 p.m., the tables in the bistro were mostly full, soft chatter and laughter filling the airy modern space. Sunshine streamed through the windows, endless possibilities of water and sand and berry tasting. Of course, Leo was more ambitious than that. He had a fifty-mile bike ride all over the island planned, including a foray up and down Turtleback Mountain.

"Well, which one do you like?" Nidhi asked.

"I dunno, they're both good." Rani impatiently pushed her sample penne in white sauce around the plate. "Also, it's a tomato. Does it really matter?"

Nidhi gasped. Katrina was suddenly very focused on cleaning a microscopic spot off a wineglass.

"How can you say that?" Nidhi emphatically speared some tomato and penne with her fork. "This sungold looks and tastes nothing like the taxi."

"Uh-huh." Rani also forcefully speared some of the sungold version. Pretended to think as she chewed. "Yes, absolutely. Let's go with this. It's so much more . . . tomatoey."

This time, Nidhi and the caterer exchanged exasperated looks.

"I'll give you girls a few minutes," Katrina said diplomatically.

Nidhi took another bite of each, savoring them. "I honestly can't pick one over the other either."

She looked so stumped that Rani had to laugh. "So serve them both?"

"Serve two very similar penne dishes?" Nidhi sounded appalled. "It would be an embarrassment."

"Totally. How gauche." Rani smirked as her phone pinged. Probably a message from Leo wondering where she was.

But actually it was an alert from Chatterbox. And three more came up as she was reading.

"Um . . . Nidhi?" Rani said.

Her big sis had her eyes closed as she contemplated another bit of taxi tomato. A true gastronome to the core. But they had bigger issues to deal with.

"Look." Rani tapped Nidhi on the shoulder. "A bunch of our relatives from India have gotten visas to come for the wedding! Do we have space for nine—no wait, ten—no, actually *fifteen* extra guests?"

Nidhi's eyes nearly popped out. "What?"

"Fifteen relatives from India are asking if they can come to the wedding. They have visas."

"What? How?" Nidhi looked completely flabbergasted. "They only just found out about it."

"Apparently, they'd been hoping to come for a visit since we got in touch. But now that they've found out about the wedding, it really does seem like the perfect timing." Rani grinned. "Actually, it's pretty exciting. We've never even seen them before! We're going to have a reunion after all this time!"

Nidhi stared at her. Stared at her own phone, pinging with alerts. At first she looked like she was going to completely lose it. Which, not a surprise—Nidhi had a thing for trying to control chaos. Fifteen extra guests would be hard to squeeze into the Songbird for the wedding weekend, Rani had to admit. Dad and Amir had insisted they be able to house their out-of-town wedding guests, and Amir had his own family coming from all over.

There was also the whole issue of whether Dad would even want them there.

But Nidhi was already nodding in agreement, her eyes sparkling. "If we can pull it off, this could be really amazing. I can't believe we're actually going to see Lalita Phua and Deepak Phupha and Lakshman Dada and Sona and Prakash and all the rest."

It was hard to imagine. They'd all just been online figments up until now. But in only a couple of weeks, they could be here on Orcas Island. They'd get to see the Songbird Inn, the only home the Singh sisters had ever really known. And though it was usually full with guests coming and going, that weekend it would be bursting with friends and a family from faraway.

Nidhi called Katrina over. "I can't decide. You choose. They're both great."

Somehow, Rani made it to her date with Leo just seventeen minutes late. His grin said he didn't mind at all. And even though spandex didn't suit most people, Leo *wasn't* most people.

Chapter Six

*W*hat should I wear?" Rani asked Avani that evening as she rooted through the depths of their too-small closet. Tonight she'd meet Vikram for moonlit date number two, and she needed the perfect look. With all the talk of the relatives coming to the wedding, it had reminded Rani that she really needed to decide who she'd ask as her date, which was only two weeks away.

"How about this?" Avani pulled out a yellow sundress.

"Yellow? At night? It's going to look weird against the lantern light."

"This?" Avani pulled out her silver Winter Ball dress, one of her few decent pieces.

"Thanks, but that feels too . . . nightclub." Rani sighed. Her sisters were so hopeless when it came to fashion. She was on her own.

"Fine." Avani rolled her eyes. "You'd think you'd be able to find something considering your stuff takes up way more than half the closet!"

"Please," Rani retorted. "How many moisture-wicking athletic shirts do you really need?"

Avani threw a pillow at her face. "A lot, okay?"

Rani threw the pillow back. "Whatever, dweeb."

"Oh, those are fighting words." Avani pulled out a moisture-wicking shirt and modeled it in front of her. "See? The height of sophistication!"

Rani laughed. "Uh-huh."

She dug through the mess of their closet, desperate for just the right thing.

INT. INN – DAY

                   RANI

How in the world can I impress my suitors when I wear
nothing but rags?

            FORTUNE-TELLER

Rags? Is that a rag?

(Pointing)

Between two of Avani's giant and completely redundant parkas, Rani spotted a bit of scarlet poking out.

It was perfect.

A strapless bloodred gown with a long, ruffled train that she'd bought on a whim. It had been horrifically expensive, and she'd had nowhere at all to wear such an extravagant, deadly thing. But she was feeling deadly tonight. Ready to make Vikram fall truly, madly, deeply for her. Ready for that epic romance she'd always dreamt of.

She slipped it on. Expertly curled her hair into flowing luxurious raven locks. Picked the most scarlet of scarlet lipsticks.

"What do you think?" She twirled for her twin.

Avani whistled. "Go get 'em, tiger."

It was close to 11 p.m. when Rani headed out. Guests were still lingering and chatting in the living room, where they'd had a live band playing earlier, a summer Saturday tradition. She noticed Raj's parents talking quietly out on the south deck. They'd left the doors open, sea air gently carrying in their voices.

"This is nice, isn't it?" said Raj's mom.

"Very nice," replied Raj's dad.

"Dinner was lovely."

"Yes."

"The tandoori fish was grilled just right."

"It was very good."

"Impressive view, even at night."

"Yes."

Then a long silence.

Rani shook her head. That was the most pathetic conversation she'd ever heard. Is that really what she had to look forward to after marriage? No, she refused to believe it. She was destined for more, for a love that transcended time, for an epic romance that could compete with the ones in the films.

EXT. GARDEN – NIGHT

> RANI
>
> Oh stars above, I have long wished upon you for a love
> through the ages. I hope you'll deliver.

Vikram was waiting for Rani in the garden when she arrived, a vase of flowers in his arms. As she approached, she realized he'd bought her a gorgeous—and very expensive—arrangement of three dozen red roses.

She grinned. He was so over-the-top, and she kind of loved it. "What, one dozen wasn't enough?"

"Not for you." He offered her the enormous bouquet. "You look amazing, by the way."

"Thanks." She tried to hold it to the side so he could admire her in the darkness, the sultry scarlet dress and roses together. But a few unruly stems kept flopping the wrong way right into her face.

Not cool, universe. Not cool.

EXT. GARDEN – NIGHT

> RAJ
>
> I call it "Woman in a Bramble."

> RANI
>
> Hush, you.

Vikram's favorite book turned out to be a nonfiction treatise on how to engage with the climate crisis.

"Fun reading." Rani chuckled, lighting the citronella candles she'd brought. She wasn't about to let any bugs get in the way tonight. She stretched her legs across the picnic blanket and arranged the dress's long train to flare out just so.

EXT. GARDEN – NIGHT

               RANI
      Dear stars, I've brought before thee Prince Charming
      #2 on Moonlit Date #2. Will we fall hopelessly, madly
      in love?

              VIKRAM
      Thine eyes art so bright, thine lips so red. Also, can you
      believe the state of the polar ice caps?

"I promise this book's not as dry as you think." Vikram took the initiative and poured them both sparkling cider. "The author has a sense of humor. Honestly, I'd love to be able to write like him someday. To make people care, but without overwhelming them with information."

Though Rani craved more compliments for her killer dress, she knew that this was who Vikram was. Someone who cared more about her thoughts on the issues than her looks.

It's a good thing, it's a good thing, it's a good thing . . .

"You do make people care." She fiddled with the scarlet ruffles on her gown just one last time before pulling out the charcuterie tray and chocolate dipped strawberries. "Honestly, I've only ordered 'for here' coffee in a mug after that video you did about how recycling to-go cups and single-use utensils is just a lie."

"You did?" He looked really excited.

Rani smiled. "Really. The inn also switched to ribbons from recycled materials for our gift baskets."

"Nice. At least until my parents really do figure out how to break down large amounts of plastic, it's great to know that I can actually make a difference."

"You are."

"Thanks." Vikram gestured at the picnic fare. "And thanks for planning all this."

"You're welcome."

He took an appreciative taste of cheese. "So what book did you bring?"

"Got it right here." Rani's hands searched her bag.

He'd shared with her, and now it was her turn. A give and a take; just what she'd wanted. And yet she felt at a bit of a crossroads, too. She'd actually brought two books. *Emma*, a favorite for certain. But there was also another book—the book she'd read over and over again—a smoldering romance between a prince and the ordinary girl he'd fallen for. And she could passionately explain how the themes transcended time and space, how there was nuance to their relationship that made you rethink what love truly was.

She hesitated. Did she really want to go into a long explanation defending a book with a hot shirtless guy on the cover? Vikram had claimed he was interested in her thoughts on romance and toxic masculinity, sort of. She just wasn't sure how sincere he was about it.

EXT. GARDEN – NIGHT

> VIKRAM
> Please, I want to know the true depths of your heart,
> dearest one.

> RANI
> Um, the true depths? Are you certain you're ready
> for that?

Rani wished that it was easier to share herself, but pulling out *Emma* to show Vikram was just easier. He peered at the special edition hardcover, Emma reimagined with gorgeous artwork.

"Oh, I think that's my favorite Jane Austen novel, too," he said.

"You've read it?"

"Well, I don't read much fiction besides what they assign in school." He munched thoughtfully on some Gutiérrez chèvre with a cracker. "But I saw one of the movies. It was cute."

She grinned. "Didn't you think her matchmaking was pretty great? Though I'm better."

"Isn't the point that it almost never works?"

"Yeah, that's why I'm better!" Rani winked. She was definitely proud of herself for herding her sisters and Dad through a year of new crushes, blossoming feelings, and kisses in the Northwest drizzle.

Vikram raised his glass. "I'm sure you are."

She clinked it with hers. "So, when do you want to interview me on all my hot takes on romance?"

He laughed. "Well, as I said, it's a very compelling topic. We'll do it soon, I promise."

EXT. GARDEN – NIGHT

> RANI
>
> Promises, promises. A true gentleman acts.

> VIKRAM
>
> Shall I extoll your virtues once more?

> RANI
>
> I suppose that would be acceptable.

It was late when Rani stumbled back to the room she and Avani shared, her head spinning once again with moonlight and poetry and brooding dark eyes. Three dozen long-stemmed roses and sparkling cider and a boy who had even invited her on his family's yacht tomorrow. Seriously—a yacht! Apparently, they were getting some work done on it, which was why they were staying at the Songbird for now. But they could still use it a bit, at least.

She tiptoed into the bedroom, but there was no need; Avani was out cold, drooling on her pillowcase. Rani giggled and took a quick photo with her phone. Each twin kept a stockpile of embarrassing photos of the other—mutually assured destruction, should any of them ever be revealed.

She wasn't planning to disarm anytime soon.

On her bed, a giant stuffed orca smiled playfully at her. There was a note attached: *Let's sail away together. Just us and the whales. Yours, Leo*

Rani squeezed the snuggly adorable thing, expelling a long, satisfied sigh. Destiny really had come her way, making up for Raj's flakiness and last year's unkissed summer. Fate had given her two suitors, and her heart pitter-pattered at the thought of both of them. It was just like in her favorite novels and films. A dream come true.

Wait. What if it was *actually* a dream?

What if someone pinched her and she'd wake up and it would be cold and wet and dreary in mid-November and she'd realize that there had never been a Leo or a Vikram?

Just to be sure, Rani pinched herself.

Nothing happened.

Everything was as before—roses on her dresser and a soft orca pressed up against her. She was still here. But so was her fear of it all slipping away.

Chapter Seven

*R*ani arrived at Sunday dinner late again, having spent the last few hours on Vikram's family's yacht. And whoa. Just whoa. She could get used to that kind of life. Maybe a little too used to it.

Fernando pulled out a chair for her, and Brie passed her the biryani. Their family had certainly grown over the year. (Due in large part to Rani's matchmaking, obviously.)

She longed to invite someone of her own to the weekly meal, but—as great as Vikram and Leo were—she didn't quite feel ready. She was still waiting for a Sign to tell her which one was perfect for her.

INT. INN – EVENING

> RANI
>
> Help, the stars have failed to reveal to me which
> handsome suitor is my true fate. What can I do?

> FORTUNE-TELLER
>
> My dear, you must discover this on your own. But one
> hint: Your true suitor will understand that which you have
> always loved. That which keeps you awake at night.

> RANI
>
> Romance novels keep me awake at night.

> FORTUNE-TELLER
>
> Indeed? Very interesting.

At least Raj had stopped texting her. He must have gotten the hint that she wasn't interested. She still saw him and his family around the inn of course, but he'd kept his distance. Well, the real him did. The daydream version of Raj kept intruding into her thoughts.

Sheesh. Like a boy for fifteen hot minutes and he'll haunt you for life.

As Rani pondered the fortune-teller's advice, the table swelled with excited chatter about the wedding. Avani was rapidly listing off songs that were vital for the playlist, Sirisha was asking Dad and Amir if there were any particular moments they wanted her to capture, and Nidhi mentioned casually that the inn would be overflowing on the wedding weekend and that she'd recommended some of their guests stay elsewhere.

Rani raised her brows at her big sis. The Songbird would only be short on rooms because of the fifteen surprise guests coming from India. But Nidhi hadn't mentioned that part.

"Eat up! Eat up!" Dad encouraged them.

"And don't forget to try the haleem," Amir added. "I'm not a professional chef like your dad, but I think it came out well."

Rani spooned some of the hearty stew into her bowl. She'd gotten used to mixing in Amir's Pakistani dishes with their usual North Indian cuisine, and there were always some surprising flavors and combinations that kept things fresh.

"For an ophthalmologist, your cooking is pretty decent," she said.

Amir laughed. "Why, thank you. I'm glad I can do something domestic around here, though I'm not much of an event planner. Nidhi—I can't thank you enough for taking over so many of the wedding details."

"My pleasure." Nidhi glowed. "We finalized the menu yesterday. It's all really simple flavors with an emphasis on local produce. The sungold tomato penne is divine!" She winked at Rani.

"Much better than some silly taxi tomato penne," Rani agreed, smirking.

"I hope they're Gutiérrez tomatoes," Fernando added in.

"Don't worry, they are!" Nidhi assured him.

Rani waited for Nidhi to mention the big news. Her other sisters had to have seen it on Chatterbox, too, but they all seemed rather busy with their food all of a sudden. Cowards.

Well, if they weren't going to say anything, she was. But maybe it was best to ease into the topic. "Hey, Dad, I really think it's time you got on Chatterbox. The relatives have been wanting to congratulate you on the wedding."

Things got quiet at the table. Dad put down his roti and exchanged a look with Amir, making it clear that he'd discussed the issue of his estranged relatives with him.

"You may thank them for the good wishes," Dad said. "I'm very glad you're getting to know our relatives—especially your cousins. Lalita Phua and I had always been close when we were kids, and she really stepped up when I asked her to. It fills my heart with joy that Nidhi is getting this opportunity with her."

"So what's the problem?" Rani asked.

Dad chewed thoughtfully before speaking. "To be honest, some of our other relatives haven't always been there for me when I needed them. The memories are rather painful, and that's why I prefer not to talk about it."

Rani fiddled with her napkin. Avani's fork clattered to the floor, the sound echoing in the sudden uncomfortable silence.

Eventually, Dad sighed. "All I can say is that family—real family—are the people who show up for you when things are hard. The Songbird isn't just how we make a living; it's always been my dream to run something like this. And I couldn't have done it without the help of so many people right here in the San Juans. The community has supported us in so many ways I can't even name, and they're the ones I want surrounding me as I tie the knot. Josie, Armand, our staff. So many business owners"—he smiled at Fernando—"especially the Gutiérrezes."

Dad looked like he wanted to say something more, but he stopped himself.

The sisters, meanwhile, began their own conversation through blinks and quirked brows.

Rani: *What are we going to do? Tell the relatives not to come?*

Sirisha: *I hope not. I really want to see them.*

Nidhi: *We'll come up with a plan.*

Avani: *Can't you see I've got enough on my mind with the playlist? And how cute Fernando will look in a suit?*

Rani: *Hmm, who would look better in a suit—Vikram or Leo? Vikram could pull off a white one, probably. Black shirt paired with black tie. And for Leo—hmm—navy. Definitely navy.*

Amir patted Dad's shoulder and cleared his throat. "I'm looking forward to introducing you all to my family, too. They're excited to meet the four very accomplished women I keep telling them about! I've bragged about each of you. Sirisha: your photography. Avani and Fernando: your chicken raising. Nidhi: your baking, and your big plans for next year. And Rani: your eye for fashion. Thanks for picking out our wedding sherwanis, by the way."

Rani shrugged modestly. "It was the least I could do."

Dad raised his water glass. "To my very accomplished daughters."

They all raised their glasses, and despite the uneasy feelings about the relatives, Rani felt a warmth inside. They *were* very lucky for all they had right here on Orcas, to have made a success of the Songbird, to have found their own interests and to have a father who encouraged them to make their own paths in life.

"Now," Dad continued, "something much more pressing: Who wants to give the speech at the reception? I think we'll stick with just one on our side, and one from Amir's family."

"Good idea," Avani agreed. "We need time to party at the reception, not a zillion speeches. But Fernando and I already have something special planned—we're going to sing a song!"

She and Fernando high-fived.

"You can sing?" Rani asked.

"Better than you!" Avani smirked.

"Hmmph." Rani sniffed. She knew she had a tendency to get slightly—just slightly!—off-key. But her twin didn't need to rub it in.

Sirisha hid behind her hands. "Please, don't pick me for the speech!"

Dad laughed. "We won't force you, I promise."

"I think Rani should do it," Nidhi said, nudging her gently under the table with her foot. "She's our resident expert in romance after all."

Rani was surprised—and flattered. Finally, her sisters were recognizing her true talents. Like a gardener, she'd spent the whole year watchfully tending all the little romances that had bloomed, watering them and making sure they had soil to grow.

And now, with two guys vying for her attention, she had to admit the truth. She wasn't just the Official Love Guru anymore. She was the QUEEN.

INT. INN – EVENING

RANI'S SISTERS
Dear and wise Rani, please tell us your secrets on the art
of love. We have much to learn from you.

RANI
Fear not, I am nothing but benevolent with my powers.

"What do you say, Rani?" Dad asked expectantly. "Will you give the speech?"

Rani tossed her hair, stood up and raised her voice as if she was already on stage, chest puffed up. "I would be honored."

Amir and Dad clapped, Fernando hooted, Nidhi squeezed her hand. Avani arched her eyebrows in twin language: *Good luck! You'll need it.* Rani arched her own in return: *Don't think I've forgotten your comments on my singing.*

The Singh sisters gathered later that evening in Nidhi's attic room, the gentle pattering of rain on the roof the perfect accompaniment to their chatter. It was evening, so at least no one was missing out on sunshine, thankfully. Summer rain was rare, but the sisters could definitely get touchy about it. Good weather in July and August was their much-deserved reward for living through all the gloom of winter and spring.

Rani caught Nidhi staring out her window, a funny little smile playing across her big sister's lips, her eyes dreamy and faraway under those jealousy-inducing lashes. Nidhi would never need mascara, that was for certain.

"Thinking about Grayson?" Rani tucked one of Nidhi's curls back up in her topknot.

"What? No." Nidhi turned to fiddle with an arrangement of daisies from their garden on her nightstand.

"Are you sure you don't want to meet up with him in Buenos Aires?" Avani asked, now getting a dreamy look on *her* face. "It would be *so* romantic . . ."

Nidhi laughed. "You're the one who said I should keep my options open!"

"Maybe I was wrong about all that." Avani put on some music—the song that she and Fernando had declared theirs after dancing to it at the Winter Ball.

Rani had never seen her twin so dang *happy*. And at peace—with herself, with her relationship. Curiosity got the better of her. "Are you in *love*?"

Avani looked sheepish. "I don't know. What even *is* love?"

Sirisha flopped on the bed, cupping her chin with her hands. "Does love make everything inside you sort of—tingle?"

Nidhi leaned against the headboard that had once saved her life. "All I know is that love doesn't have to be forever. It can be something you feel just in the moment. It doesn't mean you have to get married or anything."

Rani sat down at Nidhi's desk chair, suddenly pensive. It sort of bugged her that her sisters were all starry-eyed and wistful and discussing that big L-word, while Rani was still waiting to feel *it*—whatever *it* was. Sigh. She had two admirers. Three, if you counted those ignored texts from Raj. (Which she didn't, obviously.) Still, she was impatient for a romance that would truly sweep her off her feet.

Of course, they had other problems to discuss, too.

"We need to talk about the incoming relatives," Rani said. "What are we going to do? Dad basically said he didn't want them at the wedding."

Nidhi sighed, fiddling with yet another loose strand of hair that somehow looked perfectly tousled. "Everything's set for them to come. We just have to convince Dad he wants them here."

"At least he said he was glad that Lalita Phua stepped up for you," Avani said.

"Yeah, that's a good sign," Sirisha agreed. "We should let him know that the rest of them want to show up for us, too. That whatever happened in the past, they regret it."

"How do we know they do?" Rani asked. "We never talk about it on Chatterbox. I'm afraid to bring it up!"

Nidhi bit her lip. "I think it's time to have the hard conversations. I'll see what I can find out from Lalita Phua. Rani—you and Dad are getting your final fittings tomorrow, right? Maybe you can find out more about which relatives he was talking about. And what it is they didn't show up for. Then we have to help them make it right."

"Yeah, that sounds real easy." Rani flopped on the bed beside Sirisha.

Nidhi and Avani flopped down next to her, so they were all four sisters lying in a row, listening to the quiet, almost hypnotic pattering of summer rain against the roof. The cosmos was shifting around them, their safe little world on a small island in the San Juans expanding irrevocably. A window had been cracked open, and the Singh sisters had peeked out and realized that there were dreams to catch hold of and relationships to explore and strange new places that stretched out beyond the dusky horizon.

A warm breeze drifted in, carrying in the scent of summer blossoms and sweet, inevitable change.

Chapter Eight

Rani tossed and turned, the moon annoyingly bright outside, her dreams a blur of dashing from door to door among the guest rooms in the Songbird. Except each guest room door opened to a new and wondrous life with a different eligible suitor, and selecting just one was impossible.

When the alarm went off on Monday morning, the fog hovering over the sea seemed to have seeped into her brain. Her insides felt like Dad's double boiler scrambled eggs—a recent addition to the menu that was becoming quite popular with the guests. At breakfast duty later that morning, they actually knocked the much-vaunted eggs Benedict off the throne of most-ordered item.

The misty morning meant guests weren't as impatient to get out, and the atmosphere in the dining room was relaxed as people allowed themselves to linger over their coffee. Which made waitressing much more relaxed, too. If only she didn't have that horribly awkward task in front of her later with Dad. Once the restaurant had cleared out, Rani headed to her room to grab her purse.

The Official Love Guru had work to do.

"There you are!" Dad said, coming up the stairs just behind her. He was carrying a giant adorable stuffed deer in one arm and a vase of tulips in the other. "The deer is from Leo. The tulips are from Vikram."

"Oh, thanks." Rani took the vase while Dad walked her to her room with the stuffed deer. "They've really gone overboard with the gifts. I barely have room for them all!"

"They must really like you." Dad smiled. "Do you want to invite either of them to the wedding? We can make space for them to stay here—somehow."

Actually, with the relatives possibly coming, it would be harder than Dad realized. But that wasn't the main problem. "I don't suppose I can bring two dates to the wedding?"

Dad grinned. "That would be an interesting choice."

INT. INN – EVENING

VIKRAM

Apple of my eye, may I have this dance?

LEO

You scoundrel, you're not worthy of this fine maiden. My dearest, may I have this dance?

RAJ

You're both scoundrels. Rani, when will you realize my
love is true?

VIKRAM, LEO, and RAJ engage in fisticuffs.

RANI

Gentlemen, please, please. Compose yourselves. I will
dance with each of you.

RAJ

You will?

RANI

Well, if I must . . .

Rani shook her head. "It's hard to decide! They're both great, really."
She paused. "How did you figure out that Amir was the one for you?"

Dad's smile truly glowed. Come to think of it, he always glowed when
he talked about Amir.

"I don't know," Dad said. "I suppose we just clicked. The first time
we went out for drinks, we talked and talked all evening. He asked me
all about the Songbird, and you girls. We talked about how he was liking
Orcas. We talked about the weather. Anything. Everything. It was so easy
being with him. Before I knew it, it was after midnight. With him, time
always flies, all the worries about the inn drift away, and all I want to do
is make him laugh again."

"You two are so adorable."

How simple Dad made it all sound. If only it would feel that simple to Rani.

He patted her shoulder. "You'll figure it out. Ready to go to our fitting? I hope they've finally come out right."

"You and me both," Rani said.

"Just a sec, I need to grab my keys," Dad said. "Meet you at the car?"

"Sure."

As he started to walk away, the light in the hallway silhouetted him just so, highlighting the width of his shoulders and the sturdy way he walked. He'd always seemed so confident, someone they'd been sure would take care of them no matter what happened.

It was hard to remember that sometimes he might need Rani and her sisters to take care of him, too.

Dad stepped out of the stall into the larger fitting room lined with mirrors. He and Rani were the only ones in the dressing area at the back of the shop. His sherwani shimmered softly, fitted perfectly to his shoulders. He wore scarlet silk with gold embroidery, and Amir would be wearing gold silk with scarlet embroidery to complement. It had been Rani's idea, to symbolize their entwined love.

Dad patted the fabric nervously. "How do I look?"

Rani scanned the folds of the silk. Though they'd had to have numerous fittings since Beatrice had struggled with the fabric, today it looked perfect. "You look regal, like a prince. No, better than a prince. A king."

"Thanks," Dad said, fussing with the bejeweled traditional headgear that came with the outfit. "Come, show off your lehenga in the mirror with me."

Shyly, she stepped beside him. She'd been nervous about it, after so many past versions where the lehenga had poofed out strangely instead of falling in the graceful silhouette she wanted. But, standing next to Dad, Rani couldn't believe what she saw reflected in the mirror. The dress fit like a dream. She felt like a fairy tale princess from the stories she loved so much.

It hit her then. Dad was getting married.

It deserved saying again: Her father was getting married. They were getting a new stepdad. A salt water sea was suddenly rushing out of her eyes.

"What's this? Why are we crying?" Dad tucked her hair behind her ear, kissed her on the forehead.

She felt about four years old when he did that, and that was okay. She felt protected and loved and supported. She'd always felt that way, every single day of her life that she could remember. And she hoped he felt the same.

"We?" she asked shakily, before noticing that Dad was tearing up, too.

He chuckled. "Yeah."

Rani sniffed. "I guess everyone gets emotional about weddings."

Dad squeezed her tightly. "Yes, I suppose they do. I love you so much, sweetheart. And I know you and your sisters have been through an incredible amount. Losing your mom, losing Pop. But you've all been so great with Amir, so accepting. I want you to know that I appreciate it."

"Of course—we're so excited for you!" Rani cried harder.

The door creaked open and Beatrice stuck her head in the room.

"How's everything . . . Oh, um. I'll just give you two some more time." She smiled sheepishly and shut the door again.

Rani wiped the tears and sat down on one of the many chairs in the space. "Dad, I want to talk to you about our relatives. What exactly happened between you?"

Dad looked uncomfortable. "Honey, it's all in the past."

"Not really," she pressed. "They've asked if they can come to the wedding, Dad. They have their visas arranged. Nidhi saved them rooms at the Songbird. But they're waiting for our okay to actually purchase the flights."

Dad looked shocked. "They want to come here? I don't know if that's such a good idea."

"I think they want to make things right, Dad, but they don't know how." Rani played with the folds of her beautiful dress. A dress that she desperately wanted to wear at a wedding that included all the family that they'd lost but then found. She could picture them there: some with faces that had Dad's nose, some with the curve of his smile or maybe his chin. Hints of Rani and her sisters in their features, too. "Tell me what happened. Why did you lose touch?"

He sat down beside her, brushed his hand through his hair. "Where to begin? After your mother passed, everything was so hard for me. I didn't know if I could raise four girls all by myself. My parents had already passed, too, so I wasn't going to get help from them. Lakshman Dada called and told me to go home to India, that it would be better for all of you. That your mom's family wanted to help, and so did he. As my dad's elder brother, he'd been more than an uncle to me, and I truly appreciated the offer. I was really close to doing it. After all, I was in this country where I had no support system whatsoever. I even quit my job as a sous chef in a restaurant in Portland, ready to leave.

"But then, one day, someone told me about a property for sale on an island in the San Juans. I had never heard of Orcas at that time. Mom and

I were so busy raising you four and paying rent, we never had the time or the money to travel, even locally. But when I saw the Songbird, something clicked. The place was falling apart, just a complete mess, but I had a feeling about it. I'd always dreamt of starting my own hotel and restaurant, and Mom had supported me. Had even dreamt of helping me run it.

"I couldn't afford it on my own, but I took us all to go see it. I met Pop while we were out there. We got to talking, and we realized that maybe if we worked together, we could renovate it. Make it beautiful. It was a dream for both of us.

"And over the course of that project, Pop and I fell in love." Dad laughed, and Rani squeezed his hand. "It was such a surprise; I'd never expected that, at all. But I felt like I had life inside me again. Jonathan and the Songbird were truly a light in the darkness. And I certainly felt that Mom would have approved, would be proud of who I became and the life I built for you."

"I think so, too," Rani whispered, even though she didn't remember much of her mother. All she had were old photos, a smiling woman with long flowing black hair and gentle eyes, a patrician nose like Nidhi's. A woman who always seemed to look perfect in a sari.

"But Lakshman Dada thought I'd lost my mind. He kept insisting that I give up on the project—even when we were done and we'd put so much work into it."

"Because of Pop?" Rani asked.

"Well, he didn't say anything about Pop specifically. He didn't go that far, but honestly his silence said enough. The fact that he thought our relationship was second to his desire for me to return to India with you four. I told him he couldn't control who I was or what I dreamt for myself and for our family, but I promised to visit with you girls as soon as we had the money. Only, he was so angry that he told me not to bother. He'd been the so-called patriarch of the family for so long that he wasn't used to anyone disagreeing with him—and he didn't exactly take it well when they did. He said . . ." Dad struggled with words for a moment before continuing, his voice heavy. "He said that we weren't Indian anymore, that we'd left our heritage behind. We stopped speaking after that. In fact, I haven't spoken a word to him since that last phone call."

Rani tried to picture all this. Lakshman Dada had seemed so jovial on Chatterbox. But she'd never met him in person. Dad was describing another side to him—one she wasn't sure she wanted to get to know. But then again, what if he had changed? People could do that, couldn't they?

"Thanks for telling me the whole story," Rani said, swallowing. "But it was a long time ago. Do you think you should give him a chance? You did say family is about showing up, and he wants to come here. Maybe he wants to show you he still cares."

Dad rubbed his chin. He still looked like a king in his beautiful wedding sherwani, but one who had reached a crossroads in his kingdom.

INT. DRESSMAKER'S SHOP – DAY

FATHER

I want the world for you, my four daughters, but my heart was wounded years ago, and now I am wary of what the world has to offer.

RANI

Father, we can't change the past. But we hope to make

the future brighter—and that starts with taking on
some wrongs.

Rani and Dad walked back to the car. The morning fog had lifted, and the island felt different—expectant, as if the salty sea breeze was soft gossamer, as if the evergreens were an arbor for the ceremony, as if the twinkle of sunshine on the water was bubbles exploding out of a champagne bottle.

Dad looked out at the glimmering sea. "I'll get on Chatterbox, okay? Let's see what Lakshman Dada has to say."

Rani hugged him. "Thanks, Dad. You're really brave to face all of this."

He chuckled. "You girls make me brave."

Chapter Nine

*E*arly the next morning, before the restaurant had opened for the day, the Singh sisters gathered at a table in the dining room near the windows looking out north. A variety of pastries sat untouched in front of them, cups of chai unsipped. Dad stood outside on the north porch, pacing back and forth, back and forth. Phone in hand.

The sisters didn't press their noses against the windows like children, but they sort of wanted to.

Dad tapped a button on his phone. Waited.

And his daughters waited along with him.

Long moments felt like eons as the connection was made, packets of data hopping through cell phone towers and satellites to land somewhere on the other side of the world. A continent they'd never stepped foot on. A motherland that was theirs, and yet not theirs.

Someone must have answered because Dad started talking. The lines on his forehead grew deep like the narrow channels between islands—but he was nodding, too. Speaking carefully. His hand clenched tight on the phone. Specks of silver in his hair catching the light, his age showing the way it rarely did. Yet he didn't look lost.

How could he be?

He stood beside the inn on a craggy cliff over the sea, the one he'd poured his soul into. Tulip planters lining the edge of the porch, his beloved imported tandoori oven beside him. When he finally hung up, he looked at peace. And when he saw the sisters gathered against the window (still not quite pressing their noses against it—but close) he offered them a rueful Dad smile and a thumbs-up.

He'd formally invited the relatives to the wedding, and they'd accepted.

Chapter Ten

The rest of the week flew by in a flurry of dates and wedding planning. Rani had somehow become Nidhi's assistant, taking calls from vendors when Nidhi was too busy. Nidhi had even given her access to the budget spreadsheet so she could account for costs as they came up. Seriously, her big sister had actually learned the word *delegate*. (An extremely suspect phenomenon that prompted a secret twin discussion about possible body snatching.)

It was a lot of responsibility.

Way-too-early a.m. on Saturday July Fourth, Rani moaned when her alarm went off. Flopped around on her bed. Of course, there was barely any room to flop around, since Leo had sent her so many stuffed animals that she basically had to cocoon herself in a tiny space between them.

BUZZ. BUZZ. BUZZ.

She tried to hit the snooze button, but instead toppled over a stack of nonfiction reading from Vikram (each book intensely meaningful to him, obviously).

"Rise and shine, beautiful!" Avani shut off Rani's alarm for her.

"Why are you so perky?" Rani asked.

"Well, I wasn't up late on some moonlit date." Avani shrugged. "How many moonlit dates have you been on now?"

"Too many." Rani's eyes were still closed, but she could hear Avani moving around, opening drawers. Getting ready for the day. Which she should probably do, too.

CRASH.

The sound of glass shattering forced Rani to open an eye. Just one, because she was far too exhausted to open both. And she spied a vase full of roses smashed on the floor.

"All I did was shut the dresser drawer," Avani explained with dismay. "There are way too many flowers up here."

It was true. Vikram had really overdone it. The room looked like a Valentine's Day display.

"It's yours, so you get to clean it up," Avani added.

Rani pressed the stuffed orca over her head and moaned. "Can't move."

"Uh-huh. We've got breakfast duty."

"Ugh. We've always got breakfast duty."

"And it's a holiday, so prepare for it to be extra busy." Avani sing-songed, "It's summer! Love in the summer, summer, summer!" And promptly hopped into the shower.

Rani's phone pinged. She should probably answer all the texts that the guys were sending her. But she didn't want to do that either.

Was it possible she actually *missed* what life was like before Destiny (capital *D*) had intervened? She thought back to quiet summers of the past. Except for helping out around the inn, she'd been able to do whatever she wanted. She'd spent hours just relaxing with Raj last year—back when she'd thought he liked her. But then she recalled the disappointment of being left unkissed on that hammock. A moment that haunted her still.

Ugh. No, this year was better. Much better. If she could just manage to get up.

So sleepy . . .

Then Avani was shaking her awake. "Hey, seriously. We're going to be late." She opened the curtains and annoyingly bright sunshine flooded the room.

"Do you mind?" Rani threw a stuffed sea otter at Avani.

"Hey!" Avani protested. "Don't shoot the messenger!"

More stuffed animals went flying, and soon it was an all-out war between the twins. When they finally made it to the dining room, they were four minutes late. Not too bad, considering most of the guests hadn't even come down yet.

As they passed the espresso bar, Avani quirked her brows at her twin. *Countdown to patented Concerned Sister*^{TM} *look.*

Rani giggled. *Three, two, one . . .*

But Nidhi only rolled her eyes at the two of them.

The twins exchanged glances. *Certified case of body snatching, for sure.*

As breakfast duty came to an end, Rani realized she desperately needed to make progress on her speech. The wedding was just a week away, the relatives were officially coming, plane tickets booked, and meanwhile she had nothing written down.

Nothing.

Obviously, she had tons of thoughts on love, that big L-word that she'd spent so much time thinking about and reading about and dreaming about. She was the Official Love Guru, the Romance Queen, a matchmaker that could give Emma Woodhouse a run for her money. She'd studied the subject thoroughly in books and films—and even in her life. Growing up, she'd seen the way Dad and Pop had been together, been inspired by them. Yearned for that same simple camaraderie. She'd seen Dad fall slowly but surely for Amir over the past few months. She'd even helped usher each of her sisters into romances, the kind that made them starry-eyed and full of unnamed wishes.

So what if she hadn't personally experienced *it*—whatever *it* actually was?

Rani knew her stuff, but to get it organized into a speech was a whole other thing. Getting out of the Songbird to clear her head was the only way. Besides, a part of her was okay with taking some space. At least Vikram and Leo were both busy hanging out with their respective families today. And with the wedding this close, Rani really needed to decide which one to take as her date. Ack!

To clear her head, Rani wandered into a café in Eastsound that smelled of butter and brioche, sugar and cinnamon. (Nidhi's dream scents, probably.) The pastry display was tempting, but she opted for a sandwich and an iced latte. Settling at a corner table, she pulled out a romance novel from her bag. She was there to work on the speech, but she needed inspiration first.

"I wonder why the Skull didn't strike last night," commented a woman at a nearby table. "It almost doesn't feel like Independence Day without him."

"What a disappointment," her friend agreed. "What are we supposed to do? Be satisfied with a few fireworks?"

"I guess that's all we're getting this year."

Rani chuckled. She'd have to let Grayson know that he'd been missed when she saw him next weekend. For now, she returned her attention to her book, quickly losing herself to the sparring between a couple in the workplace. She'd read about three chapters when the bell dinged as someone walked into the shop. Plenty of people had come and gone while she'd had her nose stuck in a book, but something made her look up.

It was Raj. Of course. The guy constantly invading her film fantasies. The guy she couldn't seem to get out of her head, no matter how hard she tried.

Rani's hands trembled. Her iced coffee splashed.

"Hey," Raj said.

"Hey." She fumbled with her romance novel but decided to leave it out. After all, this was who she was, and she'd waited an entire summer for Raj to figure out that she was worthwhile last year. It was too late to keep playing games.

He strode over to her table and—infuriatingly—plopped into the seat across from her. "Look, I know you're mad at me."

Mad?

Was that the feeling brewing inside her?

Or was it heartbreak? Maybe indifference? Maybe something else altogether?

Rani wanted to keep on ignoring Raj as she had done these past weeks, but when she locked eyes with him, it was as if they were the only two people in the coffee shop. Everything seemed to quiet—no more clinks of cutlery or tourists ordering at the counter or dishwashing in the back.

Just the beating of their two hearts.

"Actually, I'm not mad," she lied. "Just busy. If you don't mind—"

"Things are messed up," Raj cut in, his voice shaking a bit.

Rani took in his expression. For the first time since he'd gotten here, she really saw it. Saw that even though he was composing himself as best he could, something more lurked in the contours of his face.

Or was that just something she had read in a romance novel? The dark secrets of a gothic hero? A flight of fancy that only occurred in fiction?

Raj swallowed. Continued. "My parents—well, things aren't exactly easy with them right now. Actually, it's been rough all year. The constant fighting was starting to drive me off a cliff. I was going to text you so many times, but then I'd hear yelling and slammed doors. Or my mom crying alone in their room. And then I didn't know what to say. After a while, I sort of gave up."

Wow. Whatever she'd been expecting—it hadn't been that. What he'd said was officially the saddest thing in the world. And suddenly, Rani felt like a jerk.

A big one.

"Well, I guess I'm sorry, too," she said softly. "For ignoring your texts since you got here. And I'm sorry about your parents. That does sound hard."

"They're in counseling." Raj fiddled with a napkin. "But things aren't really the same as they used to be. Now they're a lot more careful around each other. It's weird. But it's better than all the volatility, you know?"

"That makes sense." Rani recalled the conversation she'd overheard from his parents on the deck. Careful was exactly the right word to describe it.

She felt herself slowly, slowly, slowly letting the resentment she'd bottled up inside for the past year seep out. Raj had been through a lot. Maybe if she'd called him, she could have helped. But she hadn't done that either.

A proper romance heroine would have tried, probably.

"At least they're working on things." Raj got up. "And look, I'm not going to bother you anymore. I know you don't want to see me, but I just wanted to explain. Actually, that's why I followed you to the garden that other night—but when I saw you were planning a midnight date with someone else, I just . . . couldn't do it." His lips quirked. "Too jealous."

He was jealous? Seriously?

Oh no. Forget it, Rani.

Even though what he was saying about his parents made sense, she still wasn't sure she wanted to get reeled back in. "Maybe we can just be friends," she said, hoping she sounded very mature and casual. (Not that she actually wanted to be just friends.)

But Raj didn't seem to get that because he actually smiled and sat back down. "So . . . what are you reading?"

She sighed and held up the book. "Just a romance."

The cover didn't include a hunky undressed man, but it was candy-colored and cutesy. Rani braced herself for the usual remarks about the quality of her reading. Even Leo and Vikram didn't seem to take her very seriously. Leo wasn't judgy, but that might be because he only read the CliffsNotes versions of books assigned at school. And Vikram always seemed too busy for that interview on the toxicity surrounding discussions of romance that he'd once promised her.

"Workplace romance, huh?" Raj asked.

Rani blinked. Had he actually looked past the cover to the description?

"Yeah, it's cute." She felt exposed, like a clam dug up on the beach. She hadn't expected him to show up here—obviously—and she wasn't wearing anything special, just cargo shorts and a simple pink tank top. She hadn't done up her hair, and she wasn't even wearing lipstick.

Yes, after all those lectures she'd given Sirisha about being being prepared for romantic situations at any moment, she'd somehow forgotten to put on lipstick that morning.

Official Love Guru, indeed.

But Raj didn't seem to mind. He was looking at her in that way he had last summer—that way that she'd been certain meant something. He reached for the book, and she let him have it.

He scanned the pages as if trying to find a secret in there. "I wish romance was as easy as it seems in fiction."

"Since when is it easy even in fiction?" Rani said. "The characters usually have to overcome something really big before they can commit to the person they're supposed to be with."

He shrugged. "But it always works out alright in the end, doesn't it? Not like real life."

She crossed her arms. "Have you ever even read a romance? They're more real than you might think."

"Well, no," he said. "I feel like people would give me a hard time."

"Ugh. I hate that," Rani replied.

"Me too."

"It makes no sense to me why people make fun of romances so much. Most people will be in a relationship at one time or another, right?"

Raj nodded.

"So why make fun of reading about something that's so central to much of our lives?"

"That's a good point," he said.

She nodded, still unsure of how to proceed. There was still the matter of that unkissed sunrise on the hammock. But she felt bad for him, too.

She held up her half-eaten sandwich. "Want to have lunch with me?"

He broke out into a grin that seemed to stretch from one end of the island to the other. "I'd love to."

Chapter Eleven

*L*unch was nice.

Just the two of them chatting over sandwiches and iced coffee. Raj had always been really easy to talk to, and that hadn't changed. Rani filled him in on the major events of her year: her sisters falling in and out of love, Dad and Amir, the wedding, even the impending relatives. And Raj filled her in on his own: getting elected class president at school, placing in the state tennis championship, junior prom. He told her some more personal tidbits about his parents, too, things that you wouldn't share with just anyone.

Or at least Rani wouldn't.

They continued talking as they waved goodbye to the barista and headed out onto the street, where the sunshine was bright and intense.

Rani fished her sunglasses out of her purse and put them on. They were oversize, of course, and made her feel like Audrey Hepburn.

Maybe she needed a little Audrey to make it through this day.

"Do you think your parents will pull through?" she asked.

"It's hard to say." Raj shrugged. "Some time here on Orcas might do them good. They get so caught up with their jobs—but here, they have to actually face each other."

"It can't hurt," Rani said eagerly. "And the Songbird was named the Most Romantic Inn in America. So if there's any place to rekindle a romance, this is it."

"I hope so." Raj stopped on the sidewalk, his amber brown eyes smoky and warm.

Or maybe not. In real life, you couldn't really read that much in someone's eyes. Raj's eyes were just brown, not *smoky and warm*. That was one aspect of romance novels that Rani was convinced was pure fanciful imagination.

They walked on. Past bustling cafés and boutiques. Past the library and Lulu's ice cream parlor. Past a church and an art gallery. Tourists were everywhere, but Rani didn't actually mind. Their excitement for the island was infectious. It truly was a magical place, and she hoped for Raj's sake that the Songbird's powers really would bring his parents closer. She hoped they all had a path written in the stars for themselves. Destiny with a capital *D*. But that was one of the hard parts about finding love and keeping it—you didn't know what life would bring you. You didn't know what would tear you apart.

Dad had probably never guessed that his dream of owning an inn and restaurant would tear him from his family, that falling in love in another country would mean he couldn't really go back.

They came to the bookstore, which Rani always had trouble passing by without a quick look. "You know, if you really want to help your parents, maybe some research will help. Should we dig up some good romances? The kind where old flames are stoked again?"

Raj smiled. "Let's do it. Recommend me some literary greatness."

"I hope you're not being sarcastic."

"Definitely not. My parents need all the help they can get. Lead the way."

Rani scanned his face with skepticism, but he seemed earnest.

"Great," she said. "The Official Love Guru is on the case."

"Official Love Guru?" he asked.

"That's what they call me."

"Who is this *they*?"

She gestured vaguely. "Oh, you know. They. Them. Those folks."

"Oh. Well, if *they* say so then . . ."

"*They* do." Rani winked and led him to the romance aisle.

She grazed her fingers across paperback covers. People always said that romances were just the same formula over and over again, but the formula didn't mean that there wasn't something to learn from them. Every author put a different spin on life and love, what drew two people together, and what kept them together even when things were hard. Yes, there was silly stuff, too—the kind about eyes being smoky and warm, or the contours of a face holding secrets. But mostly, there was a ton of useful ideas on all aspects of relationships.

"This one is about a couple who've been married for ten years but are starting to feel like roommates," she said, shoving the book at him and pulling out another. "Here's one about a divorced couple who get stranded on an island together and end up falling back in love. Oh, and here's one that's about a guy who mistypes an email address and loses out on the love of his life."

"Oh, please. That's not really what it's about, is it? Besides, I thought all romances end happily?"

Rani gestured at the shelf. "Actually this is the 'women's fiction' section, a designation that's also super sexist. I mean, why is *this* fiction relegated to women only? But anyway, the endings in these books don't have to be happy."

"Ah," he said. "Apparently, I have a lot to learn." His brow furrowed as he flipped to the end. His jaw dropped. "Wait, seriously? She never forgave him after a single typo?"

"Believe it, buddy." The Official Love Guru tossed her hair and walked back outside.

The two of them wandered out to the beach, discussing his parents and more romance novels and Rani's theories on what might help. They even talked about Rani's struggle to articulate all her thoughts on the L-word for her big speech. It was kind of embarrassing to admit for the Official Love Guru, something she'd be hard-pressed to tell her sisters.

But Raj didn't make fun. He was also a surprisingly good listener.

Out on the water, sailboats rode the wind. Wakeboarders and water skiers cruised behind speedboats. A kayaking couple took photos of wildlife. But Rani was happy to stay on the shore and skip rocks.

"I lied to you, you know," Raj said, tossing a pebble over the water. It bounced three times over the surface before sinking out of sight.

"Lied about what?" She tried to sound casual and not to let all those feelings from last summer overwhelm her. He'd explained about not calling, but would he confess that he'd missed a lot more than Dad's gulab jamun since last year? Did she even want that anymore? She had Leo and Vikram, after all.

Rani found a nice flat rock and let it fly. Six skips.

"Nice," Raj said.

"It's all in the wrist," Rani said. "But you were saying?"

"Right." He paused.

Rani skipped another rock, but it only yielded a paltry four skips.

"I lied . . ." He cleared his throat. "I do like romances. Mainly in Bollywood form."

"Huh. Okay." Not exactly the confession she was hoping for, but that had probably been unrealistic. Besides, she was *slightly* intrigued. "Tell me more. And it better not just be about how hot the women are."

He winced. "Ouch. But fair. I mean, Kajol is a goddess, but that's not the point. Can I confess that I love how over-the-top Hindi films are? I mean, who wants real life, anyway? Who doesn't want to sing and dance on a grassy hilltop, with snow-covered mountains in the background?"

Rani nodded. She'd been swept away to grassy hilltops far too often.

"Not to mention," Raj continued, "I love how Hindi movies try to encompass every genre at once. You want action, mystery, and a romance all together? You want light comedy followed by the most intense drama you've ever seen? It's all there."

Rani laughed. "You could get whiplash."

"I even like the cheesy morals," Raj said. "I mean some of them are super outdated, obviously. But ultimately I do like how close everyone is to their family, how they want to do right by their parents and all. The sense that everything isn't just about you."

Rani skipped another rock. It skimmed the water—one two three, four—no, twelve skips! But she pretended like she'd known it would happen. "So how many times have you watched *DDLJ*?"

"As if I can even count." Raj picked up an oyster shell and chucked it. It did skip one time and then plopped inelegantly into the water.

"Good answer."

When Rani and Raj got tired of skipping rocks, they beachcombed for a while. Rani uncovered some beautiful shells and Raj played with hermit crabs on the beach. As they lingered in the sun, he casually mentioned that there was a video game he was convinced was actually the greatest love story of all.

"Oh, please," Rani scoffed.

"Seriously, you need to play the game. Then you'll understand."

"I suppose we could try it sometime." Rani found herself saying. Wait, was she offering to spend more time with him? What was happening?

She let it go, and together they built a driftwood fort. All the effort of moving and stacking the heavy logs made them hungry again, so they stopped at a bodega and grabbed snacks and drinks. Rani led Raj to a birch tree behind the high school, her favorite place to sit and read during lunch. They plopped down under the heart-shaped branches, fallen scraps of white bark on the grass around them.

"So this is where Rani Singh spends most of her days." Raj munched on dried mango strips. "Lucky walls."

"Uh-huh." Rani rolled her eyes, popping a potato chip in her mouth. They'd spent the last few hours together, and he'd made the occasional flirty comment. So had she. She was the Official Love Guru—she couldn't help but flirt just a teensy bit!

Still, did she really need a third suitor? That would probably just be greedy, wouldn't it?

Raj lay down in the grass. "Hey, that cloud kind of looks like Link from *Zelda*, don't you think?"

"Actually yeah, it does. And that one looks like Mr. Darcy."

"Oh, and there's Pikachu."

"Do you think about anything besides video games?" she asked.

"Do you think of anything besides romance?"

"Ouch. You got me." A breeze tickled at Rani's nose; a butterfly fluttered by. She pointed. "There's your left ear."

"Hey, what're you saying about my left ear?"

"Um, nothing. Let's move on."

"We can't move on from my left ear!"

"It's not your ear, okay? It's Barack Obama's ear."

"Now you're saying my ears look like Obama's?"

"It's a compliment."

"Uh-huh . . ."

The grass smelled like laziness and sunshine. The sky was big and blue and bright, and more open than it had ever been. Also, obviously dotted with puffy clouds that looked like Raj's ears. And Rani didn't particularly want to move or do anything besides tease him about it.

They were back at the hammock on the porch. The place where Raj had broken her heart a little less than a year ago. The place of non-kissing. Even though Rani knew now why he hadn't kept in touch, she still felt raw about it. Honestly, she wasn't certain why she'd suggested they come back here after grabbing dessert from the restaurant. It felt like returning to the scene of the crime. They'd even opted for Dad's gulab jamun, a special form of torture. Maybe she was testing Raj. Maybe she wanted to see if he remembered exactly what he'd said.

Rani looked at the first touches of gold sweeping over the sea. Having grown up at the Songbird, she was pretty much an expert on what made a sunset spectacular—just the right number of clouds to fully bring out the explosion of colors. And tonight seemed ripe for a cinematic display, the kind in films that end with kisses.

Sigh.

She was starting to regret their day together. It had been fun and easy and relaxing, but she didn't know if she could shield her heart from him. She wanted to be friends, she really did. But it was *hard*.

"You probably don't remember this . . ." Raj put down his bowl, looking as if he didn't have much of an appetite either. "But last year, we were out here on the hammock, early one morning . . ."

Her heart thudded so loudly it could start an avalanche. "I remember."

"Yeah well . . ." Raj bit his lip. Swallowed. "Iwasgoingtokissyou."

His words were rushed, but that didn't matter to Rani. She heard every one of them. She parsed them in her brain. He. Was. Going. To. Kiss. Her. She waited for him to say more, but instead a slight tinge of pink crept across his cheeks, just like the scene unfolding behind him in the sky over the sea.

"So why didn't you?" she prompted, annoyance seeping into her tone. She couldn't help it.

Raj had the grace to look sheepish. "I got nervous. The moment was just a little *too* perfect, if you know what I mean."

"No, not really." Rani bit into the gulab jamun. It tasted of sadness.

"You're not going to make this easy on me, are you?"

She shook her head. Not after he'd left her hanging like that.

He sighed. "It was straight out of a movie. The sunrise, the coffee with pain au chocolat. Your dad's beautiful, historic inn. It just . . . I mean . . . I didn't feel like myself because it felt like there was so much pressure to be perfect. I love Bollywood, seriously—but the heroes never seem to doubt themselves. Since things were already off with my parents, it was even harder to believe that I could have what all those movies promised. So when the moment came, I messed it all up. I'm such a doofus."

He hung his head.

Rani played with her hands, trying not to care. Trying not to let her heart race, though it wasn't something she could really control. So he *had* felt something for her, but he had wounds in his heart, just as Dad did.

The colors were coming out now in the west. Ribbons of golds and oranges, slashes of magenta, and streaks of crimson. It was even more spectacular than she'd expected. But despite her constant foray into fantasies, despite her dreams of running wild in green fields wearing a bejeweled lehenga, the dupatta fluttering in the breeze as she danced and sang—despite all that, this moment didn't feel like a movie to Rani at all.

The sunset might have been a cinematic glory, but in a film, she wouldn't feel the evening breeze lingering with possibilities, the salty sea air enveloping them. She wouldn't smell the cologne he used—was it bergamot scented?—or the sweet lavender on his breath as he leaned in. She wouldn't feel his warm hand clasping her palm.

She lingered in that feeling. The feeling of just being, of living her life. She didn't know what love was. Even when she found it, she knew it might be an ephemeral thing, an epic passion that only lasted for a moment. She'd been searching for so long, but the search itself swelled into her heart. That pure wanting.

"I suppose this moment is a bit too perfect, too?" she asked breathily.

Raj's amber brown eyes searched hers. "Maybe I'm ready for some perfection."

She squeezed her lids shut, feeling nothing but his hand clasped in hers, his breath on her face. "You are?"

"Yeah. Um . . . can I kiss you?"

There was still so much swirling inside her, questions about whether she still even wanted this. She had other suitors, those who hadn't made her wait a year. And yet . . .

Yet something had clicked with Raj last summer. And whatever it was had clicked again today. There was an easiness to being with him that she'd never felt with anyone else. She'd opened up to him, about her love of books and romance. And he'd opened up to her, too. The afternoon had flown past; it had felt like time was nothing. That easiness, that click, was something you could never fully capture in a film—it wasn't a meet cute or a melodramatic twist.

Rani answered Raj with her lips. It was no film scene; there was no fanfare. No song, no dance. No sweeping camera. She was just a girl kissing a boy on a hammock in the sunset.

Chapter Twelve

The Friday of the wedding weekend, they needed a caravan to pick up fifteen relatives from the ferry landing. Grayson had arrived the day before—from Chile—and he and Nidhi were up ahead in his truck. Sirisha was driving Dad's car, Avani was in Fernando's SUV, and Rani was bringing up the rear in the car she and her sisters shared. As they passed the lavender farm and snaked through shoreline and pines, Rani felt a tingle of excitement—and anxiety.

Although Dad had formally invited Lakshman Dada and the rest of the relatives to the wedding, he was still rather reticent about his feelings over the whole thing. Apparently, the confession in the fitting room was enough talk of the past.

"I just want to move forward" was all he'd said when he'd caught the sisters talking about it in the library the other night.

"Okay," they'd all chorused, not wanting to upset him just days before the wedding. Maybe what Lalita Phua had told them privately on Chatterbox was okay then: that Lakshman Dada was very proud, and he probably wouldn't just come out and apologize over what had happened.

As the Singh sisters shuttled to the ferry landing, the sun was shining in that magical way that only happened in the summer on Orcas, the air glimmering with possibilities. The breeze fragrant with the scent of salt water and pines and flowers and things happening for a reason. Rani realized then that romance didn't have to be with another person. Sometimes it was more than that. Sometimes it was simply a feeling that fluttered in your stomach when you were exactly where you were meant to be.

The ferry was just pulling up to the dock as Rani parked in the lot up on the hill.

"I hope this isn't a disaster," she said, shutting the car door. Even with her sunglasses on, the sun was blinding.

"It won't be." Sirisha squeezed her hand.

"Aren't you the one who's all about the power of love?" Avani asked.

Rani rolled her eyes. But before she could respond, passengers started walking off the ferry. Her pulse raced; her heart fluttered and fidgeted and refused to settle.

The Singh sisters walked down to the dock, holding up their handwritten banner, which they'd stayed up making with glitter markers. "Welcome to Orcas Island!"

They squealed as they spotted their relatives dragging suitcases and grinning and waving. Rani recognized the faces from pictures on

Chatterbox: Lalita Phua with her little red glasses and serious bun, jolly Deepak Phupha in a sweater too warm for the weather. Their tall cousin Prakash with his buzz cut and aviators, towering over the aunties and uncles. Sona with her camera strapped around her neck, Sirisha's mirror. Lakshman Dada with his silver hair and jovial smile. He really did look like just a friendly retiree, not some dream crusher.

Nidhi awkwardly tried to touch his feet—a sign of respect for your elders. Rani, Sirisha, and Avani reached out to do the same. But Dada shooed them all off, as did the other relatives, though they looked like they appreciated the gesture.

And then it was a whirlwind of hugs and kisses and exclamations of "Oh, you're so grown up!" and "We've missed you!" and "We've missed you, too!" and "Our four beautiful girls!" and "What a magnificent place to live!" and more, and the Singh sisters were each fiercely glad that this was happening, that they were showing the family they'd never known the only place they'd ever called home.

When the caravan returned to the Songbird Inn not long later, the sisters saw it anew with their relatives. Painted a robin's-egg blue, the historic inn jutted out over the craggy edge of a seaside cliff, boasting oversize windows and Craftsman elegance, the wraparound porch promising panoramic views, pines looming like sentinels in the distance.

Lalita Phua said simply, "Your dad has done well for himself."

"Very impressive!" "Beautiful!" "You're lucky to have had this place for your home!" the others chimed in.

"Yeah, we're lucky," Avani said.

"Very," Rani agreed emphatically.

"Yes," Sirisha added. "I wouldn't give this place up for the world."

They gave the relatives the tour: the parking lot led to the east porch and the entryway into reception. Nidhi gently herded everyone into the wide living room, with its tall, coffered ceilings, the clusters of leather sofas, the double doors out to the south deck, and beyond, the glittering sea. The relatives exclaimed at how charming the inn was, the historic chandeliers, the built-in bookshelves, the huge fireplace.

Naturally, they were drawn outside, where sunshine drenched the views of the Salish Sea. The water was dotted with ferries and sailboats. A few other wedding guests enjoyed iced tea or rosé at the tables, but the inn was still fairly empty, as most others would be coming in tonight after work.

They pulled together some tables and Avani ran to grab cold drinks for their tired guests. Nidhi caught everyone up on what they had planned: various fun events during the day tomorrow, then a ceremony down at the cove in the afternoon, dinner and dancing planned outside on the grass. Finally, a casual barbecue on Sunday to round out the weekend.

"This is lovely, but we *must* help with the wedding," Lalita Phua said. "What can we do?"

"Oh yes, we insist," Lakshman Dada said. "Tell us what you need."

"Aren't you tired? What about jet lag?" Nidhi looked surprised. "Besides, I think we have everything covered."

"Nonsense," Lakshman Dada huffed. "There's always something more to be done for a wedding. Tell me, do you have a mandap?"

"No," Nidhi said, "we weren't really planning to have one."

"Are you certain?" Dada asked. "Because I can build you one. But if there's something else more pressing, just tell me. I'm ready to work."

And he was. They all were.

Nidhi had always been adept at assigning people chores, so it was no surprise that she came up with plenty for the relatives to do. Welcome baskets for the other guests, centerpieces, flower garlands. Nidhi texted Dad—who was enjoying the day off on a hike in the woods with Amir and his family—and confirmed that they were okay with the idea of a mandap, a special gazebo to perform the ceremony under.

When Dad gave the okay, Grayson and Fernando carried what was needed down to the cove. Then Lakshman Dada and a couple of other uncles and cousins went to work. Rani watched all the hammering and nailing, thinking *this* was yet another form of what love was. Constructing something with your bare hands when you didn't have the words to say what you really wanted to say.

She, of course, had opted out of helping, since she was *extremely* busy gathering her thoughts for the big speech. Which was, sadly, still a cluttered mess. Not that Rani planned to let anyone know. It would ruin her reputation as Romance Queen. Also, observing everything was part of her brainstorming, obviously!

Soon they had the mandap put together, though it was a bit rough around the edges.

"Beautiful," Rani said a little doubtfully.

Lakshman Dada laughed at that, clapping her on the back. "Not much of a poker face on this one. Don't worry, it will look different tomorrow once it's been draped with fresh flowers."

"And who will do the draping?" Rani asked.

"Naturally, I will," Dada said. "What, you think I can't handle some flowers?"

"Not at all."

They hiked back to the Songbird, where delicious smells were coming from the outdoor grill on the north porch. But instead of Dad, Rani found her cousins hard at work cooking.

"What is that divine smell?" she asked.

Prakash held out a fluffy wrap with pickled onions and egg peeking out. "Have you ever heard of a Kolkata egg roll?"

"Street food?" Nidhi's eyes almost bulged out, and she looked like she was about to swipe a bite right out of Prakash's hand.

"The street food version is really good," Prakash said, "though I'm not sure your delicate American stomachs could handle it."

"Mine couldn't even handle it when I lived there," Dad called, coming through the doors with Amir. "Although, someone once told me that cooking was—how did he put it?—a feminine calling."

Everyone froze. The relatives looked like they had no idea what to do. Prakash laughed nervously.

Then Lakshman Dada coughed. "A very outdated notion. I'm sorry that I ever had such views. But Prakash, Sona, and all the other young people in my life have shown me that you don't have to do what people expect you to do."

Dad blinked. Then he scrambled to hug his nieces and nephews first. "You're so big, look at you. Prakash, I saw you when you were just a baby. Sona—I only saw pictures of you."

The aunts and uncles and their great-aunt each approached to coo over Dad and his silvery whiskers, and to introduce themselves to Amir—who was apparently too handsome for them not to flirt with a bit. The sisters squeezed one another's hands. It was happening: They were all meeting again, and so much depended on it going well.

Dad turned to Lakshman Dada with slightly more trepidation. He began to reach down for Dada's feet per tradition, but Dada shooed him away, too.

"Beta, stand," Dada said. "You're your own man. You always have been. This is hard for me to say—I was taught never to admit I was wrong—but I was. I shouldn't have tried to pressure you to return to India when your dreams were clearly here. I've regretted my words for many years now. I'm sorry it took me so long to tell you."

Oh wow. Rani couldn't believe that Dada had actually come out and said all that. And he wasn't finished. He talked about how he'd tried to do better with the next generation, how he'd invested in Prakash's app, and how he'd gone to protests with Sona for safety. Rani hadn't known how involved Dada was with all her cousins' lives, and she knew she and her sisters missed out on that by living so far away. But there was still time to grow closer.

"I never want to make the same mistake again," Dada continued. "Because if you love someone, you love their dreams, too. You want what they want. And I'm sorry I didn't learn it in time to help you with the Songbird Inn. But you've done beautifully without any help from us. You've raised four brilliant girls. You've found love and happiness here. For that, I'm grateful. And if there is anything I can do now to help you or your girls, I would love to be a part of your lives."

Dad looked as stunned as Rani felt—Dada was actually apologizing for everything? Lalita Phua had seemed so certain that he was incapable of it. But their great-uncle had surprised all of them.

A smile like sunshine dappling through a morning window spread over Dad's face. "Thank you. I appreciate that." He turned to the rest of the family. "And thank you all so much for coming out here. You've made us feel very loved."

Dada held out his hand. "Congratulations, beta."

Dad shook it, then pulled his uncle in for a hug. Dada heartily congratulated Amir as well, and nobody could stop from getting teary after all that. The sisters distracted themselves as best they could with the Kolkata egg rolls: flaky doughy wraps dipped in egg with pickled onions, lime, chilies, tomatoes and cucumbers inside. They also asked their cousins all about their schools, their jobs, their passions. Sona wanted the scoop on Grayson and Fernando and Brie. Naturally, Rani filled her in on her sisters' romances, embellishing the tales until others were listening.

"You're quite the storyteller," Lalita Phua said, leaning in. "I hear you're giving a big speech tomorrow."

Rani chuckled nervously. "Oh yeah, I have something fantastic planned."

Of course, Dada had completely stolen Rani's thunder, because there was no way she was going to improve on all he'd said! But that didn't matter. Rani suddenly knew exactly what love was. Because when you feel it, you know.

She'd felt *it*, here on the north porch of the Songbird, with her family.

Later that evening, Rani stared at her mess of a speech, tempted to throw it away. Why did they need a speech anyway? She could just toast the happy couple. Short and sweet.

And yet, that seemed rather a waste for the Official Love Guru. So much had happened over the course of the year. Whether they realized it or not, she'd gently shepherded each of her sisters into opening their hearts. She'd done good, and now she was determined to change how people thought of love and relationships. She wanted the world to understand why love was so important—not to ridicule it as some idealistic, unrealistic thing. This speech could be her manifesto, a rallying cry for lonely hearts everywhere.

Unfortunately, the written version she'd attempted was full of crossed-out sections and arrows rearranging the words and eraser marks that had rubbed holes through the paper.

"Writing isn't as easy as you thought, is it?" Avani asked, smirking.

"Okay, okay, I'm sorry I ever teased you about never finishing your novels." Rani doodled hearts in the margins of the page with her pencil. "But this is absolutely impossible! How can I get all my thoughts together in one little speech? If I talk for more than ten minutes, everyone will throw their tomato penne at me!"

As her twin chuckled, a knock sounded on their bedroom door.

"I wonder who that could be?" Avani asked in a tone that said she knew exactly who it could be. She flounced to open the door, and said loudly, "Why, Raj, we weren't expecting you! Also, I was just leaving." With a wink and a wicked grin, she trotted away.

Rani stood from her desk. "Raj! What're you doing here? You know I have to work on my speech."

Since the Songbird was closed to paying guests for the weekend of the wedding, Raj's family had moved to a vacation cabin down at Deer Harbor.

"Yeah, I know." Raj ran a hand through his messy hair and grinned. "Avani said that you were—and I quote—'having an existential crisis'?"

"Something like that," Rani said. "It's harder than I thought!"

He set his backpack at his feet, looking a little too good in another video game T-shirt and shorts. (How did he manage to make that hot? A mystery.)

As he took in her room, Rani realized it was still a mess of too many stuffed animals from Leo and too many of Vikram's urgent nonfiction issue books on her nightstand. Both of them were still texting her occasionally, though Leo had left for his home in Bellingham (only a ferry ride and short drive away) and Vikram for his family's yacht (they were around the whole summer).

She could have asked either one to the wedding, but she hadn't.

Over the past week, whenever she'd had a moment away from wedding planning, she'd spent her free time with Raj. Lazing on a beach and watching the clouds drift by. Playing card games under a tree. Eating ice cream and laughing and doing nothing at all. A watercolor blur from last summer into this one, as if those rainy wet months in between had never happened.

It turned out she didn't really need seaplanes and yachts. She didn't need windsurfing or moonlit picnics. She just wanted someone she could talk to, someone who was actually interested in what she had to say. And when she'd asked him to come to Dad's wedding with her, it had felt right.

"You probably don't need my help with the speech," Raj said. "But just in case, I have some ideas."

"You do?"

Raj strode over to the two bookshelves on either side of the window. One was Avani's, full of an eclectic mix of everything from science fiction to the memoir of a famous soccer player. Rani's shelf was far more consistent: top to bottom, it was full of romance. Some were funny, some were tragic, but they all explored that mysterious, magical thing called love.

"I guess I'm starting my own collection." He opened up his back-pack—and pulled out more romance novels. Some that she'd recommended to him, others that he must have picked out himself.

"Did you actually read all these?" she asked, but the answer was obvious. All of them were filled with tabs and sticky notes. She flipped through them one by one. "Whoa. You found all the little epiphanies that the characters have along the way."

INT. INN – EVENING

              RANI

Help, the stars have failed to reveal to me which
handsome suitor is my true fate. What can I do?

          FORTUNE-TELLER

My dear, you must discover this on your own. But one
hint: Your true suitor will understand that which you have
always loved. That which keeps you awake at night.

              RANI

Romance novels keep me awake at night.

          FORTUNE-TELLER

Indeed? Very interesting.

Rani often drifted into daydreams, though rarely the same ones twice. Yet that fortune-teller that she herself had created might be onto something. Surely this pile of romance novels, so thoroughly read and appreciated was a Sign (with a capital *S*).

"Thanks," she said. "For taking me seriously."

He smiled, his eyes smoky and warm. No really, they were—it wasn't just something she'd read in books. There was a world of feeling in them, in his smile, in the way he brushed her hair from her face.

And even though all she wanted to do was kiss him, she picked up her pen. And started writing.

Chapter Thirteen

For once, the Singh sisters weren't running around, making certain everything was in the right place. Various relatives and friends had been delegated different aspects of the big-day coordination, so when they walked down the beach trail to the cove, the wedding guests were already seated on folding chairs, the string quartet was already playing, summer flowers were draped everywhere.

It wasn't the extravagant affair Rani had always dreamt of for her future self, with designer clothes and a few hot celebrities, but she had to admit that the moment felt perfect. Waves lapped gently against the shore, restless children got their formal wear covered in sand, and seagulls squawked. Sailboats paraded by. The guests included all their relatives, but also so many friends from the islands. Josie, Armand, and the rest of the Songbird staff, teachers and friends from school, Dad's friends from his hiking club and the local small business association.

Summer weddings at the cove were a Songbird specialty, but it was hard to believe they were actually having one of their own. Rani sniffled into the bundle of summer wildflowers she carried, her head swirling still with thoughts on that big L-word and what it meant and what she'd say tonight. She'd finished her speech, but after rereading it and reworking it so many times, she had no idea if it even made sense anymore.

Sigh.

Seated in the front row, Raj smiled, looking at her in a way that gave her shivers. It seemed to say he knew her. And she kind of thought that he did. He'd also told her so many times that her speech would be brilliant, and hopefully he wasn't one of those dudes who said you were brilliant when they didn't really think so.

Seriously, he'd better actually think so!

Nidhi hugged Grayson briefly before taking her place to the side of the wedding mandap, which now was adorned with gorgeous, cascading flowers. Sirisha waved shyly to Brie before taking her spot. Avani winked at Fernando, and Rani squeezed Raj's hand briefly before lining up as well. The sisters stood in a row, their silk lehengas glittering in the sunshine. Nidhi in vibrant burnt orange, Avani in icy blue, Sirisha in spring green. And Rani in summery lavender, heart thudding with a kaleidoscope of emotions.

At last, the music changed, and Dad and Amir made their appearance from the trail, hand in hand, wearing their shimmering gold-and-scarlet sherwanis and elegant traditional headgear studded with jewels.

Rani mentally congratulated herself on her flawless taste, because they truly looked like royalty. Sirisha unleashed her ever-present camera as the happy couple walked down the aisle to the mandap, where Amir's parents and Lakshman Dada awaited them, elders from each of their families.

Dad and Amir turned to face the audience.

"Welcome everyone," Dad said with a huge grin.

"We're so glad that all of you can be here to celebrate with us today," Amir added.

"Those of you who live here on the island and are a part of our every-day lives," Dad said, "we're so grateful to belong to this unique and beautiful community."

"And those of you who traveled a great distance to be here on this beach with us—" Amir said.

"Even if we'd lost touch. Even if the years had come between us—"

"You're a part of this family as long as you want to be," Amir finished.

The audience cheered and hooted, and the ceremony got swiftly under way. Amir and Dad had been adamant that they wanted to keep things short and sweet, with nods at traditions from both their cultures while making it known that they were forging their own path. Rani's eyes teared up when at last the couple literally tied the knot with the chiffon scarves each of them wore draped around their necks. The entwining of gold and scarlet—and their lives—was complete.

Finally, family—both by blood and by heart—were invited to come up in batches and bless the couple themselves. Dad and Amir were showered with rose petals, and the ocean itself gave its own blessing by gently spraying the couple with a surprise wave.

"It's good luck," Lakshman Dada assured everyone, wiping the spray from his pants.

EXT. VILLAGE – DAY

RANI, her sisters, and the townsfolk gather for a wedding replete with music and color.

> FORTUNE-TELLER
> Ah, my work here is done. You and your family have followed your path through the stars and made your way.

> RANI
> You have taught me much, madam. I wonder if I, too, may one day learn to read the stars and help lonely hearts find their fates.

> FORTUNE-TELLER
> Truthfully, I am in need of an apprentice. Would you like the position?

> RANI
> I think that might be part of my destiny.

Rani's plate was heaped with sungold tomato penne, sautéed snap peas and summer squash, a salad with luscious berries. Golden fingerling potatoes and freshly grilled seafood doused with butter, lemon, and dill. The menu she and Nidhi had so painstakingly selected. She still thought a tomato was a tomato, but dang—these were some really good tomatoes!

With so much beautiful summer sun, they'd opted for dinner and dancing outdoors in the grass. Paper lanterns had been strung across trees, the tables dressed with lacy linens and an abundance of flowers, and the guests allowed to sit wherever. The din of laughter and chatter pealed over the soft dinner music that Avani had curated from among the old Hindi ballads that Dad often hummed. The sisters and their dates were together near the dance floor that had been set up over the grass. Because, as Avani had vehemently declared, they needed to PARTY!

If only Rani could relax about her upcoming speech. She was the Official Love Guru; she was going to kill it, obviously, just as Raj had said. And yet her knees trembled under the table.

"It's gonna be epic," Avani assured her.

"How do you know?" Rani asked. "You haven't heard the latest version of my speech."

"Oh, I meant my song is going to be epic." Avani winked. "But I'm sure your thing will be fine, too."

"Gee, thanks."

EXT. VILLAGE – EVENING

FORTUNE-TELLER
The village has many lonely hearts. As my apprentice,
can you divine from the stars the right path for each and
every one of them?

RANI
(Looking up at the sky)
Don't hide your secrets, stars. We need you.

Nidhi called for order by clinking her fork against her glass. "Thank you for coming, everyone. I hope you've got plenty to eat and drink. Let's toast the happy couple!"

Everyone raised their glasses toward Dad and Amir, who were both beaming and so perfectly handsome in the evening light, eyes only for each other now that the formalities had finished.

Next, Avani and Fernando took to the dance floor with acoustic guitars. Avani's voice was bold and sweet as she sang the first notes. Possibly, just possibly, she really was a better singer than Rani. The girl had too many hidden talents—skiing and poetry and even beer pong?—and Rani wished she had gotten just a few of them, too.

But she couldn't grouch at her twin for long; the song Avani and Fernando had composed was really funny and adorable, covering the happy couple's original meet cute at the small business owners association, to their next run-in at the deli and grocery store in Eastsound, then a party at a local philanthropist's estate, and finally getting ice cream at Lulu's. Clearly, you're not in love on Orcas unless you've shared a fresh waffle cone with locally made ice cream.

Up next, Amir's sister told lots of silly stories about Amir as a kid, how he'd had the most enormous coke-bottle glasses that overtook his face, and how that experience had made him want to become an ophthalmologist.

"Your office has much better selections," she assured him, "but just remember that those ridiculous spectacles led you right here. Congratulations and much love to both of you! Cheers!"

Rani clinked her glass with Raj, then took a fortifying sip of sparkling pear cider. (Another Gutiérrez venture, naturally.) The moment she'd both been dreading and looking forward to had arrived. Nidhi called her over to the microphone, and Rani rushed and stumbled a bit in her high heels, lavender silk slick against her skin.

She looked out at the guests, out at the gorgeous garden reception with so many lovely people that made her heart swell. Lakshman Dada winked at her. Amir smiled encouragingly. Dad blew her a kiss.

EXT. VILLAGE – EVENING

FORTUNE-TELLER

Apprentice, here's your chance. Share all you've learned.

RANI

Okay, here I go: Love is garbage.

"Or at least, that's what I thought just one year ago," Rani said, remembering that feeling. "I couldn't handle the heartache of it, I couldn't handle another unkissed summer." She winked at Raj so he'd know she didn't hold it against him anymore. "I've read hundreds of romance novels, watched tons of romantic movies, both from here and Bollywood. And to be honest—sometimes I think I get it, and sometimes I don't at all. Sometimes love feels like something everyone is chasing, and yet no one really knows what it is."

Her sisters nodded in agreement, and so did most of the guests. It seemed that love was mysterious to most people.

"Honestly, it doesn't matter what I say here tonight. All the best things that need to happen have already happened. Dad and Amir found each other. Somehow, they knew what love was without having to define it. But—and this is a big but! I wouldn't be me if I didn't at least try to share some of my thoughts on what it means to love." She paused. "So, can I trust you all with my secrets?"

Raj hooted, "Tell us!"

Others called: "What are they, Rani?" "What is love?" "Come on, Official Love Guru!"

Rani laughed. "Here's the thing: Sometimes, I think I know everything. Sometimes, I even meddle in my sisters' lives."

There were chuckles from the audience and knowing glances from her sisters.

"But watching them, watching Dad and Amir, I have learned a lot this past year—I've learned that the concepts of love and family are deeply intertwined. After all, when love is true, when it lasts, when you promise to be together for the rest of your lives, doesn't the object of your affections become a part of your family?"

She raised her glass to Amir. "It's really the best—to see your family grow and make room in your heart for someone new."

More cheers resounded in the evening air.

"Of course," she continued, "your family has to do the work, too. Love is when someone shows up for you, even when it's hard. Love is admitting you're wrong, acknowledging the mistakes you've made."

Her great-uncle clapped heartily, as did the rest of the relatives. Rani hoped they understood how much it meant to her and her sisters that they had traveled all that way to be here.

Next, she turned her attention to her sisters. Nidhi first. "Love is when you want something so badly for yourself, and the people around you want it for you, too. When you upend your life and let go of old dreams, and they encourage you to go for it."

Her eldest sis nodded, looking different that evening, as if she'd finally settled into her lanky limbs, her dreamy eyelashes no longer wishing for something quite so hard because she'd found some of what she'd been looking for. Older and wiser and ready for big adventures.

Rani was really going to miss her next year when she was away, though.

But no time to think about that—she locked eyes with her twin, her soul sister, her dear Avani. A girl who was both poetic and sporty, a girl whose heart was more tender and sensitive than most people knew. "Love is also when you're afraid of getting hurt, when you're afraid that you might lose someone, but you realize it's worth any possible heartache."

Avani sniffled into her napkin and Rani quirked her brows. *Aww, you're getting weepy at my speech.*

Avani shook her head. *Yeah, right. I just have something in my eye. But you're doing okay, I guess.*

Rani chuckled softly. *Uh-huh. My secretly softie twin.*

Avani: *Hush, you.*

Rani laughed and then focused on Sirisha, her little sis who'd grown up so much this past year—and had finally found the perfect deep rose lipstick (with the help of the Official Love Guru, naturally). "Love is when you're afraid to speak, but you do it anyway."

Sirisha smiled, tossed her bob, and took a quick photo.

Rani then arched her brows at Raj, even though things were just beginning with him. "Love is when someone listens to what you have to say—and even takes notes."

Raj shrugged his little shrug, modest about that small thing he'd done that had meant so, so much to her. It wasn't love with a capital L yet, but an excellent start. Perhaps it would grow into that epic romance she'd always dreamt of. But for now, she was happy with where they were.

EXT. VILLAGE – EVENING

FORTUNE-TELLER

My dear, are you finally allowing the stars to keep their secrets?

RANI

For tonight. Don't think I won't be asking about them tomorrow!

Finally, Rani looked at Dad and Amir, and again at all the guests gathered on the lawn of the Songbird under twinkling paper lantern lights in the warm summer air.

There are a few moments in your life that will stay with you forever, until you're old and gray and perhaps even beyond that, to the edges of time and space. This was one of those moments for Rani. Her heart overflowed, growing wild like roses left untended around a fairy-tale castle. And she understood.

"Love is something I've seen my whole life, something I've always felt with my family. Something I've always felt here on Orcas. Something that doesn't have to be complicated. It doesn't have to be like a movie. In fact, it doesn't have to be grand or extravagant at all. Love is home, love is family, love is community. Love is making food and eating it together. Love is watching a sunset together. Love is hopping on a plane from across the world so you don't miss a big moment with someone you care about. Love is rainy days mixed with sunshine. It's something that grows throughout the seasons. It happens in fall. In winter. In spring. And in summer."

She grinned, throwing the rest of her notecards in the air. "I'm rambling, so only one more: LOVE IS A FLASH DANCE PLANNED JUST FOR YOU! Hit it, Avani!"

At the cue, Avani played the song they'd picked over the speakers. Every guest got up and joined—on the dance floor or the grass or wherever they were—while Dad and Amir watched in delighted silence. Rani had sent everyone a prerecorded video to practice with, including the relatives from India. It was all worth it to see Dad chuckle as Lakshman Dada busted a move, his silver hair glinting like the moon.

When the song was over, another one began. Avani's perfectly curated playlist, of course. Rani dragged Raj to the dance floor—realizing suddenly that they'd never actually danced before, a missing component of their relationship in vital need of remedying.

Next to them, Fernando and Avani showed off, of course—those two just couldn't help it. Nidhi and Grayson swayed gracefully, and Grayson said something that made Nidhi laugh with abandon. Brie and Sirisha shimmied and shook it under a paper lantern, lit within like fireflies, no words necessary.

Dad and Amir kissed as guests twirled around them.

Raj's moves turned out to be adorably awkward, and Rani kind of loved it. Besides: Anyone looked good on the dance floor if they were in formal wear, in her professional opinion—even when they were doing the dreaded robot dance.

"Dork," she whispered.

"You know it." He grinned and switched to a fumbling version of the coffee grinder, hopped up for a pirouette, and then finished with a bit of flossing. He was *not* what you'd call smooth.

But he made her laugh.

Rani grazed her fingers against the nape of his neck, pulled him in close. Let the song envelop them as they slowed down, danced cheek to cheek. He smelled like bergamot and wild promises. And when his lips found hers, firm and full of warmth and wanting, she wondered if maybe, just maybe she was finally feeling *it*.

(Whatever *it* actually was.)

The air turned crisp as the evening waned and the Singh sisters' laughter twinkled in the twilight. Music glimmered around them like winking pearls and the rustle of pines played dulcet strains of violin. The breeze danced and voices carried over the roar of the sea, the echoes warm and soothing as Dad's lavender gulab jamun.

THE END

Acknowledgments

My heart is so full from all the love and support of the people who have helped me along the way and made this book of joyful representation possible. I feel so lucky to work with my rock star agent, Penny Moore. Thank you so much for believing in me and for your passionate championing of diaspora stories! I am also incredibly grateful for my editors, Christine Collins and Britt Rubiano, for loving these sisters as much as I do and for your tireless efforts to nurture their story and drizzle them with care. Kieran Viola: I so appreciate your warm welcome and cheer.

I am grateful to all the wonderful folks at Hyperion who have worked on getting this book into the hands of readers. Sara Liebling, Guy Cunningham, Jody Corbett, Mark Amundsen, Jenny Langsam, Ann Day, Crystal McCoy, Danielle DiMartino, Holly Nagel, Dina Sherman, Matt Schweitzer, Bekka Mills, Marybeth Tregarthen, Monique Diman, Michael Freeman, Lia Murphy, Vicki Korlishin, Kim Knueppel, Mili Nguyen, Loren Godfrey, and the rest of the team.

Huge thank you to Chaaya Prabhat for the gorgeous cover art, and Marci Senders for the cover design. I love it. Blair Thornburgh, Lynn Weingarten, and Marianna Baer: Thank you for seeing the potential in my writing and helping to shape this novel. Chelsea Eberly: Thank you for getting it into the right hands. I appreciate all the behind-the-scenes work from the teams at Aevitas Creative Management and Working Partners as well.

A novelist in the making takes a lot of nurturing to grow. I learned so much from my wonderful and insightful mentors, Padma Venkatraman and Jennifer Latham. You made me believe. Emily X. R. Pan and Nova Ren Suma: forever grateful to have my short story championed by you. Trisha Tobias, Cynthia Leitich Smith, Mara Delgado Sánchez, Diane Telgen, and the rest of the team at Foreshadow YA: I'm so grateful you saw something in my voice and helped me take that first big step of being published. Thanks also to Julia Rios and Racquel Henry for boosting my words.

My friends in the writing community have also provided sunshine that outlasts the gray. Rachel Lynn Solomon: Thanks so much for all the reads, support, and advice. You're an inspiration. Janine Southard: Thank you for all the cozy writing dates and long chats. Shveta Thakrar, Anuradha Rajurkar, Sasha and Sarena Nanua: I so appreciate your enthusiasm and support. A.M. Dassu: much love for being my confidante and friend. My talented critique group, you've been my rocks: Flor Salcedo, S. Isabelle, Linda Cheng, Candace Buford, Michele Bacon, and Tanya Aydelott. Grateful also for my other writing friends: Paul Decker, Zoe Fisher, Waka. T. Brown, Gayatri Sethi, Shymala Dason, Lauren Stone, and Maritess Zurbano. My fellow WNDB mentees, especially Pamela Courtney, Teresa Robeson, Joanne Wong, and Urania Smith: I love the way we lift each other up. Cosmic love to my friend and poet Kay Kinghammer. Janet Reid and Patrice Caldwell: Thank you for the excellent advice when I needed it. 22 Debuts and Class of 2k22: You've helped navigate this road with laughter and camaraderie, and I would not be sane without you. Special shout-outs to fellow debuts George Jreije, Susan Azim Boyer, Priyanka Taslim, Brian Kennedy, Derrick Chow, Anna Kopp, Stacy Stokes, Anita Kharbanda, Sathya Achia, Jen Ferguson, and Judy Lin.

Organizations like We Need Diverse Books and The Word: A Storytelling Sanctuary have done so much to help uplift underrepresented writers. I'm also thankful for all the advice and connections I've made through online communities: KidLit Alliance, Desi Kidlit, Kid Lit Authors of Color, and the DVpit fam. I've looked up to trailblazers and shining stars like Heidi Heilig and Justina Ireland for help paving the path and planting roses along the way.

To the Orcas Island residents: I hope I've done justice to your beautiful home. Thank you, Michèle Griskey, for sharing your thoughts and insights on island life.

To my parents, two sisters, and brother: I couldn't have possibly written this family story without all your love, chaos, and laughter. We navigated a new country together, with all its adventures and challenges. Thank you for making me who I am. Thanks also to our patient extended family who always made us feel welcomed, even as we struggled with how to be both Indian and American.

To Cleo: Thanks for all the puppy snuggles.

To my husband and the love of my life: I could not have done this without you. Thanks for reading all my messy drafts, for being patient with so many roller-coaster emotions, and for enthusiastically supporting me every step of the way.

To my kiddo, Commander B, my biggest fan and the light of my life: You put sunshine in every rainy day. Love you more than anything.

To the reader: Thank you so much for picking up this book and letting these sisters into your hearts.